WHO IS TRYING TO KILL THE PRESIDENT? COULD IT BE THE CANDIDATE OF THE OPPOSING PARTY?

"Special Agent Dutch Brown's job is to protect the President, and it will cost him dearly. Author Adam Tocci takes the reader on a dizzying trip of unexpected twists and turns that could easily be ripped from today's headlines. It's all there – love, sex, murder, deceit, dirty politics, and the ultimate betrayal. A great read!"—*Joan C. Borgatti, author of Frazzled, Fried...Finished? A Guide to Help Nurses Find Balance.*

"From its tense opening scene to its ripe-for-a-sequel ending, Adam Tocci gives the reader a bird's eye view of the characters, the politics, and the intrigue of Washington and the Secret Service in this action-packed thriller. Brisk plotting, colorful characters, and a dose of humor make *Bullseye* a quick and enjoyable read."—*Chris Westphal, author of The Spy Who Loathed Me*

ALSO BY ADAM J. TOCCI

LOVE ON THE LINE

HARVARD STUDENT AGENCIES BARTENDING GUIDE—
Contributor

BULLSEYE

ADAM TOCCI

Moonshine Cove Publishing, LLC

Abbeville, South Carolina U.S.A.

FIRST MOONSHINE COVE EDITION JANUARY 2014

ISBN: 978-1-937327-38-5

Library of Congress Control Number: 2013958262

For Adam Jr. and Meghan, the true muses in my life.

VISION STATEMENT

The vision of the United States Secret Service is to uphold the tradition of excellence in its investigative and protective mission through a dedicated, highly-trained, diverse, partner-oriented workforce that employs progressive technology and promotes professionalism.

MISSION STATEMENT

The mission of the United States Secret Service is to safeguard the nation's financial infrastructure and payment systems to preserve the integrity of the economy, and to protect national leaders, visiting heads of state and government, designated sites and National Special Security Events.

BULLSEYE

Chapter 1
Late October

As the sun fell behind the mountains, Special Agent Dutch Brown stared out at the Pearl River and took in the scent of the waterway, grateful for the lack of mosquitoes and other insects that would have clouded around him if he were back home.

Dutch and his partner, Harry Ludec, were in an old burrowed out enclosure mid-way up a small hill; given the discarded food containers and other trash, it was a place that smugglers had probably used for decades, Dutch figured. The vantage point afforded them a view of a small dock, and a view of the only exit leading from the parking lot at the foot of the hill.

Through a pair of binoculars, Harry surveyed the darkening horizon.

"Anything?" Dutch whispered to his partner of three years.

"Nope."

Silence set in as the two agents kept their eyes moving, Harry scanning for the approaching boat while Dutch visually checked off the men on the team, positioned around the small secluded area. Unless you knew where to look, they were virtually invisible.

He hoped the hastily put-together mission would work.

Dutch continued his surveillance. It was an unassuming place, an abandoned textile company's unloading area. In the parking lot, patches of grass grew between cracks in the asphalt. Years of wind and water blowing off the river were clearly evident in the rotted wood that hung on the few remaining buildings. Dutch estimated that the dock, just north of his position, could accommodate four boats, but it didn't appear that the place had had visitors for quite some time. An old wooden fishing boat that looked as if it had been washed up on shore twenty years earlier perched on an elevated platform. Dutch could make out the slightest shadow of moment from the wheelhouse porthole, and knew that it was Agent Fedder from the CIA.

Roughly forty-five yards to the south at the only entrance to the parking lot sat Scali and Savard, two rookie agents who had only been on the job at the CIA's Far East posting for a few months. They were positioned on either side of the one road leading into the fenced parking lot. Agent Scali was inside an abandoned guard shack, its windows boarded up and wooden fascia boards pulled loose from the foundation.

Agent Savard was situated in a drainage pipe on the opposite side of the fifteen-foot-wide road. A small bridge crossed a stream carrying run off from the surrounding area, and the pipe was sunk on the side of the bridge in such a way that Agent Savard had an unimpeded view of the dock. On the east side of the lot was a rusted chain link fence covered on top with loosely strung barbed wire. The fence terminated at the guard shack.

All in all, it's a perfect place to smuggle something in, thought Dutch.

On the hillside below Dutch counted five camouflaged members of the SWAT unit of the Beijing Police Department's Organized Crime Division. They had been uncharacteristically cooperative with the two agencies from the United States Government. Dutch liked to think his charming personality had convinced them it was to their benefit to allow the sting operation on their soil, but he knew better. It was Harry who pointed out that it was more likely the Chinese government was looking to score points with the United States in order to help ease the restrictions the President had put in place during her first week in office. The new tariffs seriously altered the favorable trade balance that the Chinese had enjoyed for the previous decade, and many pundits believed if the stiff tariffs were lifted, China would emerge as the world's economic leader.

Dutch still liked his version of the story.

About a quarter mile outside the parking lot perimeter waited members of the Beijing Police Department set strategically around the four roads leaving the dock area. They sat in unmarked cars that would be called in if things went wrong.

Earlier in the day, Commander Tu, who was in charge of the members of the organized crime division, had failed to convince Dutch to let the police officers know why they were there. Dutch stood firm, knowing full well that the Beijing police department wasn't known for their officers being above suspicion. Tales of corruption and close ties with the Triad, or Chinese mafia, haunted the department. If Dutch had a little more political backing—or time—he wouldn't have used anyone but his own men and a token representation from Beijing. But things moved too quickly once they received the tip from the CIA that the smuggled U.S. currency would arrive tonight. Dutch didn't have time to set up the ambush exactly as he would have liked.

Harry nudged Dutch. "When did Cheng say they were coming?" he said, referring to the CIA's mole in the Triad who had been working with them over the previous few months on the case.

As he answered, Dutch's eyes never stopped their systematic surveillance of the team's positions.

"Just after sunset," he said, observing the last hues of purple the setting sun cast as it fell beneath the horizon. "Shouldn't be long now."

Harry went back to his binoculars for another few minutes before speaking again. "What do you think?"

Dutch tilted his head an inch and said, "He's been right so far."

"What. Do. You. Think?" Harry asked again, emphasizing each syllable.

Dutch hesitated. "I would have felt better with more time."

"Too late now," Harry pointed downriver, where a faint light shone, clearly moving toward them.

Dutch tapped the microphone attached to his camouflage jacket. "Everyone, ready. Await my signal."

Harry focused the binoculars. "Appears to be twin motors, about a thirty footer. Two men—wait—three visible."

Dutch checked his team's positions one last time.

"Anything else?" Dutch said as the boat drew nearer.

"I'd say there are enough boxes on deck to hold five, maybe six million. A guy in a white hat is sitting on top of the boxes—I'd say five or six of them."

Dutch grunted as he calculated how much time before the boat docked. Just then he heard a truck driving down the dirt road. Dutch looked to see headlights streaming ahead of a military Humvee. The grinding noise of the gears gave away its distance to them.

"That's a good sign," Harry said, still focused on the boat.

"Yeah, they're not expecting us." He regretted saying it as soon as it came out of his mouth. Dutch wasn't a very superstitious man, but he didn't want to leave anything to chance for another major bust in his short career.

Harry gently put his binoculars down on the dirt, then reached inside his bullet proof vest for his weapon. Dutch did the same as the Humvee stopped twenty feet from the dock. Two men emerged from the front of the vehicle and stood by the hood. The lighting was too poor to make out anything but silhouettes and just enough of their faces to determine they were of Chinese descent. One of the men was much smaller than the other by about a foot.

Just then, the boat cut its engines and drifted toward the dock. Dutch could see just the trace outline of Agent Fedder's gun protruding from the opening in the wheelhouse.

The man behind the wheel of the boat maneuvered it to the side of the dock as the man without the white hat jumped out to tie it up. The two men in front of the Humvee approached the dock. Dutch couldn't tell whether anyone remained in the vehicle.

Once the boat was secured, the other two disembarked and met the men on the dock. All were dressed in dark clothes, with the exception of the one white hat, who appeared to be the leader. He stood in front and spoke with the men from the dock. Dutch was too far away to hear anything but a murmur. Dutch took a quick look again to ensure everyone was ready and waiting for his order to converge.

White hat gestured to the Humvee while the other two men who had arrived in it waved their arms as if they didn't know what he was talking about. Then white hat nodded to the two who had been aboard the boat with him. They turned and moved back toward the boat. As soon as they did, the back door of the Humvee opened and out stepped an enormous man.

Bald, he stood about six foot five, and Dutch figured he had to weigh three hundred fifty pounds. Like the other two, his facial features looked to be Chinese. He had small hands that moved back and forth as if he were cracking his knuckles. Between the man's girth and the length of the long black overcoat he wore, Dutch could only imagine what he was carrying for weaponry.

The man slowly sauntered to the group standing by the dock. White Hat approached him and the two shook hands. They spoke a few words, a few nods of the head, and whatever appeared to be the sticking point was apparently settled. White Hat turned and motioned to his men, who went to the boat and lifted the crates sitting in the back. The other two men from the Humvee assisted in the unloading process.

Dutch could feel Harry shift his position.

"Not yet," Dutch muttered under his breath. Something didn't seem right, but he couldn't put his finger on it.

White Hat and the fat man stood in front of the dock and conversed until the boxes, five in all, were removed from the boat.

Dutch's breathing became very shallow as he braced himself for the quick run twenty or so feet to the parking lot. He peered at the two leaders, who shook hands and exchanged pleasantries. They certainly looked as though they didn't expect anything to go wrong.

Just as Dutch was about to give the order to converge, a crackle came over his radio.

Dutch covered the mic with his hand and turned to Harry. "Who the hell is breaking radio silence?"

"Moving into position now," came a voice with a heavy Chinese accent loud enough to break the quiet on the hillside.

The suspects' heads all swiveled in Dutch and Harry's direction.

"Move, move, move!" Dutch yelled into his microphone as the surrounding area exploded into action.

Commander Tu's men came out of nowhere and descended the hill. One of them opened fire, and the scene quickly dissolved into chaos.

The men by the dock pulled out their weapons and began firing wildly toward the hillside.

The fat man threw off his overcoat to reveal an Uzi sub machine gun, then sprayed the hill, just below Dutch's position. Dutch took aim at the fat man and squeezed off two shots, dropping him like a boulder with two bullets in the chest.

White Hat ran toward the old guard house. Agent Scali bound out, pointing his Beretta 92 at the man's head.

On the dock, the driver of the boat began firing what sounded to Dutch like an M-42 machine gun, and two of Tu's men fell.

Agent Fedder took aim and the boat captain's head exploded.

Shots continued to rain down from the attack team, and the two men from the Humvee collapsed in a hail of gunfire.

As the gunfire subsided, a haze of smoke settled on the scene as Dutch scanned the area for the last deckhand. Harry had scrambled down the hill and was now moving toward Agent Scali, who stood in front of the wounded White Hat. Commander Tu and his uninjured men, along with Agent Fedder, inspected the dead bodies along the dock.

Dutch spotted movement to his right. It was barely perceptible at first and came from the most unlikely direction. Dutch stood still, almost as if he were afraid to scare away his prey. A shape moved on the other side of the barbed wire-topped fence, in between rows of stacked wooden crates. He estimated the man was about forty yards from Agent Scali and White Hat, but no one else seemed to notice him.

Dutch moved closer, but had no idea how the man was even able to scale the fence without anyone seeing him.

Harry stopped walking and looked at his partner, but Dutch raised a hand in an unspoken signal. Quickly and quietly, Dutch passed to the end of the fence at the exit from the parking lot, then looked around. His prey wasn't visible.

Then, like a flash, the man bolted from behind the last stack of crates and with remarkable speed headed to the trees lining the opposite side of the street. Dutch raised his Glock, instantly calculating the shooting solution in his head as his body pivoted to keep up with the man's speed. He was about to yell an order to freeze when the man began yelling as he ran. Dutch couldn't make out what he was saying, but the next thing bullets stitched the ground around him.

Dutch hit the ground and crawled toward the guard shack for cover. Looking back, he saw Agent Scali lying on the ground. Harry was on his elbows and knees propelling himself toward the fence. Keeping his head down while bullets kicked up bits of dirt and asphalt, Dutch fired blindly in the direction the bullets were coming from, but for each round he got off, it seemed another ten came back at him.

He crawled until his hand felt the wooden base of the guard shack. He moved around to the side facing the dock and raised himself up by his back against the wall. Chunks of wood spewed from the corner of the shack, preventing Dutch from getting a look at his assailants.

Harry sidled up to him.

"What the fuck!" Harry yelled over the din, as splintered wood flew in their direction.

Then, as quickly as the barrage had started, it stopped. Dutch held his position and scanned the area where Commander Tu and his men had taken cover behind the bullet-riddled Humvee. Agent Savard had retreated back to his post in the storm drain and appeared to be all right.

Dutch then looked at the spot where moments earlier White Hat had been surrendering to Agent Scali. What he saw would stay with him for the rest of his life.

Agent Scali lay face down in a pool of his own blood. Half of his head was missing, and the red blood still trickled from the gouge, mixed with a greenish liquid. Brain fluid.

Time seemed to stand still for a moment, and then movement suddenly came from everywhere. Commander Tu called in his police force from outside the fence area, and they came running. Harry ran to Agent Scali and knelt, instinctively putting his hand on the dead man's back as if there was something he could do to help. Six of the Chinese police officers, weapons drawn, stood in a line at the exit of the parking lot.

Gesturing wildly, Commander Tu screamed at the men in front of him.

"Commander!" Dutch shouted, more as an enraged statement than a question.

Tu pivoted to face Dutch, his face glowing red. He bowed to Dutch and said, "Agent Brown, my apologies."

Dutch looked at the scene and noticed that two police officers were missing. He pivoted in a circle to see bodies, injured and dead, scattered on the ground. Two team members stood with their weapons at their sides. The CIA agents walked toward them. Dutch felt his body clench as he methodically searched for the one man he wanted to see most of all, but could not.

White Hat was missing.

Chapter 2

"The Senator implied that he couldn't afford to get behind this bill as written with the mid-term election just a couple of months away" said Presidential Chief of Staff Michael Harvey, looking toward the Director of Homeland Security and the White House Legal Counsel who sat on the beige couch opposite him in the Oval Office.

The President moved the reading glasses down her nose in her trademark "I don't give a shit" look of disgust. "Do I even have to say it?" the President said.

"Madame President, I'm afraid you've got to face reality on this front. Your bill is just too controversial for Congress to get tangled up with right now. Only Congress can write legislation; the President may only recommend it. If she does so, then a member of Congress may introduce the bill for consideration. If you want to stick to your version, we've been told by more than one Representative in our party that they will delay the vote. Then you'll be stuck rolling the dice waiting to see what the makeup of the new Congress will be."

White House Chief Counsel Preston Chase, sitting across from the Chief of Staff, nodded his agreement.

"What the hell are you agreeing with him for?" the President said. I didn't ask you in here to talk political strategy."

The President turned back to Harvey. "What are the polling numbers?"

Harvey opened a folder and scanned a long list of figures. "Our projections right now are a possible loss of seven seats in the House and maybe two…" He paused, referring again to the figures. "No, three in the Senate. If that stands, it may be difficult to push through your immigration reform bill after the mid-terms."

The President stared off at the portrait of George Washington that seemed to be listening to the debate. She hoped to see some mystical answer revealed to her in the slight grin of the first President. She wondered how many men who sat in her chair had done the same thing over the years.

After a moment, she focused on her lead counsel. "Mr. Chase, what do you propose?"

A tall man in his early seventies, Preston Chase had been Lorraine Burton's personal attorney for over two decades. "I've drafted a few amendments."

Removing a document from his briefcase, Chase stood, and then moved toward the President's desk. Lorraine couldn't help but notice how well his perfectly tailored three-piece suit hung on his slender frame, and his gold pocket watch glinted under the fluorescent lights of the Oval Office

Handing the document to the President, he took two steps back, his hands folded in front of him. "From everything we've learned from the Minority Leader, the changes laid out here should be enough to carry the vote in the House."

The President read the document. "Five year waiting period?" She continued to skim down the lines of the amendment. "Application for green cards after paying a five thousand dollar fine?" She looked up. "You've got to be shitting me."

"Madame President," Harvey said as he approached the desk to take a place next to Chase. "With these changes, the flavor of the immigration reform bill you drafted stays essentially the same."

The President stood. "The same! The same? Are you kidding me? My bill says that no immigrant here in this country illegally will ever be able to request citizenship. You're telling me that you want to adopt what amounts to essentially a five-year waiting period for complete amnesty?" She stared at the two men in front of her. "Mr. Harvey, why would you suggest that I accept these alterations to the bill?"

"Because, Madame President, you'll win the support of the House and most likely the Senate. You can then add a new immigration reform bill to your list of accomplishments within the first two years of your first term, as promised."

"Really Mr. Harvey? Really?" She fixing him with a stare.

Her Chief of Staff returned her gaze with a look of quiet desperation.

"Mr. Harvey, can you please tell me what exactly I did promise during the campaign?" she asked with a feigned sweetness to her voice.

He exhaled. "You vowed to pass sweeping immigration reform for our country."

She nodded. "And do you think what is written on Mr. Chase's new draft accomplishes that goal?"

"It depends on your point of—"

President Burton held up her hand. "I asked you a simple question that only requires a simple answer. The words 'it depends on' shouldn't be heard in your reply."

Chief of Staff Michael Harvey let out a long breath before saying, "No."

"There, you see? That wasn't difficult, was it?"

Harvey's face reddened. "But Madame President, you need to keep things in perspective. You have accomplished a large amount of what you set out to do in your first two years. Your approval rating is over sixty percent, unemployment is down four points, and the Dow Jones should break 20,500. This legislation may not be what you could call 'sweeping', but it accomplishes a lot. Why are you digging your heels in trying to hit a home run with this one piece of legislation when you're already way ahead of the game?"

"Gentlemen, please have a seat." She beckoned them back to their respective couches. She took her place in one of the two caramel colored leather arm chairs that sat between the couches and in front of the glass coffee table.

"I became President of the United States so I could make a difference in this country as well as the world. I know that sounds trite, but it's the truth. According to you, Mr. Harvey, the American people seem to approve of the job we're doing so far. So why is it that you feel I should compromise on the most important piece of legislation I've introduced to date? A piece of legislation that, need I remind you, is very near and dear to my heart."

"Because it would be better to compromise to ensure passage of something that's important to you rather than roll the dice and come up empty," said Chase.

She slapped her knees with the palms of her hands and stood. "Well then, Mr. Chase, I guess that's why you'll never be President. You don't like to take chances." She returned to her desk, sat, put her glasses back on, and began reading a new folder that was waiting for her. "The answer is no," she said without looking up. "If the members of my own party are too spineless to get behind real reform just to keep their jobs, then screw them." She focused on Chase. "Hold back the bill until after the mid-terms. If they thought it was uncomfortable in the chambers before the election, you watch what I'm sending to the floor next year." Now, she focused on Harvey. "Home run, Mr. Harvey? That's small time. I'm going to hit a grand slam. My bill will

16

pass, I guarantee it." Looking again at the folder, she said, "You may all leave now, thank you."

The men stood and mumbled their customary "Thank you, Madame President" as they trudged out of the Oval Office. Lorraine Burton looked up after the door closed to find Harvey still standing in the middle of the room.

Topping off at six feet even, the chief of staff was taller than she, which she liked. He preferred to wear his white hair parted on the left side of his head. There was enough there so as not to make it look like a bad comb over. He had green eyes and a sturdy, two hundred twenty pound frame. His winning smile could catch the best female reporters off guard; a trait he used often.

She lowered her glasses and sat back in the chair.

"Ahhh, Michael, forever the worrier. What is it now?"

"Madame President—"

"Madame President? We're being awfully formal now, aren't we? It's just the two of us."

"Yes, Madame President, but we are discussing the business of the United States."

"You had no problem calling me Lorraine this morning when you woke me for round two." She smiled coyly at him.

His face reddened. "Yes, but Madame President, we're in the Oval Office."

She stood and sauntered toward him, stopping less than six inches from his face. Her hand reached up and tapped him on the chin, and then she traced a line straight down his throat, past the buttons on his shirt, lingering briefly on the buckle of his belt. She nuzzled her nose into his ear as her hand continued further down, putting to rest any doubt that he wasn't paying attention. Her Chief of Staff let out a controlled gasp.

"Now, what's on your mind?" she said.

He stared up at the ceiling and backed away from her. "Madame—" he started, but was interrupted when she raised a finger. "Lorraine, eh, listen…" he trailed off, having trouble finding the words he wanted to use, but surrendered to the moment and let loose a chuckle.

She laughed.

Harvey stepped back from her and motioned to the couch a few feet away. "Madame President," he said deliberately, "please sit."

She complied, liking this new commanding tone.

Harvey lowered his voice. "Lorraine, I know how important this bill is to you, but I'm afraid that you may be letting personal issues cloud your judgment. It's been ten years since Bill was killed—"

She darted up from her seat.

He pressed her shoulders, pushing her down. "Please Lorraine, hear me out."

She assumed he fully understood the dangerous territory he had ventured into.

"The loss of your husband was a terrible thing to have happen. I can't imagine what it must have felt like. My concern isn't your motives, but one of perception. I know you feel strongly about changing the immigration laws, but the fact that your husband was killed by an illegal immigrant gives the impression that you may be blinded by personal feelings. It will appear as if you are trying to force through what you want instead of compromising. Believe me, Lorraine, two years ago when you first took office the compromise that's now on the table would never have existed. But your track record and your approval ratings have the Minority Leaders running scared. This compromise is really a win for you. I urge you to take it and move on."

She sat quietly for a moment looking at him. "Well, thank you for being so candid." She put her hands together. "Do you understand my feelings for you?"

Michael smiled and sat back. "Well, yes, of course. But that's a totally different subject. I feel the same way about you. That's why I can see your motivations. At least I think I can."

His face relaxed, taking on a relieved look as though he thought he was finally getting through to her.

"Good," she said, then stood to her full five-foot-ten-inch frame. She slowly crossed over and sat on the coffee table so their knees were touching one another. Reaching out, she took his hands into hers and squeezed them affectionately.

She continued in her softest voice, and giving him her biggest smile, said, "Michael, if you ever try to convince me to compromise on this fucking bill again, I'll cut your balls off when we're in bed."

Without waiting for a reply, she tapped his knee quickly and flashed her best campaign smile. "Meeting's over."

Chapter 3

Troubled by the catastrophe that the mission in China had become, neither Harry nor Dutch could sleep on the trip back to Omaha. Now, back in the office, they waited for the debriefing session to begin.

"How did the talk with Maryann Scali go?" Harry said.

Dutch shrugged. "About as well as they all go. She was somber through most of it. But at the end, she was very quiet. There was a silence between us and she didn't say a word for the longest time. I wasn't sure what to do, but she looked me squarely in the eyes and said, 'thank you.' I don't know, it was the way she said it, you know? Like she really appreciated what we do and what her husband did. Does that make sense?"

Harry nodded and silently let the moment pass. After a moment he said, "How are you feeling?"

"About as good as you look."

Harry looked up, grabbed a file and examined it while rubbing the stubble on his face. "What are you talking about? I look great." The partners' desks sat face to face and the desk lamps were moved to each side to clear a passage for the multitude of folders they tossed on each other's desks during the course of a typical investigation. Each knew not to keep a cup of coffee in the "landing zone" where a mis-thrown folder might veer off course and knock over the cup.

"It'll take a while for my body to adjust to Central Standard Time," Harry said taking a long drag from his cup.

"Come on, it's a piece of cake. One good night's sleep should do it."

"Didn't you say you were headed to Alexis' tonight?"

Dutch smiled. "Well, maybe it will be an extra day before I'm back on track."

Harry rolled his eyes. "You're breaking my heart."

Two of the newest agents walked into the office. Fresh from the academy, they looked like they should still be in college. The taller of the two, Agent O'Brien, had red hair and freckles. Dutch remembered thinking the first time he saw him how good he'd be at undercover work. No one would ever peg him for a Federal agent.

His partner was pudgy around the middle, with greasy straight black hair. Dutch thought his name was Meyers or something like that. He had never really had a chance to meet him.

O'Brien said, "Dutch, Ben here doesn't believe me. Can you please show him that trick from before?"

Harry let out a sarcastic laugh.

Dutch looked at O'Brien. "How much do you have riding on it?"

O'Brien looked sideways sheepishly.

His partner spoke up. "Twenty bucks. And I still don't believe it."

Dutch stood. As tired as he was, he enjoyed the attention.

Harry had to laugh again. "Watch out son, don't be a fool with your money," he warned Meyers.

"What's my cut?" Dutch asked O'Brien.

He looked caught off guard. "Cut? I mean, sure, your cut. Well, I didn't think…."

Dutch laughed and said, "All right, but only because I need the practice. You can buy me a coffee later."

O'Brien looked relieved and smiled, nodding.

"First, a history lesson for our newest agents. Before I do anything...Agent Meyers, is it?" Dutch looked for confirmation from the Agent that he got his name right. The man nodded.

Dutch continued. "Please tell me who the person is in the picture hanging on the far wall."

Meyers peered to where Dutch pointed, an eight by eleven frameless photo of a woman hanging on the plain beige wall about twenty yards away. She had heavy eyelids bulging from a narrow face surrounded by long red hair.

"That is a photo of Lynette 'Squeaky' Fromme," Meyers answered.

Dutch raised his eyebrows, impressed. "Very good, rook. Now, bonus points if you can tell me the agent that stopped her from killing President Ford and how."

Harry raised his hand, which Dutch ignored.

Meyers furrowed his brow. "I believe he stopped the shooting by wedging his thumb between the hammer and the gun right before she took the shot with her Colt .45."

Dutch nodded and said, "That's true. But it wasn't my question. "

"Right." Meyers looked to the ceiling for help.

"Ahhhhkkk!" Dutch said, sounding like a buzzer in a game show. "O'Brien?" he asked, pointing to the redhead.

"That would be Agent Larry Buendorf."

"Bonus points go to the Irishman. Good job, rook."

Dutch reached into his desk drawer and pulled out his Arrowhead throwing knife.

"I thought you carried that under your vest," O'Brien said.

"When I'm wearing one. I'd rather not sweat while I'm in the office, if that's Okay with you."

O'Brien blushed while Meyers marveled over the knife. It had an eight-and-a-quarter-inch stainless steel blade attached to a stone black handle with double brass rivets. The tip of the blade shone in the florescent lights.

"Money on the table," Dutch said to the agents who reached into their pockets, each pulling out a twenty, slapping them on the desk.

Dutch stiffened both legs, locking his knees in place. His body was sideways to the photo of Squeaky at the end of the office. He lifted the knife by the handle, and then tossed it into the air and caught it by the sharp point on his index finger. He continued to balance the knife by the tip until he again flipped it into the air and allowed it to spin once, then caught it again by the point. One more time Dutch flipped it, only this time the knife spun twice in the air before he caught it by the tip on the same finger. Then, as quick as a flash, he let the knife drop, caught it by the handle and threw it across the office, lodging it in the forehead of poor Squeaky.

"Shit!" Meyers yelled. "That's unbelievable. Really fucking unbelievable."

He didn't even seem to mind when O'Brien reached for the twenty and pocketed it.

Dutch tried not to blush and said, "Anyone who wants to learn how to throw, just let me know. It's a great skill to have." When no one took him up on the offer, he pointed to O'Brien. "That's the last time. Next time I get half."

O'Brien nodded and smiled as the pair exited the office.

Harry, arms crossed, shook his head. "You're just a show off, that's all."

Dutch twisted his lips into a smile and said, "I may be, but that skill saved my life more than once in the field with the Seals."

There was a crackling noise, and their boss's voice echoed from the phone base. "Harry, Dutch, we're in Conference Room One."

"Showtime," said Dutch. Each grabbed a stack of files and walked through the maze of cubicles built on creaking wooden floors. The Omaha Branch office building of the Secret Service was originally a mincemeat factory that developers had converted a decade earlier into office suites. The Secret Service occupied the entire top floor. The agents would joke that the building, like the agents inside it, wasn't quite ready for prime time. It sat on a somewhat busy intersection at South and 15th Streets on the Belvedere Point section of North Omaha, which was the highest elevation in an otherwise flat topography. Agents with windowed offices were afforded a good view of the city and its skyscrapers.

Crews washed the windows every other week, but still couldn't keep up with the dust that constantly blew in off of the surrounding farmland. After windstorms, the dust on the building's windows gave a feel of the aftermath of a blizzard in the Northeast.

Portraits of past division chiefs hung in straight rows along the corridor, accentuating the uneven and sagging walls and floor. The smell of ancient wood, floor cleaning solution, and furniture polish reminded Dutch of the first day of school after summer vacation , when he would walk into the freshly scrubbed school hallways.

Entering the conference room, Dutch instinctively focused on the line of windows in one wall that looked out over the city. Walking around the heavy oak table to find his seat, he couldn't help but notice how cracked and worn the pale green paint was, and wondered if the department's budget was really so slim so as not to allow a little updating of the decor.

Division Chief Ken Needle sat at the head of the long conference table that was only half occupied. His chair, like the one that matched it at the other end of the table, was plusher and sat unmistakably higher than those that lined the sides of the table. In Dutch's mind, the idea of using furniture to dictate who was in charge belonged in the same era as the cracking paint on the walls.

Needle's sat, squeezing his hulking six-foot-five-inch frame into the old wooden chair. His hair was cropped short, and Dutch knew it was the way Needle had worn it all his life in the military.

Special agent Mark Falk sat to Ken's left. Falk was in his late twenties with a round head covered in unkempt black hair. Next to Falk was his partner, Agent Michael Langone. Also in his twenties,

22

with the exception of his sandy blonde hair, he appeared to be a young Ken Needle.

Dutch took the seat to Needle's right, and Harry fell in next to him. Both set their stacks of files on the table, and Dutch mused that they resembled stacks of pancakes at an all-you-can-eat breakfast buffet at the local HoJo's. Dutch let his eyes wander to the wall on the right, where hung a blank white screen. He thought it was rather low tech for the service, but the glamorous trappings of the agency hadn't quite hit the Omaha branch yet.

Dutch looked across the table at the "odd couple," as he and Harry referred to them, and shifted uncomfortably as he listened to them quietly talk to one another.

"Who are we waiting for again?" Langone asked his partner.

"That 'Whiz Kid,' Flecca."

"Whiz Kid? What are we, back in the seventies?"

His partner laughed and said, "It's how he got his nickname. Trust me, once you meet him you'll see why it fits perfectly."

Langone looked puzzled for a second before saying, "Isn't that the kid who was ordered to work here by the court a few years ago?"

"You haven't really got the whole story," Dutch said. He'd gotten to know Flecca very well in that time and became fast friends.

When Dutch began working in Omaha, he had hit it off with Whizzer right away. He found out that once he got to know him, the 'nerdy' exterior whittled away to expose a very smart and funny young man. Besides helping Dutch and Harry too many times to count with his prowess for the more technical skills needed for investigations, he thought much like the partners had. He certainly didn't mind taking chances or even "bending" the rules when necessary. The three of them made a great team. It also didn't hurt that on the occasions that Whizzer had dinner with Dutch, Dutch brought along Alexis. Whizzer had a mad crush on Alexis and flirted with her non-stop. She played to him like a conductor to an orchestra and they had shared tons of laughs together.

"And you do?" Falk asked.

Dutch shrugged. "Pretty much. Flecca was arrested for underage drinking when he was eighteen. But he had a history with the arresting officer, who'd been out to get him for years. Two days before he was scheduled to go in front of the judge, he hacked into the local police department's database and found the home address of the officer and sent a male stripper dressed as a cop to his house."

The room erupted into howls. "No!" said Langone.

Dutch held up his hand. "Honest truth. Flecca hid across the street and videotaped the show. Somehow the video quickly found its way to every e-mail in the precinct. Flecca even charged the stripper to the cop's credit card."

Langone's jaw hung slack. "You're bullshitting."

Harry picked up where Dutch left off. "It's all true. But the judge was so impressed he said society would be better off if Flecca's talents were used with computers rather than doing laundry.'

Needle spoke next. "That was five years ago. Mr. Flecca, feels that breaking laws while employed by the federal government was a pretty damn good job.

As though on cue, Richard Flecca entered, and the assembled agents spontaneously applauded as he took a seat.

"Wow," said Flecca. "I'll be late more often. Sorry."

Just 23, Richard Flecca was a true "whiz kid," and his nickname around the office was "Whizzer." The first thing Dutch noticed, just as he supposed anyone did, was Flecca's thick, oval-shaped bottleneck glasses that appeared too big for his head. The remnants of acne on his round freckled face did nothing to dispel his youngish looks. He slumped slightly when he walked to his seat. He couldn't have weighed any more than a hundred fifty pounds soaking wet, and his corduroy pants and partially untucked navy-and-orange checkered cotton shirt hung off his body.

Whizzer took his seat and immediately opened his laptop and began tapping away on the keys. He glanced at the bare white screen until a light blue haze began to form. Within a minute, the all too familiar United States Secret Service logo appeared. Whizzer looked up at the men seated around the table and seemed almost surprised, as if everyone had walked in and taken their seats while he was working on his laptop.

"All right, let's get started," Needle said as he placed his two hands on the table and stood, giving the impression that he needed the extra help to hoist his body out of his seat. "First of all, from an accounting standpoint I'd like to say congratulations to you both," he said, speaking to Dutch and Harry. "The final tally of the money you secured in Donguan, China totaled five million, four hundred thousand." A murmur of appreciation came from the opposite end of the table.

"Thank you sir," Dutch said. "But I would rather have brought home a person instead of the money."

Harry grunted his agreement.

"Agreed, but it's still over five million accounted for that we didn't have last week. Good job to you both. From an operational standpoint, let's break it down."

He nodded at Whizzer, who went to work on the laptop keys as the logo disappeared and an aerial view of the Human Port and Pearl River appeared.

"Mr. Flecca has a series of still shots recovered from our satellite positioned over the towns of Donguan and Guangzhou at the time of the operation."

As Dutch narrated, Flecca clicked through a series of satellite images of the night, playing out frame by frame the events of the raid.

Dutch tensed as the screen showed agent Scali, down with a bullet to the head.

Drawing a breath, Dutch regained his composure. "Once agent Scali was down, the primary suspect fled past the fence and into the street." While Dutch spoke, a new image appeared. "We were immediately shot at from an unknown number of assailants from the direction the primary headed." The photo showed all the agents taking cover on the ground.

The final satellite picture showed the aftermath of the shootout. The police, CIA, and Chinese SWAT forces were huddled together.

Dutch continued narrating through the remainder of the images, still haunted by the image of Scali's lifeless body. Finally, his part of the debriefing was over. He took his seat and nodded to Harry, who stood and continued the narration as a grid map of the area lit up the screen.

When Harry covered the escape of the man in the white hat, Langone interrupted. "So, it looks like he must've fled east, is that right?"

Dutch fielded the question. "Actually, just the opposite. We believe our suspect ran toward the barrage of gunfire."

Agents Falk and Langone scoffed. "Why would he do that?" said Falk.

"We believe one of the pairs of police officers stationed just outside the gate was really working for the Triad. When things went bad, they kept us all at bay with their gunfire but allowed our primary to run toward them. Once he reached the pair, they got into the unmarked police car and took off."

"That doesn't make any sense," said Falk.

Harry said, "Actually it makes perfect sense. What better way to let someone escape than to shoot around them, keeping everyone behind on the ground and taking cover? We didn't even know which direction he went until we saw this satellite photo of his escape."

"Hence the two missing police officers," Needle said.

"And a shitload of empty casings found outside the fence line matching those we recovered from the smuggler's Micro Uzis. My guess would be same ammo, but bigger guns based on the amount of lead they threw at us," Dutch added.

Needle continued, "Okay, what about the other suspect who sounded the alarm and fled into the woods?"

Dutch shook his head. "No luck finding him, either."

"What does Commander Tu say?" Needle said.

Harry shrugged. "What do the Chinese always say? It's an embarrassment, his department has been shamed, all the usual things. It still doesn't bring back White Hat."

Needle looked at him, one eyebrow raised. "You're not buying it?"

Harry looked at Dutch, then back to his chief. "Sir, it's no secret the Triad has agents within the police force. It's one of the most corrupt in the world. Frankly, I was disappointed when the service didn't give us more help from our own resources."

Needle slowly nodded. "Well, I'm sure with one dead CIA agent, this will now get the attention of much more than the Secret Service."

Harry leaned forward. "Sir, I've been in touch with Hannady in Langley. Their agents have been scouring the area looking for clues. They've met with all the members of the backup force and haven't turned up anything. The information they have gathered isn't worth shit. Whizzer and some members of the CIA's technical crew are trying to clean up the partial photo of the man who ran into the woods. They think they might get something we can run through our database soon. Unfortunately, we never got anything close on the face of the man wearing the white fedora. It looks like we may run into a dead end on that front."

Both Dutch and Harry sat back down.

Needle folded his hands on the table and looked straight ahead without focusing on anything. "All right. Big picture: what are we looking at?"

Dutch didn't hesitate. "Sir, we're obviously looking at more people involved with this smuggling ring than we originally suspected. Going into this, we thought that the entry point in China was a cleverly disguised area where small shipments coming and going wouldn't be noticed. Now we have strong evidence the Chinese mafia is involved. Commander Tu ran backgrounds on the three men from the Humvee that were killed. All of them have known ties to the Triad. As for the driver of the boat who was killed, he was an American. The CIA has uncovered his identity as one—" Dutch opened a folder and scanned it. "Phillip Crowthier. His record is rather unremarkable. Time in jail for petty theft, B and E, that type of thing. No known ties to any group inside or outside the states. He's just a typical gun for hire."

Needle pressed his index fingers under his lip. "So what do we know for sure as of this point in time?"

Dutch nodded to Falk and Langone to field Needle's question. He wanted them involved as much as possible with this side of the investigation, no matter his personal feelings about them. As of that moment, they were the only two resources available.

Falk sat up straight and cleared his throat. "Sir, Agent Langone and I are in the process of tracking down the payroll records from the Port of Camden in Jersey for the last two weeks. From the information Dutch and Harry gave us, this is the most likely departure point of the money that surfaced in China. Odds are that Crowthier was probably employed there as well."

Evidently, Needle didn't have much confidence in the two either because he turned back to Dutch and asked, "And please tell me again why you're so sure those crates you recovered left from the Jersey Shore?"

Dutch looked to Whizzer. Instantly a new photo of a stack of wooden crates piled on top of one another showed on the screen.

"Sir, these are the crates that contained the money. They are also available for inspection down the street at our warehouse where they're being kept for evidence."

Whizzer switched to a close up of one of the crates.

"You'll notice a red mark in the top right corner."

Dutch paused to let everyone examine what he was referring to.

"Looks like all the other marks on the crate," Langone said.

A new picture appeared, this one a close up of the mark.

"It does, but look at the shape of the mark. It's an eyeball with a red pupil. This mark is what shipping companies on the Jersey Shore use for certain cargo. When foremen on the dock see this mark, they know that particular cargo is going into the ship's hold separately and must stay on top, not stacked under all the other crates. They've used the same symbol for years."

"And how do you know this?" Falk asked.

Dutch shrugged. "Luck. I grew up in Jersey and hung out by the docks, so I picked up a few things. I'd know that symbol anywhere." He turned to Needle and said, "Sir, I can tell you without hesitation that the red eyeball stamped on the top right corner of these crates means they left from the Jersey Shore. It's impossible to forget."

His boss opened the folder in front of him and took out a still photo of the crate with the symbol on it, studied it, then slid it back.

Needle motioned for him to continue.

"Sir, Harry and I have got to get up to Jersey and look for ourselves. I'd also like to coordinate with Tim Mackenzie of the New Jersey State Police office to assist once we get there."

"Why involve the state police in Jersey?"

"Mackenzie and I went to school together. He's an old friend. He also knows more about what goes on down at the docks than anyone in our agency. He'll be able to help us find where on the dock the money left from."

"Plus," Harry said without letting Needle respond, "he's someone we can trust. He can point us in the right direction and save us days of poking around trying to find out the lay of the land."

"Okay, who do you need?" said Needle.

"Obviously we'll need a couple of agents from the Jersey branch to begin with. Harry and I will need a place to work out of for a few days as well." Dutch paused in thought before adding, "Also, sir, I'd like you to make a call and get A.J. Burke put on the case with us. He's based out of D.C."

"Burke?"

"Yes, sir. He and I came out of the academy together. He's assigned to the Treasury Department. He heads up logistics for the Bureau of Engraving and Printing. Indications are that's where the money has gone missing from. This way we've got the beginning, middle, and ending points being represented in the investigation."

"How sure are you the money is missing from there?"

"Sir, the serial numbers on the recovered money show that they were printed in D.C."

"All right," Needle said and rose from the chair. "Keep me informed as to the progress."

"Thank you, sir," the partners said in unison.

Chapter 4

Alexis lit the last candle on the dinner table, then went to the dimmer switch on her dining room wall and lowered the lights just a little bit more. Everything looked perfect. In the kitchen, she lowered the oven to a temperature to keep the baked ziti warm, just in case she and Terry didn't get to dinner right away. After all, it had been over a week since they last saw one another.

She moved through the hallway and stopped to check her reflection in the mirror. The heat of the kitchen disrupted her straight hair and she wanted to look her best tonight. She tucked one of her bangs back behind her ear. Her hair curled right below her chin, and the jet black color accentuated her large round, cool blue eyes. Though she hated her nose—it just seemed too wide—Terry said it was the feature that he liked most. He said he always liked women with "untraditional features." Alexis wasn't really sure if that was meant as a compliment.

After another final look in the mirror, she stuck her tongue out at herself, mocking her vanity, and headed back to the kitchen.

Moments later she heard the key in the lock and knew it was Terry arriving.

She half skipped and half jogged the twenty feet to the door, and when Terry opened it she leaped into his arms, knowing he would catch her. Their lips met.

When they had finished kissing, Dutch said, "Do you welcome all your guests like this?"

"Only the lucky ones."

He continued holding her, caressing her as they made their way into the living room.

Setting her down, he cradled her face in his muscular hands. "How are you, babe?"

She lowered her head down to his so she could kiss him before answering, "Better now. I've missed you."

"Ditto. We can't let this happen again."

"I'm fine with that, but I'm not the problem. You are. I never leave home." She chuckled.

He rolled his eyes. "Oh yeah, babe, you're always here. I've had more sex with your voicemail than I have with you lately."

"Oh yeah?" She smiled. "Well, we'll have to change that tonight, won't we?"

She kissed him again, this time allowing her tongue to find its way between his lips. He folded his arms to bring her tighter against his body. Even in this awkward position, they seemed to "fit" as she always put it, like two puzzle pieces.

Dutch lifted her up slightly and adjusted his pants.

She laughed. "Having a little problem down there?"

"No problem at all. Just gotta get a little more room. It's really a curse you know, needing all that room."

"Depends on your point of view, I guess. From where I sit, it's no problem whatsoever." She kissed him again, and then moved her hand down between his legs until she could feel his arousal grow.

He carefully stood, made one more adjustment to his pants, then took her hand and led her to the bedroom.

Exhaling loudly, Alexis rolled onto her back, her chest still heaving. She tried to get her breath back under control. She stared up at the ceiling as her eyes slowly began to regain their focus. She let her hand drop onto Dutch. The warm sweat that soaked both of their bodies made his chest slick. She turned her head to look at her boyfriend, whose breathing wasn't nearly as heavy as hers was.

"Was it good for you?" she said.

Dutch looked at her and laughed.

"I feel like I just ran a marathon, and you're hardly breathing hard."

"Hon, that's because I'm in much better shape than you are," he teased.

Alexis wasn't a health nut, but she was religious about hitting the gym three times a week. She turned on her side and rested her head on her hand so she could face him. The moonlight filtering through the blinds made her boyfriend's sweat-soaked body glisten. She took a finger and traced his stiff jaw line down to his chin. His face was handsome and very regal looking. His nose, unlike hers, curved perfectly. She admired his chestnut brown eyes that matched his hair. Her finger continued tracing up and onto his head, where she tried to grab a handful of his freshly cut hair, but there wasn't enough to hold. She liked the crew cut look.

He kissed her finger as it moved past his lips, past his chin, and down his chest. She liked to trace the lines in his well-defined six pack abs. As her finger caressed the sculpted lines of his muscles, his body twitched.

"Ticklish?"

He grabbed her finger and brought it back to his lips. "Down there I am." He turned on his side so the two faced one another.

"Hi, beautiful," he said, smiling.

"Hey," she said in almost a whisper.

"I've really missed you."

She nodded. "Me too. It's getting harder to spend time away from you."

He grunted his agreement and kissed her finger again.

"Do you think there's a way we could possibly do something about this problem?" The question she asked was a familiar one.

He shrugged.

She playfully jumped on him and began tickling the lower, well defined, part of his stomach. He tried in vain to grab her hands but he pretended she was too quick. He didn't really want her to stop anyway.

Finally, after much laughter from both, he was able to wrest her hands and hold them. He lifted her and turned so he hovered over her body, holding himself up on his elbows while still clutching her wrists.

"Do you have any ideas how we can decrease the amount of time we spend apart?" he asked.

Since their jobs required frequent travel, moving in together was often a topic of conversation. Alexis shrugged playfully.

"How about if we discuss it over dinner," said Dutch.

She giggled. "I'll need more candles. The others have probably burned themselves out by now.

Dutch followed Alexis out of the kitchen holding two plates full of pasta and set them down on the table. She lit the new candles and opened a bottle of wine before sitting down. Holding up a half full glass she said, "A toast."

He met her glass midair with his own. "What are we drinking to?"

She smiled. "To...possibilities."

They clinked glasses, and each took a sip.

Dutch admired his girlfriend in the flickering candlelight. She was beautiful even when she lounged around the apartment wearing his tattered "Navy" t-shirt and baggy sweats. He caught her blue eyes, which cast a spell over him in the dim light. They radiated life and love.

"You're amazing," he said.

"Thank you," she said, blushing slightly.

"So, what's new in your job?"

He had caught her with a mouth full of ziti, and she quickly picked up the napkin to wipe the errant piece of mozzarella that hung from her mouth. "Some .... Gig... mews..atullee," she managed to get out.

Dutch laughed.

She swallowed, wiped her mouth, and blurted out, "I forgot to tell you some great news! Brad wants me in D.C. to help with his presentation to Congress!"

"Wow!" His smile stretched from ear to ear, and his chest swelled with pride for her. Alexis was a rising star at Montgomery & Company and was the youngest Vice President of Mergers and Acquisitions the firm had ever had.

"I thought you weren't sure who was going. I'll bet it was you all along, This is a really big deal, Alexis. Congratulations!"

She beamed. "Thank you. I'm pretty psyched about it."

"So will I be seeing you on the news testifying to Congress with that skinny microphone in front of your face?"

"Brad's going to be testifying. I'll be next to him, though. Maybe you will see me."

"Honey, I don't know about this. Brad always seems to choose you when he needs someone to travel with. Should I be jealous?"

It was a private joke between the two of them. Alexis was twenty-seven, and Brad Montgomery—all two hundred seventy-five pounds of him—was in his late sixties. He had two ex-wives and a heart condition, and he didn't pay attention to any of them. The proud owner of a "type A" personality, Montgomery could say he had "been there, done that" twice over in the financial world.

"I could be wife number three and get my piece of that estate."

"Go for it." Dutch laughed. "But really, darling, I'm proud of you. You certainly deserve it. No one works harder in that office."

They continued eating in silence for a couple of moments. Dutch could sense that the pause caused the mood in the room to shift.

"Speaking of—" they both said in unison and laughed. They had entered that zone of thinking the same things at the same time in their relationship, and slips like that were happening more frequently.

"You first," she said.

Dutch took another sip of wine before starting. "I wanted to talk seriously about us. We've been dancing around it for months, but I think we really do owe it to ourselves to figure this out."

"I agree."

They sat staring at each other. Dutch waited for Alexis to speak. She waited for him. When neither spoke, smiles appeared on both of their faces.

"All right, I'll go first." Dutch said. "Omaha isn't where I want to end up. You know that, and I know that. Why I got stationed here I'll never figure out. It's a nice place, but it's not somewhere I want to put roots down. Once this investigation I'm working on is over, I'm going to put in for a transfer back to the East Coast. At this point I don't care which state they put me in, but I've had enough of the Midwest."

"Right. You know we're on the same page with this. I'd miss my family, but that's why they have planes. In fact, I got a call from Darrell in the New York office this week. He hinted that all I've got to do is say the word and I can be transferred to the Big Apple."

Dutch frowned. Alexis had the opportunity to move out of Omaha and go to the city, but she hesitated because of their relationship. For some time he tried to convince himself it was her family keeping her there, but he could tell she was itching for something more and he couldn't kid himself anymore.

She raised her hand to stop him from objecting. Many times in the past, he had witnessed her stubborn Italian heritage kicking in once she dug her heels in. As the only girl in a family of five, she had learned to get what she wanted.

"Sweetheart I already told you, we either move together or not at all. I've got the kind of job that I can be living in the middle of the country but still travel to where I need to be. It's not as easy for you."

Dutch said, "I know, and I appreciate it. But I don't want to hold you back from advancing your career."

She looked at him, blew him a mock kiss, and went back to her food.

"Okay, so we're both here for now. Hopefully in a few months that will change. In the meantime..." He left the thought unfinished.

"In the meantime..." she echoed, blushing and suddenly unable to meet his gaze. She had been asking him to move in with her for a month, and he had been sidestepping. She kept glancing between him and her plate of ziti.

There was a pregnant pause. She wasn't going to make this easy for him. He tried to search for the right words. "I mean, economically and all....you know."

"Um hum," she hummed her agreement, raising her eyebrows and urging him to continue.

He wiped his sweaty palms on his napkin. "Well, it would be easier...you know, with...clothes....and the whole money thing."

She banged her fork on the plate. "Terrence Brown, do you mean to tell me that you're less afraid of storming a beachhead than telling me that you'd like to move in with me?" All of this beating around the bush had gotten her worked up. "I can't believe you. For four weeks I've been asking you—"

He interrupted her tirade by standing, crouching beside her chair, and then pulling her head toward him and kissing her.

She pulled back after the first kiss and continued. "I mean I wasn't sure if you even—" He kissed her again. "Wanted to—if you weren't sure—"

This time he took both of his arms and wrapped them around her, drew her close, and kissed her hard. He could feel her resistance fall away, and she melted into him.

Finally they parted. With her eyes still closed she whispered, "I'll make room for you in the closet."

Chapter 5

Several days later, Station Chief Ken Needle tossed two plane tickets on Dutch's desk.

"Be at the airport by five a.m.," he said before disappearing around a corner.

Dutch picked up the US Airways tickets, examined them, and yelled out, "No first class?"

From his desk, Harry motioned for Dutch to hand him the tickets so he could examine them. "It's about time we got these," he said, opening one of the ticket vouchers.

"No shit. At least we're flying out tomorrow morning. That will give us the entire day to make some headway at the docks."

"What's the latest in Jersey?"

"Mackenzie said his surveillance hasn't turned anything up in the last twenty four hours. But his contact inside the union has promised us unfettered access to whatever we need once we get there."

Harry looked across the hallway at Falk and Langone's office. "Those two have really been a bust."

Dutch let out an exasperated breath. "We'll have to start from scratch when we get to Jersey. All of the intel we got from them amounts to nothing. I wish the brass had given us the okay to go a week ago. We're losing time and this trail is running cold."

"No shit. Like there wasn't a Federal judge anywhere who could have issued search warrants in less than a week?"

"It's an election year, don't forget. These judges are tied in pretty tight with union money."

Harry signed and shook his head. "Fucking politics." He stood and stretched. "I'm heading out to get a cup of coffee. You want anything?"

"Nope. Thanks for asking," Dutch said as his phone rang. He picked it up. "Agent Brown."

"I'll bet you're still one ugly mother fucker," said a raspy voice on the other end of the line.

"I may be ugly, but at least I still get laid. How's married life working for you?" Dutch recognized the voice as his friend from New Jersey, Detective Tim Mackenzie.

"You bastard!"

Dutch laughed. "Thanks for calling, Tim. What's the good word on the coast?"

"You're going to love me, that's all I've got to say."

"Tell me what I want to hear."

"If you can ever get your ass here, I've lined up Mickey Finn for you, all gift wrapped and ready to go."

"Cut the shit, Tim. How'd you do that?"

"Let's face it, he's a sucker for the old days. When he found out you were flying in, he couldn't wait to talk with you. I think he misses you more than I do."

"Oh yeah, I'm sure that's it. What did you get on him? Not B and E again. Please tell me he's not that stupid."

Mackenzie laughed. "Yup, he's still that stupid. I got word from a sergeant at Precinct 3 they picked him up a couple of days ago. He's cooling his heels in the pen now. You'd think that thirty years of that two-bit larceny crap would have turned him into an expert by now."

"How long's it been since his last stint at Bayside?"

"Let me think. I'd say he's been out about four years now. I don't think he's looking forward to an automatic return trip this time. He's got to be what, sixty, sixty-five by now, right?"

"I guess. When we were kids, he was working a forklift on the docks. How old were you when he gave you that video game that 'fell off the boat?'"

Mackenzie laughed. "I almost forgot about that. Shit, I must have been twelve or thirteen. Wow, I can't believe how long ago that was."

"So, how did you talk him into it?"

"Mickey and I had a heart to heart last night in the lockup. Believe it or not, he's mellowed quite a bit since the old days. I don't think his heart's in it anymore, but he just doesn't know how to do anything else. He was happy to see me, that's for sure. The first thing he did was ask about you. When I told him you were coming, he looked like a kid on Christmas morning. I guess he thinks the information he's got will give him his get out of jail free card this time."

"Well, it'll be good to see old Mickey Finn again. I'll bring him a couple of packs of Pall Mall for old times' sake."

"Sounds like a plan. I've got some space for you to set up shop when you get here. Make sure you find me before you head over to the 3rd; I want to go with you."

"You got it. Tim, you're the best!"

"Yeah yeah, I've heard that before. All I know is, dinner's on you tomorrow night."

"Absolutely. Now stay out of trouble. Bye, Tim."

Just as Dutch hung up the phone, Harry returned and set a steaming cup of coffee in front of him.

"Did I hear the words 'Mickey Finn' a second ago?" Harry said.

"Yes you did."

Harry sat and looked at Dutch with raised eyebrows, beckoning him to continue.

Dutch smiled thinking of the man, and told Harry how he'd known Finn as a child.

After a couple of minutes, Dutch paused to take a swig of his coffee. He could picture the events from his past as if they happened just the day before.

"Anyway, this guy Mickey catches us making off with a keg of nails one day. I was so scared I almost pissed my pants. He was this tall, thin guy with crazy black hair flying out in different directions. His face was full of wrinkles, and his hands were worn down and callused. He had tattoos all over his arms, and when he grabbed us his hands felt like sandpaper. He sat us down and asked what the hell we thought we were doing. Mackenzie and I just looked at each other, hoping the other would answer. All of a sudden Mickey breaks out laughing. We didn't know what to make of this guy. He said that he'd been watching us steal stuff for the last two weeks."

"So what did he do?" Harry asked, suddenly coming back into Dutch's focus. The shadows of the past drifted away.

"Being the model citizen he was, he said he wasn't going to tell on us if we'd help him. You see, Mickey had his own side business going on at the time. We'd be his lookouts when certain crates went missing into the back of Mickey's truck."

"So he turned you and your buddy into criminals? Sounds like a real standup guy."

"We had no idea what Mickey was doing, really. He would tell us that the crates were overstock and he was delivering them to his boss' office, but that the dock master didn't like him kissing up to the big boss so we had to keep an eye out for him. We actually believed him."

Dutch's phone rang, interrupting his story. He held up his finger and picked up. "Agent Brown."

"Dutch," a female voice on the other end said, "Ken needs to see you and Harry in his office pronto."

"Got it," he said, then hung up and stood. "Come on, we're being beckoned."

The two strode out of the office and down the hallway.

"So then what?" Harry said.

"So anyway, we got to know Mickey pretty well over the next couple of summers, and after Tim made detective, Mickey became one of his top informants. The rest is history."

They were approaching Needle's office when Harry held his hand across Dutch's chest, stopping him before they went in.

"Okay, but you've got to tell me something. Please say his real name isn't 'Mickey Finn.'"

"Nope, it wasn't. I found out years later his real name was Albert Hoff. But the guys around the dock gave him that nickname because they said he was so ugly, the only way he'd get laid was to slip a 'Mickey Finn' into a girl's drink."

Harry and Dutch were still laughing when they opened the door leading into the foyer of their division chief's office. The blonde secretary, a telephone cradled to her ear, gestured for them to wait.

"Yes—yes, sir—no, sir. I'll make sure your appointment is not canceled this time. Thank you for calling."

She hung up and pressed a button on her phone. "Sir, Agents Ludec and Brown are here."

"Tell them to come in."

Most offices in the old textile building looked the same. However, Ken Needle's was much bigger, with a picture window along the back wall affording views into the city of Omaha. The walls were covered with pictures, mostly older ones, with faded colors. From many visits to the office, Dutch knew they were of Needle's old infantry platoon. There were soldiers on top of tanks riding in the desert during the first Gulf War. Glimpses of the vast desert as well as Middle Eastern architecture were difficult to miss.

Needle rose and motioned for them to sit. The formality of it struck Dutch as a bit out of place and immediately became concerned. He didn't know what this was going to be about, especially since he had spoken with his boss twenty minutes earlier and everything seemed fine. The hair on the back of his neck rose in anticipation, something his body did automatically since his days with the Seals.

The two partners sat, but Needle remained standing. He walked from his chair to the front of his desk where he leaned against a corner, facing them, then reached out his hand.

"I wanted to be the first to congratulate the both of you."

Harry frowned. "Congratulate us?"

Needle grabbed Harry's hand and shook it vigorously, then took Dutch's hand and did the same. "Ten minutes ago I received a call from Special Agent William Polk."

"Polk?" Dutch said.

"Yes, Agent Polk from the POTUS detail. It seems the work you two have done on your last couple of cases hasn't gone unnoticed from the folks at the White House. You're on the short list of call-ups."

Dutch and Harry looked at each other, then skeptically at their boss.

"On the short list to be on the Presidential Protection Detail?" Harry asked.

"That's right."

"How long is the short list?"

"It consists of the two of you!"

"I didn't think there were going to be anymore call-ups this year," Dutch said.

Needle shrugged. "It's not my job to figure out why, just to do what I'm told. You are both expected to be at the D.C. office at noon on Thursday. Good luck."

"Thursday!" protested Dutch. "That's in two days. We're supposed to be in New Jersey tomorrow. What about this case?"

"What about it? Turn your notes and the file over to Falk and Langone; they can take lead on it. They have been working with you, so it shouldn't be much for them to take over."

"But sir—" Harry protested.

"Agent Ludec, I don't want to hear it," Needle said, holding up his hands in front of him.

"Sir, you've got to understand. We're at a critical juncture in this case. Falk and Langone—"

Needle interrupted him. "Falk and Langone are trained Federal Agents who specialize in the investigation of crimes against the United States monetary supply. They will be more than capable of taking over. You two, on the other hand, would be wise to take some advice. Bill Polk is the Special Agent in Charge of the detail that protects the President of the United States. He doesn't just pick up the phone for any ordinary matter. He specifically asked for you two to head to Washington to meet with him."

His posture softened as he pushed himself off the corner of the desk. "Gentlemen, this doesn't happen every day. Now, unless you two want to stay in Omaha the rest of your lives, I'd get your asses out of here. You've got two days to turn over your case notes and pack for your trip to the show."

Dutch looked at Harry, who returned his bewildered gaze, then stood.

Back in their office, Dutch dropped down in his chair and stared blankly across to Harry without really seeing him.

"What the fuck just happened?" asked Harry.

Dutch slowly shook his head. "I don't know. I mean, the last couple of years we've collared some high level criminals, but I didn't think—"

Harry interrupted him. "How much money do you think we've recovered since we've been partners?"

Dutch opened his desk drawer and found the scratch pad on which he kept an informal running tab of their currency seizures. "Including the five-point-four mil we just brought back, the count's up to…..shit, I didn't realize we were at that figure." Dutch looked up to Harry. "Seventy five million dollars!"

Harry whistled. "That's a lot of greenbacks."

Dutch allowed himself to smile. "I guess we have been on a roll, haven't we?"

He put the pad on his blotter and sat back in his chair. He mumbled under his breath, "Washington…William Polk. Harry, do you know what this means?" His voice grew more excited with each passing moment. "We're going to D.C. to meet with William Polk! This is fantastic!"

He looked over at Harry when he didn't hear a response to his mini celebration.

"Harry, what's wrong?" he asked. "I know you love being an investigator, but this is the POTUS detail we're talking about here."

Harry shifted in his chair. "I know it's a huge honor, Dutch, but this has always been your dream, not mine. Sure I love being an investigator, but I also have roots here that you don't. You've only been here three years, but I've lived here all my life. My family is here; my wife's family is here. Our kids go to school here and are happy. I don't know if this is a move I'm looking to make."

Dutch deflated a bit. "This is once in a lifetime, Harry."

Harry just nodded. Dutch could see the inner conflict on his partner's face.

Harry laughed. "I'm ten years older than you. Past my prime, so to speak. Sandy and I talked about this a couple of years back. She thought the possibility of my going to D.C. had elapsed because of my age. They're looking for young guns like you. Why would they want me?"

Dutch looked him in the eye. "Because you've been a top investigator for years now, and we've had a couple of really high profile cases lately. Why wouldn't they want you?"

Harry smiled. "Thanks, Dutch. I really appreciate that." He sat back. Dutch could see a small smile begin to crease his face. He started shaking his head. "Washington. Can you believe it? I never thought in a million years." His voice trailed off.

Chapter 6

The storm front that was supposed to move south stalled over Nebraska, causing Air Force One—a military version of the Boeing 747—to pitch violently starboard. Behind her desk aboard the "flying White House," President Burton continued her phone call as if the jolt never happened.

"Mr. Prime Minister, I'm sure you and I will be able to agree on the last pieces of this relief package in no time. Why don't we let our people craft the final draft and I'll call you in a few days with any changes that are needed." She paused and listened. "Of course, of course, yes." She smiled.

Michael Harvey shifted in the leather upholstered chair in front of her desk, waiting for the call to end. Chin in one hand, feeling airsick, he was amazed at her ability to remain charming while on the phone with foreign dignitaries in one minute, then slice the head off a staffer the next. He crossed and uncrossed his legs as he watched his boss work her magic.

White House chiefs of staff rarely lasted more than two years, and Harvey thought he knew why. Among all his other responsibilities, he also had to keep the voting public from seeing Burton's darker side.

"Well that's very kind of you to say, Mr. Prime Minister," she said now. "I wish you the same. Take care." Hanging up, she looked toward Michael and gave him a smile and a thumbs up.

"Congratulations, Madame President," he said.

"Thank you Michael. I couldn't have done it without you, though. It was a stroke of genius getting that language about the mining rights thrown in at the last minute. You should have heard him just now. He's so anxious to get that check that he would have signed onto just about anything."

"Well, appropriating two hundred million dollars for the earthquake relief was the right thing to do in the first place. That was your idea. I give you credit for standing up to Congress the way you did."

She quietly chuckled and looked out the rectangular window at a bright blue horizon, which seemed to sit atop a flat deck of black storm clouds.

"Congress. What the hell do they know about doing the right thing? All they care about is their next election cycle. Two hundred million is a drop in the bucket for them, but they need to make it look as if they're fighting for every last dime of the taxpayers money…that is until they need a cool ten million for someone to study the mating habits of a black eyed chinchilla that suddenly turned up in their district."

"Still, though, the hundred mil they approved would have looked good in the press. You wouldn't have taken a hit with that."

"Probably. I can't believe three congressmen from some backwater district in Idaho were able to hold me hostage like that."

Standing, she crossed to the bar against the wall, steadying herself as the plane rocked again. She poured two glasses of the thirty-year-old whiskey she preferred without spilling a drop.

"Now everyone's happy. East Timor gets a fat relief check." She turned from the bar and approached him, holding out one of the glasses.

Harvey clinked his glass with hers, drew it close to his mouth and said quietly, "And to the gold, copper, and silver mining rights we got in return," he said.

President Burton emptied her glass in one gulp. Setting it down, she looked at him and let her mind wander. She had known Michael Harvey since she was in her thirties when he was her boss at Waverly Investments. She was lead counsel for many high profile cases the investment firm found itself in, mostly due to Harvey himself.

Even back then she could tell that Harvey, ten years her elder, took a liking to her and her work ethic, not to mention the fact that she had bailed him out of more than one scrape with the Federal Trade Commission. She was also keenly aware that not only did he notice her talent for the law, but her lineage as well. Her family was well known in Arizona political circles, and her father was heavily connected with politics at the national level. He had been a Chief Advisor to President Bush Sr. He himself had been rumored at one time for a run at the White House. Like father like daughter. She correctly assumed that Michael Harvey knew full well of her political ambitions and her connections that could get it done, which is why he kept her close as she progressed along her career path from the law to politics. It had been a match born out of mutual need and reciprocity.

Harvey capped off his life in the financial world with the multibillion dollar merger with Drumm Pharmaceuticals. Many considered it to be his crowning achievement. Out-foxing his competitor at the time, now Secretary of Homeland Security Trevor Sirois, was no easy feat, and solidified not only his standing in the financial world but his financial security for years afterwards.

Later on he surprised everyone when he abruptly left Wall Street for Main Street, flying to Arizona to head up the Presidential campaign of one Lorraine Burton. She showed her appreciation of his hard work when she tapped him to be her Chief of Staff days after the election.

Harvey looked at her now, as she looked absently into the middle distance.

She seemed to snap out of her funk and returned his gaze. Then, with a recklessness all too familiar, she reached for the bottom of her shirt.

He finished his drink and walked to the door, opened it slightly, and met the eyes of the Secret Service agent standing at his post, then closed the door.

Through the door, Michael heard the agent quietly say, "Widow is bunking down." He knew the man was speaking into the communicator in his cuff to keep the other agents on duty updated.

Inside, Michael turned to find the President's ample breasts exposed and her belt and buttons undone on her pants. He admired the beauty of the most powerful woman in the world. At fifty-five, her breasts were full and firm. Her curly blonde hair, which always looked to be ready for the cameras, fell so it just barely touched the tops of her shoulders. Her arms weren't what one would call muscular, but toned. President Burton had never had children, and had always taken good care of herself, and it was paying dividends, especially with barely any clothes on.

She noticed him admiring her, and took her time removing her underwear. She turned, allowing him a good view of her rear.

While enjoying the show, he took off his pants and began working on his shirt buttons. Himself a former CEO on Wall Street, he did his best to keep up with the aging process. At sixty-five years old, his two hundred twenty pounds was a bit high for a man of his height. However, his muscles were still chiseled from years of his hobby of body building. The thick hair on his chest had turned white over time. Lorraine liked to run her hands through it, and he liked to let her.

She got to the front of her desk, turned so she could face him, and slowly took either end of her underwear and shimmied it down her long, slender legs, stepping one leg out at a time. With her left foot, she flicked it with amazing accuracy and landed it right in Michael's hands. He removed his underwear, and motioned with his head to the inner door which led to her sleeping quarters.

She slowly shook her head, smiling wickedly, then indicated the couch beside the bar.

"That doesn't pull out to a bed," he said.

"Then I guess we'll have to take turns lying down." She moved her hand down his chest, then wrapped it around his erect penis. Holding it like a leash, she led him to the couch.

"Lorraine, we're kind of close to the door."

She turned and sat, still holding him as he stood in front of her and said, "Then you'll have to make sure not to make any noise."

He quietly thanked God that the Secret Service could keep secrets.

Chapter 7
Early November

With childlike excitement, Dutch approached the nondescript building on the corner of 10th and H Street. It was a good thing he had the address, because nothing about the structure indicated it was the D.C. home of the United States Secret Service. From the outside, it looked like any other downtown building with first floor offices looking out to the sidewalk and tan bricks reaching up nine floors. In fact, the architecture was very tastefully done with a large glass façade shaped like a point jutting out over H Street, affording its occupants a nice view of the city. Other than the cameras conspicuously placed at strategic points, the only thing hinting it was a government structure were the decorative steel posts lining the front to deter any type of vehicular bomb being driven into the first floor.

He held his breath and opened the glass door that led into a bland foyer. The lighting was dim and the walls were metallic gray. There was no furniture for anyone to sit on. It was immediately evident that this was not a place in which one loitered. The middle of the entryway was taken up by a bulletproof glassed booth that reminded him of a movie theater ticket kiosk. On either side of the booth were secure bullet-proof glass doors leading to who-knew-where. In fact, the only allowance the department made to let anyone walking in know it was the Secret Service was a large steel lettered statement hanging on the east wall. Dutch paused as he read the familiar phrase, "Worthy of Trust and Confidence," the motto of the United States Secret Service.

He and Harry had different interview times, so Dutch was alone as he approached the non-descript frowning woman sitting behind the thick glass.

"Special Agent Terrance Brown to see Director Polk," he said into a slotted metal disk.

The woman found Dutch's name on a list, then pointed to her left and pressed an unseen button. Dutch could hear massive locks sliding out from the door frame to his right, and turned that way.

Once past the outer gate, as he thought of it, the hallway was brightly lit and painted in a more welcoming yellow. A slender man about his own age came out from the first door on the right of the hallway.

"Agent Brown," he said. "Right this way."

The two didn't exchange any pleasantries as they walked to a bank of elevators and ascended to the top floor. Once the doors opened, the man stayed behind in the elevator. Alone in a lavishly furnished waiting room, Dutch hoped the beating of his heart couldn't be heard by anyone else. He wiped his sweating palms against the legs of his pants.

Only then did he notice a busty blonde secretary smiling at him from a desk in the center of the room.

"Please have a seat, Agent Brown." She indicated a row of chairs lining the far wall.

As he crossed toward the chairs, Dutch took in the décor. He hoped his mouth wasn't gaping open while he took his visual tour.

There was the obligatory picture of the sitting President hanging in the center of the wall. Lorraine Burton stared down at him with what had become her trademark million-dollar smile. It made her seem accessible to the common man. He wondered if that facade were true. He hoped he would find out soon.

The seal of the United States Secret Service was embossed on the thick blue carpet. A large glass coffee table was positioned over the seal, giving it a larger-than-life look. The white painted walls were strewn with pictures of Secret Service Agents on duty. Each wall seemed to have a different theme. The center wall had pictures of agents guarding different Presidents taken over the years. From what he could tell, the history of the wall spanned back to the Kennedy era, not an era the service was most proud of. John F. Kennedy was the last sitting President that was lost while in office. A mistake the Service was hell-bent not to repeat.

The photos were taken in and around Washington D.C. with many familiar backdrops such as the Capital building, the White House of course, the Jefferson Memorial. The list went on.

On the left wall hung more pictures of agents surrounding various Presidents, only these were taken in foreign countries. The Eiffel tower, Tiananmen Square, and other prestigious destinations were well represented.

Hanging on the wall behind him were photos of the different Presidential Movers, as they were referred to. Marine One, Air Force

One, and the Presidential limo nicknamed 'The Beast' were all photographed in various stages of motion. Dutch tried not to turn his head too much and make it obvious he was enthralled by the pictures. He would glance occasionally at the secretary to make sure he wasn't getting caught. He thought he saw a smirk on her face once or twice. He was sure he wasn't the first one to be in awe of the surroundings. To hell with it, he thought and kept looking.

The phone rang, and he could hear the receptionist say something into her headset, then she looked up. "Agent Brown, Director Polk will see you now."

As he entered Polk's spacious office, Dutch was struck by the magnificent view of the District of Columbia nine stories below.

Hanging along walls on both sides of the office were various pictures of its occupant working at different Presidential events throughout his short career in the Secret Service. Dutch could see Agent Polk walking with President Burton along the South Lawn of the White House. Another photo showed Polk speaking into his lapel microphone at a function honoring a grouping of past Presidents. Next to that was a photo of the Queen of England walking alongside the President, Agent Polk in step behind them. The photos went on.

Other photos showed Polk in combat gear, posing in front of military helicopters, on top of tanks, and on patrol. Most of the backdrops appeared to be from the Middle East, but there were a few with greener backgrounds.

Dutch couldn't help but wonder whether the whole display had been created to make the visitors of this office feel outmatched.

Special Agent Polk entered through a side door. "Welcome, Agent Brown. Please, sit down." Polk motioned toward a comfortable-looking dark leather chair in front of his desk. "May I call you Dutch?" he asked as they shook hands. It was perhaps one of the firmest handshakes Dutch had ever felt.

"Please do, Agent Polk."

"Before we begin, that's an interesting nickname you've got. How did you get the name 'Dutch,' anyway? In the military? You were a Navy Seal, right?"

Dutch smiled. "Yes, I was. But I got the nickname back in high school, actually. I dated a girl who was a transfer student from

Holland. She said that back in her country her family always insisted that she pay for herself whenever she went out with a boy. Therefore—"

"You went 'Dutch,' " Polk finished.

They shared a laugh as Dutch looked about the office. "Quite an impressive photo gallery you've got." He hoped the remark didn't seem like an attempt to get on the man's good side.

Agent Polk smiled. "Thank you, Dutch. I have seen a lot over the years. Both the military and the Secret Service are jobs I've been blessed to have."

"That's an interesting way of putting it. I've heard it described other ways."

Polk let out a booming laugh. It surprised Dutch, as he would have thought that all agents' goals were to be as inconspicuous as possible. Although from looking at Polk, that wasn't an option.

"And you're bold enough to admit it to me! That's priceless; you've got balls. So it's true what they say about you: no bullshit, just straightforward?"

Dutch shrugged. "Is that what people say?"

"Why do you think you're here today? It's not just that people are talking about you, Dutch, but the right people are talking, if you catch my drift."

"The right people?"

"Yes. And your track record is tremendous. These last two cases…" He paused and picked up a folder in front of him. "You cracked a counterfeit ring in Oklahoma that had been operating for what looks to be five years. You had that closed within four months of getting the case, after two other agents couldn't. That's impressive."

"Well, sir, I did have help. In fact my partner, Harry—"

Polk interrupted. "Yes, I know about Agent Ludec. He will be coming into my office later. We're here to talk about you right now."

Dutch shifted in his leather chair. He wasn't used to this type of attention.

Polk picked up the folder again. "And this trip you just returned from in China. You recovered over five million? That's what I'd call a good trip.

"Yes sir, but unfortunately we lost a member of our CIA detachment and we didn't capture our mark. We're still working on that." Dutch shifted again. "May I ask how word spread so quickly?"

"You may. Many people keep a close eye on the job our agents do in the field. We look for the best and brightest in the hopes of tapping into that talent for one of the most important jobs in the world." He paused, Dutch assumed for effect.

"By 'we,' you mean...?" Dutch asked.

"Well there are many really, but in your case you've attracted the attention of some very notable people. In fact, one in particular. Dutch, have you ever met Trevor Sirois?"

"The Director of Homeland Security? Yes, I have." Sirois was from Dutch's home state of New Jersey. "He and I met at a function at the Wilshire Hotel a couple years back. He was the keynote speaker for a dinner I attended with my girlfriend."

"Quite a date."

"My girlfriend is a Vice President for Montgomery and Company. She was there for work; I just tagged along for the ride. I wanted to show her where I grew up."

"Sounds pretty serious. Is it?"

Dutch paused and said, "Sir, I appreciate your asking about her, but I'm sure you have a complete security background check on Alexis sitting in that folder you have your hand on. In fact, maybe you could remind me when Alexis and I met. She's a stickler for anniversaries."

Polk laughed. "Okay, that was fun. But now back to business. We were talking about Trevor Sirois. How well do you know him?"

"Not very. I never spoke with him since that night in Jersey."

"Well, you must have left an impression. Evidently he likes to keep abreast of anyone from Jersey serving in an official capacity within the Federal Government ever since he began serving the President."

Dutch raised his eyes. "Well, I'm honored."

Polk smiled. "You should be. You're the first agent he's ever recommended. However, since the Homeland Security Department has been formed, whenever its Director recommends someone for the POTUS detail, it's usually automatic."

Dutch could feel his stomach tighten. His goal was suddenly within reach.

Polk watched him for a moment before continuing. "Agent Brown, the question you need to ask yourself now is an interesting one. Before we start the process of vetting you for the Presidential Protection Detail, you need to tell me if you're ready to take on the challenge of a life altering job." Although it was a statement, his voice rose at the end in the manner of a question.

Dutch could have recited the demands of the job: eighteen hour days, being on call 24/7, a solid year's training, a job in which every moment would be spent focusing on one task, and the obligation to give his life if necessary to protect the president.

Instead, Dutch looked the man in the eyes and gave an unwavering, "Yes."

Bill Polk smiled. "Good answer," he said, closing the file in front of him and slapping it for good measure. "We'll get started on our end and be in touch." He stood and held out his hand.

As the two shook, Dutch asked, "Sir, may I ask what drew you into the Secret Service after your time in the Army?"

"You've done your homework on me, I can see." Polk chuckled. "My story is like most. I wanted to serve my country the best way I knew how."

Dutch released the man's hand. "But I would imagine the work you did while with the Army Rangers was a great service, as well."

The smile left Polk's face. "That's not public knowledge. How did you know I was with ops?"

Without breaking eye contact Dutch said, "Behind me to my left against your back wall is a picture of your Army unit."

"That photo doesn't show that I was with the Rangers. It's just a picture of my unit."

"The thin black ribbon on the bottom right side of the picture frame does."

Polk squinted to see if he could see the ribbon in question from the distance at which he stood. "Well done," he said.

Dutch smiled. "Thank you again for your time and consideration."

He turned and walked away, tapping the back wall as he left the office and into the next chapter of his life.

Chapter 8

Alexis, and Harry's wife Sandy, flew into Washington to surprise "the boys" and commemorate their interview, and both couples met for dinner at a trendy D.C. restaurant.

Afterward, still a little surprised to be in Washington at all, Dutch leaned against the door frame of their hotel bathroom wearing only his boxer shorts, watching Alexis wash her face. She was dressed in only her underwear, and he admired her curves as she bent over the sink and scrubbed her face. She was constantly trying new lotions for things ranging from preventing dry skin to anti-aging and wrinkling cream, and the strategy worked. She had beautiful, soft skin, and Dutch couldn't wait to rub his hands over it.

"Sandy doesn't want Harry to take the job, does she?" Dutch said.

Alexis finished moisturizing. "Nope," she said, pressing a towel to her mouth.

"Really?"

Alexis laughed. "Yes, really. Why do you sound surprised?"

Dutch took a deep breath. "Harry's on the fence, too."

Now it was Alexis's turn to be surprised. "You're kidding."

"No. Wish I were." He stepped closer, watching her face in the mirror. "I mean, I know he likes the idea of the job. What agent wouldn't? But I think he's seriously waffling back and forth. I know he's afraid of the impact it will have on his family. I feel bad for him."

Alexis pursed her lips and moved to the bed and sat.

"What do you think?" he said.

"About you or Harry?"

"About my taking the job. We really haven't talked about it yet."

"Well," she started while reaching behind herself to unclasp her bra.

Dutch stopped her. "I'm having enough of a hard time keeping focus on the conversation while you're in your underwear."

"Pig." The bra fell off. "I'm just getting ready for bed," she said, then reached for a long t-shirt and slid it over her head. She turned to him. "Better?"

"For now."

Alexis sat beside him and nestled her head against his bare chest.

"I appreciate your thinking of me in all this, Terry, thank you. I love you for a lot of things and your thoughtfulness is just one of them."

He pulled her closer and kissed the top of her head. "So, how would you feel if I was offered the job?"

She looked up at him. "This is what you've been shooting for. What kind of a person would I be if I stood in your way?"

"It's a lot of long hours. I'd have to move to D.C. The job is dangerous…" His voice trailed off.

"Honey, I work a lot of long hours. I'm on the road constantly. Your job now is dangerous. All these things I can deal with. But I want you to take it, because it's what you've always wanted. We'll deal with it. There's nothing that we can't overcome, no matter how difficult or challenging."

Dutch's smile widened. He took her shoulders in his hands and gently pulled her away from his chest. "You really mean that, don't you?"

She nodded.

He fell into the pool of her light blue eyes, her shining black hair framing her face, her smile, the way she smelled. Everything about Alexis Jordan was perfect, including their love for one another.

"Lexi, I love you." He leaned in to kiss her.

Their lips met as their bodies melted into one another. She moaned softly and pressed against his lips harder. Then, swinging her legs over and moving them to either side of his body, she used her upper body to flatten him against the bed. With a devilish look in her eye, she pulled the bottom of her night shirt over her head.

"Have we ever made love in D.C. before?" she asked.

Chapter 9

Agent Byron Meadows, Deputy Director of the Presidential Protection Detail, looked out past the fence line running parallel to Pennsylvania Avenue. The protesters were lined up three deep, swinging their signs back and forth.

"Paulsen, I'd like one more in sector eighteen," he said over the two-way radio mic concealed in his sleeve.

"Ten-four," his earpiece crackled. "The natives are getting restless tonight, huh?"

Meadows didn't reply. He wasn't one for needless chatter over the air. Instead he dropped his arm and checked his Service issued Sig P-229 once more. He had been warned about times like this by his mentor, Marcus Reed, the longtime PPD Director prior to Bill Polk.

Looking back toward the protesters, Meadows remembered a story Marcus told him about a time during the Nixon years when things got really challenging protecting the President. Right after Watergate the protesters were out in force even when the President wasn't in the White House, which was the case once again.

"If you want to take the temperature of the public, look out past that fence," Marcus would say.

That night, while he was on duty, Byron Meadows knew the country was running a fever.

"Nat, how does it look up there?" he said into his mic.

"All clear," was the immediate response.

Of all the agents currently on the Presidential detail, Meadows had worked with Agent Nat Shakalis the longest. He was the best sniper the service had ever seen. Currently he was positioned on the roof of the White House. Nat's instincts were unequaled and if he said it was all clear, then there was nothing special about the impromptu assembly outside the fence line.

It was unsettling, though. From a security standpoint, President Lorraine Burton's term had been unremarkable so far. Her approval rating was good. The economy was doing well. But Burton had aroused a lot of dissatisfaction by advocating sweeping immigration reform. The initiative had struck a nerve with the public—a very dangerous one. A shutter went through Meadows's body. He felt in his bones that there was a storm coming, and it wasn't the one blowing in from the west that concerned him.

He turned and continued his patrol through the sacred hallways of the West Wing until he reached a door leading down to the Secret Service offices directly beneath the Oval Office. Meadows slid the key card through the computerized reader, then turned the latch handle two times down and one time up to open the door. There are one hundred thirty two locks in the White House, and each one has a different trick to open the door other than the key. No one agent other than himself and Bill Polk knew how to open all the doors.

He descended the long staircase, turned the corner into his office, and sat down to read the evening briefs before he would call it a day.

Two reports waited for him. The first told him that Widow was still in the air. Widow was the nickname given to her by the Service when she became President. Depending on who you spoke with, it stood either for the loss of her husband or the symbolic black widows who ate their counterpart after mating.

President Burton's return was delayed due to the weather. Meadows smiled, thinking of Max Ford who piloted the President on every trip and hated any type of turbulence to disturb his passengers, and had probably rerouted the flight for a calmer approach to the East Coast. He was still upset about the last trip's weather and didn't want there to be any problems on this one.

The second memo was from Bill Polk, alerting Meadows that two new agents, Ludec and Brown, were to be promoted from the Omaha branch to the POTUS detail. Agent Ludec he didn't know, but he remembered hearing about a Dutch Brown.

He opened Brown's file, which was included in the report. Brown had only been on the job three years but had a fantastic record with investigations. He flipped the pages of the personnel report. Ex-Navy Seal, five years in the service, specializing in explosives.

Meadows had learned about Brown from other sources, too. A friend, John Connors, had served with Dutch about six years back. When Brown submitted his application to join the Secret Service, John picked up the phone to Meadows, the only person he knew in the Service, to make a personal recommendation. Meadows remembered the conversation.

"Our group came under heavy fire on a beachhead. It was a black op, so not even the Navy would confirm it was happening. We were stuck in Corinto, Nicaragua. I was laying down suppressing fire from the trees lining the beachhead so the rest of the team could get back to the sub when I was hit in the arm and leg by enemy fire. Dutch and the rest of the team had made it safely into the water and were on their way. I thought I was a fucking dead man when I looked up and saw Dutch running back toward me. Bullets were exploding all around him as he zig zagged to my location. It looked like something out of a James Bond movie. He took my grenade belt and pulled out all the pins. I thought he had gone mad. He hurled it as far as he could behind us, then bent over to shield me. Then came this huge explosion. It was so unexpected the bastards shooting at us thought there was another Seal team headed to the beach. In the confusion, Dutch picked me up and slung me around his shoulders like I was a rag doll. We made it into the water and back to the sub. I had to ask him why he came back. I mean, I was dead and he shouldn't have been racing back to me like that. Do you know what he said? 'Because I don't leave anyone behind.' Can you believe that? You're crazy if you don't take this guy."

Meadows put the file on his desk. He had quietly watched Dutch throughout his training. He was close to the top of his class in just about every category. On graduation day, Meadows was curious where he would be assigned. He thought for sure that he'd be based around Washington D.C., close to the action. When he found out it was Omaha, he was stunned. Not much ever happened in Omaha, but he chalked it up to the wonderful government bureaucracy working at its finest. He himself had experienced that first hand, had he not?

Most around the inner circle of the Secret Service thought Meadows, not Polk, should have been named head of the PPD when President Burton was sworn in. Meadows, though, never let his own disappointment show. He wasn't the type to let personal feelings get in the way of performing his job to the fullest.

He sat forward again and looked once more at the file on his desk. Well, if anyone could make it out of Omaha and onto the POTUS detail, it didn't surprise him that it was Agent Dutch Brown. He looked forward to working with him in a year when he would get out of PPD training.

It was past midnight when the Presidential motorcade rounded the corner outside of Andrews Air force Base and began the ten-point-eight-mile trip back to the White House. The rain fell heavily, so Agent Clyde Rolleston opted for the motorcade instead of the usual trio of VH3 Sequorsky Sea King helicopters to escort the President home.

Rolleston sat opposite the President and Chief of Staff in the back of The Beast. He kept his eyes impassive to give the impression that he wasn't paying attention to the conversation taking place in front of him. After a while, Presidents got so used to their protective detail they ceased to see them. This was the case with Widow. At the halfway point of her first term, it had become apparent that her security detail seemed to disappear in her mind. Although it was true that the Service defended her from any harm, they were also tasked with defending the office from any harm as well. That included not discussing any scandalous behavior they observed.

Rolleston's boss, Byron Meadows, constantly harped on that point, particularly since it was obvious to all that the President was involved in a love affair with her Chief of Staff. It wasn't the first scandal that the PPD had suppressed, nor would it be the last, and thinking back over the years it was amazing to Rolleston how little information actually got out to the public regarding what went on behind closed White House doors.

It was more than the scandalous behavior that made Rolleston chuckle; it was the conversations that he heard. It was true that the President had to be free to discuss anything and everything while her security detail was present, but Rolleston had to laugh inwardly at how valuable the information he heard the President speak would be to her political rivals, as was the case that night regarding all the strategy, hustling, and last minute deals for this immigration reform. Then next year will come the campaign stops, speech content, talking points for the press, and all the necessary things for ramping up another campaign, her final one.

He watched as Harvey hung up one of the three phones in The Beast.

"Madame President, that was the House Majority Leader."

"Don't tell me. I don't want to hear what that sniveling coward has to say."

Harvey looked at Rolleston and rolled his eyes, but Rolleston did not smile. The entire security detail liked him. The Chief of Staff was the first to step in and act as a buffer between the President and her rampages at the Secret Service, especially when she disagreed with Bill Polk, who ultimately called the shots when it came to defending her.

"Madame President, you're not going to win this one," Harvey said.

"Mr. Harvey, this was a good trip. I don't want to ruin it before I even make it home. Let's not go over this again." She fixed him with an icy glare.

Harvey nodded. "Okay."

Better him than me, thought Rolleston. It didn't seem like President Burton would be easy to deal with in the office, let alone in bed.

Chapter 10
One year later

Dutch opened the wrapper folded around his sandwich. "Roast beef with butter and Swiss cheese. Mmm, that's good. You know me too well," he said to Alexis.

"Don't I know it, babe," Alexis said, opening her own ham and cheese.

Their voices echoed a bit sitting beneath the Capitol Rotunda with its acoustic properties. Dutch and Alexis met there twice a week for lunch. Dutch insisted on going so they could watch the sculptor working on completing a statue that had sat unfinished in the rotunda for more than ninety years.

They were watching what had been an unfinished rectangular block of marble sharing the same base alongside busts of Lucretia Mott, Elizabeth Cady Stanton, and Susan B. Anthony slowly take shape into Lorraine Burton, the nation's first female President. The statue had been added to the Capitol collection in 1921 as a tribute to the passage of the 19th Amendment giving women the right to vote. Until now, it had sat unfinished until the historic election three years ago.

One of the Capitol security guards came by on his route through the rotunda. The guard was new and wasn't used to the couple's semi-weekly routine. Stopping in front of them, apparently planning to issue an order for them to move along, he was about to speak when Dutch preemptively took out his credentials and flashed them to the guard. The guard immediately stepped back. "Oh, I'm sorry sir!" Tipping his cap, he continued along his way.

Alexis chuckled when the man was out of ear shot. "You just love to do that, don't you?"

"Yeah, I kind of do."

"So, you've just completed training and already you're out of control and blinded by power."

"Exactly."

Dutch's new posting consisted mainly of "Mansion duty," which meant he was posted at the White House. His hours could change depending on when the President was home or away from the Mansion.

Usually when she traveled, his hours were on more of a set schedule, but when she was home it could change on a moment's notice. Usually they could plan ahead when the President had travel plans that were public knowledge. But when there was a chance that a trip was canceled or added without public knowledge, everything changed. Including what he could and couldn't say to his girlfriend.

"And I've got authority to have you arrested."

"For what?"

"Uh, being disrespectful."

"That might be fun, too."

He laughed and shook his head.

"But seriously, when do you think you'll know about your schedule?" she said.

"Let's see, today's Wednesday. I'd say no later than Friday morning."

"Okay, that works. I know Sandy was planning on flying out without the kids for a quick visit this weekend but she canceled because she wasn't feeling well. I was going to ask her if she wanted the extra ticket if you couldn't come but she didn't make the trip. I'm sure I can find a date, though," she said.

Dutch nodded and took another bite. "I'm sure you can."

The sculptor's chisel made a loud clang, and a small piece of marble hit the ground.

Only a few hundred yards away, President Burton entered the Oval Office through her private office door, then surveyed the people seated on the couches as she strode to her desk.

In front to her right was Trevor Sirois, Director of Homeland Security. Sirois' impeccably tailored grey Hugo Boss suit accentuated his long, slender figure.

Next to him was Glen Seeley, Senate Majority Leader and Chairman of the Senate Committee on Finance.

Across from Senator Seeley was Patti Harris, the White House Press Secretary. Patti had been with President Burton since she was Lorraine Burton, Chief Litigation Attorney for Waverly Investments. For President Burton, Patti had been a no-brainer for Press Secretary. It was her subtle way of giving the finger to the media who got plenty of shots in during her campaign to become the first female President in history. Patti was considered by most to be a knockout, and her thirty-six years made her old enough to be respectable, yet young enough to hold the attention of the men in the press corps. She was just a shade under six feet tall with straight natural blonde hair that shone almost white under the bright lights of the media room. Her bra size was 36D, something she would occasionally remind the press corps by her choice of blouses at particularly tricky times during Burton's administration. She had a narrow waist that curved perfectly into her fitted skirts. Anyone who met her for the first time would assume she was a dumb super model. However, her quick wit surpassed her natural beauty, and she often caught men off guard. The male journalists desired her, and the female ones detested her. The President loved every moment of the rivalry.

Next to Patti was Chief of Staff Michael Harvey. The seating was strategic, as Harvey and Sirois couldn't stand each other, never mind sit next to one another.

Lorraine took in the group, which included some of the finest minds in the economic world. Her inner circle of financial advisors, Seeley, Sirois, and Harvey were nicknamed the "Billionaires Boys' Club," which was a dig at her being a female. But she liked the name.

"Let's get started," the President said.

Immediately, folders were opened and pens stood at attention.

"Mr. Seeley, what's the latest you're hearing from the Fed?" she said.

Seeley adjusted his glasses and skimmed over a report from his staffers.

"Well, speculators are betting long on the dollar. We're estimating the Fed's position will be at thirty billion by month's end." He flipped a page. "Meanwhile, the same speculators are shorting the Euro, which should continue its decline, setting up a favorable situation for the U.S. over the next fiscal quarter."

"Mr. Seeley, what does that mean for interest rates?"

"If the trend continues I can see interest rates staying level for the next half year or so. But please keep in mind that I can't promise—"

The President held up her hand. "You can't promise anything, I know. But all indications point in that direction?"

"Yes, Madame President, they do."

"Mr. Sirois, what do you hear out there?"

"Madame President, my contacts in the trading houses are telling me they are going to be trading heavily against the Euro. It backs up what the Senator is telling us."

"Mr. Harvey?" she turned to her Chief of Staff.

He tilted his head in Sirois's direction. "Madame President, if what we're hearing continues, then it's good news for our economy." He turned to the Press Secretary and added, "Patti, you can keep the positive spin going with the media. That should also shut up that putz Roger Graham for a little while anyway." He referred to the President's opponent, the Congressman from New Mexico and odds-on favorite to become the Democratic Nominee for next November's Presidential election, only one year away.

President Burton tried to keep the sour look off her face that her Chief of Staff said she showed every time Graham's name was mentioned.

"It looks like you just sucked on a lemon," Harvey would say.

"They're going to want our prediction on Wall Street and how we plan to deal with the unfunded student loan debacle that's still lingering out there that we had to cover," Patti said, looking at the President.

"Unbelievable. That wasn't even my administration and they're haunting me about that debacle."

"The press has a long memory."

The President glowered at Patti. "It's your job to shorten their memories. Tell them the President doesn't give a rats ass about ten billion in unsecured loans that we're never going to get a dime back on!"

Harvey leaned over to Patti and said quietly, "The official position of the President is that we're doing everything we can to watch out for the taxpayers' dollars and are working closely with the banking industry to close out that dark chapter in our history."

Patti nodded and jotted down the note.

Chapter 11
March

Roger Graham jogged along a path parallel to the Potomac, and he could feel his heart beating harder than it had for weeks. The white smoke from his breath in the cold March temperatures kept blowing back into his face. His assistant, Frank Tipper, or "Tip," jogged beside him, occasionally glancing at a clipboard.

"Damn, I can't go this long without jogging again," Roger panted as he made his way around a bend.

"How's your knee feeling, sir?"

"So far, so good. I think this time the rehab did the trick. Tip, the next time I want to play in a charity basketball game, slap me in the head, Okay?"

Tip laughed. "You got it, sir."

A female jogger approached from the opposite direction and smiled at the Congressman. Although he was in his late forties, his rugged good looks still garnered glances from women half his age. It embarrassed him when he heard himself referred to as "tall and handsome,' but a compliment was still a compliment. His sandy blonde hair hadn't begun to show any signs of white yet. His face sported well defined cheek and jaw muscles. But it was his dimples that showed when he smiled that had women swooning. His campaign manager never missed an opportunity to exploit that feature in the papers or on television.

Roger became bored too easily in a gym and never took to the spinning craze that was so popular in fitness centers. Jogging had always been his mainstay. He normally ran forty miles a week, although the previous four weeks were spent rehabbing his knee preventing him from running at all. To finally get back out on his first run that day felt good. He liked to do most of his brainstorming while jogging, so most of his staff was in fantastic shape as they had to keep up with him during what he called their "mobile staff meetings."

The pair ran another half mile before the Congressman stopped and hunched over with his hands on his knees, breathing loudly.

"Shit. It doesn't take much to fall out of shape," he gasped.

"No sir, it doesn't. But you did well for your first time out. Two miles is nothing to shake a stick at."

Roger looked up and noted that Tip had hardly broken a sweat. But Tip was half his age. Roger wouldn't want anyone else as his right hand man, especially during a Presidential campaign. Tip wasn't actually calling the shots; that job belonged to Greg Underwood. But Tip was an organizational genius, and the schedule always hummed.

"Give me time, Tip, and I'll run circles around you again," Roger said, still winded.

"No problem, sir, I'm sure you will. Now about the dinner tonight at the Crowne Plaza. Will Mrs. Graham be attending?"

Roger managed a quick grin in appreciation for the faux reassurance from his staffer. "No, Meghan called just before we headed out and said she won't be back in time and to go without her."

Tip made a note on his clipboard before continuing. "What time should I tell the advance team you'd like to meet this afternoon?"

Roger looked at his watch as he ungracefully made his way to a bench and collapsed. In between large gulps of air he said, "Let's say five o'clock. That should give us enough time, don't you think?"

Tip screwed up his face and moved his lips slightly as he silently counted. After a moment he said, "I think so. We're going over the Midwest trips, so that should give us enough time."

Tip's cell phone rang and he reached into his pocket.

"Hello," he said, and then went silent, nodding his head from time to time.

Roger tried to glean something from listening to one side of the conversation, but there was nothing to hear.

"Okay, thanks," Tip said, then hung up and turned to his boss.

"That was Greg with the latest polling numbers."

Roger held up his hand, and nothing else was said. All of his staffers knew his convictions about polling. Throughout his political life, Roger Graham loathed polls. He held strong beliefs that polls had too much influence over public opinion. Also, too many politicians easily forgot what they were elected to do when polling figures came out. He was determined not to turn into one of them.

He did, however, try to sneak a glance at his staffer to try and get a read on the news he received.

"Sir, I'll only say that after your primary win in New Hampshire last month, you are riding the wave that would be expected of the front runner."

Actually, Tip was understating the obvious. Roger had 775 of the 2025 delegates necessary to secure the nomination. His closest competitor had seventy-two. It was fast becoming a mathematical certainty that Roger would be the Democrats' choice to run against Lorraine Burton in November.

Roger drew a deep breath, then slowly released it.

"Well, I guess that's good news. But I'm sure Greg has a hundred reasons why we can't take our eyes off the Murray campaign." He referred to his chief rival for the nomination. "Where was Murray last night?"

Tip glanced down at his clipboard as he pulled the car keys out of his jogging sweatshirt's inside pocket without looking. "Kansas. Overland Park, Kansas, to be specific."

Reaching the car, Roger pulled open the passenger door and said, "Why Overland Park? Am I missing something?"

Tip climbed into the driver's seat and turned the car on. "Overland Park, Kansas was voted the seventh best city to live in the United States a few years back." He slowly backed out of the parking space.

Roger looked at Tip, open mouthed in amazement. "And you know that how?"

"Because you pay me to."

Tip put the car into drive and headed out.

Chapter 12

"Keep your eyes open at all times. I know I've said that a thousand times before, but things are really heating up now because of this immigration bill that Widow is pushing."

Dutch and Harry, sitting next to each other during the afternoon briefing, shared a smirk. They had been dealing with the protesters outside the perimeter of the White House for weeks. Their assignment was the front gate leading to the closed portion of Pennsylvania Avenue, which had the largest congregation of protesters. The camera operators all knew where to go when looking for some B-roll, or fill in video, of protesters in front of the Mansion.

"Sir, can you fill us in on the latest intel of the recent threats made against Widow?" asked an agent in the back of the cramped briefing room in the basement of the White House.

"You'll have to be more specific," replied Agent Ronald Gillespie, Special Agent in Charge of the afternoon shift that was about to begin.

Chuckles echoed through the room. Since there had been a Secret Service, there had been threats against the President of the United States.

"Sorry, sir I meant the multiple tips about the upcoming trip to San Antonio."

"The advance teams are tracking down those leads. Your only concern for the next five hours should be guarding the occupants of this house," Gillespie answered firmly, then turned to face Dutch and his partner.

"Ludec, Brown, you two keep a close eye on the fence line along Pennsylvania Avenue. Those protesters are really testing us now that CNN has set up camp across the street. They're willing to do anything to make the six o'clock news."

Dutch nodded, and saw Harry do the same.

"Okay, that's it for now. Keep on your toes. Dismissed."

The sound of moving chairs and low murmuring could be heard as the agents stood and headed for the door.

"How's Sandy doing?" said Dutch as he and Harry were waiting for the agents in front of them to filter through the room's single cramped door.

Harry grimaced. His wife had had surgery for a kidney stone two days earlier. "She was upset that I couldn't come home while she was going through this."

Dutch looked at his friend. "She still hasn't warmed up to you working in D.C., has she?"

Harry shook his head. "Things are getting worse. I don't think we've said more than two sentences to each other about anything else the past week."

They exited the briefing room and headed up the stairs, then continued down the red carpeted hallway toward the west wing. They both buttoned up their coats and put their sunglasses on as they headed out into the sunny, yet cool, March afternoon.

"And how's your perfect relationship going?" Harry said.

"It's not perfect."

"C'mon. Weren't you going to remind me how your perfect girlfriend thinks it's a turn on that you protect the President?"

Dutch laughed. "I didn't want to keep rubbing it in."

"Asshole," Harry muttered under his breath.

They made their way along the concrete walkway leading to the gate house guarding one entrance to the parking lot reserved for Secret Service vehicles and select dignitaries who happened to drive to their meetings at the White House. Dutch noticed the three solid steel cylinders sunken in the ground installed after 9/11. They could rise to their full three feet within ten seconds after someone hit the alarm button located in the guard shack. He felt sorry for anyone who tried to ram those.

As they approached the gatehouse, two security guards greeted them.

"Good afternoon, gentlemen," said Dutch.

"Afternoon, sir," replied one of the guards, who handed Dutch a clipboard with the names of people who were scheduled to be admitted during their shift. Dutch pulled out a sheet of paper he received from the briefing and compared the two. The names matched up.

"Looks good," Dutch said, handing the clipboard back to the guard.

"How's everything been?" Harry asked the other guard.

He paused before saying, "Word got out that CNN is doing their live shot for the evening news just outside the gate. That should liven things up."

They watched the immigration bill protesters jostle one another in an attempt to stake out their positions on the sidewalk in front of the long, black wrought-iron fence that was so familiar a backdrop on television reports outside the gates of the White House. Some were carrying the requisite signs, some had whistles around their necks, and some wore t-shirts that were partially concealed by their unzipped coats. Dutch couldn't make out what was on them. However, he wasn't concentrating on the shirts, but rather the faces in the crowd. Dutch's training taught him to look at the faces. People's eyes could reveal so much.

The thing that struck him about that day's crowd was the ethnic leanings. Most of them looked to be of Central American descent. One protester even carried the Guatemalan flag.

"Maybe someone should call the ICE Agents," cracked one of the guards referring to the Immigration and Customs Enforcement branch of the government.

Harry and Dutch didn't respond.

"All right, we'll keep close to this area. Let us know if anything changes," Dutch said without breaking his concentration on the mounting crowd.

The pair of guards nodded and took their place back in the security shack.

"Great. Just when I thought it would be a quiet afternoon," Harry said.

"Look on the bright side, you'll probably make it on TV again." Dutch smiled.

"Oh sure, won't Sandy love that."

In the Oval Office, President Burton looked down at her itinerary as the Secretary of State and the rest of the attendees of her previous meeting left the room, leaving behind only Michael Harvey. She hated Wednesdays. When she wasn't traveling, it was the day Harvey loaded her up on meetings. This Wednesday was no different. She glanced the clock on her desk. Five thirty p.m. She leaned back in her custom fitted leather padded chair, stretched, and yawned.

"My feelings exactly," Harvey said.

"Hey, it's your fault. You're the one who draws up this schedule."

"One more, Madame President, and you will have earned a night to yourself."

The door opened and in walked Trevor Sirois, followed by Preston Chase and, to the President's surprise, Special Agent Bill Polk.

"Welcome gentlemen," she said quickly glancing from the Secretary of Homeland Security to her Chief of Staff. "And Agent Polk, this is a surprise. I didn't know you would be sitting in on our meeting about immigration."

"Madame President." Polk headed toward her desk while the others took their seats. "I apologize for attending without your prior knowledge, but it is important that I am here for the beginning of this meeting."

Burton had locked horns with Polk many times before over things such as her movements among the people, as Polk dictated which exits and routes she used. With three years in office under her belt, though, they had seemed to reach a détente, instead coming to expect what each wanted and trying to compromise. Still, the United States Secret Service was the only department with which she had a losing record in negotiations.

Polk's unexpected presence probably spelled bad news for her, and she imagined it had to do with the immigration issue and security. She motioned for Polk to take a seat. "Well, Agent Polk, should I start this meeting or just let you say what's on your mind and get it over with?"

Polk looked as if he'd eaten something that didn't agree with him. "Madame President, your upcoming trip to Texas has presented us with some…challenges. We'll need to change parts of the standard protocol."

"Challenges? Isn't it your job to find ways around challenges?"

Polk's face reddened, but his voice remained calm. "That's why I'm here this afternoon. I'm afraid I must insist on—" As soon as the words left his mouth, he regretted it. She had goaded him into making a mistake right off the bat. The self-satisfied look on her face before she exploded betrayed her pleasure.

"Insist? I'm sorry, did you just say insist?" She asked, her voice overly loud. "Mr. Polk," she said, intentionally leaving out the "agent" as a subtle dig. "I'm not sure what you need to insist on, but in case you forgot, people don't insist I do anything."

Seeing himself in a familiar spot, Harvey leaned forward to take up his role as referee. "Madame President, I'm sure Agent Polk has come in here because of a pressing need for a change in security, not to insist you do anything, did you?" he asked, eyebrows raised and gazing meaningfully at Agent Polk.

Polk begrudgingly nodded and mumbled something incoherently.

"But Madame President, I think we'd be remiss if we didn't wait until Agent Polk fully explained the situation that his department is faced with."

Polk looked at Harvey appreciatively while Lorraine rolled up her eyes in surrender to the seemingly never-ending tug of war.

Polk continued. "There has been a credible threat to your life, specifically aimed at your visit to the Mokara Hotel in San Antonio."

"And this is something that you've never encountered before." Three years of feeling surrounded by an army of black-suited men and women were wearing on her. It had stopped feeling like security and become more like being babysat.

"For this trip only we believe it's necessary to take additional measures to care for your safety."

"Agent Polk, I'm in the middle of a reelection campaign. Face time is of the utmost importance—"

Harvey interrupted loudly enough to be heard over the President's protests. "What type of changes did you have in mind?"

Bill Polk turned to face Harvey. "We want the President to enter the Mokara through the underground parking garage, then up the service elevator. It's a short walk from the elevator exit to the backdrop and up to the stage where she'll be speaking. It's the most secure way we can get her in and out."

Burton knew that Harvey usually sided with the Secret Service. If she put up too much of a fight over Polk's suggestions and lost, she'd lose face in front of Sirois and Chase. She had to pick her battles, and that one might be one not worth fighting. Currently her polling numbers were favorable in Texas.

Harvey looked at her. "It seems like a logical request in light of their intel, wouldn't you agree, Madame President?"

Lorraine held her chin between thumb and index finger, sizing up Polk. "Agent Polk, in the coming weeks I've got a number of campaign stops through the Midwest. These are some very important states I'll be traveling through, and I need to carry them in November. Will you be coming into these meetings with the same request before every trip?"

"Madame President, it's impossible for me to predict all the variables so far in advance."

Lorraine looked at her Chief of Staff to make sure he got the message.

"Agent Polk, surely you can see where the President is going with this," Harvey said. "Where does your department feel these threats are coming from?"

Polk couldn't see a way out of the trap. "Sir, it comes mostly from the southern border states."

Harvey lowered his head slightly, maintaining eye contact with the head of the Secret Service. "So, what's the likelihood that stops in Nebraska and Ohio will yield that type of attention from the Mexican border?"

"Sir, we have large numbers of illegal immigrants in every state—"

Harvey spoke a notch louder. "So, the threat is equal in every state?"

Polk knew when he'd been snookered. He looked from the President to her Chief of Staff. "No, sir, as of now I have no reason to believe that."

"Okay then, give and take, the heightened security will only be for San Antonio. Harvey stood and slapped Polk on his shoulder, a subtle gesture to let him know he should probably leave while he was ahead.

Lorraine watched a flicker of recognition show in Polk's eyes. "Thank you for the time," he said, then exited.

Lorraine noticed that on his way out he met eyes with Agent Meadows, who had been stationed at the door for the afternoon. The two seemed to convey an unspoken frustration. She tried to keep her satisfaction from showing.

"Let's get down to business," she said and sat next to her Chief of Staff on the couch.

Chapter 13

"Breech in sector three!" a voice yelled in Dutch's earpiece. He bolted out the door of the West Wing. Harry had been walking the perimeter when the alert was given and was a good fifty yards in front of him, running toward the gate. Dutch could see that a protester, wielding a sign that read "Immigration Will Kill the Economy," had scaled the White House fence and was gaining speed as he headed across the lawn. Dutch ran, calculating that he could cut him off about a hundred yards further down.

Agent Gillespie's voice crackled over his earpiece, dispatching additional agents to the area of the breech. Gillespie was in the control room and could direct the action using the multitude of camera angles available to him.

Dutch neared the protester's projected path as Harry closed in on him from the other direction. For a moment he thought about going for his gun, but there was really no need. This guy wasn't going anywhere and it wouldn't look good to gun down a protester in front of the cameras.

In a matter of seconds, Harry would be in reach of the protester. Suddenly the man threw his sign backwards. Harry tried to dodge out of the way, but the sign cart wheeled and Harry tumbled over it.

Dutch was nearer now, and dove at the runner, catching him around the waist like a linebacker. They both hit the ground hard, and Dutch heard the man grunt as the breath was knocked out of him.

Dutch kept rolling until he was on top. He was aware that they were probably on live TV across the nation, but he didn't know if this guy had a weapon or not. He swung his right fist and made contact squarely in the man's face, knocking his head into the frozen White House lawn. The protester didn't try to get back up as Dutch scanned the grounds, making sure no one else had used the diversion to crash through the gate.

Three other agents arrived, panting, their weapons drawn. Dutch turned the man over on his stomach and jammed his knee into the small of his back, then retrieved a plastic restraint and fastened it around the man's wrist. Standing, he removed his weapon from his coat. He turned the suspect over onto his back and saw blood seeping from the corner of his lip.

Agent Gillespie appeared on the scene and spoke into his mic. "Area secured; stand down."

Two of the other agents pulled the protester off the ground while the third checked him for weapons. Agent Gillespie began reading him his rights.

Dutch looked behind him for Harry. His heart skipped a beat when he noticed he was still on the ground, face twisted in pain while he held his leg. Dutch looked back to the protester to see if he had missed a weapon, but all he saw was the guy with his cuffed hands behind his back.

Dutch ran to Harry, scanning the area as he went to see if there was something or someone he missed.

"Harry, what the hell happened?"

"The fucking sign tripped me and I ended up falling on the pointed end," Harry said between gritted teeth.

Harry tried to sit up while holding his calf, attempting to stem the flow of blood. Then Dutch could see it. A piece of the wooden handle of the sign protruded out of his leg.

"We need a medic on the west lawn. Agent is injured," Dutch said into his sleeve.

Agent Gillespie swung around quickly. "Ludec, are you all right?" he called.

Harry nodded, still clutching his leg and wincing in pain.

Dutch surveyed the crowd. Many were moving down the fence toward their position, digital cameras out, to get a better view. The CNN camera seemed to be fixed on Harry.

Three more agents arrived, one carrying a medical bag, and quickly knelt next to Harry.

"Hey, how about me? I'm bleeding!" shouted the protester.

Dutch noticed the agent's hands on the guy's neck tightening. The man quickly quieted down.

"Get an ambulance in here," the agent attending to Harry's leg said. "This gash is pretty deep."

Harry's face turned pale as the blood continued to gush from his wound. The medic tied a tourniquet around his leg, but the bleeding continued.

In the Oval Office, Agent Meadows, his arm gripping President Burton's arm, listened to his earpiece, then loosened his grip. "All secure," he said. He nodded to the additional agents, dismissing them.

Lorraine wasn't sure if she should defiantly rip her arm from the grasp he still had on it or not. She also hoped that the slight tremble she felt go through her body wasn't evident to her protector.

"What the hell just happened?" Sirois said.

Meadows told him what had happened. Finally, he released Lorraine and returned to his post at the door.

"Thank you, Agent Meadows," the President said in more of a clipped voice than intended, then looked at her guests as if nothing had happened. She turned to the others. "Shall we continue?"

Preston Chase spoke up. "Madame President, use what just happened as a barometer. People are angry. Maybe you should consider lessening some of the more harsh immigration reforms."

"Mr. Chase, Congressman Graham also has an immigration reform plan. I won't soften anything. I want the voters to have a clear choice between Congressman Graham and me on this issue."

"Yes, I can understand that, but the perception of this bill being tied with what happened to your husband is inevitable."

Measured and civil, the President said, "No matter what I include or don't include in this bill, Mr. Chase, people are bound to make that connection. I can't control that." Her gaze bored into him, a silent but lethal challenge for him to say anything else.

"Honey, I'm fine," Harry said, clearly trying to keep his voice steady through the pain as the ambulance raced along 21st Street toward George Washington University Hospital. He tried to make it sound as if he weren't lying on a stretcher. "It's just a scrape," he tried to assure Sandy.

Dutch sat beside him, cramped into a corner of the ambulance.

"Listen…Sandy…please hon, I've got to get going. What? No, please…honey…all right, here's Dutch." He handed the phone to his partner.

"Hi, Sandy," Dutch said in as upbeat tone as he could muster.

"Terrance Brown, don't you bullshit me. How is he?" asked Sandy, her voice shaking.

"Wow, you sound like Alexis now."

"Dutch!"

The EMT began changing blood-soaked dressing on the wound. "Sandy, he's going to be fine."

Sandy had watched the entire event on CNN. "Do you know what it's like watching your husband go down while chasing a criminal on live television?" she said, her voice shrill. "Just be straight with me, Dutch!"

"Sandy, I'm not going to lie to you. A piece of wood nicked his femoral artery. He lost a lot of blood, but he's got the best medical staff in the world looking after him and I'm not leaving his side, I promise. I'll call you once he gets assessed in the emergency room."

He could hear Sandy take a deep breath. "Thank you," she whispered, then hung up.

He turned back to Harry, who had a new white bandage around his leg. Dutch didn't like the pale face looking back at him. He wondered just how much blood his partner had lost.

He smiled and said, "Look on the bright side," he said. "You'll probably get a commendation for this."

Harry managed a wan smile, nodded, then turned his head to stare at the ceiling of the ambulance. He closed his eyes in obvious pain. The siren shut off as they turned into the parking lot of the hospital.

Chapter 14
April

Harry's surgery was successful, but in the weeks since it had happened two infections had landed him back in the hospital. With the second infection, Sandy insisted he go back to Omaha for the surgery as well as the rehab because the recovery would be lengthy. He had been hospitalized in Omaha for almost a week.

Dutch dialed the hospital's number from memory. Sandy answered. "Hi, Dutch."

"Hey Sandy. How did you know it was me?"

"Because you're as predictable as the rain. You're probably just getting to your desk and about to sip your coffee. No one else would call the hospital here at seven o'clock in the morning."

Dutch put down the cup he was holding and grimaced. "How's our patient doing?"

"The test results showed he has the MRSA type of staph infection. So they changed the antibiotics, and he should be out of here in a few days. That's the hope anyway. We're cautiously optimistic here. It's been a long four weeks."

Dutch could hear some noise in the background. "When am I going to get my partner back?"

Harry, sounding groggy, came on the line. "Hey, buddy! Thanks for calling. I wanted you to know I dropped by the old office."

Their time together in Omaha seemed like decades ago to Dutch. "Yeah? What's up?"

"Nothing much. Talked to Langone and Falk." The two younger agents had taken over Harry and Dutch's investigation of the money recovered in China.

"How's the case shaping up?"

"Ha!" Harry said, and Dutch could hear him wince with pain. "Those douche bags haven't made any headway at all!"

"I can't say I'm surprised. Money's been bleeding out of the country and the Service is chasing its tail."

"If they'd let me out of here I'd go over there and help them out," Harry said.

"We'd rather have you back in Washington," Dutch said, hoping Sandy wasn't listening.

Once again Sandy came on the line. "He's going to need one to two months' worth of rehab to build back the strength in his leg before he can return to active duty."

Dutch detected a hint of satisfaction in her voice, but knew better than to argue. Just then, he heard a voice from the hallway: "Hey Dutch, Meadows wants you pronto!"

"Listen, Sandy, I've got to run. Tell the patient we all miss him and hope he gets his ass back here ASAP. Do you guys need anything?"

"No, we're fine. Believe me, the kids are loving having their dad back home."

Dutch smiled and tried not to sound disappointed. "That's great, Sandy. All right, I'll talk to you guys soon."

"Okay, take care, hon."

Dutch hung up and hurried to his meeting with Agent Meadows.

"Roger, don't get too cocky. Heading south from the Carolinas as Burton is moving north toward us could be construed as instigating," Greg Underwood said. "Don't get too cocky."

"Cocky? Is that what you think it is? I just want to come across as confident. I'm not afraid of her because she's the incumbent. I think it's important to display that image," said Roger.

The two faced one another in the Spartan conference room of Roger Graham's Washington campaign headquarters. Joining them around the table were Frank Tipper, Joanna Davis, and Darrell Robinson.

Darrell was a tall, handsome African American who had worked with Roger during his Senate campaign and stayed on his staff afterwards. Darrell was tasked with the enormous job of travel secretary. He oversaw everything from flight and vehicle transportation to hotel and meals.

Joanna Davis was relatively new to the team. Greg admitted during the hiring process for a Press Secretary that her ice blue eyes, long blonde hair, and runner up as Miss Teen USA five years earlier entered into the screening process. He needed someone to rival Patti Harris on the President's side.

"And how is it going to look when our motorcades pass one another on I-95?" Greg said.

Tip stopped his note taking and lifted his head. "Sir, that's a great idea!"

Everyone around the table looked up.

"A photo op. Of course. Two campaigns moving in different directions. It's perfect! If the theme of the campaign has unofficially turned into 'a clear cut difference,' then that's great optics."

Roger gave Tip a high five. "Tip, I love it. That's great."

Joanna and Darrell smiled and nodded as well, but Greg sat as stoic as ever. "Are you done yet? This isn't a pep rally for your high school football team."

Tip shrugged. "It's just a matter of timing. Finding out exactly where Burton's motorcade will be."

Roger turned to Darrell. "How about one of these Secret Service guys assigned to us?" Roger asked referring to the team of agents assigned to him once he secured the Democratic nomination for President a week earlier. "You've gotten to know them by now, haven't you?"

Darrell nodded. "Give me a little time. I think I can get some inside information."

In recognition of Dutch's text-book-work, weeks earlier, tackling and subduing the protester on the lawn of the White House, Polk assigned Dutch to the Secret Service's most prestigious detail, Air Force One.

Now, as his first flight approached, Dutch tried to hide his anticipation, as he and Meadows drove through the gates of Andrews Air Force Base and headed toward the lone unmarked hanger containing the world's most recognizable airplane.

Meadows pulled up to the last of several security checkpoints and flashed his credentials to the Air Force guard on duty who inspected it, then waved him through.

"God I love the Air Force," Meadows said.

"Why's that?"

"They never deviate from protocol. That guard who just checked my credentials is Frank Marshall. I've gone to dinner with him and his family half a dozen times, but he still scrutinizes my Secret Service ID like he's looking for a defect.

Meadows parked the black Crown Victoria and they got out and approached another guard at the door of the hanger. Once again they showed their credentials and were waived in.

Meadows continued, "I admire it. Not just Frank's dedication, but the entire Air Force. I think that other than the Secret Service, the Air force cares more about the safety of the President of the United States than anyone else in our nation. Dutch, do you know that the Air Force personnel on the Presidential Airlift Group were handpicked, and are the best the Air Force has? They spend their first two years on duty with the PAG hand waxing and polishing both the inside and outside of the aircraft under their protection and never complain. In fact, they consider it an honor."

Dutch had to stifle his excitement. This was his first detail aboard Air Force One. Of course he had seen countless videos and photos of the nation's mobile national landmark, but to see it up close was a sight to behold.

As they passed through a final door into the hanger, Meadows slapped Dutch on the back. "It's okay; you can let your jaw drop. Unbelievable, isn't it?"

The two stood and looked up at the pair of VC25 military jets parked in a "V" in the hanger. Dutch's jaw did, in fact, drop. Slowly and methodically, his eyes took in every square inch of the two aircrafts. He was sure he wore a goofy smile but couldn't help himself.

An Air Force staff sergeant approached and greeted the pair.

"Good afternoon, gentlemen," said the tall sergeant. Her brunette hair was tied back in a neat ponytail that protruded from her Air Force cap.

"Hey, Cheryl, how are you?" said Meadows.

"Fine, sir. But as you know we just went on the clock. Chief of Staff Harvey called to confirm we're a go, so it's T minus eight hours before departure."

"I'm glad we were able to get here before they pulled out of the hangar."

Meadows's timing was perfect. Eight hours before each Presidential flight, the planes with identical tail numbers 29000 taxi out to the runway for final preparations before receiving their precious cargo.

Chapter 15

Standing in front of the familiar blue pedestal with the Presidential Seal, addressing an audience of more than eight thousand at the University of Miami campus, President Lorraine Burton was in her element as the crowd cheered. Then, reading effortlessly from the scrolling teleprompters positioned on her periphery, she continued. "Florida has always played a critical role in national politics. You are truly the pulse of the American people, which is why I'm here today."

Most pundits in the press agreed that she, above every other President, could deliver a speech without seeming to ever look at either her notes or the teleprompter itself. The range of directions she looked seemed to defy the angles necessary to read the constantly moving dialogue.

Dutch, whose adrenalin was still rushing from his first trip on Air Force One, was positioned to her left and thirty yards toward the back of the BankUnited Center. He wasn't listening to the speech. His eyes moved constantly, and he listened to a stream of updates from the earpiece.

"Sector 5, report," came Meadows's steady, evenly-paced voice in Dutch's ear.

"All clear."

"Sector 2, report."

"Sector 2, eyes on male, salt and pepper hair, third row back, second seat from right."

"Roger," Meadows said.

The nearest agents around the perimeter of the President glanced in the direction of the person described by Agent Martin. Dutch was halfway up the auditorium and didn't have a good vantage point of the third row, so he continued his surveillance.

"Sector 8, report."

Silence.

Dutch's body tensed. He turned his head slightly toward the back of the room where Agent Nat Shaklis was stationed among the crowd. He was dressed as a student and occasionally shouted with the rest of them as if on cue.

"Sector 8," Meadows repeated evenly.

"Sector 8, clear," came Nat's response.

Dutch let out a breath and continued scanning. During the mission brief, they were told that the president wasn't going to spend any time on the flash point topic of immigration, especially in Miami where Dutch guessed that a large percentage of its residents were in the country illegally. But it certainly didn't sound like she was heeding Harvey's suggestion. A palpable tension seemed to hover over the crowd. It was just like the President not to back down.

Dutch searched for the occasional body, head, arms, or whatever that moved during unexpected times, watching for people whose focus was anywhere but on the President. There were a couple that concerned him, but they had already been pointed out by the more senior agents who had worked hundreds of these events.

As his gaze drifted to his right, movement caught his attention. He focused on the area. Nothing. He continued scanning. There it was again, something that just wasn't right. This time he was ready for it. It was coming from the far right side of his line of sight.

He spotted a buxom blonde co-ed dressed in cut off blue jeans sitting in the front row of the back section of the auditorium. The seams in her white t-shirt struggled to stay intact. What had she done to attract his attention? She was staring at him. As the crowd around her moved in either applause or discontent, she sat staring at him.

Dutch turned his head so she was directly in his line of sight. That's when she made her move. Like a flash, her hands grabbed the bottom of her t-shirt and it lifted off of her chest. Her huge, round, braless breasts bounced out.

As quickly as she lifted her shirt, it was back down. She sat with a self-satisfied look on her face and winked at him. Dutch suppressed a chuckle and went back to scanning the crowd.

Burton's voice grew louder. "And I ask you, is it fair to provide amnesty to those who entered this country illegally while thousands of others who have patiently waited to become citizens of this great country are told their wait was all for naught?"

For the first time during the speech, boos could be heard over the applause. It was mostly coming from the back. But Dutch could also detect a smattering of dissenting voices coming from various points around the auditorium. The sudden shift in the mood caused the hair on the back of his neck to rise. His eyes moved a little quicker over the sector he was responsible for.

Suddenly, someone seated in the middle of the foremost section about fifteen rows back stood.

"Tango up front…what's he doing?" Meadows blurted out, his voice no longer sounding measured, but alarmed.

Dutch watched as agents in the aisles on either side of the row moved closer. Time seemed to freeze and everything went into slow motion. Dutch watched the man bend down then snap back up.

Dutch's training kicked in. He was about ten rows behind the standing man. Agent Martin was closer, but she wasn't moving.

Dutch didn't hesitate. He immediately sprinted down the aisle, lurched past Martin and into the row. He shoved people out of the way who were blocking him.

"Amnesty! Amnesty! Amnesty!" the man yelled while punching the air above his head in a motion that conjured up memories of protests from the sixties.

A nervous voice in his ear said, "He's got something in his left hand."

All at once the agents on stage converged in front of the President as something was lobbed high in the air. An agent in front of the President jumped from the stage and caught the airborne object.

Dutch abandoned trying to move through the obstacles between him and the target. It looked as though the man was reaching for something else. Dutch jumped up, balancing himself on the tops of the seats, took two large strides then launched himself at the target.

The man didn't see him coming. It felt as though he was tackling a bag of flour when they collided. Dutch's shoulder crashed into the man just under his ribcage, forcing air from his lungs as they tumbled to the ground. Dutch pinned him to the floor, hands working fast as he knelt on the man's stomach

Two other agents dove into the fray as Dutch wrenched the man's arms behind his back. His earpiece chattered, but his focus was on the man under him.

"Dutch, any weapon?" asked Agent Martin who was standing behind him with her Sig P-226 drawn.

"Nothing! Anyone see a weapon?" he had to yell to the other agents around in order to be heard above the throngs of people yelling and trampling over each other trying to get out of the way.

One by one they chimed, "Nothing."

Dutch stood and pulled the man, arms cuffed behind him, to a standing position. He was still hunched over from the blow Dutch had inflicted on him. Two agents pulled the man, who could barely support his own weight, along the now empty row of seats. Dutch could hear President Burton's voice. "All right, everyone, there's nothing to worry about. The Secret Service has things under control. Well, I can see that not everyone agrees with my message today," she added.

A din of subdued nervous laughter greeted the comment.

"But that proves my point. You deserve a leader who isn't afraid to make decisions and who sticks with her convictions, regardless of the vocal minority. My job is to represent what the people ask of their government. And unlike my opponent…"

Aboard Air Force One an hour later, the President and her Chief of Staff stared blankly at the three televisions screens, each set to a different news network channels. The sound was turned up on only the farthest screen to the left so they could hear the reporter over the roar of the engines on Air Force One.

"You could say it was déjà vu tonight at the BankUnited Center on the University of Miami campus when a yet-to-be-identified man threw a shoe at the President during a campaign stop."

Video of the man throwing the shoe and the agents taking him out appeared on the screen, showing two different angles. The perky blonde with big blue eyes and perkier chest replaced the footage on the screen.

"Unlike the incident in Iraq when President Bush actually had to duck to avoid airborne shoes, the Secret Service reacted quickly and at no time was the President in danger."

A slow motion shot of Dutch airborne and tackling the man played over and over.

There was a rap at the door. "Come in," Burton said, then muted the television.

Agent Meadows walked in, closed the door behind him, and stood between the flat screens hanging on the wall.

"Agent Meadows, thank you for coming so quickly. We wanted to say what an excellent job you and your agents did tonight," Harvey said. "Truly professional. Please give your team a thank you from me.

I'm sure the President will come out shortly to express her gratitude to Agents Cross and Brown for their heroics."

The President looked at Meadows without saying anything. Harvey knew that if she did say something, it would only go toward reinforcing Bill Polk's caution about the campaign swings down south and the dangers they presented.

"Thank you, sir," Meadows said without looking at the President. "That's our job." He crisply turned and left the office.

Outside the President's Air Force One office, Agent Meadows proceeded down the narrow staircase, then walked the forty-five feet to the bank of wide seats where the Secret Service agents sat when not tasked with a job. As he made his way, he thought about the gratitude, or lack thereof, the President just showed him. It caused him to remember the other Presidents he had protected over the years and how they all differed from one another. When he arrived at his seat, he sat, stared across at the empty seats, and reflected on his time in the Service.

Dutch appeared in the hallway interrupting his thoughts. "You wanted to see me, sir?" he asked politely.

"Yes, I did. Agent Brown, please sit down." Meadows motioned to the seat directly across from his own. "Agent Brown..." he said, the last word hanging out there like bait on a fishing line.

Dutch looked uncomfortable at the use of his last name. He responded slowly, "Yes, sir."

"Dutch," Meadows said in an attempt to ease the tension.

"Yes, sir?" Dutch repeated.

"Nice job today. You let your instincts and training kick in before any of the others. Hell of a feat on your first day outside the Mansion. It was impressive."

Dutch smiled. "Thank you, sir. I appreciate that."

"However," he said in an ominous tone, "here in the Service we try not to pat ourselves on the back for just simply doing our job, so with each compliment comes an area to improve on."

Dutch sat silently, his eyes a little wider as he seemingly waited for the other shoe to drop, so to speak.

Meadows smiled and said, "Next time, don't stare so long at the tits."

Dutch's face worked as he clearly tried looked like he was trying to keep the smile off his face. He stood and said, "I won't, sir. Thank you."

Chapter 16
Early June

Roger Graham sat under the oversized multi-colored umbrella. His table afforded him a magnificent view of the crystal clear water of the infinity pool nestled in a corner of the plush hotel resort garden. A light breeze slightly cooled the already seventy degrees, cloudless June day as the sun continued its rise in the east. He took a deep breath of the clean southern California air as he sipped his iced coffee and closed the book he was reading.

As if on cue, Frank Tipper appeared out of nowhere and sat across from him.

"Sir, I've got the daily polling results for you."

Roger held up a hand. "Tip, it's only six-thirty in the morning. Can I please slowly work myself into the day before getting hit with polling results that I'm probably not going to look at anyway?"

Tip gave his customary sigh, but rebounded by pulling out the clipboard that was never more than an arm's reach away.

"Speaking of today, in a half hour you've got an interview with the *New Yorker* magazine. They were hoping to do some photos as well."

"I love that magazine. I even submitted a cartoon years ago, but it was rejected."

Roger noticed as the weeks flew past how easily frazzled Tip had become and was beginning to worry about his health. Tip had been too busy the previous couple of days for the afternoon run which, Roger was sure, could be of great benefit to his assistant.

Tip continued as if he hadn't heard his boss. "After that, Agent Rolleston requested a few minutes with you on the way to your eight-thirty rally in Miramar San Diego."

"What does Rolleston want now?" Roger asked in a tired voice, not wanting to deal with his Secret Service detail's requests.

Tip hunched his shoulders and adjusted the glasses on his head.

"Tip," Roger said, like a father catching a child in a lie.

Tip squirmed in his seat before saying, "I think he may want to discuss tomorrow's agenda with you."

Roger knew exactly what he was talking about. He picked up the cell phone, punched a number, and was connected to his campaign manager.

"Greg, get the hell out here," he barked and hung up before receiving an answer.

Roger and Tip sat silently. This needed to be cleared up before Tip could proceed with the daily briefing.

A minute later, the rotund figure of Rogers's campaign manager meandered out of the back door of the hotel and sat next to his boss under the umbrella. He already had a white handkerchief out and was wiping the perspiration from his thick neck.

"How the hell can anyone live down here? I feel like I'm in a brick oven," he complained.

"Greg, were you aware that Agent Rolleston wanted a word with me this morning?"

Greg Underwood immediately changed his posture, sitting up straight and propelling himself into defense mode.

His voice was stern. "Roger, listen. He's just doing his job. You've got to go easier on the Secret Service team assigned to you."

Roger raised his voice as he once more reached for his cell phone and angrily punched a button.

"I don't give a rat's ass if he is doing his job; he's not listening to me. He's not in charge here, I am."

Greg recoiled from his uncharacteristic outburst.

Roger put the phone up to his ear and barked one word, "Simon!"

At the mention of the name, Roger noticed his staff shift uncomfortably in their chairs. He knew they disliked this newest addition to his team. What he wasn't sure about was if it was the man's mysterious background that bothered them or his looks and demeanor that they couldn't warm to. He knew his entire staff shared the same feelings of unease, but wouldn't bring it up directly out of respect for a decision that had never been up for discussion.

Within moments a slender figure emerged from the sliding glass doors of the posh hotel. Standing roughly six feet tall, Simon's physique was rather unremarkable for a man in the CIA, which added to the questions everyone had about the person they only knew by a single name, Simon. His hair looked to be thinning from what one could only guess had been a thick head of light brown hair when he was younger. Guessing this man's age had become somewhat of a game among the staff. Most people had their money on around fifty-five years old, but the speculation ranged wildly from late thirties to early sixties. The "age pool" was like so many other things that didn't make sense about this mystery man. The fact that he couldn't be described the same way by any two people really ruffled the staff. Roger told them to stop prodding, which only fueled the mystery.

However, the feature that no one could ignore was his face. His eyes were grey, and his skin was marred with pock marks and scars. But the thing that stood out most about Simon was the dent in his left cheek. A huge chunk of it had been removed by a bullet that nearly ended his life. compliments of, as Roger described it, "a difficult mission in Central America."

Simon and Roger had worked together years before in the CIA. That's all Roger would let his staff know along with the fact that none of their missions were declassified, so no one could ask about them.

Tip stood and pulled out a chair, which Simon declined, choosing to stand in a militaristic posture instead.

Without acknowledging either Tip or Greg, Simon addressed Roger in a very quiet voice, seemingly knowing what he was called out to discuss.

"Roger, Agent Rolleston is concerned about your safety. He wants to implement a buffer zone of at least ten yards around you when entering or exiting your vehicle. The unrest along these border states is palpable, and he's worried because it's next to impossible to determine who is a friend and who is a foe in the crowds."

Roger listened without interrupting, a fact that didn't go unnoticed by Greg, who shifted uncomfortably in his chair and wiped the perspiration off his face with his handkerchief once more.

"Simon, I understand the need for—" Roger began before Simon's upturned hand cut him off.

"Roger, you've got to pick your battles. I happen to agree with Agent Rolleston on this point. This is a very…" he paused and cast his first sideways glance toward the occupants of the table before continuing. "...sensitive time in your campaign. It's best to play it safe."

Greg lurched forward and said, "Excuse me, but do you know something we don't? And if you do, could you please share it with us?" The agitation in his voice was evident.

Simon slowly turned and bore his eyes into the campaign manager. He said in a tone that sounded like a teacher speaking to a student, "Mr. Underwood, there is a great deal of unrest in Central America. We happen to be less than fifty miles from the Mexican border."

Greg tried to match his condescending tone. "Yes, Simon, that's right. However, Roger Graham's campaign message is to make the naturalization process much easier for those who would like to become citizens. That happens to be a very popular message fifty miles from the border."

Simon shot him a glare that would freeze lava. He responded with a forced measured response. "That's true, Mr. Underwood. However, Roger Graham also is a proponent of legalizing marijuana, which in turn would free up the funds necessary to patrol our country's borders. I'm not sure if you are aware who controls the drug trade, but they are people who aren't afraid of executing anyone who would stand in the way of their business. That includes a Presidential candidate within the borders of the United States."

Simon kept his gaze on Greg, who sat back with a heavy thump that moved the entire table. His eyes wouldn't meet those of Simon, but stayed on Roger.

Roger nodded at Simon and thanked his CIA liaison. All watched as Simon spirited back inside before they spoke.

Greg was first. "With all due respect, Roger, may I ask once again why you insist on having a CIA attachment on top of the Secret Service detail to protect you while on the campaign trail?"

Roger allowed himself a chuckle looking at the incredulous looks he was getting. With tension building and the breakneck pace the campaign had taken on with roughly five months to go until the election, he wouldn't admit his guilty pleasure in enjoying the effect Simon's presence was having on his staff.

Roger smiled and said, "I understand your frustration. I don't want either of you to take this personally. It's just that there are some aspects of my campaign for which I need to rely on some of my old contacts. In no way is that a reflection on the confidence I have in either of you. Trust me."

He could tell by the dejected looks on Greg's and Tip's faces that the tired explanation, no matter how it was delivered, was starting to wear thin.

To Roger's surprise, Tip spoke up. "Sir, you've told me from the beginning to voice my opinion." Roger nodded silently and Tip continued. "Sir, I think it's time you let your staff know why you insist on keeping a CIA presence with you. The reason I ask is that questions are beginning to filter through to us, and I'm afraid it will just be a matter of time before you will have to address them in public."

Roger smiled and said, "Nicely put. I like the way you worked your question to make it sound like a campaign issue. Tip, I'm proud of you. You're getting better at this political game."

"But sir, the question still remains. Also, and this may be a more difficult thing to explain, but the CIA doesn't have jurisdiction over domestic issues in the United States. That's the job of the FBI."

"Again Tip, you are correct."

The three sat silently for a moment before Tip said, "Sir, are you going to answer the question?"

Roger took a sip from his drink and sat back in his chair with a smug look. "No, I am not."

"Roger, the media will begin to press you on your time spent working in the CIA. These are questions we've been able to deflect in the past, but the appearance of impropriety by having an agency cross jurisdictional lines may be too much to ignore."

Roger opened the newspaper and said from behind it, "Please get me when the reporter from the *New Yorker* is here."

And with that the meeting was over. Tip and Greg gave one another a frustrated look as they stood and walked away.

"Here's to you, partner," Dutch said, raising his glass. Harry, Sandy, and Alexis clinked their glasses. "It's good to have you back."

"Here, here," Alexis said.

"Thanks, partner. I appreciate it," Harry took a drink from his Guinness.

The dinner rush at Citronelle in Georgetown was in full swing, but with just one phone call Alexis was able to snag a table. Montgomery and Company Vice Presidents and Directors were frequent patrons, so the management was more than happy to accommodate a last minute request by one of the company's rising stars.

The dinner was elegant, and delicious, but Dutch couldn't help but notice that Sandy kept glancing at her husband, as if she were waiting for him to say something. Finally, as dessert was about to arrive, Dutch said, "All right, you two, what's going on?"

Harry looked chagrinned. Then Sandy tenderly took her husband's hand and drew him closer, kissing him on the cheek. She continued rubbing his arm as Harry sat back and took a deep breath.

Alexis and Sandy exchanged a look. Dutch felt as if he were the last one in on a secret.

"Harry, what's going on?" Dutch said, leaning forward to encourage him to speak.

Harry looked at his hands, clearly having difficulty meeting his partner's eyes. "Dutch, I'm out."

Dutch waited for more. Getting none, he asked, "What do you mean, 'out?'"

Harry drew a deep breath, then let it out. "Listen, it was a fun run while it lasted, but I'm not cut out for the POTUS detail. I'm an investigator. That's what I love." He gazed lovingly at Sandy. "But I really want to go back to Omaha."

"Well, shit," said Dutch. "I guess I should've seen it coming. Have you told Polk yet?"

"No. We're getting together at the end of the week. I'll tell him then."

"What's your assignment this week? I looked at the duty roster and we're not paired together."

"I'm supposed to be staying at the Mansion all week, lying low until I get my feet back under me."

"That's smart. How long do you think it will take to get transferred back to Omaha?"

"Ken Needle told me transfers from the POTUS detail to somewhere else is like going against traffic. Not many people look to come off that detail. I expect it will happen right away."

"So you've already spoken with Needle?"

Harry nodded, and his expression showed the finality of the decision.

Dutch felt conflicted. He was sad to lose his partner, and embarrassed he had missed the clues that everyone else at the table seemed to know. Looking back, though, he had to admit to himself it wasn't a big surprise. Harry had been reluctant to take the job in the first place.

"Needle must be pretty happy to have you coming back."

Harry shrugged.

"Yes, is an understatement," Sandy said.

Dutch watched Harry and his wife share a loving look. "Well, good for you," he said. "You'll do a great job and I know you'll be happy to be back in Omaha."

"Thanks, Dutch. I'm glad you understand."

This time Dutch shrugged. Sitting back, he looked at his partner for a long moment before asking, "Any regrets before leaving?"

Harry looked thoughtful. "I really would have liked going on one of the travel teams just once. Flying on Air Force One must be a rush."

Dutch smiled. "It really is. I can't lie to you, it's right up there."

Harry reached into the breast pocket of his suit coat and pulled out a cocktail napkin with the Air Force One logo on it.

"At least you got me a souvenir. I guess that'll have to do."

He gazed at the cocktail napkin for a moment, then looked up. "Other than that, no regrets." He took Sandy's hand.

Dutch raised his glass. "I will miss you terribly, but here's to you both. There was only one good reason to leave D.C., and that's it. Here's to family."

"Here, here!" the others echoed, raising their glasses once more

Chapter 17
Late June

Alexis looked at her cell on the side of the bed and decided against turning it on. Work could wait. She picked up the remote control then settled into her pillow. Dutch was in the bathroom, and would be back any second. She pulled the sheets up to her neck and savored the memory of their lovemaking. Then, for the millionth time, she glanced at the sparkling diamond ring on her finger. The dinner was perfect. The proposal was perfect. Their life would be perfect.

She clicked on the television.

Moments later, when Dutch entered the room, Alexis was sobbing, the sheets stretched up to her mouth, eyes locked onto the television screen.

A video clip replayed over and over, showing the President, standing in front of the familiar podium with the Presidential seal, delivering a speech. Out of the left corner came an agent's body flying through the air, stretched out horizontally in a full dive. A black object connected with the Secret Service agent, and it looked like his neck was ripped apart as he continued across the screen.

It happened so fast the activity didn't even register on the President's face until two agents threw her to the floor and others came rushing in from every conceivable angle. They covered her with a human shield as agents immediately fell into a horseshoe perimeter on stage, their Uzis out and searching for a target.

Another camera angle showed people scrambling in all directions, but the dark suits of the Service stood their ground.

Dutch grabbed his phone and turned it on. He frantically scrolled through more than a dozen messages and keeping one eye on the television. What Secret Service Agent had just given his life for the president? Dutch's stomach clenched. No, it couldn't be.

Dutch and Alexis stopped what they were doing when the replay slowed and moved in to see a close up of the agent whose neck had exploded.

"Oh my God!" shrieked Alexis, burying her face and continuing to sob.

Dutch froze, unable to move, seeing Harry's face on the screen, his neck ripped away.

Three days later, Dutch stood in a row of men he served with on the PPD. As bagpipes played, and guns saluted, Dutch looked at Sandy Ludec, who winced at each shot. Her face was a mask of sorrow as she watched the American flag being removed from the top of the black coffin suspended above the grave.

Marine Corps officers folded the flag, and then one of them ceremonially marched over and awarded it to Sandy, who took it from the soldier without looking.

Junior looked straight ahead at the final resting place of his father. Hunter watched the Marine guard salute his mother.

Dutch wept openly, not even trying to wipe the tears away, as Alexis pressed her face into his shoulder and sobbed.

As protocol dictated, the President had spent a moment with each of the Ludecs, then left the graveside flanked by a larger than normal contingency of agents. Once her motorcade was away, the remaining mourners dispersed until all that was left were close family, which included Dutch and Alexis.

They had stayed the previous few days with Sandy and the kids, helping to plan the more personal moments of Harry's wake and funeral, but a full military funeral at Arlington National Cemetery was strangely turnkey. At Sandy's request, her church broke tradition and allowed a second eulogy after the obligatory one from the President. It was delivered by Harry's older brother and was much more personal and family oriented.

Dutch choked up again thinking of the Ludec family. It was the central theme in Harry's life. How could this have happened, and why?

"Thank you, Terry. For everything," Sandy said, snapping Dutch out of his trance.

She stood next to him as he stared at the coffin, lost in his thoughts.

"Please, Sandy, you don't need to thank me."

"I wouldn't have even known where to begin getting those pictures of him while he was serving in the Army. I really appreciate your reaching out to find them."

Dutch took Sandy's hand. "Harry was one of a kind." His voice cracked. "He'll really be missed."

Then Sandy did something Dutch didn't expect. Taking his other hand, she pulled him in close and turned him so he was facing her. They were close enough so no one else could hear what she was about to say.

"Finish his work," she said, staring directly into his eyes. "Don't let anyone get this President. Then Harry's death won't be in vain."

At this moment it was easy to see that Sandy Ludec was first and foremost an army wife. Though she may have loathed Harry's job, she understood its importance.

Now, he locked eyes with her. "I promise."

Chapter 18
July

Joanna Davis's long hair gently blew past her face as she stood on the stage next to Roger Graham. The June sun shone on the campaign team standing on a makeshift wooden stage on the outskirts of Phoenix. Joanna pointed to a reporter from the Los Angeles Times and said, "Last question."

Roger took her cue and turned to the reporter who remained standing while the others sat, pens poised to quickly jot down his response.

"Congressman Graham, in light of the killing of Secret Service Agent Harry Ludec last week, do you feel a need to take a second look at the policies you've proposed regarding immigration reform?"

"First off, our hearts and prayers go out to the Ludec family. There is no higher honor than dying in the service of one's country." He paused dramatically before continuing. "Our country owes a great debt to Special Agent Harry Ludec. He epitomizes everything good about our country."

He paused for applause.

"The message both I and my opponent have about immigration reform may be different, but it's of paramount importance to remember a tenet on which our country was founded, which is our ability to peacefully work out our differences. The actions of one man cannot and will not derail the democratic process. Thank you very much everyone, and God Bless America!"

The few hundred people surrounding Roger's stage bellowed out thunderous applause. The press was eating up this candidate. His good looks combined with a unique ability to effectively convey his message had garnered favorable media coverage, evidenced by his continued rise in the polls.

He waved to the crowd and exited stage left surrounded by his security detail that encircled him all the way to the bulletproof limo. His closest campaign staff members were already inside.

"Great job, Roger," Greg Underwood said, who was seated next to him.

"Thanks Greg, and to the rest of you as well. Fine job all around," Roger said.

Joanna Davis and Tip were across from him. A member of the Secret Service detail sat in a fold-down jumper seat against the far door. Simon sat next to him.

They lurched forward a bit as the caravan of vehicles began their drive North. In front of Roger's limo was a black SUV carrying Secret Service agents. Behind the limo were two additional black SUVs. The first carried more agents and the back tailgate was raised with a sniper buckled in who could react to a threat while moving.

Once the caravan was underway on its trek to the airport, Roger announced he was making an unexpected stop, without his Secret Service protection detail. He tilted his head toward the driver's side. "Simon and I will meet you on the tarmac at eighteen hundred hours."

The Secret Service agent shifted on the leather seat, making a squeaking noise. He sat forward a bit further and glared at Simon but kept his mouth shut.

Tip pursed his lips. Such unscheduled trips were becoming more frequent during their southern campaign stops.

Sensing Tip's discomfort, Roger said. "Take a deep breath, Tip. We have the time built into the schedule. I promise I won't be late."

Tip glanced at his watch and Roger knew he was wondering what he would be doing for the next four hours while out of contact with his campaign staff.

"Sir, I feel the need to ask what is so important that you need to make an unscheduled stop?"

Roger appreciated Tip's obsessive compulsiveness about his campaign schedule. But his job was keeping the campaign on track and had nothing to do with the work at hand.

"You don't need to know. All you need to know is that I'll be back in four hours."

Tip pursed his lips and made a notation on his clipboard. Roger had always been true to his word. There was nothing left to say.

The line of SUVs stopped in the middle of a dirt road they had turned onto three miles from the main highway. Amid a copse of trees, Roger stepped out and shielded his eyes from the still swirling dust. From another vehicle, Agent Rolleston approached at the same time Simon and two other agents from the CIA stepped up alongside Roger.

"I suppose my asking you not to do this would fall on deaf ears," Rolleston said.

Roger nodded. "Agent Rolleston, I know you probably don't believe me, but I truly am sorry that I need some time without the Secret Service. My hope is that one day I will be able to include you. But for now it's for your own good."

The orders from Langley superseded the Secret Service, and Rolleston knew he was powerless to do anything. But he had to try. "Is there someplace I can station my team that can assist your return? We're less than a mile from the Mexican border. You don't know what's around here."

"You worry too much, Agent Rolleston." He extended his hand and the men shook. "We should be back in less than three hours. Thank you again for your service."

Roger and Simon, along with two CIA agents, left in one of the SUVs.

Watching them disappear in the dust, Clyde Rolleston couldn't decide if he hated or admired Roger Graham. The dossier on him was full of blanks for sensitive and national security clearance only. From what Rolleston had been able to learn from asking around, at one time Graham had been into some "heavy shit" as one of his friends at the CIA told him.

"It's best if you steer clear of trying to figure the man out," his friend cautioned. "I'm not even going to try to go digging because he'll find out about it before I hit the first key on my computer. Let's just say that he's been around the block doing shit no one will ever find out about."

Graham was well insulated, and kept the right political connections to keep his past a well-guarded secret. What was public knowledge was his time in the airborne forces in Iraq and Afghanistan. There were rumors about Iran as well, though he knew he could never verify those.

Having served in the Army himself, Rolleston respected anyone who ever put on the uniform, especially Special Forces. He was alive today because of the work of so-called "black ops" behind enemy lines. He recalled his deployment years earlier in Afghanistan. His platoon had been cut off from their battalion under heavy fire from snipers in the Korangal Valley. Running low on ammo and losing a man every five minutes or so, things didn't look too good. Suddenly the gunfire ceased. After twenty minutes, Rolleston and two other scouts ventured out to find an Airborne Ranger standing atop the hillside and giving them the all clear sign. As quickly as they saw him, he was gone. To this day he never knew who was in the squad that had saved their lives.

Rolleston stared out at the area where moments before Roger had been and whispered under his breath, "Good luck, sir."

Chapter 19

Dutch had liked Meadows since he began on POTUS duty. But his admiration soared when Meadows allowed Dutch a temporary transfer from the PPD to the investigation of the attempted assignation of Lorraine Burton.

Meadows said it was because of Dutch's strong investigative background, but obviously Meadows knew of Dutch's friendship with Harry and his family.

Now, Dutch sat at one of four rectangular tables arranged in a square that were filled with agents in a windowless room at the D.C. headquarters of the Secret Service. At the far end of the room, three large screens ran video captured during that fateful day. Each person had a laptop and was tasked with a different aspect of the investigation. Dutch's assignment was to study the steps his partner took in saving the President's life. From the beginning of the speech to the fateful end, Dutch retraced everything that Harry saw and did.

Before he could even begin, Dutch met with Polk to find out what the hell Harry was doing there, just days before his transfer back to Omaha. Polk explained that they he had tried to talk Harry out of the transfer but once it was evident he was serious about going back to Omaha, Polk offered him something he couldn't refuse. In light of his brave and dedicated service during the fence jumping incident back in March, he wanted to "throw him a bone" as a way of saying thank you. He offered Harry a one-time spot on the POTUS away team for a quick campaign jaunt to Florida.

Sandy had agreed to the one-time detail, and felt deeply guilty, despite countless reassurances that she had no way of knowing the consequences.

Now, after hours of concentrating on the video screen, Dutch rubbed his eyes. Reading something would offer a needed break. The Mexican government had sent over some files with information about the shooter, a Mexican national. Harry reached for them. An old booking photo showed Juan Diego Martinez: thick black hair, hard eyes. He had a dark complexion and pock marks around his cheeks from what looked to be some type of lingering psoriasis.

A lifelong criminal, Martinez had spent time in the Mexican underground working for various drug lords as a hired gun. It seemed not to matter the target as long as the money was right.

A notation from the Mexican government referenced a CIA workup on Martinez, indicating that he was implicated in the murder of at least two government officials in Mexico who were attempting to crack down on the out-of-control drug trade along the border. Dutch flipped through the pages of the entire file but couldn't find the referenced CIA report.

Dutch looked toward Agent Nat Shaklis "Where's the CIA report on this bastard?"

Nat shook his head. "Not in hand yet. Harvey says we should have it by the afternoon. Langley is slow getting it to us."

"Slower than Mexico?"

Nat shrugged.

Dutch went back to the report. One of the many questions the team was working on was a motive. From all indications, Martinez was making a decent living as a hired gun. Why he would turn his attention to the leader of the free world was a mystery.

The early theories were that he was mentally unbalanced. Perhaps he viewed Lorraine Burton as someone who was trying to oppress the Mexican people by keeping them from a better way of life. Dutch didn't buy it. Perhaps the question, Dutch thought, is who would have hired Martinez to carry out the hit? Who in Mexico would have benefitted most by the murder of Lorraine Burton?

Whatever the case, it was a suicide mission. Martinez had taken a shot at the President, and killed Ludec, but he had paid the price: A sharpshooter's bullet to the head, and two others in his heart. Getting one shot off at the President was unlikely enough, but the service made sure that a second one wouldn't fly. None of this made Dutch feel any better since his partner was still dead.

But how did Martinez make it into the crowd with a weapon? That was answered right away when Dutch opened the next file containing the report on what killed his partner. It had been a dart saturated with lethal amounts of Epibatidine.

The dart itself wasn't metal, so it didn't set off any of the metal detectors screening everyone in attendance. The needle on the dart was made of coated carbon fibers. The dart had been fired from a crude blow gun. Each component was concealed so one person could quietly, without drawing attention, assemble the weapon virtually unnoticed.

The open file included pictures of each part of the blow gun. It was made from bamboo and was small enough to fit in most people's hands undetected. It consisted of two, three-inch segments which screwed together. Another picture showed the black paper fins attached to a small needle projectile no longer than an inch. Most of the needle bore the unmistakable blemish of Harry's blood. The next photo showed the tissue-like material resembling a handkerchief in which the shooter carried the lethal dart meant to kill the most powerful woman in the world.

The lab report indicated that the poison on the dart, Epibatidine, was an alkaloid extracted from the skin of a phantasmal poison frog which is indigenous to the Andean slopes of the central Ecuadorian Bolivar province. It is about two hundred times as potent as morphine and at one time was considered a replacement for the popular painkiller. However, the line between a therapeutic and toxic dose was so fine that it was considered too dangerous for use with humans.

At high doses, the effects were hypertension and paralysis in the respiratory system, seizures, and then death. In Harry's case the reports indicated he lived approximately five minutes in brutal agony.

Dutch pushed the folders away in anger.

This was information he would make sure Harry's family never learned. Harry died a hero, but right now that's small consolation when he remembered the looks on Harry's children's faces at graveside. Closing the reports, Dutch returned to a file on his laptop containing fifty-five still photos grabbed from various video sources. They showed at least five angles on the scene. He put them in chronological order.

The Wildlife West Nature Park's amphitheater seated one thousand people, and the stage on which President Burton stood was in the center of the venue.

The first grouping of photos was from a CNN camera placement in the center of the amphitheater, positioned on scaffolding behind the seats, about forty feet above the President.

Martinez, circled in red, was visible in the photo. He was seated in the third row about ten feet to the left of center stage, allowing for a perfect shot at the President.

According to reports, everyone admitted to the rally had gone through the metal detectors that always accompany the President, and had been subjected to pat downs and dogs trained to sniff out bomb making materials. Martinez had balls, that was for sure, Dutch thought as he opened another computer file.

Another vantage point showed still photos of Martinez making his move. The crowd had parted, giving him about a foot of open space three hundred sixty degrees around him. The photo in this sequence which was most helpful was taken from a FOX news camera set up on a ten foot metal scaffolding to the right of the stage pointed toward the crowd. According to the time stamp on the bottom right corner, this photo occurred one second after the photo from CNN's video. He could see Martinez face and eyes focused on the President, and his left arm in motion raising a tubular device.

The next image showed the agents beginning to move, alerted by the parting of the crowd around Martinez.

Dutch opened another series of shots that were taken from a local ABC affiliate whose camera was set up in the far left hand side of the venue slightly behind the bleachers, with a shielded view of the crowd and a partially obstructed view of the President. It was evident this local station didn't get the choice camera placements as did the networks, but for Dutch's purposes he couldn't have asked for a better shot of his partner.

According to the time stamp in the bottom corner, the first photo from the ABC affiliate was taken about the same time as the last one from Fox. The service had been deployed in a standard horseshoe perimeter consisting of three layers of security. Harry was located in the innermost circle, just to the left of the President. In fact, Harry's position afforded him the chance to be one of the first to see the shooter make his move. Dumb luck, thought Dutch.

The next photo in the sequence showed Harry's head turned in the direction of the unexpected movement. Next showed Harry's head still focused on the crowd, but his legs were moving. Dutch had hard copies of these photos, which he fanned out on his workspace so he could switch from the laptop digital display and the ones he could pick up and move around.

Next was Harry, his eyes still fixed on the shooter, beginning to move his arms in front of his body. Harry was moving fast. He easily covered the twenty feet within two seconds.

The next two were the hardest for him to study. Harry held his arms in front of him as his knees recoiled, preparing to launch his body in front of the deadly shot. The next image Dutch stared at the longest. Harry was airborne horizontally at the perfect angle to shield the President. The dart had buried itself in his neck. Blood—frozen in time—exited in two directions. Harry's face hadn't yet registered the pain. Dutch closed his eyes and looked away from the photos for a moment.

Nat, who had been watching from the corner of the room, approached and put his hand on Dutch's shoulder.

Without looking up, Dutch said, "How quick was it?" He knew he'd get a straight answer from Nat.

"Reilly and Marks were the first to him after the perimeter was secured. It had been around thirty seconds since the impact. They tell me he was grabbing his neck trying to stop the blood. His breathing was labored. The fin of the dart was still wedged between his larynx and spine."

Dutch nodded for him to continue.

"They called for a medic, but it took another minute before anyone got there. The President was long gone by then and the crowd had scattered." Nat paused and tapped the folder he had given Dutch moments earlier. "You'll see there was enough Epibatidine on the dart to kill an elephant. Looks like our shooter knew he only was going to have one shot at Widow. He was right."

"Was Harry able to talk at all?"

Nat shook his head. "The dart hit him perfectly in the throat. Bad luck really. He was dead about three minutes after the medic reached him. Nothing anyone could do."

Dutch expelled a breath. "Luck. Sure."

A palpable silence hung in the air for a moment before Dutch said, "Who took Martinez out?"

A morbid chuckle escaped Nat. "Who didn't? Coroner said he was hit from three different angles."

Dutch looked over at Nat. "I sent one through the bastard's skull. I heard his fucking face blew up from the impact. I just hope the mother fucker felt it go through the whole way before he bit it."

Chapter 20
Fourteen weeks before the election

Off stage to the left, Lorraine Burton looked at Roger Graham, who was on the other side, as Sam Shepard, the debate moderator finished his opening remarks.

This was the first public appearance since the attempt on her life. She looked at the Secret Service Agents deployed around her. It was the first time she ever remembered noticing them and where they were positioned. But somehow after seeing the agent get struck down mere feet in front of her, she was a little unsure if they could defend her again. Her heart beat hard against her chest.

She closed her eyes tightly and took a deep breath, then distracted herself from thinking about the assassination attempt by recalling what her sources had told her about Graham.

Graham's rise to political prominence didn't follow the typical track. He came from a non-political background; in his case, the Army Rangers. From the classified reports she managed to get about him, he excelled in covert and stealth missions. During the Afghan war, his task force had been dropped into a heavily saturated Al Qaeda stronghold near the Pakistan border and stayed undercover for weeks relaying intelligence that proved crucial. The information he and his team gathered was so vast and diverse that after his tour of duty Langley came calling.

Much like his time with the Rangers, Roger Graham didn't take long to distinguish himself within the CIA. After training, he immediately went undercover. He was assigned to the task force working to stem the illegal flow of drugs coming into the United States from the Mexican border. Upon receiving this posting, what he did was classified and stamped for only the highest of security levels, out of reach of even Lorraine's covert sources.

After ten years in the CIA, Graham suddenly resurfaced in the U.S. He tendered his resignation, claiming a desire to give back to the country, moved back to his home state of New Mexico and entered the hotly contested race for the Congressional Second District.

The press labeled him "the James Bond candidate," who vowed to lift the veil of secrecy from government. He was a democrat but proclaimed to have very independent leanings. He won the election in a landslide and was off to Washington.

Now, as a candidate for President, he offered a unique problem for seasoned politicians like Burton because they had a hard time penetrating his CIA past. Most of what he did was still classified. As President she could give an executive order and have the reports on her desk, but the request must be made part of the public record. That was the last thing Harvey wanted. He didn't want it to be known they were digging into a hero's past.

So the mystery around Graham's time in the CIA would remain just that. Langley ran by different rules, and this President didn't enjoy a favored status within the agency. Early in her Presidency she let slip that she thought the "toys the boys" used in the CIA were too costly. That was all it took. Now she had no friends who could pull strings to keep such requests off the front page.

"Madame President, it's time," said Harvey from behind her, snapping her from her thoughts.

Lorraine timed her walk from stage left at precisely the same moment Graham entered from the opposite side. They met in the center and shook hands.

In the wings, the candidates' respective handlers watched anxiously. Weeks had been spent preparing for the debate, learning their opponents vulnerabilities, and crafting pithy sound bites that would convey their talking points. But the debate was a gamble. One never knew what the opposing candidate had in store.

Midway through the debate, after President Burton had confidently fielded a question about the economy, Harvey leaned into Patti and said, "She's getting too comfortable."

"How can you tell?"

"Did you hear her? She wasted forty-five seconds of her response to say absolutely nothing. She better watch out, because she may not be able to switch gears quickly enough if he pounces."

"How else did you want her to answer the question? The economy has done well these last three years. Why shouldn't she brag a bit?"

Harvey turned just enough to keep the President in his peripheral vision but still answer Patti directly. "The President does her best when she's giving specifics. When she starts spewing bullshit about nothing, people can see through it. She's better when her back is against a wall."

"Isn't this a good thing then? Her back hasn't been against the wall all night."

Harvey sighed uneasily. "I just don't feel good about it."

At the opposite side of the stage, Tip was in full swing. He was timing how long the President talked, amazed at how long politicians could go without saying anything. It frustrated him to no end that more people wouldn't see through the façade.

"What do you think?" he asked Greg Underwood, who stood rigidly at this side.

"How long?" Greg asked, barely moving his lips.

Tip glanced at the stopwatch once more. "She's got thirty seconds left," he said without looking up.

Greg's lips tightened as the veins in his forehead began to bulge. "Now," he spat in a whisper.

Tip moved his arm out from his body and extended the fingers on his hand, attracting Roger's attention.

Roger took a deep breath, then interrupted.

"I'm sorry, Madame President—"

The President raised her eyebrows in surprise, almost as though she'd forgotten he was still on stage with her.

Sam Shepard stepped in quickly, as if he expected something like this because the debate had been going too smoothly. "Mr. Graham, she still has fifteen seconds left."

"Mr. Shepard, and for that matter Madame President, excuse me but another fifteen seconds of needless banter isn't going to kill us if we forego it. We have real problems in this country, and I don't want to waste even fifteen more seconds of America's time."

Sam Shepard sat speechless.

"I beg your pardon?" President Burton said. "I would hardly classify our debate as a waste of time."

That was it. She bit and Roger had her. Greg smiled.

"Madame President, I'm not saying the debate is a waste of time. I'm just saying listening to you talk about nothing is a waste of time."

An audible "Oohh" rose from the roughly three thousand gathered at Hill Auditorium on the campus of the University of Michigan.

"Mr. Graham—" she began.

"That's Congressman Graham, just as I refer to you as Madame President."

Judging by the cacophony of camera clicks and flashes, this was a moment none of the photographers missed, and would be splashed all over the front pages of newspapers and websites the following morning.

"Madame President, you never even answered the question. Please don't patronize the American public by lecturing us about how fragile the economy is. I think the 6 percent of people currently unemployed already know that. I think the 47 million people relying on food stamps already know that. I think the—"

The President cut him off this time, her tone shrill. "Congressman Graham, I'm not going to lower myself or this debate by bringing it to a street fight. The American people don't deserve—"

"Actually, they do deserve a street fight if that's what it takes to begin talking about the matters that will affect every one of us in the coming four years."

Sam Shepard's head shifted from one candidate to the other, his mouth agape.

"Let's stop taking the softball questions from reporters who have been in the tank of the political machine far too long," Graham said. "Let's you and I just talk in the time we have left, shall we?"

An unexpected round of applause arose from the crowd. Lorraine Burton looked out, looking unsure of what to say. Sweat beaded along her hair line.

She drew herself up to her full height, puffed out her chest a bit and said, "All right, Congressman Graham. Let's do just that."

Backstage, Patti didn't realize just how hard she had been squeezing Harvey's arm until he plied it off of his suit jacket.

On the opposite side of the stage, Tip and Greg exchanged a silent high five.

Both camps braced themselves for a fist fight.

High atop the catwalk that traversed the stage, Meadows said into his mouthpiece, "Stay sharp everyone. Stay sharp."

He had protected Presidents and presidential candidates during debates before, However, he had never seen emotions run so high. Unbridled yells and claps reverberated throughout the hall as Burton and Graham traded barbs.

Meadows looked down to the side exit of stage right and made eye contact with Rolleston, whose team of Secret Service agents was working together with the POTUS detail since they were both in the same place. Rolleston raised his eyebrows and puffed out his cheeks as he returned a concerned look.

"Keep focus and work the room, people," Meadows said into his microphone that transmitted to all the agents in both details.

The debate only grew more heated as the candidates talked about trade policy, economic stimulus, and Chinese expansionism. To the left of the President, Harvey threw his plastic bottle of water against the exit door.

Then the debate turned to U.S. drug policy.

Graham said, "Legalizing marijuana would have a cascading positive effect for our economy." The audience, largely made up of college students, cheered.

"Roger Graham, how can you be serious about that? I know you don't like to rely on facts and figures, but do you know the rates of addiction, overriding health costs, and the multitude of crime that would ensue? And that's just off the top of my head."

"Excuse me, but I thought we were going to have an open and frank dialogue for the American people tonight?"

"That's what we were doing."

"Then let's get back on track and stop wasting everyone's time pretending that the enforcement of illegal marijuana use isn't a joke right now."

His face reddening, Harvey stormed to the cyclorama curtain surrounding back stage, balled up a fistful, and shoved it into his mouth. Patti looked around to make sure no one from the press would be able to see this open display of frustration.

"Madame President, if I wanted to right now I could go out on any street in America and buy pot to roll my own joint. Legalization will mean greater tax revenues, a better relationship with our neighbors to the south, and significant savings in law enforcement. You know it and I know it. The quicker we can agree on the obvious the sooner we can solve the problem."

Lorraine played it safe and didn't respond. Too many police unions supported her during the last election cycle.

"Perhaps most importantly though," Graham continued, "the freed up law enforcement personnel tasked to the failed 'war on drugs' can be deployed to patrol and protect our territorial borders, keeping out criminals, and creating a fair system of immigration for those who come to our country to contribute to the economy, and who benefit the thousands of businesses who employ them."

At home with Alexis, Dutch clicked off the TV and threw the remote control over the side of the bed.

"Honey, what's wrong?" said Alexis. "I thought you wanted to watch this."

"I did, but I was hoping it wouldn't come down to immigration again."

"Well, you knew it had to come up."

"I was told it wasn't going to. Typical friggin' politicians. Always going back on their promises."

"Terry, I thought what Graham said had merit, don't you?"

Dutch considered his reply. "It's not that. Every time Graham cranks up the immigration issue, it makes our job harder."

"You miss being on the POTUS detail, don't you?"

Dutch sighed. "Yeah. But finishing the investigation and getting answers will certainly help Sandy and the kids."

"I know it's been difficult for you, Dutch. Did you talk to the department psychologist?"

"Yeah. It was good." He sighed.

Alexis knew that the final report on the assassination attempt and Harry's death would be released the following morning. "Are you comfortable with the final outcome?"

A pregnant pause, then, "Yes."

Alexis pulled on his ear a bit and they both chuckled.

"All right, I'm 98.8 percent comfortable with it."

"I thought so. So what is it, do you think Martinez didn't act alone?"

Dutch sat up and turned so he could lean against the headboard. He took Alexis' hand in his own.

"No, the evidence says he was alone. I'm comfortable with that part of it. His file gave plenty of background of his past criminal acts. He had used blow guns to commit murder before. Not only was he proficient with them, but he knew how to make them as well. No, this attempt had his name all over it."

Alexis lowered her head a bit but kept eye contact.

"Between you and me, right?" Dutch said.

She took her index finger and traced an X over her heart.

"There's something about Martinez, but I just can't put my finger on it."

"How so?"

"I don't know. He was a pro; there was no doubt. But something about the job doesn't add up."

"Do you think there's something you missed, or do you feel guilty because you weren't there?"

"I don't know."

Silence set in until Alexis pulled him to her chest and rubbed his temples.

"Ouch, don't move so much," she said when he adjusted his head on her breasts.

"What's wrong?"

"My boobs are sensitive."

"Is that why you're wearing flannel in August?"

"It's just what feels comfortable tonight. I've been cold lately."

"Oh" he said.

She smiled, ran her hand through his crew cut and hugged him.

Chapter 21
Eleven weeks before the election

"The numbers are in. It was just as I said it would be, dead even," announced Greg Underwood. He grabbed at the seat next to him in an attempt to steady himself as the custom fitted campaign bus hit a pothole.

Joanna and Tip put their hands up defensively as the hulking campaign manager tried to right himself. Roger leaned over and gave each member of his staff a high five as they rode along Interstate 395 at seventy miles per hour.

"Lots can change in a short period of time" Roger said. "We have to remember that," He reclined in his plush leather seat in the corner of the "war room." "We pulled even because of a good showing in the debate a few weeks ago, but polls can be fickle. And in three weeks we haven't taken the lead. We can't let our guard down—even though the debate did go pretty well."

The staff cheered, still elated that polls had judged Graham the clear winner.

"But the debate is history, folks. We still have eleven weeks and one more debate before the election," he said.

Looking over the edge of his ever present clipboard, Tip said, "Okay, new subject: Congress is scheduled to debate Burton's immigration bill in roughly three weeks. The press says it could go on for a long time. But you'll only be in D.C. for three days when it's scheduled to come to the floor. Are you sure you don't want to extend your stay there?"

"Absolutely. The President wants this immigration bill put to rest as quickly as possible. Trust me, she's given everyone in her party the word to wrap it up quickly."

The bus swayed once more and Greg used the momentum to land in a seat. He said, "I spoke with Frank French at the DNC headquarters last night. He promises me the Representatives in the assembly are ready to pull every trick in the book to delay. All we have to do is give him the word."

Roger shook his head. "That's exactly what Burton wants. I'm not going to do it. I'm sure she's chock full of leaks and sound bites that will slam the Democratic leadership for stalling."

"So?" Tip said.

Joanna moved to the edge of the couch and tried to straighten her pencil skirt Roger suspected she must have regretted wearing as it rode up her long legs a bit too much.

She said, "it will come across for what it is, a cheap way of using the parliamentary process to forward political ambition."

"I disagree. When it was—" Greg started before Roger looked at him and held a finger up to check him.

Joanna continued, "our message needs to revolve around more than the immigration debate. If we appear to be stretching things out in Congress just to curry support from the American people, it could backfire. With what I'm sure would be a good dose of help from the administration, it could be viewed for what it is, a tactic."

Roger smiled and said, "I knew it was a good idea to hire her."

Everyone in the bus laughed.

Darrel nodded and made some notes on his iPad, as their bus hurtled toward the Nation's capital.

Back in Washington, Harvey was in the Oval office, having just concluded a meeting with himself, President Burton, and the Chairman of the Joint Chiefs of Staff. The polling data had not improved since the disastrous debate.

Lorraine stepped to her desk, opened up the top drawer, and removed a pack of cigarettes. As she pulled one out, she glanced at Harvey. Then, she fished out a lighter from the drawer. Harvey didn't move. Lorraine lit the cigarette and took a long draw, then exhaled tiredly.

Her head tilted back and her eyes rose to the ceiling in apparent pleasure. She inhaled again and held her breath, keeping the blue smoke inside her mouth for an extra moment before exhaling and bringing her head back down. A swirl of blue gray smoke circled her head as she took a seat and stared at the clock on her blotter. Harvey had given it to her as a gift when he was her boss.

My how the tables have turned, she thought, again looking at her Chief of Staff. Out loud she said, "Well Michael, I know you've been dying to say it for hours now. Out with it."

She took another drag from her cigarette and held it between her index and middle fingers alongside her face.

Harvey sat back, the sofa molding to his body.

"What do you want me to say? The polls don't lie."

Another puff on the cigarette as she measured what to say next.

"Michael, don't take this the wrong way, but how much of your polling is affected by the attempt on my life?"

Harvey looked surprised at the question. "Madame President, I think we need to keep our focus on the present."

She shook her head. "No, I don't think so. Since Mr. Martinez's fifteen minutes of fame ended so abruptly, we haven't taken the time to really measure how much that could have affected the campaign."

Harvey sat quietly and listened.

"If you allow yourself to think outside the box, has our polling changed since the attempt on my life or are they still asking the same questions as if I weren't nearly killed?"

"So if I understand you correctly, you want to gauge how your numbers could have dropped because of the assassination attempt?"

She took another long pull, held the smoke in again, and then slowly released it before saying, "Yes, that's exactly what I'm saying."

"Madame President, historically when an attempt is made on the life of the President, the approval numbers go up." He sifted through another folder laid out in front of him. "According to the polls taken daily since the attempt..." he silently moved his lips, counting to himself. "It doesn't look like there was a spike at any time."

"How about after the final report on the attempt was released by the Secret Service?"

Again he shuffled the pages in front of him shaking his head back and forth while doing so.

He looked back up to find her staring at him.

"What does that tell us?" she softly said.

He shifted uncomfortably. He felt as if he were being set up. "Well, you could look at it a number of ways."

"Stop bullshitting me, Michael." She slammed her flattened hand on the desk.

Harvey raised his voice in retort. "Your performance in the debate is what turned it, and the immigration policy you're trying to ram through Congress isn't sitting well with the public. Is that what you want to hear?"

She stood slowly and said quietly, "Of course that's what you think."

Harvey stood, no longer comfortable being lower than she. "What are you trying to say?"

"Let me make it clearer: you're not doing your job."

"Come on!"

"It's true, Michael. Your job is to make what I do work in our favor. It's called politics. Instead of playing politics, you're thinking of ways to make me change.

She jabbed a finger at him. "What you need to do is focus the public's attention on the fact that I almost got killed. If you had, then maybe everyone would be talking about that instead of all the poor immigrants who run through our borders by the thousands every day. Michael, have you even once tried to shed light on the fact that it was an illegal immigrant who almost killed me?"

Harvey glanced down at the carpet for a moment, then back up at her. "You're right, I haven't."

The two stood silently, avoiding one another's glare. The President searched for a place to rest her eyes and saw Agent Meadows, ever vigilant, standing at his post by the grandfather clock. Their eyes met and she gave him an uncharacteristic smile.

Lorraine walked toward Harvey and stopped a foot in front of him. She took his hand and squeezed it tightly.

"Michael, I know I can be tough on you." She continued squeezing his hand. "But you know me, and I know you."

They laughed as she put her arm under his and locked them in an embrace. Then she leaned back and fell into the couch, taking him with her. In unison they put their feet on the coffee table. They laughed again and she turned toward him and admired his profile.

She knew the buttons to push with this man. There was definitely a time for a hard stance, but other times for a soft caress. This was one of the latter.

"You know I'm hardest on you when I'm scared, don't you?"

He nodded. "I know."

She ran her hand up and down his arm. "I'm sorry if I go too far sometimes."

He turned to look at her. Their eyes were inches apart. His seemed to soften when he said, "Wow, an almost apology. Circle the date, folks."

She playfully slapped his arm. After a period of silence she said, "What do you think?"

The question hovered in the open. Finally he said, "I think that you're right and wrong."

She waited for him to continue.

"You're right, I should have pressed the victim issue harder. I didn't. I can change that. But I didn't want to call attention to your husband being killed by an illegal immigrant. That's why most people think you're trying to push this bill through Congress." He paused and looked at his feet. "But again, I see your point. I should have pushed it."

He shifted and increased the distance between their legs so he could look at her squarely.

"Lorraine, you're doing fantastic in an impossible job. I really believe that and so does over half of the American public. If I can keep them on cutting the deficit, we're in good shape."

Her eyebrows shot up. "Only in good shape?"

He moved his head to one side. "Lorraine, Graham is good. We didn't see him coming. He hits certain buttons with the public. He's handsome, well spoken, and doesn't back down from his opinions even when they may not be popular. His track record in Congress backs up the way he's campaigning. We're in for a tough eleven weeks."

Michael took her hands and kissed them. "We can win this. But you've got to help me. The immigration issue is hurting us, and it's getting worse. The angrier people get, the worse your polling numbers get. Yes, it's almost like a mob mentality, but it's also reality. Graham is turning this into a fight for the American dream, and it's working."

She sat up straighter. "Michael, this legislation is important. Even he'd admit it. Something has to be done, and I'm the only one in position to do it."

"Yes, Lorraine, you're right. And I admire your convictions. But there is reality and there is perception. Now I don't want you to take this the wrong way because it's going to sound bad."

"Okay. Don't beat around the bush."

He took a deep breath. "Lorraine, if there is another attempt on your life, your numbers are going to take a big drop."

She paused for a moment, carefully considering his words. "So, even though I really believe in it, I should back off on the immigration issue. If I don't, someone will try to kill me, which will make me so unpopular that I'll lose the election. Is that what you're saying?"

He looked at her blankly. "Uh…" Then he burst out laughing. Lorraine joined him. "I guess it is," he said.

"Yeah, I guess it is!"

Stifling his laughter, Michael said, "and, by the way, I hope they don't succeed."

"Good point. I'm sure you're far too busy to plan a state funeral. I wouldn't want to put that on you by dying!" She laughed even harder. "Maybe I could help out by planning it myself."

"That would be nice of you."

"I just want to make sure the Speaker of the House doesn't deliver the eulogy! He's such an asshole." Then after a pause she turned to him, "Michael, what do you want me to do?" Her voice betrayed a helplessness she hadn't felt in years.

"Lorraine, pick up the phone and contact Congressman Danby. The Minority Leader would jump at a chance to meet and try to water this bill down."

She looked hesitant. "Let me sleep on it, will you?"

He nodded.

"Speaking of sleeping…" She stroked his arm.

"Madame President,.." he asked innocently.

Chapter 22
Ten weeks before the election

Standing with the staff sergeant who was escorting him, Dutch looked up as the enormous doors of the unmarked hangers slowly opened. The twin VC25 presidential airplanes were inside. It was exactly eight hours before takeoff.

To Dutch's right, a voice said, "Excuse me!" Dutch turned and narrowly dodged out of the way as a bicycle raced by.

"Gotta keep your eyes open there, rookie," the staff sergeant said to him.

"What is that person doing on a bicycle in here?" Dutch asked as he and his escort passed the hulking frames of the jets being prepared for takeoff amid a swirl of activity.

The sergeant laughed. "That was corporal Reverdy just coming back from the market."

"In civilian clothes?"

"Whenever we need to supplement our food order for any trip, the kitchen staff dresses as civilians so as to not draw attention when shopping for the President. When we've got a last minute request for something, Reverdy usually goes because he's the fastest on a bike."

Dutch shook his head in amazement at the inner workings of the PAG.

They approached a metal door, which the sergeant opened. Dutch walked along wooden paneled walls with pictures of Air Force One on different runways throughout the world.

The sergeant moved ahead and opened a thick mahogany door to the cavernous PAG briefing room. On one side of the room, windows overlooked the airfield. Maps covered the entire surface area of the other three walls. Commander Max Ford sat at the head of a long conference table surrounded by twenty support officers. Ringed around the outside were about fifty more air force officers taking notes.

"For our last leg of the trip, we will be using runway two-four as our primary once we touch down at Maxwell Air Force Base. This gives POTUS a quick ten minute ride to her campaign stop." Ford looked across the long table and continued. "Viper, I want you to radio a status update the instant you touch down on the secondary landing zone at Cairns Army Airfield. If we hear there is a problem with two-four, I'm immediately switching to LZ 2."

The captain nodded without looking up as her pen flew across her notepad.

"Now we haven't been to Cairns since they upgraded their runway. Niner-two-three will be the landing strip where the backup VC-25 will be waiting, if needed. The advance team reported that it held up fine when the C-17 transport planes landed there yesterday, but I don't want to assume anything."

The sergeant leaned into Dutch so he could whisper.

"Viper is Commander Aimee Fox. She's sitting at the opposite end of the table." He motioned with his head to a tall, attractive brunette whose hair was pulled back into a tight ponytail that poked out of the back of her Air Force cap. "She'll be piloting the VC 25 running ahead of the President and landing at Cairns." Last year they upgraded their runways to support the weight of Air Force One. We land heavy because of the extra fuel needed in case we need to abort a landing and takeoff again in a hurry."

"Land heavy?"

"Yeah, most planes take off with lots of fuel but land light because of everything they burned off during the flight. We need to keep that extra fuel, just in case, so we land heavy, about 830,000 pounds heavy. Most commercial runways can't take that kind of stress. It would crush them. Since this is our first time using this airfield, the commander is a bit more jiggy than usual."

As liaison officer for this trip, Dutch had been briefed on all the details of the trip. The Beast and its decoys were flown in a day earlier, along with eighty-five tons of equipment, and he knew by heart the route they would take, along with the security set up along the way to the campaign stop and fundraising dinner.

Commander Ford said, "Officers, I see that Special Agent Terrance Brown has joined us. He will be the Secret Service liaison for us during mission one-three-five."

Dutch wasn't sure what he was supposed to do. This was his first time as liaison to the Air Force crew assigned to the PAG. He held up a hand but didn't smile, hoping he looked the part.

Commander Ford gave Dutch a wink before looking back to the ocean of Air Force personnel and said, "Are there any questions?" He paused for a long moment.

Dutch could tell this wasn't the typical cursory question asked at the end of most meetings. Commander Ford wanted his officers to truly think of any lingering doubt they may have before he dismissed them.

Ford nodded and said, "Ladies and gentlemen, I have received a go from the Chief of Staff, and we are on the clock for one-three-five."

"It's the one hundred and thirty fifth trip for this President on Air Force One," the sergeant whispered to Dutch. "Each trip is considered a mission."

Commander Ford added, "I know I don't need to remind everyone in this room, but this is a Zero Fail Mission. Let's keep it that way. Dismissed."

Chairs moved and scraped across the tiled floors as everyone seemed to rise at once to exit. A few of the officers nodded at Dutch on their way by.

Commander Ford remained, stepping over to extend a hand to Dutch. Dutch admired the firm grasp of the pilot.

"Agent Brown, it's a pleasure," Ford said with a smile.

"The pleasure is mine, Commander."

"Since this is your first stint as liaison agent, you need to meet Bonnie before you do anything else. She's the one who keeps things running around here." He turned to the sergeant. "Jerry, please show Agent Brown to the hub and introduce him, will you?"

The sergeant nodded then saluted his superior as Ford walked out. Suddenly the room felt smaller.

The sergeant once again held the door and they headed down the hallway to meet Bonnie. As they turned a corner, Dutch almost knocked into someone who was rushing the other way.

"Kevin?" Dutch asked when the man tried to squeeze by him.

"Dutch? What are you doing here?"

"I'm the liaison agent for this trip. But what about you? You're a long way from home, aren't you?"

Agent Kevin Brady and Dutch had graduated together the year before. Kevin had been assigned the security detail for Graham back in March.

Kevin looked a little out of sorts. Dutch thought it may have been his surprise in seeing him.

"Yeah, you can say that again. I'm the errand boy today. Ghost sent me to get the weather report of the Northeast corridor for tomorrow.

Ghost was the official nickname for Graham since he'd been declared the Democratic candidate for President.

"All right, well you look like you're in a hurry. Let's catch up soon" Dutch said.

Kevin nodded and turned to leave, then paused. "Hey, Dutch, uh, do you have a minute right now?"

"Sure, I guess. What's up?"

Kevin expelled a breath and looked around. "Come with me."

Dutch turned to the sergeant and said, "Can you excuse me for a minute?"

They zig-zagged through a maze of hallways until they came to a metallic outer door. The bright daylight hit them full on when they exited. Kevin looked around then pointed Dutch to a section of the building without any windows.

"What's going on, Kevin?"

Kevin stood uncomfortably close to Dutch's face, then peered around before speaking. "Listen, I haven't had a chance to talk with you since…Harry…" The sentence hung in the air.

Dutch let the silence stand for a moment, partly because he didn't know how to respond, and in part because of the lump in his throat that formed every time he received condolences for the loss of his partner.

"I'm real sorry about that, Dutch. I know you two were close."

Dutch nodded and took a step back, but Kevin remained close. Again, he looked to either side, then lowered his voice. "Dutch, how much do you know about Congressman Graham?"

Dutch couldn't read the look on Kevin's face.

"You're on his detail, Kev. You know more than me."

"That's just it. I've been with this guy for months, and I don't know any more about him than how he takes his coffee and his time per mile on those insane runs we take daily. He doesn't talk to his detail about anything."

Dutch shrugged. "Big deal. The President has only spoken with me once. Guys who've been on her detail since the beginning tell me she's not too chatty with any of them."

Kevin shook his head. "Dutch, it's not that. I mean that I don't know anything about him other than what I read."

Dutch waited while Kevin took another look around.

"You do know that he has a few CIA guys on the detail with him, right?"

Dutch nodded. "Yeah. I wouldn't be too happy about that if I were you, but what can you do? I heard Langley signed off on it."

"Well, that's just it. I'm sure Meadows could tell you Widow's favorite sexual position if you asked. Graham? Nothing. He doesn't open up about anything other than the campaign when the Service is around."

Dutch looked at his watch, hoping to speed Kevin up to the point he was building up to.

"Did you know that Graham takes unscheduled trips without his Secret Service detail?"

This got Dutch's attention. He turned to Kevin. "No, I didn't know that."

"Good. You shouldn't. We're under strict orders not to tell anyone about them."

"But who—"

"He disappears with his friends from the CIA for hours every time we're near the Mexican border."

"Well, that is weird," Dutch said. "What does—"

"Rolleston went ballistic the first time it happened. Word has it that he went all the way up to Polk, who made a couple of calls himself. A day later word came down to let Graham call his own shots with security."

"How many times has this happened?"

"Four. None of us have any idea where he goes or what he does. He's back exactly to the minute when he says he will be. From what I can tell, his CIA bodyguards pack heavy wherever they go, which is small comfort for Rolleston."

"Why are you telling me this?"

"Look, I don't want to be the one who, you know, breaks the 'code.'"

Dutch knew he was referring to the unspoken code that no Secret Service agent ever let on what is said or done by their protectees.

Kevin continued. "But we're at the point where we just don't know what to do. If something were to happen to him and it was leaked that the Secret Service wasn't with him, you know whose balls will be in a sling."

"Your whole detail."

"Right. So off the record Dutch, and I mean strictly off the record?"

Dutch nodded.

"Rolleston had a real heart to heart with Polk about it. From what Rolleston tells me, Polk is just as pissed off as we are. He asked Rolleston if he knew anyone who could covertly poke around. When he and I brainstormed, your name came up."

"Me? What do you want me to do?"

"You're the hot-shot investigator. You have more training than anyone I know."

A pair of pilots from the briefing came around the corner, duffle bags in hand, and walked past. They gave Dutch and Kevin a cursory nod as they continued toward the jumbo jets being towed out to the tarmac.

"Kevin, what do you think is happening?"

"I don't know. But being charged with protecting someone and not knowing their activities… it puts everyone in a bad position."

"Okay, Kev, let me think about it."

"Thanks, Dutch. And Rolleston told me to thank you for considering it. Anything you come up with would be appreciated by the entire detail."

The pair shook hands and Kevin turned and began walking away. He had gone about ten feet when Dutch said, "Hey, any guess when he may do this again?"

Kevin turned to face Dutch. "I can't be sure. None of us ever are. But if the pattern holds, then around—" he paused for a moment. "I'd say this Wednesday. We're slated to be in the southern part of Texas. Odds are he'll do it then."

"You got an approximate time?"

Kevin shrugged. "It's usually after the morning campaigning, most often around noon."

"I think I have an idea. I'll drop you a line if I come up with anything."

Kevin gave him thumbs up. "Thanks, man. Stay safe."

Dutch watched Kevin turn the corner, then took his cell phone out and dialed a number he knew by heart.

"Hello, I'd like to speak with Mr. Flecca, please."

Chapter 23
Nine weeks until the election

Roger Graham sat alone inside his limousine as his staffers waited for him to complete his phone call. He shifted his cell from one ear to the other as Simon spoke.

"Is everything still on track for today?"

"Yes," Graham said. "Tip has us on track as usual, and we're going to be far away from the President so there should be no issues. None of this is your concern, though. What about that other matter?"

"Nothing has been confirmed as of now—"

"Damn it, Simon, I need you to confirm so we can stay ahead of it. You know what would happen if this leaked out."

"Yes, I do."

"All right, let me think for a minute. What do we know so far?"

"Well, my sources tell me that a satellite was tasked without authorization. No one seems to be able to account for its whereabouts for thirty minutes."

"No one has an idea? How can a CIA satellite just disappear for 30 minutes without anyone knowing how?"

"Roger, you know as well as anyone about that flyover region. It's chock full of possible hot spots…too many to guess. I'm hearing they are going to focus on how it happened, not why."

"Okay, for now that will have to do. What do you propose moving forward?"

Simon paused. "I need a look at the data from the hard drive for the time period during the hack."

"Won't that tell where the satellite was tasked to?"

"No, it won't. But it will give me a path leading to who broke through the firewalls."

"And you're certain you've got access?"

"One hundred percent. My source is flawless."

"How long?" Roger envisioned Simon working through a mental calculation.

"I'll need a couple of days."

"And the Agency?"

"Longer. Much longer, if at all. Chances are that investigation will lead to a dead end. Whoever did this was good; I can tell you that without even getting the details from the hard drive. There's only a handful of people that could pull something like this off."

"Find that person, Simon. Quickly."

"I will, but I need to know if you've considered what to do once we find whoever did this."

"Just find him, or we can kiss everything goodbye."

"You're assuming that anything can be traced back to you."

Roger's voice was much louder now. "Damn right I am. And don't try to handle me, Simon. I know a shitload more about how to play this game than you do. This very thing is why I insisted on having you on board. Now go do your job."

Before he could say anything else, Simon heard Roger Graham hang up.

Chapter 24

Alexis was at a business conference on the west coast during the president's campaign trip, but happened to catch Dutch during a lull in the activity.

"Hey, you. How are things on the left coast?" Dutch said.

"Lonely. I really miss you."

"I guess so."

"Why do you say that?"

Dutch paused, sensing a trap. "Because this is the third time you've called me today."

"Oh," Alexis said. "I'm sorry, I didn't know I was bothering you."

Dutch laughed. "Honey, you're not bothering me. I've just never known you to call so many times when you're on a business trip. How are things going, really?"

"Fine, I guess. My heart's not really in this one." Her voice sounded distant.

"Is everything all right?"

"Sure. No. Really, everything's fine."

"Can you fly back early, or does Brad need you to stay for the duration?"

Her voice perked up a bit. "No, he really doesn't need both James and me. I've already given my presentation." Now she sounded almost giddy. "Terry, that's the best idea you've ever had, other than asking me to marry you, of course."

"Of course." He laughed.

"What're you up to?"

"I'm posted on limo duty," Dutch told her. "For some reason the powers that be felt it was important to make a real show when we left the hotel, you know, the old fashioned way. We're slated to walk alongside the Beast as she makes the trip to Air Force One. It will look 'very Presidential,' or something like that."

"Well, I'll look for you on the news, then. Make sure you're smiling."

"Yeah, like that could ever happen. Listen babe, I've got to fly. I love you. Hopefully I'll see you tonight."

"Be careful. I love you, too," Dutch heard her say just before he pushed the button to hang up.

Dutch checked his watch as he walked back to the foyer where the President would be coming through in a few minutes. About ten other agents milled around, looking calm and in control. Dutch wondered if any of their hearts raced as much as his did. It was rare to have this type of pomp and circumstance when the President of the United States was on the move. After they encircled and escorted the President as she exited the hotel, his assigned position was just in front of the Presidential Seal on the door of the Beast. In fact, he would be the one to open it for her. He chuckled, thinking that it would guarantee him some TV time.

"Stay sharp. Widow will be done in two minutes," sounded the voice in all the agents' ears.

Meadows didn't sound his usual calm self, but the level of tension was only discernible to those who had his voice in their ear every day for months. Dutch knew Meadows didn't like this idea and wondered how Polk was allowing it. It must have been one hell of a negotiation during the planning phases for this trip.

There was only about thirty yards between the rear exit of the Renaissance Montgomery Hotel and the Beast, but assuring the president's safe passage across that short distance would be the most difficult time for the Service, because it was where the President would be closest to the crowd.

From the advance mission briefing, Dutch knew that the people along the route were already primed with waving arms full of American flags and their loudest cheers. It was all very well orchestrated for the evening news.

What the Service couldn't control were the pockets of protesters. Just a few feet behind him were several protesters, already yelling. He tuned out the noise and scanned the crowd, and saw mostly Latino faces. No surprise, Dutch thought. Controversy over the immigration debate had not abated. Hopefully it would die down once the Senate voted on the controversial bill, which had already passed the House.

"Widow is on the move," came Meadows' voice through his earpiece.

Dutch stiffened a bit as his eyes kept returning to a clutch of protesters directly in front of him, behind Agent Coyle's right shoulder.

Many of them held large photographs—Dutch didn't know why. And there was something about them that put him on alert.

Applause and shouts erupted as the President emerged from the building behind him. Dutch tapped his jacket out of habit, feeling his P-90 sub machine gun he chose for the trip, ready to raise it on a moment's notice if anyone even flinched in the direction of the President. She walked toward them and was only fifteen yards from Dutch's position, but it felt like she was a mile away.

Dutch saw Coyle stiffen as they caught each other's eyes.

"Thank you! Thank you!" Lorraine Burton yelled to the crowd, flashing her best smile and waving enthusiastically.

It had been a good fundraising stop and yielded her campaign coffers another cool two million. For that, she didn't have to fake her smile as she approached her limo. When she reached the end of the line of people, agents converged on either side of her as well as behind, forming a wedge of protection. The agent on the right, whom she vaguely remembered was one who had tackled the shoe thrower in Florida, stepped ahead and held the door open for her. One last smile and wave before she expertly pivoted and gracefully collapsed into her seat as the door, which weighed the same as a 757 cabin door, closed behind her with a whooshing sound, sealing the soundproof cabin.

She slid over the soft leather to the middle until she was facing her press secretary across from her. As requested, they were the only two occupants in the back of the Beast. This would be the only time she and her Press Secretary could spend ten uninterrupted minutes comparing notes.

Heading up the rear gave Meadows the chance to double check everything as the Presidential convoy waited for the rest of the Secret Service to enter their vehicles. At least that was how it looked. In reality, Harvey had made a deal with Polk to allow the Beast to sit for an extra couple of seconds to make sure the network cameras were in place for their slow crawl onto Tallapoosa Street for all to see.

In discussions during the planning of the trip, Meadows learned that Polk hated the idea of the slow three-mile drive to a waiting Air Force One. But part of the compromise with the Chief of Staff was to ensure the President stayed inside the armored limousine. Harvey argued that the extended photo opportunity was good to show that the President wasn't afraid because of the attack on her life. It seemed to be a somewhat new strategy, but the Service tried to avoid getting involved with these types of election year politics decisions.

Meadows was the last to reach the black lead SUV, and took in the sight. Having the Service flank the Beast, even for purely symbolic reasons, was an impressive sight, and he had to concede that Harvey was probably right on this one.

Meadows got the signal to climb in and begin the convoy.

"Madame President," said Patti as Lorraine settled into her seat. "That Secret Service agent who held the door for you is Special Agent Dutch Brown."

Lorraine was puzzled for a second, then recovered as she tried not to let her Press Secretary know she had forgotten the name of one of the agents who had successfully thwarted the protester in Florida.

"Yes, I remember the agent. Quiet fellow. Why do you mention it?"

"Well, ma'am, the agent who was killed in New Mexico had been his partner for three years."

The two sat silently for a moment, waiting for the limo to start moving.

"What do you think?" the President said.

Patti reached up to the bridge of her nose and took off her glasses.

"It may be a nice piece of PR if you invited him in with us for the short trip to Air Force One as a way of expressing your condolences over his loss. I think it will play quite well."

The President cracked a wry smile. "Good thinking, Patti. Please call the agent in."

"We're a go," came the order in Dutch's earpiece. The limo inched forward and Dutch's heart raced as he jogging alongside, remaining abreast of the Presidential Seal.

According to the plan, the Beast would travel at a constant five miles per hour for the first and last quarter mile, and ten miles per hour for the middle half mile. During the middle, the Service would stand on running boards that would hydraulically extend out from under the car with a push of a button from the driver's seat.

The jogging was a piece of cake for Dutch, who tried to get in at least four miles every day. He settled in for the first stretch.

Suddenly the Beast and everyone around it stopped. Dutch instinctively reached toward his jacket so his hand could be closer to his P-90. The agents had their choice of weaponry, and Dutch hadn't left things to chance, loading the weapon with 5.7 x 28 mm armor-piercing ammunition. Now, his eyes darted around warily, looking for any movement out of the ordinary.

"False start everyone," came Meadow's voice over the earpiece. "Agent Brown, you have been requested to join the President for the ride. Please step inside the Beast."

Dutch tapped his earpiece to make sure he was hearing correctly. Another agent stepped forward to take his position and opened the heavy door for Dutch to step through and enter the unknown.

"Hello, Agent Brown," the President said as Dutch bent awkwardly to climb into the car. He wasn't exactly sure where he should sit. Finally, he sat back ungracefully when the convoy moved and forced him backwards, right next to the President. An awkward silence set in as he looked from corner to corner in the vehicle, not really knowing where he should focus his attention. Did they need extra security in here?

Patti Harris sat forward and began. "Agent Brown, the President would like to thank you for joining her."

Dutch nodded at them both. "Oh, my pleasure, Madame President." He wondered if the look on his face was as goofy as it felt.

The President angled herself in the seat to face him more directly. "Agent Brown, I can't tell you how truly sorry I am for the loss of your partner. He showed a tremendous amount of courage. I'm sure the loss has been difficult for you."

Dutch tightened his lips and sat back, allowing a slight nod toward the President.

"Thank you, Madame President. I appreciate your kind words. It has been difficult."

Lorraine sat forward a bit more and turned slightly while straightening her skirt.

"How is Harry's family handling things?"

Dutch held her gaze and replied, "His wife, Sandy, has been a rock. Her kids are really looking to her during this time."

"Sandy has—" the President paused for the briefest of moments. Dutch picked up Patti out of the corner of his eye with four fingers pointed downward.

"Four children. My God, this must be so hard for her."

Dutch wasn't sure now how much the President really thought of the loss of his partner, but appreciated the gesture just the same. He would convey the conversation to Sandy and the kids.

"Yes, it has been tremendously difficult. However, she's surrounded by family and many friends back in Omaha. My fiancé and I made it out there a couple of times since Harry's death. All things considered, she seems to be keeping it together the best she can."

Through the window, Dutch could see the agents jogging alongside the vehicle. He settled into the plush leather of the seat.

"Detail ready," came a voice in Dutch's ear, giving the cue that the first quarter mile was just about done.

He watched through the window as the agents jogged slightly away from the vehicle. At the appointed mark on the road, all of them simultaneously hopped onto the running boards on each side as the vehicle doubled its speed. This was the mile long stretch of Day Street that had no curves, so the convoy could go faster.

"Agent Brown," the President said as she swiveled back toward the front, "please be sure to let Sandy know that I meant it when I said if there was anything I could do to help her through this, I am more than happy to."

"Thank you, ma'am, I will be sure to tell her that."

"Patti?" the President said, turning to her Press Secretary and letting Dutch know their conversation was over.

Dutch chided himself for being so easily taken in by her seeming sincerity. He sat back and enjoyed the view as the President and Press Secretary discussed the minutiae of their schedule. Dutch tuned them out, focusing on the crowd passing by at a perfect ten miles per hour.

It felt surreal seeing the faces of shouting Americans as they drove past. The vehicle was soundproof for security reasons, but the speakers could be turned on or off if the President wanted to hear what was going on outside. Dutch didn't peg Lorraine Burton as a "speakers on" kind of gal, but he was grateful for the oversight.

"Detail ready," came Meadows's voice again in Dutch's ear as he felt the limo slow down for the last quarter mile jaunt to Air Force One. He watched the agents step off the running board in unison and return to their choreographed jogging. This must make for one hell of a video clip, Dutch thought, taking it all in.

Just then, he heard a familiar twang through the limo's speakers. Adrenaline shot through him, and suddenly, instinctively, switched to combat mode. Without thinking, he dove toward the President.

Time seemed to crawl, and everything switched to slow motion. He was reacting to something his brain hadn't processed yet. He felt both legs hit the floor of the vehicle. No. The floor of the limo was rising up!

A bright light emanated from over his right shoulder. An explosion. The sound seemed to come much later after the flash, but that didn't matter. It was still an explosion.

His feet left the floor and he felt his body crash into the President's. He instinctively wrapped his arms around her, shielding her from whatever was coming next.

Something was pushing his back. No, pushing was the wrong description. Ripping was more like it, but there was no pain. Dutch remained focused on the President, wrapped safely underneath him.

He felt the limo continue its twist up in the air and for a moment he wondered if they would flip.

Then time returned to normal and things began to move much faster. He could hear screaming, but it wasn't the President. He was vaguely aware that Patti Harris lay crumpled in the far corner. Dutch took a quick look and saw blood.

The limo came crashing back down on all four wheels, then sped forward. Dutch lifted himself but couldn't see anything outside but a blur. His earpiece had been lost in the blast, so he was disconnected from the rest of the Service and didn't know what was happening outside.

He tried to push himself up further, but pain shot through him. He fell back down on the President who had, until that moment, remained quiet. He looked at her face. Terrified eyes looked back at him.

Again he heard Patti's cry of pain. He turned and got a better look at the Press Secretary, who was lying on the floor of the limo, arms and legs twisted at awkward angles. Shards of shrapnel protruded from her cheek and neck.

As Dutch attempted to pull himself upright his hand touched a pool of something he could only surmise was blood, although it was difficult to discern against the red carpeting.

He turned and rolled off the President, who remained on the floor. Painfully, he hoisted himself into the seat she had occupied just moments before. Looking through the open divider, he caught a glimpse of the tail of Air Force One as they sped by at what Dutch could only estimate was at least sixty miles per hour.

"Madame President," Dutch said.

She continued looking around wide-eyed, but didn't respond.

"Madame President!" he shouted much louder, which seemed to snap her out of the shock.

He knelt and tried to ignore the hot pain shooting from his neck down to his toes. He slowly lifted her up on the seat. Despite his best effort, he let out a cry of pain. Next he went to Patti, who rubbed at the glass lodged in her face. Dutch forced her arms away so she wouldn't do any more damage to herself.

He turned and pulled out the emergency medical kit stowed under the passenger seats. Flinging it open, he grabbed for a package of gauze then tore it open and pressed it against Patti's face. "Hold this in place," he said. "Press hard."

He quickly turned back to the President and gave her a visual assessment. Other than the shock still registering on her face, she looked the same as she did before the explosion.

"Madame President, are you all right?"

She stared blankly at him.

"Are you hurt? Do you feel any pain? Madame President, it's important you answer me," he said, raising his voice.

Her eyes seemed to regain focus. "What? W...w...what happened?"

"Madame President, are you injured? Do you have any pain?"

She shook her head. "Pain, no. No pain. I—I think I'm all right."

Ignoring his own pain, Dutch searched for the dangling earpiece. Wind whistled through the rear of the car, and he guessed that the window had been breached.

What the hell happened? he wondered. Finally, he found the coiled white cord behind his neck. Wincing in pain, he clumsily inserted it into his right ear.

"HMX-1, HMX-1, you have the ball," Meadows's voice boomed out. Wherever he was, there was still plenty of background noise that made it hard to hear him.

Then a calm, static-free voice answered, "HMX-1, roger, we have the ball."

Dutch knew in an instant that one of the backup plans had gone into effect. His experiences back at the Rowley Training Center resonated in his head like it was yesterday. The multitude of scenarios of an attack on the President of the United States played out in his head. When an area near the departure point was deemed unsafe, the Marine Forces waiting standby would take the lead on Presidential security. Dutch knew they were speeding toward the pre-arranged pick up point away from Air Force One where the VH-3 Sikorsky Sea King helicopter would be waiting, rotors blaring, ready to move out the moment the President was on board.

Dutch painfully shook his head in an attempt to keep focus and remain conscious. It was becoming more difficult by the second. The lingering smoke in the limo was quickly being replaced by fresh oxygen automatically pumped in from the separate supply kept in the trunk, aided by the hole in the window created by the blast. This helped him think.

"HMX-1, Cadillac One ETA nine zero seconds," came the voice of Gil Hogan, who was driving the Beast.

His voice had a steadying effect on Dutch. Although he still hadn't processed what had happened, he knew Gil could drive through anything safely.

As if on cue, he heard Gil's voice speaking to him through the intercom system. "Dutch, is everything all right back there?"

Dutch leaned forward past the divider and into Gil's line of sight in the rear view mirror and motioned a shaky thumb up. He noticed his hand was covered in crimson red as he tried to keep it steady. Was the blood his? No time to find out.

He leaned across the President to where the wireless phone had wedged itself between the seat and the door. He picked it up and hit the green button. "Gil, Widow is Okay, repeat, Widow is Okay. But we do have injuries back here."

"Roger. Please advise, does Widow need medical attention?"

Dutch looked at the President again. She had her head in her hand, but he still didn't see any visible injuries.

"Nothing visible, but cannot confirm."

"Roger. ETA to HMX-1 is three zero seconds."

Dutch put the phone back in place and moved to tend to Patti, who seemed to be slipping in and out of consciousness. He lifted the beet red gauze and saw a gash in the side of her neck. He took out a new compress from the medical kit and pressed it against the wound.

He turned to the door he had entered through minutes before and confirmed what he had thought. A hole the size of a fist had been blown through the armored window.

"Widow is here. Move, move, move!" came a loud voice in his ear.

Both doors were wrenched open and bodies flooded the limo. Dutch watched as in one motion the President was lifted up and disappeared out of view. The sound of the Sikorsky's blades made a deafening noise. He peered out the door and saw Marines everywhere, semi-automatic machine guns drawn and ready to shoot at anything that didn't belong there.

A medic launched himself into the limo. Dutch pointed at Patti and said, "Her first." He then leaned back against the leather seat, a hot searing pain shooting through his back. In a moment the sound of the helicopter's blades were fading into the background.

He sat watching the medic attend to Patti Harris, still listening to what was unfolding in his ear. He closed his eyes and listened to every step of the mission carry itself out perfectly.

He heard Viper's voice next. "Two niner zed zed zed, spinning up engines now." The backup VC25 jet that would shortly become Air Force One was waiting at the alternate landing field. We caught a break, thought Dutch. Cairns Airfield was a quick five-minute flight for Marine One.

"Roger that. Marine One, ETA two minutes."

"Please advise Widow's status," came another voice Dutch didn't recognize.

"Widow is all right. Repeat, she is all right," shouted the Marine medic onboard the helicopter, barely audible over the wash of the rotors. "Advise on wheels up."

Viper again. "Marine One, we are takeoff ready. Wheels up on your ETA plus three zero seconds."

A new voice joined the cacophony over the radios.

"Two niner zed zed zed, be advised you will have four F-18 escorts once you are airborne."

Dutch guessed the new voice was the military air traffic controller who undoubtedly just cleared the air space surrounding them.

Shit. The first time since 9/11 POTUS needs air support. What the fuck is going on? Dutch thought. His head was spinning and he was having trouble focusing on the voices despite his best effort.

"Medic, over here," yelled someone running toward Dutch. He tried to lift his hand to wave them off but couldn't. His head lagged to one side, but he willed himself to stay conscious. Hands reached in and pulled him from the vehicle, and he felt the hard tarmac of the jump off point for Marine One against his back.

Dutch's shirt was ripped off as he was rolled over on top of an orange blanket, exposing his back to whoever was working on him. He tried to ignore the pain and the voices shouting around him. He wasn't sure if they were yelling about him or someone else. He didn't care. He only focused on the sound coming from his earpiece as the Marines gave their updates.

"HMX-1 reporting: transfer is complete."

Dutch smiled. The President was on her plane.

"Air Force One reporting: Widow is on board. Preparing for combat take off."

Dutch stifled a groan from the shooting pain. But as his eyes closed, he smiled thinking of Widow, who wasn't too keen on bumpy flights. A combat take off meant that the additional 16,000 pounds of thrust that Air Force One is capable of would have her cruising at 630 miles per hour at 45,000 feet within 60 seconds.

Someone was trying to say something to him. Or was he imagining it? All he knew was that Widow was safe. He smiled. The last thing he remembered was hearing the roar of the fighter jets overhead before he surrendered to quiet blackness.

Chapter 25
Eight weeks before the election

"Hanson, Coyle, and now Porter," Agent Nat Shaklis said as he sat on the side of Dutch's bed, which had folders strewn all over it.

After a few days in the hospital, he had been sent home to continue his recuperation. "Porter? When?" Dutch said.

"He didn't make it through the second surgery. He died a few hours ago."

Dutch balled up his fists. "Fucking bastards. If I ever—"

Nat nodded in agreement as Dutch released his anger.

After a moment Nat said, "We've got hundreds working on this. We'll catch them; don't worry. Right now, all you need to do is focus on getting better."

Dutch took a deep breath, held it, and then slowly let it out. "Sorry, Nat. I'm all right. Then shifting his attention to another file he asked, "What else do you have for me?"

Nat brought the folder closer and spread out some pictures.

"This is what the Beast looks like now," he said pointing to a picture of the black custom-fit Cadillac.

There were dents along the passenger side that absorbed the blast, and the window with the fist-sized hole was visible. Other than that, Dutch couldn't tell much had changed.

"Son of a bitch. Can you believe that's the only damage? What a fucking vehicle to absorb that explosion."

"You can say that again. Personally, I always wondered if those 'run flat' tires would work. But those suckers took the punch and kept on spinning. Between that and the foam-sealed fuel tank is the only reason you made it out of there alive."

"That and Gil at the wheel. Man, he was terrific."

"You can say that again. He had you guys moving while two wheels were still in the air. Talk about training. Shit, he was out of there like it was a routine mission."

"Tell him I owe him a steak."

"Tell him yourself. He's going to be over here tomorrow with the President."

"She's still planning on coming?"

Nat rolled his eyes. "Yes, she wants to personally thank you for saving her life. You know as well as I that Harvey is going to bilk this for all it's worth." He shifted on the edge of the bed and placed a finger to his ear, attempting to look like a news anchor. He said in a mock deep voice, "The President is making house calls, news at eleven."

"Nat, I didn't save her life. I got in the way of some shrapnel. It wouldn't have killed her."

Nat raised his eyes. "You never know, Dutch. Shit, how it got through that glass is beyond me. I mean think about it, that shrapnel had to travel through eight layers of glass and plastic. It was supposed to fragment before it made it through the last layer. Hell I wouldn't even call that glass. More like see through armor plating."

Dutch shook his head. "They got lucky."

"Speaking of which, I saved the best for last." Nat leaned over and grabbed the furthest folder at the corner of the bed. He handed it to Dutch and said, "You were right. Son of a bitch, you were right. It was a Bouncing Betty."

Dutch opened it and skimmed the ballistic reports of the explosive device that had almost taken the President out. The report identified the explosive as an S-mine, invented by the Germans before World War II, and commonly referred to as a Bouncing Betty. It was designed to be buried just below the surface, with the trip mechanism protruding. Once tripped, a Bouncing Betty wouldn't explode immediately. Instead, a black powder charge would propel it upwards almost three feet before detonation. Most of these mines were filled with steel balls and other fragments designed to inflict maximum damage to the widest radius possible.

In modern times, the mine was modified for more urban use. The remnants of the bomb shown in the pictures that Dutch now examined looked as though there had been nothing protruding from the surface, and it was concluded that the mine had been remotely activated. Fortunately for those in the crowd, the brunt of the blast was focused on the Beast. Pictures of the explosion zone were littered with red arrows highlighting points of interest. The spot where the mine had been buried showed a circular hole roughly an inch or two under the pavement of Day Street. A black tar cap was believed to have been placed over the mine, although no signs of that had been found as of yet.

Because of the height of the mine at the moment of detonation, it had inflicted damage on the vehicle's windows rather than the eight inch armor plating on the side. The blast cut through the windowed armor of the vehicle. The two agents on either side of it were literally cut in half.

Dutch could only look briefly at the photos taken at the scene showing the severed bodies of his friends. He shuffled back to the more antiseptic photos of the fragments of the mine itself.

"How did you know?" Nat said.

"I got lucky. But not Rogers, Coyle, and Porter, along with, how many?"

Nat looked somber as he reported the death toll. "Ten civilians killed, twenty-five more wounded."

"How's Patti Harris doing?"

Nat's expression brightened a bit. "She's going to be fine. Most of what she caught was deflected on the way in. Superficial stuff mainly, except for her neck. I heard she'll have some scarring, but nothing they can't fix. She'll probably have the best plastic surgeon flown in, and a month from now you'll never know she caught shrapnel."

The two sat quietly as Dutch replayed the explosion in his head for the hundredth time. He could still feel the lurching of the vehicle under his feet and the burning sensation in his back. He closed his eyes and heard Patti's screaming and the blood and glass surrounding her on the floor. He felt the Beast lurch back on all four wheels as Gil Hogan deftly swung the steering wheel around to balance the tipping car.

After a moment, Nat broke the silence. "Dutch, really though, how did you know enough to lunge for the President before the blast?"

"Nat, I used to have nightmares about that sound. When those fuckers are tripped, the propellant used to shoot them up in the air sounds almost like the fast uncoiling of a spring. In the Seals, we worked once with an explosive ordnance disposal detachment out of Pendleton. They were called in to clear a section of jungle we had to traverse. The place was full of those fucking Bouncing Bettys, and they scared the shit out of me. The worse thing about those mines is that you see them before they kill you. Once they shoot up in the air they look at you before they explode. You can't outrun them; you just stare at what is about to kill you. When I heard that twang, I only thought of one thing, and that was to cover the President."

Nat shook his head. "Shit. You've got balls, man."

Dutch leaned over to his night table and picked up the clear plastic container holding the deformed steel balls the doctors had removed from just left of his C4 vertebra.

He shook it and said, "You're right. And here they are."

The two laughed. It was the first time Dutch laughed since...he wasn't sure when.

"How close was it?" Nat said.

Dutch held up two fingers spaced about a quarter of an inch apart. "That much further and Lexi was going to have to wheel me around the rest of my life."

"Shit man, you've got someone watching out over you." Nat moved off the bed and into the chair next to Dutch. "So now we're reviewing the video of the crowd and the approximate radius that someone would have to be standing in order to detonate the mine. So far though, no one stands out."

"Of course every detail of this trip had been made public, so deducing who could have known will be next to impossible."

"Yeah, and let me tell you, Polk is going fucking ballistic on Harvey. Meadows tells me he ripped him a new asshole in the Oval Office yesterday before Widow had to break them up. My guess is there won't be many more negotiations for future campaign trips."

Dutch screwed up his face and shook his head. "I hope not, but isn't that always the constant battle between POTUS and the Service?"

Nat nodded. "Usually, but for whatever reasons which are far above my pay grade to know, Widow's taken a hit in the polls after this last attempt. My guess is Harvey's not going to take more chances because it's not worth it. That's what I hope anyway."

"Amen to that," Dutch said and held out his fist for Nat to bump.

"All right, man, I've got to get going. I'm on duty at the Mansion tonight. I'll keep you in the loop if anything develops. Keep your cell on."

"Okay, Nat. Thanks, I really appreciate it."

Dutch painfully leaned forward to collect the files on the bed, but Nat held out a hand to stop him. "Those are all copies. Keep them for some light reading while you recuperate."

Of course, huge red "Classified" and "For Your Eyes Only" were stamped all over them. Dutch knew that Alexis knew not to even ask.

Dutch pointed to the files. "Does Polk know about this?"

Nat laughed. "It was his idea. Having another trained pair of eyes looking on only helps, especially since you were in the middle of it."

"Tell him I said thank you."

"You got it. Get better, will ya?" Nat said, pointing at Dutch as he left the room.

Once alone, Dutch tried to work himself into a position he could be comfortable. Despite Alexis' best efforts, nothing seemed to work until finally he reached behind him to the two overstuffed pillows he kept trying to move around and threw them to the floor. Then he gingerly moved his butt back until it came in contact with the headboard and straightened his back. The cool oak felt good against his spine, and there was nothing pulling at the sutures on his back when he sat like that.

Unfortunately, once he finally found a comfortable spot, he noticed the remote control was out of his reach. He contemplated moving again but decided it wasn't worth the effort. Besides, this was one of the first moments of quiet he had since arriving home from the hospital early the day before, and he wanted to enjoy it. He glanced at the files lying at the foot of his bed and decided against those as well. He'd have the next few days to digest everything in them. For the moment, he just wanted to enjoy the quiet.

"Terry, what are you doing?" Alexis said from the threshold of their bedroom door. She was carrying a tray with a plate of something Dutch couldn't make out.

"Honey, I'm fine, really. This feels comfortable to me."

"Nonsense," she said, putting the tray on the dresser and walking over to the pillows that he had just thrown down. She picked them up and stood, one in each hand, pursing her lips and looking him up and down, apparently trying to decide the newest placement so her fiancé would be comfortable.

"Lexi—" Dutch started, but was interrupted by a coughing fit. He winced in pain.

"What?" she looked at him innocently. "I just want you to be comfortable."

"Sweetie, I am comfortable just the way I am. Really. Now please stop fussing and come over here and sit for a moment. You haven't stopped since I got home."

He held out his hand and she took it as she made her way around the bed and delicately sat next to him. Then she gathered the folders and stacked them neatly at the foot of the bed, out of his reach.

"Terry, what else can I get you?"

He could sense her nervous energy. It became worse after Nat's visit. But how could he possibly tell her that she was driving him crazy? He also noted the subtle movement of the folders. He knew she was bothered by his working while at home. She seemed to be bothered about everything.

"Do you want the remote?" she said.

"Nope, I just want you. Is that possible?"

She gave him a suspicious look. "What do you mean by that?"

He laughed and coughed at the same time. "Get your mind out of the gutter, girl. I just meant I wanted you to sit with me. Let's talk."

"Let's talk? Talk about what?" she said, trying to avoid eye contact.

"What's on your mind? Come on, level with me."

"I'm fine," she said over her shoulder. "It's you I'm worried about."

"Me? I'm fine. The doctor said I'll be up and about in another few days."

Suddenly tears began to stream down her cheeks. She reached up and brushed them away with the palm of her hand.

"There, is this what you wanted to see?"

Dutch's heart melted. "Honey, of course not." He held his arms out and tried to draw her close to him, but she shook her head and wouldn't budge.

"No. I don't want you to move and break open the stitches. Besides, it hurts, doesn't it?"

He shook his head and smiled.

She laughed despite herself and in doing so inadvertently blew snot out of her running nose. "Oh my God!" She grabbed for a tissue to clean her face. Her voice was laced with a mixture of crying and laughing.

Dutch smiled watching her blow her nose.

"I'm sorry I'm being such a mush," she said.

"Don't worry about it. But I wish you'd tell me what was bothering you."

She moved her hands away from his and scooted backwards, increasing the distance between them. She held a new tissue to her face, wiped, then stared up at the ceiling. Her eyes were red.

"Lexi," he said, his voice rising. "Come on, out with it. There's nothing you can't tell me

With a loud blowing of her nose and a couple of fresh tissues, she lowered her head and looked at him. Her deep blue eyes were magnified through the tears.

"Terry, I just want to make sure that my fiancé is all right."

He smiled. "I am."

She moved closer. "Terry, I just want to make sure that my husband will be all right."

"I will be."

She moved even closer and put her hand on his chest. She spoke softer and slower. "Terry, I want to make sure the father of our child will be all right."

"I will be."

She didn't move. He didn't move. He wasn't sure what she wanted him to do. He smiled again. She remained quiet, so he smiled wider. Her eyes never left him.

She moved closer still and rested her hands on either side of his face and said, "Terry, I want to make sure the father of our child will be all right."

He tilted his head a bit like a dog when trying to comprehend something.

"Terry." She kissed him. "I want to make sure—" She kissed him again. "The father—" a finger poked into his chest, "of our child." She turned her finger and pointed to her stomach. "will be all right." She nodded quickly to drive home the point.

His eyes widened and a huge smile burst out. "Ohh, you mean—I mean, you—I mean, that's me—now? Really?"

She smiled and nodded quickly.

He flung his arms around her and drew her in for a giant bear hug.

"Honey, why didn't you tell me before? Ouch. I'm so happy. Oh, shit that hurts. How are you feeling?" He couldn't seem to stem the rush of things racing to get out of his mouth.

"Easy. Don't hurt yourself."

"Forget about me! How about you? You're pregnant! With our child! Alexis, that's fantastic. How long have you known?"

"Well, I thought something was up for a couple of weeks, but I shrugged it off."

"Shrugged it off!"

"For a while actually. But then I finally went to the doctor, who confirmed it. Terry, I'm four months pregnant!"

"How far along? Four months! Why didn't you—"

"I tried to, but we were both traveling so much. I didn't find out for sure until I was two months along. I kept trying to find a good time to tell you, then Harry, then this. Well, I just—" she looked at him hesitantly, but relaxed when she saw how happy he was.

"Darling, this is great! Is it a boy or a….how do you feel….what, when…"

The doorbell interrupted him. Alexis stood and headed out to answer the door.

Dutch leaned closer to the end of the bed to try to hear who she just let in. Their voices were muffled, but Alexis sounded happy to see whoever it was.

After a few more moments, their voices grew louder and he recognized the voice as Rich Flecca. Dutch smiled.

Alexis peeked around the corner. "Guess who came to visit you?" she said in a melodically teasing voice.

"I give up."

"Oh, you're no fun." She stepped aside to let in their guest.

Whizzer's familiar freckled face peered around the corner. Then his string-like body launched itself into the center of the room in one jump.

"Ta daaaaa!" he said loudly, one knee on the floor and his arms stretched diagonally outward.

"Whizzer, you son of a bitch! What the hell are you doing here?" Dutch boomed.

"Well I heard you got shot up pretty bad so I wanted to be the first to make a play on this little lady who broke my heart in Omaha."

He reached out, grabbed Alexis by the hand, spun her around and rested her on his knee.

She complied by pulling her legs up on his lap and throwing her arms around his scrawny neck, kissing him on the cheek.

"Sweetie, you know you're the first in line once I get rid of the big guy over there."

Whizzer blushed. "Awww, now you're really killing me, babe!" He returned her kiss.

"All right, is the love fest over?" Dutch said.

Alexis stood, and Dutch pointed to the chair for Whizzer.

Alexis offered to get Whizzer something to drink.

He held up his hand. "No thanks, darlin,' I only came by to check on our friend here. I'm actually in town on official business."

"Ooh, sounds important. I'd better let you two have some privacy then," she said and left the room.

"Damn it's good to see you, man. How's it going?" Dutch said.

Whizzer ignored Dutch and continued to look at where Alexis had been moments earlier.

"Hey," Dutch said, sitting up straighter.

Whizzer raised his hand and continued to look at the door until he was sure Alexis was far enough away. Then he turned to Dutch, his smile gone and his features twisted in anger.

Dutch's breath caught in his chest.

Whizzer unbuttoned the middle of his shirt, reached in, and slid out a brown manila envelope that looked like it had been folded a dozen times. He flattened it out the best he could and threw it unceremoniously on Dutch's chest.

He reached for it but Whizzer said sternly, "Don't open that."

Dutch wasn't sure if Whizzer was playing a prank on him until he saw the look on his friend's face. It was steel cold serious. Dutch sat up straighter and cleared his throat.

"Whizzer, what's going—"

Whizzer interrupted him. "What the fuck did you get me into?" he said in a harsh whisper.

Dutch felt the blood rush to his feet. The moment of euphoria he had experienced upon hearing he would become a father a moment before was a distant memory.

"Whizzer, I have no idea what you're talking about."

"Next time you ask for a favor, you better well fucking tell me what you're getting me involved in first."

Dutch thought back to the phone call he had made about Roger Graham.

"Whizzer, I seriously don't know what you're talking about. A friend of mine on Graham's detail said some things weren't adding up, that's all. He asked if I could look into it. What did you find out?"

Whizzer pointed to the envelope on the bed. "That's what I found out."

Dutch looked but didn't reach for it. His friend was pissed and obviously wanted to dictate how this was going to happen.

Dutch looked Whizzer squarely in the eye. "I have no idea what you could have come across. I didn't think it was going to be a big deal." He held his friend's gaze without blinking.

Whizzer took a breath, then said, "All right. I believe you. Sorry about that, but I'm just fucking rattled about this whole thing. I couldn't send this to you via e-mail or talk to you about it over the phone. As it is now, I'm not entirely convinced I didn't leave behind a trace. When I heard about a courier delivery to the D.C. office, I grabbed the run so I could have an excuse to come here and see you."

"Rattled about what? Trace? Whizzer, what the fuck is going on?"

Whizzer pointed to the envelope. "Dutch, if you open that you're going to be in a situation where there's no turning back. How good a friend is it that asked you to do the digging?"

"Not like you and me, Whizzer, but he's someone I work with. Come on, cut the shit. You know I've got to see what's in there."

Whizzer looked around the bedroom as if he were expecting someone to jump out of the shadows. "Fine, but I want to give you something first."

He reached into his shirt pocket and pulled out a cell phone. Handing it to Dutch he said, "We're not going to have time to talk about this here today. And I've got to be back in Omaha tomorrow afternoon. That cell phone has one number programmed into it, mine."

"I already have your number."

"No, don't call me on that one. Use this new number. It will connect you with another cell phone that, like this one, isn't registered. We'll be able to talk if we need to, but only if we need to. And after a few calls, I wouldn't trust it anymore."

"Whizzer, what's with all this cloak and dagger shit? I need to see what's in here."

Whizzer held up his hands submissively. "Okay, but it's all yours now."

Dutch hesitated. He tried to read his friend's eyes but they weren't giving away any clues as to what lay inside. He pinched open the clasp, then tore open the flap. Reaching inside, he felt the unmistakable glossy smoothness of photographs. He paused before pulling them out. As Whizzer looked on, Dutch removed the photographs.

The first was obviously taken from a satellite. It was focused on a small clearing in what looked to be an area of dense trees, someplace tropical. Two people stood facing one another. Others were placed around the perimeter of the clearing, which was about the size of a baseball diamond. The shot was too far away to make out faces. At the corner of the photo was a time stamp reading, "30-8: 21:00 GMT." Dutch remembered that was around the date that Kevin Brady told him Roger was likely to depart from his campaign itinerary and security detail.

He turned the next photo over and saw an enlarged image showing just the two people standing face to face. The first was someone of Latin American heritage. The second one was the unmistakable face of Roger Graham.

"Who—" Dutch started, but Whizzer was ahead of him.

"The person the Democratic Nominee for President of the United States of America is meeting with in that photo is Otto Torres, one of the biggest drug lords in Central America."

Chapter 26

The late afternoon Texas sun shone on Roger Graham, who stood on a wooden stage with American flag bunting draped around it. Wiping his forehead for the third time in ten minutes, he continued his speech.

"I join my opponent in condemning this horrific act of violence that threatened to disrupt the election process of this great nation. And I extend my deepest condolences to the families of the brave Secret Service agents who nobly gave their lives in defense of the President. And also to the loved ones of those who lost their lives as innocent bystanders along a motorcade route, excited to catch a glimpse of the leader of our great nation."

Roger paused. The only sounds were the continuous clicking of the cameras trying to capture every moment of what was undoubtedly history unfolding during this tumultuous Presidential campaign.

"Out of respect, I agree to join my opponent in suspending this Presidential campaign for one week in order to let our security agencies ensure this type of horrific violence doesn't happen again. Ladies and gentlemen of the press, I will not be taking any questions at this time. Thank you."

Roger stepped off the podium, ignoring the barrage of questions from the sea of reporters, and walked with the members of his staff to his protected convoy.

For the first time in anyone's memory, the Secret Service agents tasked with the security of a Presidential candidate did not try to hide their weapons. Agents were fanned out around the line of SUVs, boldly displaying their sub machine guns as they scanned the area.

Roger chuckled, thinking that for once he didn't have to worry about the press hounding him all the way to his car. Greg Underwood, Frank Tipper, and Simon were already inside the SUV. Joanna Davis followed Roger into the back seat, and then the door closed.

Everyone began talking at once until Roger held up his hand.

"Folks please, just wait. We have one week out of the public eye, so please, I don't want anyone having a conniption fit over anything on my schedule." All around people smiled and sat back in their seats.

"That's better. Now Tip, you're up first so get your clipboard out of your butt and begin."

The joke seemed to fit the relaxed mood.

Tip moved forward and adjusted his glasses, but before he started Roger interrupted him.

"Before you begin, however, I want to give you fair warning that there will be one deviation from our new schedule which will happen—" he paused and looked to Simon, who looked back and nodded. He glanced at his watch and said, "Today, in roughly three hours."

Everyone but Simon and Roger began talking at once again. Stern words of protest and questions hit him like a barrage of gunfire, making him feel as though he were back on the podium in front of the press.

He raised his voice and said, "Folks, this is non-negotiable. The good news is it will most likely be the last time. So there, good news and bad news. Can we please move on and not harp on this?"

Two hours and forty five minutes later, Roger Graham's black SUV and two trail cars were on another dirt road, miles from the highway. The rest of the vehicles in the convoy were still moving toward their overnight stop at the Embassy Suites Hotel in McAllen, Texas.

The occupants of the trail cars exited the vehicle first and fanned out, weapons in hand. Clyde Rolleston walked to Roger's limo and opened the door for him and Simon.

"As requested," Simon said, handing Agent Rolleston a single folded sheet of paper with the official seal of the CIA adorning the top.

Rolleston took his time reading every word of the order before folding it and placing it carefully in his breast pocket.

He stared at Simon, then Roger for an uncomfortable amount of time before saying, "Sir, let me reiterate one last time that I would feel much better accompanying you with a small detachment of my agents in addition to the members of the CIA."

Roger nodded and politely smiled at Rolleston. "Thank you, Agent Rolleston. Your point of view, opinion, and strong urgings have been duly noted. I appreciate the diligence with which you perform your duties. My sincere hope is that this will be the last time you and I will need to disagree on security issues surrounding my campaign."

He extended his hand. Rolleston reluctantly took it and the pair shook. Then Roger turned and the CIA agents fell in behind him and disappeared through the thick brush. Rolleston stood watching. He heard three engines roar to life. From the pitch, he guessed they were Jeeps. He continued to watch as the sounds disappeared.

Dutch painfully and slowly swung his legs off the side of the bed. Alexis stood next to him and took an arm to help him stand. After a couple of muted grunts, Dutch stood. "Terry be careful."

"Listen, Terry," Whizzer said, "I've got to run. I still have that load of junk from the office I need to drop off downtown."

"All right, Whizzer. Are you staying at the Grand Hyatt tonight?" Dutch referred to the hotel next door to the D.C. office where visiting agents generally stayed. The fact that it was a five star hotel was beside the point.

"Yup, but I'm flying out at noon. I've got to be back in the office tomorrow afternoon. Give me a call if you want. You've got my number."

"I've got a better idea. The downstairs restaurant there makes the best Belgian waffles. How about breakfast? Let's say eight o'clock?"

Whizzer considered, and then nodded. "It's a deal. Now, can I get one last squeeze from my girlfriend?"

Whizzer met Alexis and put his arm around her as she showed him out.

Dutch looked at the pillow where he had stuffed the envelope. He and Whizzer weren't through yet, but nothing could be done about that now.

Chapter 27

"Let's use this time to our advantage," Lorraine said. "We've got a one week respite from the campaign, so starting tomorrow I'm going to be hitting the phones hard to make sure I have the votes by the end of the week when the bill goes to the floor."

Lorraine Burton was in her element, seated in one of the two mahogany armchairs in front of the fireplace in the Oval Office. Michael Harvey and Preston Chase sat to her right, Glen Seeley and Trevor Sirois to her left. She lifted her curly hair to allow the air conditioning to hit her neck for a moment, then swept it behind her and let it drop.

"Glen," she continued, "I'm going to need updates from you every three hours for the next two days. I need to be sure the votes we already have don't fall away for some reason. Understand?"

Glen straightened in his chair. "I wouldn't worry about that, but yes, I do understand. Changing the waiting period requirements was just enough to get McKinley and Ladas on board."

"I want to remind everyone that the last minute concessions still aren't going to be enough to stave off the inevitable legal challenges to this bill," Chase said.

The President rolled her eyes. "Yes, yes, I'm fully aware of that, Mr. Chase."

Trevor Sirois sat forward. Managing to look anywhere but at the President, he said, "I've got staff finalizing my remarks once this bill goes through. I'll have Gladys send it to the Chief of Staff's Office later today." He said the words "Chief of Staff" through gritted teeth.

Lorraine looked at Sirois and said, "Are you two not playing nicely in the sandbox again?" The President chuckled. She truly enjoyed the drama the two men could provide.

Before coming to Washington, Trevor Sirois' lifestyle kept the New York gossip columns entertained for years. They dubbed him "The Emperor" for his Roman-like style of living. However, it came with a price which was three ex-wives that greatly cut into his bottom line, and rumored children out of wedlock curtailed his wild penchant for spending money as the years rolled on. However, he was still considered the kingpin on Wall Street until he leveraged his company and risked everything on a takeover of Drumm Pharmaceuticals. The deal would have netted his stockholders millions. But he lost the bid in the eleventh hour to none other than the man sitting across from him at that moment, Chief of Staff, Michael Harvey.

So Sirois packed up and decided to move out of the fast lane and announced his intention to "give back to the country that served me so well." At least that was the public version. Most New York insiders suspected he was just running away from Wall Street where he had been labeled a pariah.

"Once I get the comments from the Secretary of Homeland Security's office," Harvey said, ignoring her comment, "I'll make sure to integrate it into our speech. I've been promised by all four networks that we can have thirty minutes starting at eight o'clock Eastern, provided it passes."

"All right, everyone. Let's keep our eyes on the prize. If all goes according to plan, we'll have our first step toward serious immigration reform by the end of the week. Thank you everyone for your hard work on this. I appreciate it."

At that, everyone stood and filed out past the two Service agents. They had been doubled since the last attempt on the President's life. Lorraine thought it overkill, but Polk had demanded it.

Harvey stopped when he approached Byron Meadows. "Hey, Byron, how's everything going?"

Meadows took the hand offered him and shook it. "Fine, sir. We're making progress."

"I didn't mean that. I meant, how is everyone doing? You guys in the Service are unbelievable. I really mean that. Losing three of your own." Harvey shook his head. "I mean, you haven't missed a beat. I just want you to know that the President and I truly appreciate everything you've done for us."

Meadows flashed a rare smile while on duty. "You're very welcome, Mr. Harvey."

Harvey tapped him on the shoulder as he walked past. "You just let me know if there's anything you need."

Lorraine watched them from behind her desk. When Harvey left, she busily drew together some folders and tapped them down in an effort to straighten them into a uniform pile. She never made eye contact with the agents.

Chapter 28

The next day was the first day Dutch had been outside in the fresh air for almost a week. As agreed upon the day before, he and Whizzer were meeting for breakfast.

"Are you all right?" Alexis asked Dutch. She held tightly to his left arm while he gingerly stepped out of the car.

"Yeah, I'm fine. It's getting easier to stand."

"No, I don't mean that. But you're acting kind of funny today. "

They walked in silence for a moment before Dutch screwed up his face and said, "Funny? What do you mean?"

They emerged from the elevator that led from the parking garage up into the foyer adjacent to the Grand Hyatt.

"You didn't say two words to me on the way here."

He shifted his weight. "Well, you had the radio on. I didn't want to bother you listening to music."

She looked sternly at him.

"Ahhh, give me a minute. I'll come up with something better."

"How about the truth?"

He thought for a moment. "All right. Whizzer and I have to discuss something going on at work. But I can handle it."

"I'm sure you can. I just want you to know that I'm here if you need me, even if it's just a shoulder to lean on."

He said softly, "Thanks Lexi, I appreciate it. I'll let you know if I do."

Across the restaurant, a hand went up, beckoning the pair to Whizzer's table in a back corner. He had taken a table which sat under the overhang, shielding them from the expansive atrium the restaurant sat in. Faux palm trees surrounded the area where the table was giving it a distinct detached feeling from the rest of the restaurant.

"Geez, you couldn't get a more remote table if you tried." said Alexis.

Whizzer flashed his youthful smile and said, "You know I hate the sun. I like dark corners."

He rose and kissed her on the cheek, then shook Dutch's hand.

The men sat, but Alexis remained standing. She noticed Dutch grimace as he sat.

"All right you two, I'm going to get some work done" she pecked Dutch on the cheek. "I'll be in the lobby making some calls. Come get me when you're ready."

"Do you want me to bring you anything to eat?" Dutch said.

Her morning sickness had continued into her second trimester, although it wasn't as bad as it had been. But she still wasn't up to anything heavy for breakfast.

"No, thanks, I'm fine."

She walked from the restaurant to the escalator and took out her cell phone to check the time, then did the familiar calculation to figure out how late it was in Stockholm.

Her heels clicked against the polished floor as she made her way past the check-in counter with the mannequin-like stoic figures of the hotel concierge and manager watching as she walked by.

Past the front desk was a hallway leading to a grouping of eateries located just off the main atrium. She searched past the crowded Starbucks and found a table large enough for just her and her briefcase opposite a red neon sign advertising the Zephyr Deli. She turned her seat so it faced outside to the horseshoe driveway where valets ran back and forth retrieving guests cars. It gave her a perfect vantage point to observe the comings and goings of the busy five-star hotel. She was a people watcher at heart.

She pulled out a writing pad and pen from her black leather briefcase and rested them on the table, then sat back and dialed a number from memory.

A man's voice answered in Swedish. *"Hej."*

"Eftermiddag herr Jacobs. Hur mår ni idag?" Alexis replied.

"Okay, show off, I haven't been here that long to know anything other than 'hello' and 'Where is the bathroom?' What did you just say to me?"

Alexis laughed. "I said, 'Good afternoon, Alan. How is your day today?'"

Alan returned to his faux Swedish accent. "Ahhh, Miss Jordan. Why it is much better now that I am on the phone with you."

"Oh, you're too kind."

"No, no, no, you are like a breath of fresh air whenever you are here. Maybe you are willing to, how do you Americans say, have that tryst we spoke about last time?"

Alexis laughed. "You are so full of shit, do you know that? I think you've been over there too long."

The man on the other end lost the accent and converted to his native Brooklyn. "Maybe, but the women over here all buy it."

"Alan, you're a dog." She continued laughing.

Suddenly, a pain shot through her that felt like a white hot poking iron was thrust into her spine and lower back. She stifled a yell and clutched at her stomach and back simultaneously. Her phone dropped with a clatter onto the hard floor.

She tried to take a deep breath as another pain shot through her. She was overcome with a wave of intense heat, and she was suddenly dripping with sweat.

Alexis barely heard the muted voice coming from the cell phone by her feet. She saw white lights as the lobby swirled around her. A third pain hit, this one reaching all the way to her toes. She tightly grasped the arms of the chair, almost ripping the fabric in the process.

After a minute she was able to take a deep breath and the pain began to subside.

"Hello? Hello?" she heard Alan saying.

She took another deep breath and used her sleeve to wipe the sweat off her face. She sat still for a moment longer as things began to right themselves. Then she gingerly bent and picked up her phone.

"Hi, Alan," she said between measured breaths. "So sorry about that. Bad connection".

"Oh, I thought we lost each other."

She pulled the phone down to her chest for a moment and looked up at the ceiling, trying to focus. "I'm sorry, what were we talking about?"

She looked around. No one had noticed her. Whatever just happened didn't last long enough to attract attention.

"I was saying about —"

She interrupted him once more as her stomach tightened again.

"Alan—can—can I call you right back? I've—ahh—I've—I mean, I need to get my notes. I don't have what I need right now."

"Sure, I'll be here." The tone of his voice sounded somewhat suspect.

"Thanks."

She hung up and tentatively walked to the buffet lining the Zephyr Deli's walk up restaurant. A wave of dizziness hit her, and she had to steady herself against the metal shelf along the buffet line. She got the attention of a man working the sandwich-making-station on the other side of the glass divider.

"Excuse me, could I please get a bottled water?" she said.

"So why do you think you were traced? All you did was task a satellite. It's not an uncommon request for the Service to make."

Whizzer continued stirring the thin straw around his second cup of coffee. Dutch watched him open five sugar packets and empty them into the swirling liquid.

"Well, it's complicated. First of all, you've got to remember that these satellites are in ultra-high demand. The schedules they're on are set months in advance, and you practically need an act of Congress to change it. So the first problem was finding a satellite that was passing over the area you wanted me to look at on the day you told me. The smallest changes I could make to any of these, the better my chances of not being detected."

Whizzer stirred his coffee faster, obviously gearing up for a fantastic story. "You see, one of the problems was calculating the time it would take to make the course corrections and move it to the proper elevation and direction. The ESCAN axis is aligned with the direction of motion of the satellite. It's necessary for this to be the case, because the scan rate in the MSCAN axis is insufficient to keep the radar bore sight aligned with a specific area on the ground while it's being imaged. Further constraints are—"

Dutch held up a hand. "Whizzer, please. In English."

Whizzer sat back. "Oh, sorry." He looked dejected but plodded on undeterred. "Well, long story short. I got a clear picture. I recognized Graham right away but not the guy he was standing with. I knew you'd ask so I figured I'd run a simple trace to find out. I opened the facial recognition database and plugged in the image I grabbed from the satellite. It took longer than usual, which could have meant it was having a problem finding a match. It did; it came back empty."

Dutch eyed Whizzer suspiciously.

"So, I thought for a minute. Here was a candidate for President of the United States who just happens to have a background in the CIA."

"Whizzer," Dutch said.

"So, you know, it's not like I haven't done it before."

"Whizzer," Dutch said a little louder and sterner.

"I remembered a back door I used once to get information we needed really quickly from Langley. So I tried it and it was still working."

"You're an asshole; do you know that?"

Whizzer had raised his cup of coffee to his lips, but didn't take a sip. "What? Why do you say that?"

"Because I didn't get any sleep last night thinking I got you in a shitload of trouble. But you did it to yourself."

"Oh bullshit, you asked me to find out. What did you expect, that I'd stop halfway through?"

"Come on, Whizzer, you know you're not supposed to—"

"Oh right, and you're a saint. I remember when you had me—"

Dutch looked to his left and right, realizing they were making a lot of noise. He held his hands palms up in front of him and said, "Okay, Okay, shhh, let's just bring it down a notch. Fine, we're both to blame. Now, go on."

Whizzer didn't look like he bought into that presumption one hundred percent, but eyed the sparse customers in the restaurant and continued quietly.

"Anyway, I used a few keywords like Mexico, Rio Bravo, which by the way is where they were when the satellite found them, all that bullshit. Well, I get a hit almost immediately. But whatever was in the file was so hot it set off all kinds of alarms. I mean, it almost blew up my friggin' screen. So now I know I've got about fifteen seconds to enter some bullshit password or the whole pipeline I used to get in was going to be exposed, and me along with it. That's right, I said me, Dutch, not you."

Dutch nodded dismissively and wound his hand in a circular motion telling his friend to continue. He knew that his not showing interest with the inner workings of computer espionage aggravated Whizzer, but he didn't want to waste time talking about things he wasn't ever going to understand anyway.

Whizzer looked frustrated and stirred his coffee faster, adding more sugar.

"Sure, Whizzer, take this chance. Sure, Whizzer, you can do it; you won't get caught. You're the best, Whizzer." He mimicked voices from his past.

Dutch rolled his eyes and said, "Sorry Whizzer, you're right. You are the best. I'm sure somehow you saved yourself from being caught by using some miraculous computer trickery."

Whizzer took a deep breath. "Fine, I won't go into how I did it." His face broke into a wide smile. "But it was genius."

Dutch cleared his throat.

Whizzer began speaking more quickly. "Anyway, after I got myself out of that mess I was still curious. I remembered a cipher this guy once taught me and thought I'd give it a try. It was a hybrid version of the Schnorr signature. He said it would work for every file document in the world. Well, long story short it did, and just like that I was in!" Whizzer raised his hand and snapped his fingers for dramatic effect.

The waiter brought the bill and set it down between them. Dutch picked it up and reached for his wallet.

"Damn straight," Whizzer said approvingly.

Dutch took out a twenty and handed it back to the waiter saying, "Keep the change."

The waiter nodded and left.

"Whizzer, I'm sorry, but can you get to the bottom line?"

"Bottom line, I was able to access a deeply buried file belonging to Roger Graham that was still classified as active. The file was about Otto Torres."

"Still active? What does that mean?"

Whizzer shrugged. "Your guess is as good as mine as to how the CIA runs its shit. But I do know it's a file he continues to go in and out of. It's got a rundown on this guy Torres and his whole operation. Talk about big time shit. This guy accounts for a big chunk of the drugs coming up from south of the border

Dutch sat back and whistled, then took a sip of his own coffee.

Whizzer said, "Now can you answer a question for me?"

"I can't promise anything, but give it a try."

"Can you please tell me how Graham finds time to continue working a job that he supposedly retired from years ago, meets covertly with a drug kingpin, be a United States Representative, and run for President?"

Dutch knit his eyebrows in thought and stared distractedly behind Whizzer. Almost to himself he said, "I can't, but I may know someone who can."

"Did I miss something?" Dutch asked Alexis as they drove out of the parking lot of the hotel. She didn't reply. "Hello, are you there?" he asked, waving a hand from the passenger seat.

"Huh, what? I'm sorry, sure," Alexis reached to adjust the volume on the radio.

Watching her, Dutch said, "The radio's not on."

"I'm sorry Terry, what did you say?"

"I said am I missing something? Are you all right?"

"Oh, yes. I—I'm fine." She put her hand up to her forehead.

Dutch noticed how flushed she looked. He leaned over and put his hand on the back of her neck. It was soaking wet

"Alexis, what's wrong?"

His tone seemed to bring her out of a trance. "Wrong? Oh, I'm sorry. It's probably nothing."

He sat forward, seat belt straining against his chest.

"Probably nothing?"

Once they stopped, she turned and looked at him. "I got this pain a little while ago. It shot through me here all the way down to my feet." She indicated around her stomach and down her legs.

"Pain? How bad?"

She shrugged and didn't respond. Dutch knew that couldn't be good.

"All right, take a left here instead of a right," he said with a hard edge to his voice.

"Hey, what? Why? No, no, no, no. I'm not going to the hospital. No way."

Dutch was used to her stubborn Italian rants. He took her right hand off the wheel so she would look at him.

"Lexi, I don't want to argue with you, so let me put this another way. I would like you to go to the hospital to get checked out. If not for you, will you please do it for me?"

He knew he had her.

"That's not fair."

"You're right. But I'm still asking."

The two stared at one another until the light turned and a horn brought them back. She let out an exasperated breath and switched her directional to the left, surely to the dismay of the driver behind them.

Dutch followed Dr. Shea to the examination area. The antiseptic smell was unmistakable. Recent visits to hospitals swirled around in Dutch's head. If he closed his eyes he could almost see Harry's room that he had been in so much.

Alexis was perched up in bed with multiple pillows behind her back. She was smiling, something Dutch was eternally grateful for. Stretched around her exposed stomach was a thick brown belt with a black disk in the middle. Dutch could hear what sounded to him like a saw being bent back and forth.

"It's a fetal monitor. You're hearing your baby's heartbeat right now," an older nurse said with a smile as she adjusted the strap around Alexis' stomach.

Dutch tried to wrap his arms around this notion. A smile enveloped his otherwise concerned face.

The doctor looked again at his chart. "All her blood work came back fine. The bleeding she experienced earlier had been very light."

"Bleeding?" Dutch exclaimed, looking between Alexis and the doctor.

Dr. Shea gently held up a hand to give reassurance. "As I said, it wasn't much. But as a precaution we ran an ultrasound. Everything came back fine. It's not uncommon for women in their second trimester to experience these types of pains. It's probably just muscle separation."

Something in the doctor's voice gave Dutch pause so he said, "What else do you think it could be?"

Dr. Shea's expression didn't change, but paused before answering as if choosing his words carefully. "Now I don't want you to become alarmed. The chances are slight."

Dutch focused on the doctor's eyes and said, "What are you worried about?"

The doctor took in a deep breath and held it until he spoke. "What you need to remember is that as a doctor, I have to make you aware of everything that could go wrong. That doesn't mean I think it will, but it's my job."

Alexis was sitting up straight in bed now. Dutch remained silent.

Dr. Shea continued. "The bleeding bothered me a bit. Bleeding is not common during the second trimester of a pregnancy; however, it's not unheard of. It just raises a few red flags."

"Red flags? What the hell does that mean? What are you worried about?" Dutch said.

The doctor hesitated before saying, "A condition called placental abruption. Now I want to stress that I'm not saying this is what she has, but it's something I can't rule out, either."

Dutch opened his mouth to ask what that meant, but the doctor held up his hand and continued. "A placental abruption is a serious condition in which the placenta partially or completely separates from the uterus before the baby's born. The condition can deprive the baby of oxygen and nutrients and cause severe bleeding in the mother. Believe it or not, placental abruption happens in one out of 200 pregnancies. Again, I want to emphasize that I'm not saying this is what she has, but we're going to keep her in overnight and monitor her just in case."

Dutch reached for Alexis' hand which was cold and clammy. He squeezed it reassuringly as the two shared a look. Dutch smiled and said, "It's going to be fine."

Later that evening, Dutch was sitting in the chair next to Alexis' bed. It was a recliner that was upholstered in what felt like plastic. No matter where he moved he couldn't find a comfortable spot. The television provided background noise in the private room Alexis had been admitted to.

He yawned, stretched his arms out in front of him, and said, "Is this what I'm going to have to sleep in when you're in labor?"

"Yup. You'll survive. I thought you were used to sleeping on dirt and rocks when you were in the Seals? Or was that all trash talk

Dutch grimaced as he stood gingerly. "I think some of the places I've slept were more comfortable than this damn chair." Reflexively he put his hand on the small of his back. He didn't want to let on just how much pain his back was in, especially since Alexis was the one in the hospital bed.

"Ohh, poor baby. I'll try to make the delivery go as quickly as I can so you can sleep in your own bed." She paused and glanced at her watch. "Speaking of which, when are you going home?"

"What, you don't want me to stick around tonight?"

She shook her head. "Actually, I wouldn't mind a quiet night."

A teaser for the late news came on. The anchor man's deep voice talked over a video taken earlier that day.

"Only on channel four, new video of the attempted assassination tonight at eleven."

Dutch watched as a different camera angle of the President walking out of the Renaissance Hotel showed on the screen. He saw himself standing at attention looking across the way at the crowd behind Agent Coyle.

"Shit. I forgot about that!"

Alexis looked startled. "What?"

He stared blankly, trying to remember.

"Terry, what is it?"

Without moving his eyes he said, "What the hell was it? I saw something just before—"

Alexis said something, but Dutch was only vaguely aware of it. He continued trying to work through realization.

"It was—what was it?" He snapped his fingers loudly. "Whizzer, that's who can do it!"

"What?" she said.

He pointed to the screen. "The video they just showed. With everything that happened recently, I totally forgot."

He began walking in a tight circle.

"I saw something just before Widow, er, the President got into the limo. After she invited me in, then the explosion, well, it totally slipped my mind until I saw that video clip."

"What did you see?"

He looked off in the distance again, "Something about the faces in the crowd. The pictures....."

"How can Whizzer help you?"

"He can get a copy of that news video, crop it to show different angles, and shoot it off to Nat in the operations center faster than anyone I know. That might be all I'll need."

"Right now? Honey, it's almost nine o'clock."

"Are you kidding me? The operations center has been going twenty-four seven since before the President's limo cleared the smoke. I guarantee Nat's in there working tonight. I'll give him a heads up to expect something soon. In the meantime—"

"Oh sure, one minute you're worried sick about me, the next you're off on a case."

"Sweetie, you said you didn't need me—no wait, you said you didn't want me here tonight. I'm just doing what I do best. Oh, and for clarification purposes, it isn't a case, it's the case."

"Oh, sorry about that. Come here so I can give you a kiss."

His excitement palpable, he kissed her then turned and gave a wave behind his back and disappeared around the corner.

Chapter 29

Roger Graham had missed this, his favorite thing about being a Congressman. He soaked in the surroundings as the subway underneath the United States Capitol Building quietly made the short trip from the Capitol to its only other destination, under the Rayburn House Office Building housing the Congressmen's offices. The little known subway system dated back to 1909 when it was serviced by an electric bus. It was a quick and efficient way of getting the members of Congress from their offices to the Capitol while sheltering them from the elements—the press and the public included. Over the years the system has undergone multiple upgrades. But what remained on the House side were the electric powered trolley's small cars, whose sides reached waist height, almost like a carnival ride. The other thing he liked about the trolleys was the human factor. It was still driven by a conductor.

He was the only one on the train other than Mabel Hale, who was that night's conductor and an institution among members of Congress for decades. From what Roger knew about Mabel, she had been working in the Capitol for over forty years and was the first African American allowed to operate the trolleys. She was easily over sixty-five years old with a rotund figure, short cropped white hair, and a smile that could light the tunnel.

It was past midnight and he was enjoying the ride, head resting on his fists. He was disappointed when the trolley pulled into the station under his office building.

"'Night, Senator Graham." She nodded politely at Roger as he stepped down onto the concrete floor.

"Thank you, Mabel. You have a good one."

As he walked through the underground entrance, he decided to take a right instead of his usual route straight ahead to the elevators. A rigorous climb to his office on the third floor would be good for him, he decided.

Due to the lateness of the hour, few people passed him in the stairwell. Those who did gave him short, clipped statements like, "Good vote tonight, Congressman" or "Sorry about tonight,

Congressman" or "Good luck in November; you can get rid of the damned bill then."

Roger only heard bits and pieces of what was being said as he tried to maintain a curt smile and nod to the well-wishers. He was grateful to find the long white marble hallway leading to his office empty. He read the nameplates on each frame next to the floor to ceiling doors announcing which office belonged to which Congressman. Some had the flags of their home states proudly displayed on pedestals in front of their entrances. He didn't know why he still read the plaques because he knew them all by heart. On multiple occasions he had to pay impromptu visits to one colleague or another's office while trying to push some type of legislation through.

He wondered if it was all worth it. Of the eight years he had been working these hallowed hallways, what had he accomplished? The government was broken. Too much money, power, and greed soaked into the very souls of the inhabitants of this building. Votes were taken not on what would be best for their constituents, but rather what would be best for their reelection campaign which always seemed to be the primary focus for most politicians.

He arrived at his office, the only one still fully staffed at this hour. Lately that had been the norm. They looked up when he walked in and he was greeted with a chorus of "Congressman."

He did his best to give an upbeat smile. "Why are all you people here this late? Your boss must be a real jerk."

Smiles and laughs permeated the room. He looked past the front desk to the walls festooned with pictures of him at various events throughout the country, but mainly focusing on his home state of New Mexico.

A red headed intern no older than nineteen sat behind the desk. She looked like she had just stepped out of a salon, her perky smile rivaled only by her tight fitting sweater that her perfect posture accentuated.

She smiled widely and said, "Ms. Davis is already in your office."

Roger could hear the fatigue the young girl was trying to hide. "Thank you, Melissa," he said, suddenly feeling very old.

He walked behind her desk to the entrance to his private office and twisted the knob of the large oak door. Inside, he saw his press secretary seated in one of three chairs set in front of a fifty-five-inch television screen hanging on the wall between two ornately carved wooden book shelves.

"Why is it—"

Joanna held up her hand. Her other grasped the remote control that she feverishly worked, flipping between the various networks' coverage of the historic vote taken on the floor of the House not more than an hour before.

He sat in the high backed leather chair behind his desk.

He struggled to read a memo on his blotter in the dim lighting. He leaned forward and clicked a metal chain to turn on his green-shaded banker's light.

He tried to focus on the memo but couldn't get the voices of the talking heads on the television out of his head.

"Tom, I think tonight's vote has to be viewed as a major win for President Burton. Even with her party holding the majority, six Republican congressmen broke party lines and voted against the bill."

"Yes, Brad, that's something that's been over looked this week."

"Tom, what have you heard from Congressman Graham's people?"

Roger watched the screen as it zoomed in for a close up of the anchor's face.

"Well, Brad, I had a chance to speak with Joanna Davis, Congressman Graham's press secretary, just minutes after the votes had been counted. Here's what she had to say."

The screen switched to a shot of Joanna from the waist up as she said, "Well Brad, there were really no surprises tonight. Representatives Duchi, Laughlin, and Marks contacted Congressman Graham's office before the roll call vote was taken."

"What did they say?"

"They explained why they were going to break from party lines and vote with the President on the immigration legislation."

"What was the Congressman's reaction?"

Joanna paused dramatically and the camera zoomed in closer to her face, which conveyed concern.

"The Congressman appreciated the phone call. They knew how strongly opposed he was to this bill and wanted to reach out to explain their reasons."

"And what were those reasons?"

"Brad, the Congressman would like to keep private those conversations."

"Any speculation from the Congressman's campaign?"

Joanna flashed her trademark smile that the press ate up. She tossed her long blonde hair back and let out a laugh.

"Brad, I told you the Congressman did not say a word to his staff. But personally speaking, you do the math. What we have here is back room dealings of the highest magnitude. Of course, that's nothing new with this President."

Joanna snapped off the television screen and hit a button on the remote that increased the lighting. She stood and turned to Roger, holding her hand high in the air above her head.

He leaned forward and slapped her a high five.

"Joanna, you're the best."

She pumped her fist in celebration. "I love how they zoomed in on me during my pause. That couldn't have been scripted better."

"Was it scripted?"

She smiled but didn't say anything.

"How the hell—?"

Joanna cleared her throat and said demurely, "Well, a certain camera man and I did have drinks together the other night."

"Joanna! You didn't—"

She tossed the remote, and it bounced on the desk in front of him "Congressman Graham, how could you even imply that I would prostitute myself out for a good head shot?"

"I find your description of a head shot rather interesting in this case."

"Pig!" she spat out, throwing her arms up in disgust and storming out of his office.

He laughed, watching her curvy frame in a size two dress bustle away from him.

"Congratulations, Madame President," Michael Harvey offered as she rose to turn off the television in her bedroom.

"Michael, it's just the two of us in here. You know the rules about calling me that in private."

"Yes, but I'm speaking about a monumental piece of Presidential work, therefore the title fits the praise."

She walked toward him and leaned down to kiss him on the lips. "Thank you," she said quietly and moved to sit on the end of her bed.

Michael turned in his chair. "That should give us the kick we need in the polls by tomorrow afternoon. Graham must be grinding his teeth tonight."

Lorraine looked off in the distance and didn't respond.

"Lorraine, what's wrong?"

She slowly shook her head and said, "I'm just thinking of the cost."

"What cost?"

"The cost this Office demands."

"According to the accounting branch of your campaign, so far it's been north of four hundred million."

She smiled without losing her faraway look. "You know what I mean."

He looked at her. Her green eyes appeared to have grayed in the last three-and-a-half years. The grey was also assaulting her hair, something magazines noted in every issue. She couldn't do anything about that for fear of being called vain. Wrinkles creased her eyes, and her neck was showing the wear and tear as well.

It had never been a surprise how much the office of President of the United States aged the few who ever held the title, but this was the first time a woman sat in the Oval Office. Her aesthetics would be the baseline for all other women who would follow.

"May I suggest a weekend at Camp David?"

She took a deep breath, held it for a second, and then exhaled loudly. "Maybe."

Michael stood, walked to the bed, and sat down next to her. He reached for her hand while they sat, enjoying the quiet.

She watched as he sat next to her, then became lost in her thoughts. He had been there for her in every way since she had become President. Hell even before she became President. He had been both the man she needed as well as the perfect Chief of Staff. She thought back during her first year in office and how she treated him. She knew it wasn't justified but she was trying so hard to prove she wasn't going to be anyone's door mat. Becoming the first woman President carried with it the burden of her actions being the measuring stick. Maybe she was trying too hard to be someone she wasn't? But his loyalty had no equal, and she was grateful for it.

"Lorraine, what are you thinking about?" Michael asked.

She paused for another moment before saying, "Do you think it's all worth it?"

He looked at their intertwined hands. "Yes."

More silence. She turned and gave him a long, tender kiss. "Thank you for being here for me, and for putting up with me."

"Lorraine, it's my pleasure. But we still have lots to accomplish."

She looked down. "I'm tired."

"Well, let's turn down the bed and watch Jay Leno make fun of you. That's always a fan favorite."

She smiled and held his hand tighter. "No, not that kind of tired. This job takes so much from you. I don't know if it's worth it."

He looked at her tenderly and reached a hand up and stroked her hair, brushing back some strands that found their way in front of her face. "Hey, hey, that's not like you. That's not the Lorraine Burton who broke barriers all her life and fought for what she believed in. What's this suddenly all about?"

Her eyes glistened, and she appeared to be fighting back an urge to cry.

Michael put his arm around her. She buried her head and gave into the sobs that had obviously been building for some time. He tenderly stroked her hair and squeezed her shoulder.

"Michael," she said slowly. "What happened tonight…it just…it just wasn't as I imagined it would be."

"How did you imagine it?"

She stood and walked to her cherry wood bureau and grabbed a couple of tissues. Dabbing her eyes, she began to pace, tracing semi-circles back and forth around the bed.

"Countless protests, some turning violent, hours upon hours of commentary from every conceivable media outlet, my being cast as a villain, two attempts on my life, dead Secret Service agents and innocent people, a numbing amount of phone calls and arm twisting, and for what? Just to get a piece of legislation through that I believed in but had to water down at the last minute? Is that what I'm pouring out my heart and soul for?"

"Lorraine, this job is unique; you know that. It's not like the financial world. This country is a needy one. It's not easy running a democracy. What you did tonight was move us a little closer to making things better for everyone.

She held the tissue to her nose and blew, then looked at him and smiled. "Michael, I love you."

He stood and the two embraced. Slowly their bodies rocked to an unheard beat. He tightened his grip around her and they kissed again

Fifteen blocks away, Dutch sat in the busy operations room on the corner of H Street and 11th. The windowless room effectively hid the time of day. The only hint was a clock over one of the two doors leading in and out of the rectangular room. The lights were kept intentionally low for the purposes of viewing the three large screens hanging against the far wall. Each screen served its own purpose. The one in the middle was usually kept to one of the broadcast news stations. The two screens on either side were available for agents who wanted to call up something they were working on for others to see.

The room was full once again due to the ongoing investigation of the latest assignation attempt. This one took on more urgency because of the use of a Bouncing Betty as well as continued loss of life, both within the agency and out. The theory that Mr. Martinez's attempt on the President's life three months before was isolated was now viewed as unlikely. The FBI, local law enforcement, and Secret Service were all cooperating with the latest investigation. Dutch had been a big factor driving this newfound intra-agency harmony. His in-depth analysis of the first attempt on the President's life was proving pivotal in this investigation and helped advance the theory that the attempts on the President were related to the immigration bill from the speculative phase. Now the direction was focused on domestic illegal immigrants who may or may not be aided by outside interests.

His feeling about what he saw on television tonight may finally tie things together and give them people to put in the crosshairs of the investigation.

"Hey, Dutch, phone's for you," called out Agent Chip Castner from the FBI, holding up his phone receiver.

"Transfer it over."

"I can't. Your system is different from ours. I don't know how."

Dutch wondered why systems within the same government would be different and shook his head. Typical government bullshit. He stood quickly and winced in pain. "Shit!"

Two agents next to him stopped what they were doing and looked over.

"Hey, Dutch, you all right?"

"That friggin' hurt," he said, reaching behind and feeling the incision where the shrapnel had been cut out of him.

Nat walked over with concern etched on his face.

"You want me to see if it's bleeding?"

Dutch shook his head. "I know it's not. This fucking rip in my back has been killing me the last couple of days."

"Have you had a doctor look at it?"

Dutch shook his head.

"Oh that's smart. Why the hell not?"

"Hey, Dutch!" yelled Castner, who was still holding the phone in the air.

Dutch left Nat without answering and hurried over. "Yeah, Brown here," he said into the receiver.

"I'm sending you the file now. You should have it in a second or two. I was able to get three different angles. You'll be able to play with it once you load them onto your laptop."

Dutch smiled. "Whizzer, you're the best."

"I know, but I wish you'd forget I was. Peace!" As soon as Whizzer delivered his typical farewell, he was gone. Dutch chuckled, knowing that for all of Whizzer's cranky facade, the young man loved having an excuse to show off his technical prowess.

Dutch went back to his slice of the table, still smarting and trying not to reach behind him.

Dutch opened his e-mail. Whizzer's file waited for him.

He clicked it and read, "You suck. You owe me a hell of a lot more than dinner. Whizzer."

Dutch chuckled and clicked on the attachment. It took a few moments for the blue bar to make its way across the screen before announcing the file had been successfully downloaded.

He clicked it and three different angles of the news camera feed displayed, each in their own boxes. He looked up to the front of the room and saw the screen to his right wasn't being used.

"Hey Nat, can you come over and take a look at something?"

Nat walked around the table. The two agents working with him followed out of curiosity.

Dutch punched a couple of buttons, and the first image appeared on the big screen. The other agents on his side of the room looked up to see what new piece of information could have come in.

"That's Widow making her way out the back of the hotel," Nat said.

On screen was a head-on view of the President waving to the crowd. To her right stood a row of agents, Dutch at the end.

"Roll it," Nat said.

Dutch started the video. They watched as the President made her way among the throngs of people shouting both encouragement and slurs. As she progressed down the walkway, the camera zoomed out until the bottom of the screen showed the top of the Beast. A moment later she passed Dutch, who continued staring straight ahead while the other agents turned to follow the President. He stopped the video.

Nat looked at him. "What caught your eye?"

Dutch stared at the screen for a long while. All of the agents had turned except for him. He hadn't been aware at the time how long he stared at—what?

He pushed the play button and the video continued. Dutch watched himself turn and follow the President toward the limo. He had only been distracted for an extra second, but in Secret Service time that was an eternity.

Dutch froze the screen again, but the video clip didn't show enough on the right side of the screen where he had been looking.

He moved the cursor on his laptop over to the second file and double clicked it.

The new video appeared to be the same time frame as the one before but from a different angle. The CNN logo was prominent on the bottom right corner of the screen. This view was from the President's left. It showed her emerging from the exit and waving. Dutch got a better view of himself as the camera panned. This camera angle was useless because it didn't show what he had been looking at.

"This won't help," he said and froze the screen.

He paused before he minimized it. All the agents watching this video took notice of the two agents to Dutch's left. Porter and Rogers were two of the three killed in the attack. Everyone stood stoically as they took a last look at their fallen brothers.

"Hey Dutch" one of the agents who was watching said. "We've all seen this a thousand times. What are you looking for?"

Dutch ignored the question and minimized the video, calling up the last file Whizzer sent him. This footage was taken from the opposite side of the CNN footage. Dutch saw it was from Fox News's B roll. This angle clearly showed the President coming out of the hotel, only it was shot from her right. The camera followed her until she reached the last of the agents standing in line. Dutch hit a button to freeze the image. He stopped the video just as she walked in front of him.

"That's it. Perfect!" he said loudly.

All around him leaned in a little closer to see what Dutch was looking at.

"Who's the tech in here tonight?" he yelled out.

From the other end of the room, an older man approached the semi-circle of agents huddled around Dutch.

"What do you need, Agent Brown?"

Dutch pointed to the screen. "That head on the bottom right of the screen is mine. Someone in the crowd caught my attention. I was looking directly at her in this frame. Can you clean up the clarity and zoom in to get a face?"

The tech took Dutch's chair and hit a series of buttons. The screen momentarily went blue while he worked. The next image showed the President much closer but off to the left. In the forefront was Agent Coyle, who had been stationed across from Dutch.

Over Coyle's shoulders were the protesters. Angry faces, fists pumping, signs and photos seemed to be everywhere.

Dutch shook his head. "No, that's not close enough. Can you bring it in more?"

"Which side?"

Dutch pointed. "To the right of Coyle, over his left shoulder."

Dutch was vaguely aware of the agents around him. He felt as though he were in a trance, just staring at the image. Suddenly he blurted out, "It's her!"

Everyone looked to the screen but no one seemed to notice anything special. Dutch was very excited. "The woman in the t-shirt with red lettering, about," Dutch counted out loud, "one, two, three. Three people to the right of Coyle."

"His right or our right?"

"Our right."

Agents alternated between looking at the screen and looking at Dutch as a close up of the woman took up the screen.

Dutch continued to stare at the woman. Her face didn't ring a bell. She had thick shoulder length black hair with just a hint of grey running through it, dark skin, and very round brown eyes that were accented by worry lines.

"Mort, can you get us a facial recognition trace on this subject?" Nat yelled over to one of the men in the back.

Dutch shook his head. "No. It's not her face. It's something else."

He continued to examine the woman. Her hands caught his attention. They were in plain view, almost folded in front of her body. She held a picture. The picture was rectangular and creased, as though it had been folded a few times.

"It's the picture!" he yelled out. Tapping the man's shoulder he said, "Can you zoom in on the picture she's holding?"

A moment later, every agent yelled out profanity. The large screen was taken up in its entirety by the face of Juan Diego Martinez.

Chapter 30

The next morning, Dutch drove through the busy streets of Washington D.C. He had become quite good at talking on his cell while driving. Nat was briefing him on the latest about the woman now considered a "person of interest" in the investigation.

"We found her file in the CIA database. Her name is Roberta Diego Aguilar. She's the wife of Juan Diego Martinez. They're sending us the file this morning by currier. We should have it in the next hour or so."

"How current is the information we have on her?"

"CIA said it was old. Mostly the information was gathered as a byproduct of their investigation into Martinez."

"Okay Nat, thanks for the update. Keep me posted."

"Where are you, anyway?"

"I'm on my way to see a friend."

Nat sounded like he didn't entirely buy into that, but let it go. "All right. Call me when you're on your way back to the office."

"You got it. Thanks," Dutch clicked off of his cell phone.

He noticed the outside temperature was an unseasonable eighty-seven degrees before he shut off his car and stepped onto the newly seal-coated parking lot of the United States Treasury Building. The smell of tar wafted up, and he took in a long breath. New tar and gasoline were his two favorite smells. They reminded him of growing up in Jersey near a gas station. It always seemed as though the city was digging up the street for a broken pipe or problem with the drainage. The street was paved fresh every summer.

He waited until there was a break in the traffic before crossing 14th Street. He descended into the lower parking lot of the Bureau of Engraving and Printing and entered through a side door.

Once inside, a gush of cool air hit him. He approached the security station and began the all-too-familiar routine of emptying his pockets. He made sure to show his identification before removing his gun. Still, the guard stiffened when he pulled out his Glock. Dutch chose not to carry the standard issue Sig Sauer P229 from the Service. He was attached to the Glock. Although the Sig is technically better for accuracy, no one in the Agency needed additional engineering help from a gun manufacturer on that front. Simply put, Dutch liked the lighter weight and grip of the Glock.

Two other guards immediately walked over to assist him with the security process.

"Good morning, gentlemen," Dutch said casually.

A tall African American guard picked up Dutch's wallet and examined it closely before saying, "Morning to you, Special Agent Brown. May I ask who you're here to see today?"

"Director A.J. Burke. Could you please let him know I'm here? He's expecting me."

As Dutch walked through the metal detector, another guard, this one female but every bit as big as the first guard, motioned him over and held up a wand.

The guard took her time as she passed the wand over every inch of his body once, then twice.

"And I didn't even bring you any flowers," he said.

She continued the sweep without smiling or acknowledging that he even spoke.

"Tough crowd," he said under his breath.

She pointed him back to where his belongings waited in a grey basket. He put his shoes and belt on first, but didn't see his gun.

Before he could ask about it, the large guard who greeted him said, "Treasury policy, Agent Brown. No weapons allowed into the building." He motioned over his right shoulder and said, "It's safely locked away in the gun box against the wall."

"Dutch Brown!" boomed a loud voice from the bank of elevators situated directly in front of him.

A.J. Burke held up his hand, even though he was the only one getting off the elevator. A.J. was shorter than Dutch by about four inches, balding, with a round face and expanding waistline. Dutch knew the man was in his late fifties but thought he looked much older.

Dutch met A.J. a few years before when he was working his first case in Omaha. He needed a crash course on the distribution patterns of serial numbers of a batch of newly minted currency. A.J. was the person who helped educate him. Dutch had been blown away by A.J.'s encyclopedic knowledge about the United States currency.

The men exchanged greetings and A.J. firmly slapped Dutch on the back. Dutch tried not to wince.

"Welcome to my kingdom," he said jovially.

"Thanks. It's a—er—impressive place."

A.J. jabbed a finger into Dutch's midsection. "That's being kind. Don't judge though, this is just the lowly servant's entrance. The people on the tours get to see a much more ornate entryway into the hallowed halls of our money production facility. Come on. I'll give you the private tour." He said and motioned back in the direction he came.

Once in the elevator, A.J. took out a key ring holding about twenty keys and inserted one of them into a lock next to the button that read "LL." The button lit up as the doors closed and the car began its descent.

The elevator stopped at the lowest level and the doors opened. A.J. pointed to the left, and they stepped out into the floor three levels below the street. Although it was well lit, the concrete floors, dull pastel green painted walls, and lack of windows gave the place an eerily dark feel to it.

"This is where the magic happens," said A.J. gesturing proudly. "This lowest level is where all the machines are that print our currency. The floor is broken up into many different rooms, each of which has its own job."

A.J. held a door open for Dutch, and they walked into a room about three thousand square feet in size, most of which was taken up by a large yellow machine standing about twenty feet tall. Dutch noticed a continuous feed of marked paper being fed into one end of it.

The pair passed men and women wearing blue jumpsuit uniforms with their name on one side and "Security Printing" on the other. Some looked at random sheets of uncut bills under microscopes, while others folded, stacked, or bundled the money without even looking at it as if they were carrying a sack of potatoes.

"When you think of it, we run twenty-four hours a day, seven days a week. At any one time we have between fifty and one hundred million dollars drying in our racks."

Dutch's eyes bulged. "Did you say million?"

A.J. chuckled and pointed toward an employee playing to a crowd of tourists watching from a glass enclosed hallway two floors above.

He stood in front of a pallet of uncut sheets of twenty dollar bills that reached about five feet high. It had been shrink wrapped and labeled with barcodes and serial numbers on top. He made a hand printed sign using a black marker at one of the tables. The sign read "$64,000,000." He held up the sign and pointed to the pallet of money in front of him.

"Would anyone notice if I slid one of those sheets out and cut them up myself? It might fit in my pocket."

A.J. smiled. "What the hell do you think I do here, anyway? This place is sealed up tighter than a virgin on prom night. Everything we do here is accounted for in triplicate. See these readouts?" he asked, pointing to the ever-changing LED lights on computer screens located at multiple points on each machine they passed.

Dutch nodded.

"Reports are generated for everything that is printed, packed, weighed, and shipped out the door. It always agrees. If it doesn't, then it's my ass."

When they left the room, their attention was diverted to the end of the building where a large metal door was rolling up and a truck was entering.

"What's that truck bringing in?" Dutch asked.

They walked over as a forklift began unloading huge pallets of something wrapped in brown packaging. A.J. walked over to a pallet that had just been taken down.

"Have you ever seen money before it's printed?"

Dutch shook his head.

"Take a look at this." A.J. sliced open the packaging on one of the stacks.

Dutch looked at the blank ivory paper.

"There are watermarks on it. How did you get paper with watermarks already embedded in it?"

"It arrives like this from the Crane Paper Company in Dalton, Massachusetts. They have the only machines in the nation that can apply the multitude of security features woven into the fabric of the paper we use for our money."

"The only machines?"

A.J. nodded. "Yes. They have been the nation's only paper supplier for one hundred twenty-seven years. It's a third generation family-run business. We supply them with the updates to our watermarks and seals, and they make the paper so it comes to us looking like this."

Dutch looked at his friend and laughed. "That's pretty cool. I've got to hand it to you A.J. You certainly run a tight ship around here."

"Don't be fooled, Dutch. The Treasury isn't immune to the mundane problems all other branches of government have. I'm constantly running around trying to track things down and put out fires, like cost overruns and how to find them before they happen, overtime cutbacks, and budgeting. As a matter of fact, right now I'm working on an ink supply that's inexplicably been running short. There's always something. It drives me crazy, but I love to problem solve. Believe me, this job has no shortage of them."

A.J. directed him toward a steel door and took out what appeared to be a small credit card and swiped it across a black pad. The locks on the door loudly slid to the side.

After walking through, A.J. said, "Last one on the right," pointing to a door at the end of the corridor.

Dutch walked into a windowless room about the size of the briefing room beneath the Oval Office. Along one wall were monitors of what he guessed were every conceivable angle of the factory.

A.J. pointed to a chair. As he sat, A.J. took the seat next to him.

"Okay Dutch, it's just the two of us now. Cut to the chase." A.J.'s voice had taken on a very serious tone.

"Roger Graham. What can you tell me?"

A.J. shook his head. "Nope, I said cut to the chase. No bullshit. What drives you down here to see me?"

Dutch paused as he thought of how to restructure the question. "No easy way to ask without my knowing what you think of him."

A.J. exhaled. "Look, I worked for the man for two years. Straight shooter, no skeletons that can be shared—"

Dutch held up a hand. "What do you mean by that?"

A.J. readjusted himself in the leather backed chair. "Look, Dutch, Graham spent a lot of time undercover with some very bad people. People that America would rather not think about. I didn't know half of what he was involved with. But I do know the shit he's seen and done he doesn't share for damned good reasons."

"Not self-serving?"

A.J. shook his head.

Dutch looked at the bank of screens again.

"Out with it, Dutch. You came here to ask me something. I don't know what it is, but ask."

"A.J., it has to stay in this room."

"No worries. If what you want to know is stuff I can't discuss, I'll tell you flat out. Now shoot."

Dutch hesitated as he sized up the man next to him. Fuck it, he thought, I have to trust someone. Out loud, he asked, "A.J., why is the Nominee for President of the United States meeting with a Mexican drug lord along the border without the knowledge of anyone other than a select few CIA agents he used to work with?"

If the question surprised A.J., he didn't show it. His face remained impassive. Dutch made a living out of watching faces, and this one he just couldn't read. However, the silence that seemed to stretch on was disconcerting. Yet, Dutch didn't want to break it.

After some time, A.J. said, "Dutch, I have no idea."

Dutch slammed his hands on the table. "Cut the shit, A.J., how can you give me a fucking poker face while you do mental calculations for a question you didn't expect?"

"How do you know I didn't expect the question?"

"Did you?"

"I didn't know what you were going to ask, so any question was going to be unexpected."

Dutch stood and began pacing back and forth. "A.J., you told me to cut the bullshit so I did. Now it's your turn. Answer the damned question!"

Instead of standing, A.J. leaned back in his chair and folded his hands across his stomach, twirling his thumbs around one another. He had no smile, and he looked thoughtful and introspective before he replied. "Dutch, I didn't lie to you. I have no idea why Graham would be doing that."

"Don't you want to ask how I know? You don't seem surprised that I even asked the question." His voice rose out of frustration.

"No, Dutch, I don't know how you found out this information. My guess is if I asked you, you'd tell me something I'd be obligated to report. Since I don't want to do that, I'd rather not know."

Dutch could feel his blood pressure rising. "A.J., how can you sit there, calm as hell, throwing these rhetorical answers back in my face?" Dutch leaned in close to his friend and said slowly, "What— is—Roger—Graham—doing—meeting—with—a—Mexican—drug— lord—outside—of—this—country?"

Finally, it was A.J.'s turn to be loud. "Dutch, I don't fucking know, all right?" He stood and ran his hand through what was left of his hair.

He turned his back to Dutch. "You've got to tell my why you want to know this."

"Let's just say that I've heard concerns that he would leave the protection of the Secret Service for hours at a time to go to parts unknown."

"But you found out where he was going?"

Dutch nodded.

A.J. pursed his lips tightly. "Fucking A Dutch, why do you care? Your job is the President, not Graham. Can't you just let it drop?"

Dutch's eyes grew wide. "Let it drop? A.J.! People are dying trying to protect the President. If Graham has something to do with it, you think I should just let it drop?"

"Do you think Graham has something to do with it?"

"Honestly?" Dutch waited until A.J. nodded. "I didn't think there was a connection until I had this conversation with you. Now I'm not so sure."

A.J. loosened his tie and unbuttoned the top of his collar. He walked around to the other end of the table to distance himself from his friend.

"If that's the case then, Dutch, I'm sorry. The last thing I wanted to do was give you the wrong idea about Roger Graham."

"Then tell me what I need to know."

"Damn it Dutch, that's the problem. Most of Graham's past in the CIA I can't talk about. But even if I could, I only handled logistics for his undercover work. I wasn't actually in the field with him. I supplied him with what he needed."

"Then why all the cloak and dagger? Just tell me what I want to know!"

A.J. sat and rested his elbows on the table and put his head in his hands.

"Dutch, look. I know Graham. He's a guy who made it out of deep undercover work for the CIA in once piece, where most people don't have as much luck. I don't know why he'd be still going to Mexico."

"But—"

A.J. stood again. He gave Dutch a steely-eyed look and said, "But I do know that he was deep undercover in the drug trafficking industry. He had the most success of any agent in the field by the time he was pulled."

"Pulled?" Dutch looked surprised. "Why was he pulled?"

A.J. took a long look at his friend. "I only heard rumors."

Dutch remained silent.

A.J. exhaled. "Because it was felt he had become too close to the people he was supposed to be working against."

Chapter 31 – Seven weeks until the election

Meadows silently observed the scene. The President was huddled with her closest advisors around the great seal of the United States of America on the plush carpet. Couches and chairs were filled, bodies leaning inward as if they were trying to keep a secret, but no one else was in the room to hear them. Meadows was part of the woodwork and he preferred it that way. It meant he was doing his job correctly.

"Polling shows you've received a bump in the southeastern states, specifically Alabama and Mississippi," Harvey told President Burton.

"The fundraiser given by Governor Mitchell didn't hurt," Sirois added.

Impassive, Meadows watched as the radio chattered in his ear. Reports from positions around the mansion that usually didn't need to check in were becoming increasingly common. Polk had tightened things up so much the tension was palpable. Meadows could hear it in the voices of agents during briefings and planning sessions. The amount of added layers that earlier would have been considered overkill were now commonplace. What probably bothered him the most, though, were the looks on the faces of the agents he passed in the hallways. No one smiled or exchanged any pleasantries. Brows were furrowed and creased lines seemed to be more pronounced. It was troubling.

Meadows tried to mentally keep track of all the agents and where they were in the mansion. Listening to the communications was like trying to listen to a ball game on the radio.

"Sector 3, keep an eye on the east parking lot. We're supposed to be receiving members from the Minority Caucus in ten minutes. Take them directly to the Roosevelt Room."

"Roger that. How many vehicles?"

"Two. Repeat, two."

"Roger."

Meadows looked at his watch and tried to remain focused, but it was difficult not to hear what was being discussed at any given point in the White House. The meeting in the Roosevelt Room had something to do with a line item budget addition for Capitol security. Members of

Congress were not immune to the protesters of the immigration law that had just passed.

"Thank you for your time, Madame President," Harvey said, standing. Generally, this was the cue that a meeting was either ending on a sour note or ending prematurely due to some contentious issue.

Man, this guy has her back in every way, thought Meadows.

He watched the occupants file out and the President move back to her desk. Now it was only the two of them. She began reviewing a folder Harvey had dropped on her blotter before he left. She picked up her glasses and opened it, quickly scanning the first page before closing the file and throwing her glasses down in a disgusted manner.

Must be bad news, Meadows thought.

She swiveled in his direction. "Agent Meadows."

He tried not to look surprised. "Yes, Madame President."

"May I ask you a personal question?"

This was a first. "Of course you may, Madame President."

"Who did you vote for last election?"

The question came from left field and was so unexpectedly random and out of character that he couldn't help but laugh. Equally surprising, but pleasantly so, was a wide smile she returned.

"Ma'am?"

She continued. "I mean it. I'd like to know who you voted for."

"Madame President, I have to say this is a first. No President has ever asked me that question."

She reached her arms out to either side, giving him a view of her full figure. "Hey, I'm a first on many levels."

"Yes, you are. But Madame President, in this country we tend to keep our votes private."

She smiled at him. "Agent Meadows, please don't make me issue an Executive Order to have you answer the question."

They shared another laugh as she held up one finger. "But I insist on one thing. You tell me the truth."

Meadows smiled and nodded. "I voted for you, Madame President."

She cocked her head to one side as if surprised. "Really? Well, thank you for your vote. May I ask why you did?"

He smiled and shook his head again. She was full of surprises. "Madame President, I thought that you would bring the change in economic thinking that our country desperately needed." The two were silent for a moment before he continued, "And I was right."

185

"Thank you, Agent Meadows, for your honesty."

She stood and walked behind her desk chair to look out the window. As if speaking to herself she said quietly, "But I'm afraid that the national discussion has changed, and I may be on the wrong end of public opinion."

Meadows didn't respond. He left the President to her thoughts.

"Agent Meadows, I'm in the outer office. You are relieved," came a voice in his earpiece.

He quietly turned and opened the door, changing places with Agent Sommers. Meadows took one last look at the President, who was still staring out the window, before closing the door behind him.

"Agent Meadows, please report to my office."

Polk's voice echoed in Meadows's ear. He casually depressed the transmit button from under his sleeve and replied, "Yes, sir, I'll be right there."

It never fails, he thought, looking down at the tray holding his lunch. He had been relieved only five minutes early by Sommers.

"Nat, are you going to be here for a little bit?" he asked Nat Shaklis, who sat two seats down from him.

"Sure, I'll make sure no one cleans it up. When will you be back?"

He pointed to his ear. "Polk's office. Who knows?"

Nat grimaced. "I'll do my best, but no promises if it's more than half an hour."

Arriving in Polk's office, Meadows was surprised to see Dutch Brown seated at the corner of the desk.

"Hey Dutch, how are you doing?" Meadows asked, extending his hand.

"Great," he said sarcastically. "Thanks for asking."

They all sat. Polk leaned forward on his elbows. "Agent Meadows, Agent Brown just came back from the Bethesda Naval Hospital with some bad news. He's got an infection from his surgery, and it has spread. Unfortunately, he won't be cleared for active duty for another two weeks. I wanted you to be the first to know for scheduling purposes."

Meadows nodded.

"I know we're on the clock for the next campaign stop in California and you were hoping Dutch would be there, but that is now out of the question."

"You'll be missed, Dutch," Meadows said.

"Thanks."

"But there's another reason I wanted you to be here, Agent Meadows." Polk turned to Dutch and nodded.

Dutch cleared his throat, looking uncomfortable. "Just before we left for Alabama, I was approached by an agent, who I'd like to keep in confidence at this point, to look into something regarding Roger Graham."

Meadows's eyebrows lifted, but he remained silent.

Dutch looked to Polk, who nodded, then continued. "According to this agent, Congressman Graham has occasionally left his agency detail behind and gone to places unknown with only a contingent of CIA security with him."

Meadows shifted in his chair. "Dutch, that's not the best guarded secret in the Service. I've been getting updates from Agent Rolleston frequently. He's mentioned it multiple times. We've been ordered hands off. I don't think any of us have been happy about it, but we have no choice."

Dutch said, "That's true. But I did some digging and called in a few favors."

Meadows smiled. "Once an investigator, always an investigator."

Dutch pointed to an envelope on Polk's desk.

"I was able to obtain this satellite photograph of the Congressman taken three weeks ago. The man in the picture with him has been confirmed to be Otto Torres, one of the biggest Mexican drug lords in the country, and someone who is wanted by both the CIA and FBI."

Meadows quietly examined the picture.

"Go on," Polk said to Dutch.

"I wasn't sure what to do at this point, so I contacted a friend who works at the Treasury Building."

"A.J. Burke?" Meadows guessed.

Dutch nodded. "He worked in the CIA for many years. More specifically he worked with Roger Graham. A.J. was pretty tight lipped about his time with him, but he did tell me about rumors within the CIA concerning Graham."

Dutch recanted the meeting with Burke at the Treasury.

Polk turned back to Meadows. "Dutch just brought me this information. I felt it was necessary to get you in on it right away. Obviously, there have been no laws broken by Congressman Graham. The only thing we can accuse him of is poor judgment at this point, but I think it's important that you begin a new dialogue with Agent Rolleston. Perhaps even initiate an internal investigation to see if the Congressman has done anything in the last few months that could be linked to the social unrest we've experienced."

Meadows noted how careful Polk was to not say the words "assassination attempts." He looked at Dutch. "What's your take on this? You've got the heavy investigative background."

Dutch paused and seemed to consider the question carefully before answering. "I'm not sure. I'm not on his detail, so it's difficult to judge. I don't like speculating."

"But…" Meadows prompted.

Dutch tilted his head and said, "But with the evidence we've collected on the two attempts on the President's life, I think there's enough here to broaden our way of thinking."

Polk laughed. "That's a clever way to say, 'Leave the CIA the hell out of our investigations.'"

Dutch smiled. "Well, sir, not in so many words. But I think we should be careful what we share moving forward. The CIA hasn't been quick to help us along the line here."

"Yeah, but that's nothing new at Langley. They don't trust anyone. They're worse than the fucking NSA," Meadows said.

"But I think what Dutch just brought us is information worth heeding, at least quietly for now," said Polk.

"Agreed," Meadows said before turning back to Dutch. "May I ask what made you think to go see Burke?"

Polk leaned in, obviously interested.

"He's someone I've worked with in the past when I was stationed in Omaha. His attention to detail is impeccable. I knew even if he wouldn't be able to share direct information with me, he'd find a way to let me know what I needed."

Meadows shook his head. "A stroke of genius. Good job."

Polk stood and the others joined him. He held out his hand to Dutch.

"I agree; great thinking on your feet. Hopefully this is much ado about nothing."

"Thank you," Dutch said shaking his boss's hand.

"And Agent Brown, you are to stay out of here for two full weeks, is that clear?"

Dutch looked hesitant.

"I mean it. You need to let that wound heal and let the antibiotic do its work. I want you back one hundred percent or not at all. Is that clear?"

"Yes, sir."

"Leave the investigations to us. I think it's best if you clear your head and leave the office behind. You've had quite a year, the most eventful for a rookie in recent memory. I think this time off will do you a world of good."

"Thank you, sir. You may be right."

Chapter 32
Six weeks until the election

As Alexis made her way through the lobby of the Ritz-Carlton, she recognized a man who was crossing toward the exit. It was her former boyfriend.

"Peter! Peter Flynn!" Alexis raised her hand excitedly and waved, pointing to a cluster of chairs off to the side.

Peter turned, and it took a moment him to recognize her. "Alexis?"

As he came nearer, she beamed. "What are you doing here?"

"Alexis, I can't believe it's you," Peter said, then scooped her up into a bear hug and spun her around.

She giggled and hugged him tighter. "Oh Peter, it's so good to see you. How are you?"

"I'm fantastic. What a small world!"

"Do you have a minute?" She motioned for him to sit in the plush crushed velvet chairs surrounding them.

"Sure. But forget the lobby. Let's get a drink. We can catch up."

"Okay," she said, smiling widely.

Alexis noticed how empty the hotel lounge was. No surprise really for two o'clock in the afternoon in the middle of the week.

Peter held her hand as she hopped onto the metal collar of the tall black bar stool, which really wasn't a stool at all but a chair.

"Thank you."

"My pleasure," he said taking his seat. "Wow, Alexis Jordan. How long has it been?"

"Six, no… seven. Has it really been seven years?" she asked in astonishment.

"Wow. Time flies. You look exactly the same as the last time I saw you."

She noticed his desperate attempt to keep his admiring eyes from her breasts, which looked, she had to admit, better than ever. She wore her favorite terracotta Tory Burch dress with a deep V neck that was just able to hide her growing secret.

"You too. Wow, you must be living at the gym."

"You're too kind," he said, hands going to his stomach and tapping it loudly. "But I could use some firming up down here. It sucks getting old."

"Oh please, you look damn good to me."

"Alexis Jordan, you're still a great bullshitter," he said not trying to hide his glance this time.

"What in the world are you doing in New York?" he said.

"I'm working for Montgomery now. I'm here on business."

"Really? I didn't know that."

She smiled. "How about yourself? Where are you now?"

"I'm working in Trevor Sirois's office as a number cruncher watching over the billions of tax payer dollars keeping us all safe at night."

"Wow, I didn't know you moved into the government sector. And working for Trevor Sirois? Congratulations."

"Thank you. It's a great opportunity."

"Well, you were always great at your job, and word does get around in the financial world."

He laughed heartily. "Jordan, you haven't changed a bit. You're the only woman who could melt me in seconds." The bartender approached, and Peter said, "Two Jack Daniels, neat, with a side of ice."

"Oh, not for me. I'll just have a glass of ginger ale please."

"Ginger ale? What happened to the Jack Daniels?"

She smiled and flattened out her dress over her stomach.

His eyes widened and his posture straightened. His mouth hung half open for a moment before saying, "You're pregnant?"

She lifted her left hand.

He whistled. "What a rock. Do I know him?"

She couldn't wipe the smile from her face. "Nope. His name is Terrence Brown."

He hesitated, suddenly unsure, before saying, "Congratulations," and leaned over to hug her. She thought it was a bit forced, which made her feel even better.

The drinks arrived interrupting them for a moment.

"Terrance Brown. Why does that name sound familiar?"

"He works for the Secret Service."

Peter's face changed to a look of awe.

"Your fiancé is the agent who saved the President's life?" He leaned back in his chair. "Cut the shit!"

She tried to downplay it. "He was on the detail that was working that day."

Peter dropped all pretenses. "Alexis, you're marrying a hero."

She beamed. "Thank you. We're very happy."

An old fashioned telephone bell ring tone sounded. Peter held up a finger and reached into his pocket to pull out his cell. He looked at the screen and said, "Excuse me."

She took in the ambiance of the nearly empty lounge while he spoke.

"Alexis, I'm so sorry but I've got to run. The secretary needs me for a quick briefing before his meeting. Listen, I'd love to catch up with you later. How long will you be in town?"

"We're beginning to wrap things up. My guess is we'll be flying home in two days."

He finished his drink, jumped off the chair and gave her a hug. "I'm going to be here until tomorrow morning. Maybe we can get together for dinner later?"

She frowned. "I'm sorry, but our executive team is dining together tonight."

"That's no problem. Where will you be?"

"We'll be at the Mandarin Oriental."

"Great. I'll convince the guys to go there tonight. Maybe you and I can hang back at the restaurant and catch up."

She smiled. "If you can swing it, I'd like that."

"See you tonight, then." He flashed a smile, then left.

The concierge was certainly no fool. He was a man in his fifties who had worked for five star international hotels most of his adult life. The only way Dutch was going to get Alexis' room number was to flash his badge, which he did. Not wanting to cause any more attention, he left the lobby for ten minutes, then came back in and walked straight to the elevator. Two minutes later he pulled a key card Whizzer had given him a while ago that would open any hotel room door in the U.S. It worked like a charm and he was in his fiancé's room.

He found the radio and put on some soft music. Opening his duffle bag he produced a bottle of champagne and a couple of candles to set the mood. After getting ice and putting the bottle in the bucket, he lay on the bed and dialed her cell.

"Hello?" Alexis answered.

"Hey sweetheart, it's me."

"Hey you, what's going on?"

"Nothing. I'm bored sitting around so I went online and ordered something to be sent to your hotel room. When are you getting back? I want to be sure it gets there before you do."

Dutch could almost hear her smiling on the other end.

"Terry, you're a hopeless romantic. I should be back in about a half hour. We're just finishing up dinner now."

"Ok, great. Call me and let me know what you think of your surprise."

"Can't you give me a hint?"

"I'll wait for your call. Love you. He hung up, then he looked at his watch and lay back on the bed to wait.

"Oh fuck yeess!" Alexis screamed.

"Already?" Dutch panted as his fiancée pumped her hips harder up and down.

Alexis' face contorted in pleasure as she nodded and bit on her lip trying to contain the next scream. Dutch grasped her hips and moved them faster back and forth. He could feel her tighten as she let out a scream of ecstasy.

She collapsed on him, the top of her head beneath his chin. She let out a long, satisfied breath. He wrapped his arms around her and she shuddered a bit. He could feel her heart beating against his chest as she took in another deep breath, then slowly let it out.

"Ummm. That was...umm..." she said.

Dutch chuckled. "I knew I was good, but this must be a new record." He looked over at the clock. "Five minutes? Wow!"

She kept her face in his chest and laughed. "Do you have a problem with that?"

"No, not at all."

She turned to him and smiled. "I told you this whole pregnancy thing is crazy. Just feeling you inside me is..." she paused, "Just...wonderful."

"Honey, I just want to make sure you're all right. No pains, everything feels normal?"

She smiled and lowered her head, allowing her hair to brush against his face. "Darling, trust me. This has never felt better. I'm fine. She kissed him and whispered, "ready for round two?"

She rolled off and lay next to him, their sweat-soaked bodies melded together. He put his arm around her as she pulled the covers up and snuggled into her favorite "spot" under his arm. She let out a long, contented sigh that sounded more like a coo.

"My thoughts exactly" he said.

"This was one of the best surprises you've ever given me."

"I aim to please. I was going crazy staying home alone and the ten minute phone calls with you just weren't cutting it." He positioned himself on an elbow and turned to face her. "So how's the trip going?"

"Great actually. I'm wrapping up all the big stuff I needed done while I'm here before I go out on maternity leave."

"That's smart. I must be rubbing off on you."

She half chuckled and half snorted, causing them both to laugh.

Then she gently slapped his bare chest and said, "Oh, I knew there was something I wanted to tell you."

"What?"

"You'll never guess who I ran into today at the hotel?"

He raised a finger but she cut him off.

"Forget it, I told you you'd never be able to guess. I saw Peter Flynn today."

"Flynn?"

"Yes, you remember I told you about Peter Flynn. I dated him when I was an intern at Montgomery. Actually, he was my boss."

"I don't remember hearing about him. How old was this guy?"

Alexis gave him a crooked smile and rolled her eyes. "He was barely middle management. I was 21 and he was, I think, 25 when we went out. Anyway, we sat and had a drink."

"Your day was full of surprises. Did you two catch up?"

Alexis looked confused for a brief moment. "Actually we didn't get a chance. He's working for Trevor Sirois and was called out. But he told me he'd try to meet up with me at dinner but never showed. I guess he couldn't make it."

Dutch leaned over and kissed her. "Well, his loss is my gain." Then he turned on his back to let her settle back to her spot as he drew her in closer.

"What do you say we get some sleep?"

Alexis nodded and let out a long, contented sign. Her breath warmed his chest as he stroked her hair.

He stared at the ceiling thinking he couldn't remember a time he was happier. He felt her breathing begin to slow as he gently stroked her head and shoulders. In no time, he heard Alexis's rhythmic breathing that indicated she had fallen asleep.

Dutch jerked up, woken out of a deep sleep. His breathing was heavy and his heart beat wildly, but he didn't know why. He looked at the clock. It read four in the morning. The room was pitch black. He sat still, trying to let his eyes adjust, and rubbed his face, trying to convince himself it was just a bad dream that woke him. Then he reached to the other side of the bed. No Alexis.

"Lexi?" he called out.

No answer.

He felt the bed again. It was warm, but not hot. She'd been out of bed for more than just a few minutes.

"Lexi," he called again, this time a bit louder. Again, no response.

He threw the covers off and sat up. He could make out faint outlines of the bureau, the corners on their four-poster, and the door to the hotel room with the dimmest of light showing through the peep hole. The green numbers of the clock cast an eerie glow.

Dutch looked to the far end of the room to the bathroom. He could see a light on under the door. He clumsily stood and walked over.

"Lexi?" he said knocking softly.

No response. He looked down at the glare reflecting on the carpet. He expected to see the light intermittently broken by a shadow, but there was none.

He knocked louder. "Alexis?"

He opened the door slightly and listened. Nothing.

He looked in and saw the steam on the mirror. The bathroom was hot and the only thing he could think of was she was in the bathtub. He took a cautious step in and turned to look toward the tub, and his heart stopped. Alexis' pale, naked body lay motionless in bloody water.

He yelled her name and lunged forward to pull her upright, feeling her cool skin that was cast eerily white from the loss of blood. Her eyes were open, but they didn't seem to register he was there. He felt for a pulse but couldn't find one. With a shaking hand, he pushed on her neck a little harder. He could feel the feeblest of a pulse.

"Alexis! Alexis! Can you hear me?" He shook her limp body, causing more blood to seep from underneath her. "Alexis!" he screamed again.

He felt as though he was observing someone else cradling Alexis' limp body. He was brought back to reality when her eyes moved and opened slightly. There was no smile, no hint as to what was going on.

He cradled her head and held her close. He could tell she knew he was there, but she couldn't seem to show any expression or speak. His eyes darted to the bloody water, and he tried to calculate how much she had lost. He wanted to rush over to the phone by the sink but was afraid if he let go she might leave him.

She seemed to momentarily focus on him, then he watched helplessly as her eyes rolled back in her head and the life drained from her.

"NO!" he screamed, hoping it wasn't too late. He lifted her out of the bloody water yelling, "No, no, no!" He held tightly to her lifeless body, not wanting to let go.

Chapter 33

After Alexis's coffin was lowered into the ground, most of the people dispersed, leaving only family and close friends. In a misty rain, they embraced and shared words of condolence. To Dutch, it had all been a blur.

A hand reached up and clutched his left shoulder. Dutch turned and saw his boss, Bill Polk.

"Dutch, this was such a terrible shock. I want you to take all the time you need to put everything in your life back together the best you can. Your job will be here when you're ready."

Dutch smiled with gratitude while fighting back the rapidly rising lump in his throat. "Thank you, sir. I really appreciate it."

Dutch watched Polk walk to his car. It seemed like half the Secret Service had attended the funeral. He had overheard more than one person lightheartedly mention that they hoped the President was in the White House because there wouldn't be enough agents to protect her if she ventured out.

The agency cars pulled away. Dutch watched as they disappeared, grateful for the support of his colleagues. Another hand grasped his right shoulder. He turned to see a very grim-faced Michael Harvey.

"Mr. Harvey, I'm sorry. I didn't realize you were here."

Harvey held up a kind hand and said, "Please, call me Michael. And of course I wanted to be here to give you my support, as well as the President's. Dutch, I can't tell you how much your loss has reverberated around the White House. Alexis was a very special woman."

Dutch nodded and watched the Chief of Staff choke up a bit as he spoke. "Every time I met her she always seemed to light up the room. Dutch, I'm so, so sorry."

Dutch was touched at this genuine display of emotion.

"Oh, before I forget." Harvey reached into his coat pocket and pulled something out. "The President wanted me to make sure I handed you this."

Dutch took a folded piece of stationary with the Presidential seal on the front. He glanced under the fold and saw it to be a handwritten note from the President. He accepted it without reading and tucked it in the breast pocket of his overcoat.

"Thank you, Michael. This means a lot to me." He turned and motioned at the various family members gathered around in a semi-circle. "As well as our families."

Michael patted him a couple of times on the shoulder. "Please know that if there is anything we can do for you…." The rest went unsaid. It wasn't needed.

Dutch felt himself getting choked up again. The quintessential politician most likely knew the time to exit had come and deftly turned and walked away.

Another arm slid under his and grabbed his hand tightly. It was Sandy Ludec. She had been a rock throughout the entire ordeal. Without her help, he never would have gotten through this.

"How are you doing?" she said softly.

He looked and saw her crooked smile and deep, caring eyes watch him. They were the eyes of someone who knew exactly what he was going through.

Dutch nodded silently.

Her free hand tapped him on the lapel of his suit and the two stood quietly as the remaining mourners filed past.

After some time Dutch said, "A placental abruption. What were the chances again?"

Sandy quickly said, "Terry, don't do this to yourself. The doctors said there was nothing more that could have been done. She didn't do anything wrong, you didn't do anything wrong." She paused for a few more seconds before continuing, "Sometimes…sometimes bad things just happen. There's no right or wrong explanation for it. But beating yourself up over it won't help."

Dutch nodded solemnly. He heard the words, he just didn't believe them.

Dutch took one last look at the coffin, flowers overflowing from the passing mourners. He and Sandy soberly walked to the waiting limousine. As soon as they stepped inside and the door closed, the heavens opened up and the steady rain turned into a downpour.

Roger Graham's limo stopped and doors on either side sprung open. His staffers began to climb out, umbrella's unfurled.

Roger motioned for Simon to stay as he leaned toward the door and shouted, "Everyone go on, I'll be right out."

Once the doors closed, Roger said, "What do you have for me?"

Simon kept an impassive expression on his face. It conjured up an image of a tribal mask Roger had seen in some museum.

"His name is Richard Flecca. Within the agency he goes by the nickname of 'Whizzer.'"

"Whizzer?"

"My sources tell me it stems from a derivation of 'whiz kid.' He's worked with the Secret Service for seven years."

"That's quite a long time for someone in his mid-twenties." He paused and considered. "Do we know for sure it was him?"

Simon nodded, but otherwise betrayed no emotion. His unperturbed attitude was beginning to get on even Roger's nerves. He chalked it up to the pace of the campaign.

"Do we know how he did it?"

Simon shook his head. "We got lucky when we ran a trace for sealed files hacked into at the same time as the satellite re-positioning. Otherwise, we wouldn't have known it was a computer from the Service that hacked our database. It took a while to narrow which state it originated from. Once we hit on Nebraska it was easy. Everyone I talked with said it could only be one person."

Roger took a moment. "All right, you know what to do next."

Simon began moving, but Roger shot out a hand and grabbed him by the forearm. Even this didn't draw any emotion from the stone-faced man.

Roger looked him squarely in the eyes. "Simon, make sure you get this done quickly, all right?"

Simon nodded and reached for the phone behind his head as Roger stepped out. He was welcomed with a roar of applause. He put on his best campaign smile and waved to the crowd.

Chapter 34
Three weeks before the election

"A statistical dead heat? What the hell does that even mean?" Lorraine Burton asked rhetorically, throwing a copy of *USA Today* on the coffee table.

Patti Harris began to raise her arm in response but Harvey held it down, silently shaking his head. He tried not to touch the last remaining bandage on her arm that was the only visible remnant from the assassination attempt in which she was injured.

"Michael," the President said in an almost desperate tone.

Harvey motioned for her to sit.

"Madame President, these polls can be very misleading. According to our calculations, the key demographics in many of the battleground states favor you."

"Favor me? That means about as much as a statistical dead heat." She stabbed a finger at the paper.

"What it means, Madame President," began Patti, "is that Congressman Graham's surge in the polls may have peaked, and he is beginning to lose ground in those key precincts."

Lorraine looked at Patti and let out an exhausted breath. "So with three weeks left, what do we need to do?"

"Madame President, all indications are that your last campaign swing through Florida, Louisiana, and Texas next week will go a long way in determining the outcome of this election. Polling indicates if those southern states begin to swing back in your favor, you may see the trend continue with the rest of the Southeast. If that happens, then Graham is sunk."

Lorraine looked around the room, not wanting to share her feelings on the matter. Although the news from her press secretary was encouraging, she didn't relish the thought of traveling to the southern region of the United States again. Two attempts on her life were enough to keep the undercurrent of fear front and center in her consciousness. She made quick eye contact with the secret service agent standing post at the door, then quickly looked away, hoping no one could read her mind. This insecurity was something she couldn't even share with Michael in private. A crack in her armor in front of the people in this room could be a big mistake. She needed to focus on the matter at hand and put aside, for now, her hesitations.

She looked at Harvey. "All right, I can buy that. So what do we need to focus on during this trip?"

"It's time to pull out all the stops. Our team feels that the focus of these last stops should target your strongest suit, which of course is the economy. Beyond that, highlighting the successes you had in trimming the national deficit and identifying and cutting the traditional 'pork barrel black holes,' as you coined the phrase during your last campaign."

Lorraine nodded thoughtfully. "Bring in Trevor Sirois for the last push?"

Harvey held his hand to his chin and nodded. "By having the Secretary of Homeland Security accompany you on this trip, it will underline one of the biggest successes you've had in managing the out-of-control spending Washington has suffered from for years. During your term, for the first time since its inception, Homeland Security has not requested a budget increase."

Lorraine looked off in the distance and tried to clear her mind. She could feel her muscles loosen and her shoulders lower.

"I see where you're headed with this. I like it. It's different. It's flashy. It will make for good sound bites. How about the local politicians who'll meet us along the way?"

Harvey looked at his notebook. "The Governor at each stop would love some face time with you. That's a lock."

Lorraine allowed her first smile of the day. "That's good. That's really good. I like this idea more and more. Who's writing for Sirois?" she asked her Press Secretary.

"I've got Hammill on it. She's completing the last of three speeches the Secretary can choose from. He may edit as he feels necessary, but—"

The President cut her off. "Bullshit! Sirois couldn't improvise his way out of a paper bag once the cameras are rolling. I want those speeches bulletproof, no room for editing. Do you understand?"

Patti made a note and nodded.

Harvey rose and said, "All right then. Patti, you have your marching orders. Madame President, thank you for your time."

Lorraine looked at them. "Let's make sure this trip is flawless. My reelection may just depend on it."

She couldn't help looking at the agent in the corner once more, hoping that the Service felt the same way she did. Only instead of an election, it was her life on the line.

Dutch clicked off the television. He had been watching a news clip of the President delivering a campaign speech. He used to watch these clips with a discerning eye, seeing if he could pick out the faces of fellow agents who were on the security detail. Now he couldn't care less.

It had been a three weeks since Alexis died. Dutch looked around the living room that used to be kept meticulously neat. Now, fast food wrappers were strewn on the floor and the glass coffee table had rings where wet containers had carelessly been placed. He was on the couch wearing a loose fitting pair of boxers and his Navy t-shirt that he hadn't washed because there was still a trace of Alexis's scent on it. It had been her favorite shirt to wear when they were kicking around the house.

The doorbell rang. Dutch yelled out, "It's open!"

Byron Meadows entered, closed the door, and walked to the middle of the dimly lit room. Dutch watched him look left to the kitchen, where a table full of various meals in different stages of decay sat unattended. Then he turned to his right where a mantle held pictures of Alexis and Dutch. It was the only part of the apartment that wasn't in disarray. All the curtains were closed, keeping the sunlight of a beautiful day out of this depressing setting.

"Hello, Byron."

Meadows didn't say anything. He didn't even make eye contact, instead choosing to place his hands on his hips and continue his visual assault of Dutch's apartment.

"Can I get you something to drink?"

Meadows walked past him, kicking away the clothes that littered the floor. "What the fuck are you doing?" His voice was loud, almost yelling.

Dutch's eyes shot open in disbelief. For weeks he had a parade of people coming by expressing their condolences, being kind, being quiet. He had grown accustomed to it. What was this all about?

"Excuse me?"

This time Meadows did yell. "I said what the fuck are you doing? This place has become a shithole, and you've let yourself go to hell. You should be ashamed."

Michael's stomach twisted and his heart skipped a beat. It felt like his blood was pooling at his feet.

"Byron, I just lost my fiancée."

"It's Agent Meadows to you! You call yourself a Secret Service agent?"

"Well, right now I'm—I mean, I haven't been out in—"

"Cut the bullshit! I don't want to hear it. Do you think you're someone special? Do you think you're the first to ever lose someone? Do you?"

Dutch shook his head.

"Where the hell have you been? How come you haven't been at work?"

"Agent Polk told me to take my time coming back."

"Agent Polk?" he asked incredulously. "Agent William Polk?"

Dutch nodded. "He's even offered to bring by files on the open investigations."

Meadows waived his hand agitatedly. "Never mind, I don't want to get into this now. What about the Service's shrink? What did he say?"

Dutch shook his head. "I haven't seen one."

Meadows looked stunned. "What? You haven't had to come in and sit with Doctor Nyberg? Who the hell has been working with you these last few weeks?"

"Well, no one sir. Just Agent Polk."

Meadows looked dumbfounded. "That all ends today! Go take a shower, then get dressed for work."

When Dutch didn't move, Meadows yelled, "Right now, Agent Brown!"

Dutch spun and walked quickly to the bathroom.

The President didn't even try to conceal her yawn. She had been sitting at the conference table in the situation room for an hour listening to a security briefing for her upcoming campaign swing down South.

Bill Polk droned on and on about all sorts of security arrangements.

"We leave the Hilton Bentley from the underground garage. Since it will be no secret where we'll be emerging from, Major Hadley I want to be sure we have the best anti-terrorist detachment on that quadrant looking for anything even remotely considered a threat. They need to be stationed here, here, over here, and here." Polk shined the laser pointer over the entry points to the parking garage.

The President looked over to a thirtyish-looking major in an army uniform, who furiously scribbled what she assumed were names as he took note of the locations indicated.

Bill's brining in the big guns, she thought to herself as she pursed her lips and let a "hum" escape under her breath.

"Excuse me, Madame President?" said Harvey.

She shook her head dismissively.

"I thought you'd appreciate having input for security on this trip."

"Michael, I haven't had input since my car got blown up. Everyone else has, though. And while we're on the subject," her whispered voice grew louder, "don't think for a moment the voting public hasn't noticed. Statistical dead heat Michael?"

The President sat back in disgust. The polling was troubling, but what was worse was this security briefing. Without knowing it, her Chief of Staff was making her sit through her worse nightmare. She could feel her fear growing exponentially. She was trying her best not to let it show, but she wasn't sure how long that would last.

Polk stopped for a moment, then said, "Madame President, would that be to your satisfaction?"

The President smiled. "Yes, that does sound like a good idea." Lorraine hoped she just agreed to something worthwhile because she never heard the question.

She leaned back and tried to shake off the re-occurring thought of her head being blown off while speaking on the podium.

Harvey, sensing Lorraine's discomfort, got Polk's attention.

"Ah, Bill, if you don't foresee anything else that would need the President's input, we've got some pressing issues back in the Oval Office."

"No, that's fine. Thank you for your time Madame President."

Lorraine stood, and a cacophony of scraping chairs echoed around the room as the occupants stood with her.

Dutch had to work to keep up with the fast pace Meadows set as they walked along the concrete sidewalk leading into headquarters. He fumbled in his shirt pocket for sunglasses. He hadn't had them on since he was last on duty, but the sun hurt his eyes. He hadn't been outside much lately. Even the brisk pace was causing him to breathe heavily. He cursed himself for falling out of shape so quickly. But sitting on a couch watching movies and eating take out for weeks could do that to a person.

Re-emersion into the workplace and the well-wishers was the part Dutch dreaded. Enough people had expressed their condolences. He just wanted to get back to work and not have to think about Alexis.

Meadows didn't let up as they rounded the corner. Dutch didn't know if he was in trouble. But the shower, dressing in a clean suit, and taking in the fresh air had done wonders to clear his mind.

While Dutch was following Meadows to the office, he actually began thinking about work again. It had been a long time since that had happened. Suddenly he found himself wanting to get back to work, needing to get back. The cold slap across the face Meadows had figuratively applied seemed to shake the gloom off him.

Dutch was still breathing heavily as they reached the office and headed inside. Meadows stopped in the lobby and pulled Dutch to the side, out of earshot.

"All right, here's what's going to happen. I got you here, now you're going to head upstairs to the third floor, get to your desk, say hello to everyone, and then get your ass back to work. Agent Brown, do you have any questions?"

Dutch looked nervously at Meadows. Suddenly Meadows's face twisted into a beaming smile and his eyes brightened. A rush of relief hit Dutch like a ton of bricks. He held out his hand, and Meadows took it firmly and warmly, patting him on the shoulder as they shook.

"Thank you" Dutch said meaning it.

Meadows turned and threw his hands over his ears and walked away. The message was clear; his job was done. He didn't want thanks for helping out a fellow agent. Dutch watched him walk back outside, headed for the White House. He wondered who Meadows had lost in his own life that could give him the insight to know exactly what Dutch needed.

There wasn't time to think about it. Dutch was eager to get back to work. He smiled and flashed his credentials at the guard, wished him a good day, and walked through security and into the elevator.

He grimaced at the avalanche of paperwork and phone messages on his desk that greeted him. He sat down hard and laughed out loud at the mountain of work.

A steaming white styrofoam cup was thrust in front of him. He looked up to see Nat standing there with his own coffee in hand, smiling.

"Welcome back," Nat said. "We've missed you."

Dutch lifted the cup. "Thanks. It's good to be back." Then he pointed with his free hand to the pile on his desk and said, "At least I think it is."

Nat motioned to the right with his head. "Come on, that can wait."

"Where are we going?"

"You need to get brought up to speed. I'm not going to be your nursemaid while you take your sweet time getting back in the groove of things."

They descended to the room Dutch had spent so much time in during the assassination investigations. The room had about a quarter of the people than the last time he was there. The far right side was still occupied by agents continuing the investigation of the attempt on the President's life. Dutch saw some familiar faces.

They looked up and smiled at Dutch, exchanged pleasantries, and buried their faces back in the files. Dutch took another sip of coffee and was grateful for there not being any mention of Alexis during the banter. It was all business as usual in the room. He had never been more grateful for that in his life.

"Dutch, these guys have prepared a folder for your review. Basically, it sums up where we're at since you were last here."

Nat pointed to a pair of thick folders bound together by a large rubber band. "Agent Brown" had been scribbled on top in black marker. Dutch reached for them, but Nat held up his hand to stop him. "Hold on a minute. There's plenty of time for you to pore over everything."

"Well, can you give me the abridged version of where we're at?"

Nat motioned to Agent Zimmerman, who put down his file and leaned back in his chair, twirling a pen with the White House logo printed on it.

"Basically Dutch, we're not where we expected to be this far into the investigation."

Dutch laughed. "Come on, Zimmerman. Really, where are we at?"

The man didn't smile. "Oh, so you didn't like the abridged version?"

Dutch looked from Zimmerman to Nat.

Zimmerman said, "Well, that's not one hundred percent true. We're nowhere closer to finding out who planted the Bouncing Betty. But we do know a little more about the device itself. We were able to piece together some of the larger fragments that survived the explosion and found partial serial numbers on some of the components. But even the partials can tell us a lot. We now know it belonged to the U.S. Military. According to records, the Bouncing Betty that almost took out the President was supposed to be locked up in a weapons depot at the White Sands Missile Range in New Mexico."

Dutch raised an eyebrow. "No easy feat to get that kind of weapon out of an Army base."

Zimmerman continued. "Now here's where you come in. We finally got a hit on Roberta Diego Aguilar."

"Show me what you've got" Dutch said.

Zimmerman slid a thin manila file toward Dutch who opened it and removed a single sheet of paper.

"350 Allen Place, Apartment 3, Washington D.C." recited Zimmerman as Dutch read the address written on the paper. "She's all yours Agent Brown."

Dutch looked between the two agents.

"Do you want some company on the trip?" Nat said.

Dutch eyed him suspiciously. "Is that a genuine question?"

Nat laughed. "Actually no, but I thought it would sound better if I asked. You need someone with you when you go interview her."

"You don't trust me?"

"Yes, I do. But it's standard protocol."

"All right. When do you want to head out?"

Nat looked at his watch. "Give me ten and I'll be ready."

"I'll wait for you outside."

Dutch exited the building and headed to the newsstand on the corner. He paid for the Washington Post and opened the paper, feigning interest. He walked a few steps to the side of the newsstand and sat in a fold up chair that was always there. He unbuttoned his coat and leaned back with the paper, enjoying the warm sun on his face.

Just off to the right of him was a hunched, slovenly looking man who was sweeping the cracked concrete sidewalk. He was the real reason Dutch frequented this particular newsstand.

Willie Tanner was a fixture in and around the square block of H Street and 9th, located one block from the Secret Services offices. The owner of the newsstand allowed the homeless man to stay and "earn his keep" by sweeping up and straightening the magazines and newspapers that people left unceremoniously askew.

Upon first laying eyes on Willie, it was apparent there was something wrong. He stood an extremely hunched, almost bowing, five foot seven with thin, wispy grey-brown hair and a sunken face. The wrinkles made him look older than the fifty-five his driver's license would have said he was, if he had one. Willie's eyes never came into direct contact with anyone who spoke with him, and he nervously shifted from one foot to the other, mumbling frequently.

Willie possessed two unique traits, however. The first was he was legally blind. Although he could see things close up, once he tried to focus on anything outside of his reach they became blurry shapes. Ironically, his physical limitation helped fuel his second curious trait.

The most unique ability Willie Tanner possessed was something most didn't take the time to learn about. Dutch did, and it paid dividends ever since he first started working in D.C.

Willie was an idiot savant. He could remember pieces of conversations that he heard and could recite them verbatim years after the fact. What might be innocuous babble between two people could live in the recesses of Willie's brain for years afterward.

To the untrained, it might have seemed like a computer with an overloaded hard drive full of useless spam. To Agent Dutch Brown, it was an invaluable resource. Particularly since Willie spent fourteen hours a day within a thousand yards of the Secret Service offices.

"Hey Willie, what's shaking?" Dutch said to the man.

"Ha—he—hello Agent Terrance," said Willie."

Dutch shook his head. Beside Alexis, Willie was the only other person who called him by his given name. He dismissed the thought quickly and focused on Willie.

"Willie, how have you been?"

"Fi…fine. A.agent T.t.ttt.terrance, I'm sorry t..to hear about Alexis." Willie fidgeted a bit quicker. Even he was uncomfortable with the subject.

"Thank you Willie" Dutch said, continuing to feign reading the paper.

"Ag..agent P.p.pp.Parker said you, you, you weren't coming b.b..back. I..I..I'm glad he was wr..wrong."

"Putz," Dutch whispered under his breath. If half the agents knew what Willie picked up by just walking around listening, they'd shit.

"Well Willie, I'm back now. What's the word on the street?"

"Wi..Widow is n..ne..nervous. P.Polls aren't good ne..ne..news for her."

"Yeah, it looks like it's going to be a close one."

Dutch lowered the paper and watched the man methodically sweep around the newsstand. It was good to see Willie again.

Nat approached him. "You ready?"

"Yup, be right there." He waited until Nat was out of earshot and turned to Willie and handed him a five dollar bill. "Keep it real, Willie."

"Always do," Willie said taking the money without ever making eye contact with his friend, Agent Terrance.

Chapter 35

Dutch stood outside a weather beaten door badly in need of a coat of paint. He pushed the cracked doorbell and heard a faint chime inside the apartment. After a moment he and his partner could hear rustling, then a figure peeked through a ripped curtain. Dutch recognized the face immediately.

Roberta Diego Aguilar slowly opened the door, just enough for her face to fit between the frame. She was of modest height and looked to be in her late fifties with heavy wrinkles and dark eyes.

"May I help you?" she said in a thick Hispanic accent.

Dutch held up his Secret Service credentials and said, "Ms. Aguilar, my name is Agent Brown," he pointed behind him to Nat who also had his credentials opened. "And this is my partner, Agent Shaklis. We're from the United States Secret Service. We would like a minute to speak with you, if you don't mind."

Dutch knew it wasn't really a question. They had the authority to bring her into the office to question her if she refused to speak to them here. He fully expected her to be difficult and was prepared with a multitude of arguments to ensure her cooperation. But he never expected what came next.

She threw open the door and waived them into her apartment.

"Good, good. Yes, yes, I'm glad you're here."

Dutch looked at Nat who shrugged, and they entered.

She escorted them into a small dining room furnished modestly with a simple oak table, two chairs, and a small cabinet that held a few decorative plates. By the look of things, it appeared Ms. Aguilar lived by herself and wasn't used to getting company. She momentarily left the room and came back a minute later with a third chair that she put opposite the agents and sat down. She motioned for them to do the same.

"Why you take so long to come?"

Dutch tried to hide his surprise. He said, "Ms. Aguilar, were you expecting us?"

"Si, yes. Because of my husband. You know my husband? He was killed. His name was Juan. Juan Diego Martinez."

Dutch shot a look at his partner who looked just as confused.

"Ms. Aguilar, we do know about your husband," Nat said.

She looked at the two agents. "So, you will help?"

"Help you? Help you with…" Dutch started, but Nat tapped his foot and interrupted.

"Ms. Aguilar, what may we help you with?"

She looked surprised. "My husband, he was murdered by the government."

Neither agent hid their surprise.

"Yes, he was murdered. The government promised my family green cards. But they killed him."

"Who promised you green cards Ms. Aguilar?" Nat said.

"The government. The U.S. government."

"Ms. Aguilar, the government doesn't promise green cards to anyone," Dutch said.

She held up a finger and shakily stood and left the room. The pair exchanged looks but she was back in a moment holding something.

"Here" she said, thrusting the green card to Nat, who examined it then passed it to Dutch.

He turned it over, flexed it, and could tell it was authentic. After reading the information on it, he slid it back to Nat keeping his finger next to the issuing date. It read one week before the assignation attempt that killed Harry.

Dutch said, "Ms. Aguilar, who gave this to you?"

"The government."

"Yes, but who in the government?"

She shrugged her shoulders. "I don't know. My husband, he talks to the men from government. He came home with green cards for our family."

"Who in your family received them?" said Nat.

"Me, my sister, my..um, *sobrinas*, I mean Nieces."

"How about your husband?" Dutch said.

She shook her head. "No, the government, they say he had to do a job before he got his. That's all he told me."

"Who told you this, your husband?"

"Si."

"Who did you speak with in the government?" said Nat.

211

"Me? No, I no speak with the government. My husband, he speak to them. He got green cards for us and sent us here. He say he come in a week, but he never come. They kill him."

Dutch and Nat shared a look before Dutch said, "Ms. Aguilar, do you know how your husband was killed?"

She grew louder and sounded more desperate. "Si, the government."

Dutch shook his head and interrupted her. "No, I mean do you know how he was killed?"

"A man came here, from the government. He said my husband was dead. He said it was an accident, but I no believe him."

"Why did you not believe him?" Nat said.

"My husband tell me before he died, no trust these men. He said he not do job until we were in United States. He say goodbye to me, but I know something was wrong. I know he knew something bad was going to happen."

Dutch decided to switch gears. He pulled out an envelope containing still photos of the protesters the day the Bouncing Betty went off.

"Ms. Aguilar, who were all those people yelling at the President, and who were in the photos they were holding?"

See briefly looked at the photos. "We are Americans. We have rights. We no like this President, no like the law she passed. We just want to come to America and live, work, be happy."

"Did you know these people?" Dutch asked pointing at some of the faces in the photos.

She looked curiously at Dutch. "Some, yes, not all. Some live near here. We do nothing wrong. We no try to kill the President."

"Can you tell me where these people live?" Dutch said.

She looked skeptically at him, but seemingly wanting to cooperate she wrote a few names and addresses on a piece of paper sitting on the table.

"And who were the pictures of these people you were holding?" Nat asked while she was writing.

Without looking up she said, "Family who are dead."

When neither agent said anything she stopped writing and looked up. "Dead, *muerto*. These people in the pictures, they all dead."

"How did they die?" Dutch asked.

She resumed writing. "They all died trying to come to this country. Some die trying to swim across Rio Grande. Some die because they carry drugs and were sent back to Mexico. The drug lords, they kill them because they get caught. Some die in desert because no food or water. It's bad, very bad. We want to show this President faces of real people who die to come here."

"Ms. Aguilar, did you watch any television and see who tried to kill the President this summer?" Dutch said. He wanted so badly to be furious at this woman but she may not even know what her husband tried to do.

"Television, no, me no watch television." She pointed around the room. From the looks of things, there wasn't a television to be seen anywhere in the cramped apartment.

"Ms. Aguilar, I have one more question, and this is very important." She looked at Dutch.

"Have you spoken with anyone from the government since you've been here in Washington?"

She shook her head. "No, but I call. The number, it's no good."

Dutch shot Nat a look. "Do you have this number?"

She held up a finger and stood, leaving the room once more. In a moment she was back holding a business card. She handed it to Dutch.

He turned to Nat and read, "Casey Ondrus, United States Department of Naturalization and Immigration. His phone number is on the card."

Ms. Aguilar shot back, "That number, it no good. I try it. You try it, it no good."

"Who gave you this card?" Dutch asked.

"My husband. He said this man will help us when we get here. I call, but the number is no good."

"Ms. Aguilar, may we keep this card?" Nat asked.

She shrugged her shoulders. "It's no good, it's trash. You keep."

Nat pocketed it and the two agents stood to leave. Dutch reached into his jacket pocket and pulled out his business card and handed it to her.

"Ms. Aguilar, if anyone from the government comes here to talk with you, please call me. That's my number, and it works."

She looked skeptically at it, but put it in a pocket.

"What the fuck?" Nat exclaimed once they were back in their car.

Dutch, still holding the fake business card said, "Well, I think we're a lot closer to a motive now. It was a suicide mission just to get his family to America. That explains a lot."

"Sure, but now it brings more questions than it answers."

"True, but at least we have a direction to go in now."

Nat looked puzzled. "Direction? What direction? Did I miss something?"

Dutch paused, making sure to choose his words carefully.

"Nat, who can produce green cards without going through the normal channels?"

"I suppose the INS since they are the ones who approve them."

Dutch laughed at his partner and said, "Even the INS gets bogged down in their own red tape. They can't move that quickly. Think again. What is the one agency in our government that can cut through any departmental red tape, legally or illegally, whenever they want?"

Nat shrugged his shoulders.

"Okay, let me take it a step further. Which agency can do all that and have the ability to identify and work with assets residing outside the United States?"

Nat's face dropped. "The CIA."

"Bingo!"

"Son of a bitch. Dutch! You're right."

"But now this opens up a series of problems that we have to be very careful with."

"Series of problems? What do you mean?"

Dutch pursed his lips and said, "I'll put this as bluntly as I can. What would happen in this country if the Secret Service launched a public investigation into the CIA for possibly having a hand in the attempted assassination of the sitting President three weeks before an election? Now pile on the fact that her opponent for the nation's highest office has direct ties with said agency?"

"Mother fucker! So you're saying Roger Graham is behind this?"

"We're talking a total breakdown in the confidence of the American democratic process. Just think what would happen if Roger Graham were implicated. The public would immediately assume he was trying to kill his competition. Whether it turned out to be true or not wouldn't matter. It's the appearance of impropriety. And with two weeks to go until the election, Nat, we're talking about something unprecedented in the history of our country."

"Then the conspiracy theorists would take it to the next level and accuse the CIA of trying to manipulate the government to its own advantage—"

"And the fact that Graham has a CIA attachment along with the Secret Service. You see where this is going?"

"Dutch, you're brilliant. But if you're right, then we've got to move fast on this. What should we do next?"

"First, I'll need you to take a detachment of agents to follow up on those people on the list Aguilar gave us. My guess is you'll find her story checks out, but we've got to follow protocol, especially if this thing blows up on us. We're walking a tightrope here. I'll also need you to let Polk know what we've found out."

Nat nodded and said, "Okay, where are you going?"

Dutch allowed a slight smile as he flicked the fake business card between his fingers.

"I've got to meet someone who can quietly kick over rocks faster than anyone I know."

After dropping Nat back at the office, Dutch pulled into an empty parking lot and dialed the number from memory. It wasn't part of his saved contacts or address book in his cell phone. Whizzer made him promise to never put it in there. At the time, Dutch laughed and called him a wacko for having conspiracy theories. But through years of observing the number of things Whizzer was able to find out using his computer, Dutch was slowly coming around to his eccentric friend's way of thinking.

The phone rang five times. It was strange for Whizzer not to answer his cell phone. Dutch checked his watch. It was eight o'clock. With the one hour time difference, it was still just seven o'clock in Omaha.

On the sixth ring, the voicemail picked up. There was the familiar silence where there should have been an outgoing message as was Whizzer's trademark, then the beep associated with leaving a message.

Dutch punched off, waited a moment, and then hit redial. Whizzer always told him he didn't check his voice mail because it was too easy to hack. Therefore, anyone who needed him had to get the message to him some other way.

Again on the sixth ring came the silence. Dutch snapped shut his cell. He knew Whizzer didn't have a home phone for reasons he never fully explained, so that wasn't an option. He looked at his watch again.

Maybe Whizzer had been called into work for something. Dutch opened his phone and dialed another number.

"Omaha Secret Service," a matronly woman's voice answered.

Even at seven o'clock there was always someone on duty to answer the phone at the Secret Service.

"Hello, Dottie. It's Dutch Brown. How are you?"

"Dutch! Gosh, it's good to hear your voice. When are you coming back to visit us? It's not every day we get an honest-to-God hero stopping by."

Dutch ran a hand through his short cropped hair and smiled.

"Soon, Dottie. I promise. I miss you guys. But listen, I've only got a couple of seconds to talk. Is Whizzer in the office? He's not answering his cell."

She paused. "It's funny you should ask."

Dutch's heart sped up at the tone of voice Dottie used. It took a lot to rattle her, but she sounded like something was wrong.

"He hasn't reported in for a week. Ken Needle's been furious. Plus, he can't seem to find out which branch borrowed him. And you know Whizzer, he never thinks to call in when he gets temporarily reassigned on short notice."

"Well, you know how in demand he is." Dutch said, almost trying to convince himself everything was all right. "But even for Whizzer, that seems a bit long."

"I know, and so does Ken. He sent someone to his house yesterday hoping to get lucky. He wasn't home, and from what the agent said it looked like he hadn't been home in a while."

Now Dutch was really concerned. "Dot, do you know what was he working on the last time he was in the office?"

"No, but let me find out, just give me a second. Now let's see…" Dutch heard drawers opening and papers being shuffled. "Ah, here it is. He was working on a project for Mike Naylor."

The blood in Dutch's veins froze and he almost dropped his phone.

Mike Naylor was a decoy name he and Harry used when they needed Whizzer to work on something sensitive in nature. Most of the time the work put in the Mike Naylor file had something to do with bending the law to its breaking point.

"Ah, Dottie, how long ago was this?"

More shuffling. "According to his time log, he had been tasked to begin working on something classified for Agent Naylor…, hmm, that's funny. He began working on something and no one has heard from him since."

"All right, Dottie, thanks. It was good talking with you." He hung up before hearing Dottie's good-bye.

Dutch's heart was racing. He tried to think of a way to find his friend. He watched cars on the street drive past, people going about their evening without the crashing weight that Dutch was beginning to feel descend around him.

Suddenly he snapped his fingers and remembered the cell phone Whizzer gave him when he first uncovered the photo of Roger Graham meeting with Otto Torres. He reached into the glove compartment and found the disposable cell. He quickly opened it and punched the number one. Whizzer's private phone he bought with this twin was the only one programmed into the memory.

Dutch could almost hear his heart beat as the cell connected, but a recorded voice sounding mechanical said, "The number you are dialing has been disconnected."

Lorraine could sense Harvey tense when she began to speak. Minutes earlier, their lovemaking was interrupted by one of the night operators who informed the President that Roger Graham was on the line. After making him wait a couple of minutes, she sighed heavily then lifted the receiver.

"Congressman Graham, how are you?" she said with feigned interest.

"I'm doing well, Madame President. Thank you for asking. I hope you are the same?"

"Better than well. As a matter of fact, right now I'm enjoying the plush mattress on my Queen Elizabeth four poster looking directly across from my prized Portici Villa mirror. I'd say that I'd love you to see it one day, but it would be disingenuous."

The two rivals shared a forced laugh. Although the President was insanely curious what the call was about, she was determined not to ask. He was the one who called her, and she didn't want to appear desperate.

"Madame President, with just a few weeks to go until the election, I wanted to check to see how you're holding up."

"Holding up?" she said, almost spitting as she spoke.

Harvey grabbed her elbow and motioned for her to calm down.

"Congressman Graham, I'm not sure what you mean by that."

Another short laugh. "I don't mean it in a derogatory way. I studied your first Presidential campaign and know how difficult these last weeks will be. I just meant because of the added pressure of these attempts on your life. I don't remember a President who has had this extra concern during the final stages of a campaign. You've got enough to worry about without having to look over your shoulder."

The President swallowed hard and felt a wave of heat run from her head to toe. She glared at the phone. Was he just fucking with her head, or did he mean to come across as a condescending son of a bitch who would like nothing better than to have someone put a bullet between her eyes? Or was it something else? Something she couldn't put her finger on. The phone call itself was highly unusual, almost as if he knew something she didn't. It was unsettling. Could he sense her unease about her security?

She pulled herself together. "Well, that's very kind of you to check on me, Congressman. But I assure you I haven't given it a second thought. I have total confidence in my Secret Service detail."

She was proud of delivering that dig perfectly.

Roger paused, "I'll definitely keep that in mind."

"Is that all you called about, Congressman?"

"Basically, yes. But I did want to take a moment, because neither you nor I will have one later." Pause. "Madame President, I wanted to wish you good luck. You're a worthy adversary."

"Well, Congressman, I'm flattered. But I don't know if I'd choose the word adversary. After all, we are both looking out for the best interests of this country, even if we disagree on how to get there, are we not?"

"Touché, Madame President. And thank you for taking my call at this late hour."

"You're welcome, Congressman. Have a wonderful evening," she said and hung up quickly, ensuring she'd get the last word.

"What the hell was—" Harvey said.

But Lorraine wasn't listening. She leaned across the bed, picked up the phone base, and hurled it against the far wall.

Roger Graham reached back and hung up the phone in his limo. He and Simon sat alone in a deserted park just outside of Washington. Upon arrival, he had instructed the driver to leave and stretch his legs for an hour. Roger preferred to stop in remote places for private business.

"Why do you revel in playing with people's heads so much, Roger?"

Roger looked across at Simon, whose blonde hair provided a sharp contrast to the black suit he wore.

"Old habits die hard, Simon. You of all people should know that."

Roger had a gleam in his eye during moments like this. He would never let his staff see it, but with Simon it was safe to let down his guard. He looked at the notepad sitting on his lap. Written on it was a list of things to do that night. He put a check mark on the third line down that said, "Fuck with the President."

"Right, then. Now, how about our friends down south? Is everything in order?"

Simon pulled out a smaller note pad from a breast pocket and flipped some pages. "According to our intel—"

"Fuck the intel, Simon!" Roger snapped. "I need to be sure they are ready to move on this. Everything depends on it."

Simon calmly looked up. "Mr. President, I assure you they will be ready."

Roger stared at Simon for a long time. He broke into a smile despite himself and the two shared a laugh.

"That does sound good, I have to admit."

Roger leaned toward the door, but Simon stopped him. "Roger, just one more thing."

Roger sat back.

"I've confirmed that President Burton's Secret Service detail is requesting ten agents from our detachment."

"Ten?" Roger asked.

" Part of it is in retaliation for using our own CIA security. Bill Polk is basically giving us the finger for that. But the other part is for added security surrounding the President until the end of the campaign."

"Tell him no, but he can have five."

"May I ask why?"

Roger shrugged his shoulders. "Because he asked for ten."

Simon leaned forward on the leather seat, squeaking all the way.

"Roger, if you want to get into a pissing contest with Polk, that's your choice. But look at it another way. This is our chance to—let's say—lose a few agents who haven't exactly been playing ball with us."

Roger thought about this. "Good point. Give them some of the assholes who would like to see me torn apart in a crowd. Any names come to mind?"

Simon flipped more pages, then said, "Adams, Joyce, and Kennedy."

"Okay, that's three."

Simon moved a finger down the page. "I don't have a preference who the others will be." Simon looked up and met Roger's eyes. "Except for two, Brady and Rolleston."

"Clyde Rolleston?"

Simon broke from his calm demeanor. "Will you please keep it down? This limo isn't the Beast. It's not entirely soundproof."

"Yes, I know that Simon, but Clyde Rolleston? He's the detachment chief. Why do you want him and Brady gone?"

"I don't trust those two. I've been hearing things. Don't forget, Mr. Flecca's involvement coincides with Kevin Brady's meeting with Dutch Brown at Andrews."

"I thought you said we don't have to worry about him?"

"We don't. But why should we keep these two around if they won't play ball? This is the perfect opportunity to shed them, and it doesn't make it look like it's our idea."

Roger thought for a moment. "Do you think you can sell it?"

Simon nodded.

"Okay, then it's yours to handle."

"Good, but speaking of Agent Brown, there's one more thing."

Roger glared at Simon. "He's back at work?"

Simon nodded.

Roger stared at a crystal glass hanging on a rack. "This could be good or it could be bad." He continued to stare for a long moment. Then he looked at Simon and said, "Let's deliver a message to Agent Brown."

Again a nod.

Roger stared out the window for at least a minute while Simon sat motionless. Then he reached for the handle and stepped out of the limousine to get some air.

Chapter 36
Fifteen days before the election

Dutch put the file down that he was reading and rubbed his eyes and face. The information they received from the people Ms. Aguilar listed who were at the protest with her proved to be exactly what he thought. They were a typical group of legal immigrants who had lost family members trying to come to America. Full background checks were done on them and, it appeared, they all received their documentation legally and through normal channels. The only one who apparently didn't was Ms. Aguilar. Dutch and his team had been knee deep in the background checks for days and were coming up empty.

More concerning, however, was the unknown whereabouts of Richard Flecca. He had been in touch with Omaha and a few other branch's Whizzer normally was subbed out to, but no one had seen him.

Because Flecca worked for the Secret Service, the FBI's investigation was being kept very quiet. But Dutch received updates daily from his contact's in the bureau.

Dutch decided he needed a break, so he reached for his sunglasses and strode into the cool autumn air. Despite everything else that was going on, for the first time in a month he felt himself moving out of the dark well of depression he had been living in.

He felt like a walk, so he circled a couple of blocks to stretch his legs, and after some time he turned the corner and approached his favorite newsstand.

Willie Tanner started bouncing around as Dutch approached.

"A—a—agent Brown. Agent Br—br—Brown. Sooo good to—to—to see you."

"Hey Willie. What's shaking?"

Willie didn't answer and was fidgeting more than usual.

"What's the good word, Willie?" Dutch asked again, and this time watched him while he waited for a reply.

Uncharacteristically, Willie looked around. If Dutch didn't know him better, he would swear the man was afraid of something. His head turned from side to side so quickly it looked as if it were going to unscrew and fall off of his neck.

"Willie?"

Still no answer, but Willie began nervously twirling some loose fabric on his shirt between his fingers.

Dutch knew enough to wait, so he took a seat in the chair next to the newsstand. Willie walked to the pushcart and picked up the weekend edition of *USA Today* and handed it to him.

He opened the paper and scanned the pages. He wasn't reading anything, just biding time for Willie to say or do something.

"Agent B-brbbrown. P—Please go to see Gh—gho—ghost."

Against his better judgment, Dutch dropped the paper and asked incredulously, "What?"

Willie started walking away nervously until Dutch picked the paper back up and held it in front of him.

"Ghost wa—wants to s—s—s—see you."

Dutch snapped the pages in front of his face to straighten them out. "Willie, what are you talking about?"

Willie took an audibly deep breath. Under the paper, Dutch could see Willie's shoes rocking from side to side. Willie was upset, that was for sure.

"Agent Brown, you—you need to m—me—meet with Gh—gho—ghost. He wants to—to—to see y—y—you."

This was too much for Dutch. He put down the paper and stood. Willie backed away.

In a calm voice Dutch said, "Willie, please tell me again."

Willie avoided eye contact but furiously pulled and ripped the loose stands of cotton on his shirt. Dutch turned so he wasn't facing Willie directly, but stood beside him. Willie seemed to relax a bit. "Willie, are you telling me that Congressman Graham wants to meet with me?"

Willie nodded his head while tugging on his shirt.

"When does he want to meet?"

Willie moved his head back and forth almost as a horse would.

"He said, when I—I—I s—s—saw y—y—y—you, then Th—thr— Thursday night at ten o—o—clock."

"So this Thursday night at ten?"

Willie moved his head up and down quickly.

"Where, Willie? Where does Graham want to meet me?"

Willie let go of the fabric and pointed toward the Washington Monument.

"The monument?" Dutch asked. "He wants to meet me at the Washington Monument this Thursday night at ten?"

Willie nodded.

"But Willie, how will he know you gave me the message?"

Willie switched to a side-to-side motion with his head. "Don't kn—know. Just said to—to tell you he'd—he'd be th—th—there."

Dutch was confused. He couldn't see anyone watching them speaking. He took another look around, his trained eyes settling in all the likely spots someone would be when trying not to be seen. "Willie, who told you to give me this message?"

Without looking up, Willie said, "Gh—gh—ghost."

Dutch felt flushed. Willie had always been dead on with his information in the past, and Dutch couldn't remember a time when he saw him so agitated. Was Willie imagining this or was it real?

Willie grabbed his sleeve. Dutch looked at him in amazement. This was so far out of character it bordered on the impossible.

"Agent Brown, v—v—very imp—im—important. Don't tell any—anyone. C—c—c—come alone."

Willie's eyes were focused on Dutch's. This confrontational conversation was a first, and it unsettled Dutch. Willie didn't break eye contact as he continued to hold onto Dutch's sleeve. Dutch could see the urgency in his eyes and in his tense, jerky movements.

Dutch didn't know what to say. Finally, he managed, "Okay, Willie, thank you for telling me. I'll—I'll be there."

Dutch pulled from Willie's grasp and walked away, still full of questions.

He didn't even turn around when he heard Willie call out, "Be careful."

As Dutch turned the corner headed toward his office, he heard Nat call out, "Hey Dutch, I've got a message for you."

Dutch turned and took the phone message Nat was carrying. He looked down and read that Bill Polk wanted him to call in immediately.

"What do you think this is about?" Dutch said.

"Dunno. Marge handed it to me about five minutes ago and asked that I find you."

Dutch turned to a phone hanging on the wall. "Let's find out." He picked up the receiver and punching in the numbers to connect with the main switchboard.

"Hello, this is Agent Brown."

"Hold, please, for Agent Polk," said a monotone voice.

There was a pause before Polk's voice came booming through. "Dutch! I'm glad to hear you're back at work. I'm sorry I haven't had a chance to come by to say hello. Things have been pretty busy around here. How are you feeling?"

"Fine, sir. Thank you for asking."

"I've been kept up to speed on the investigation you're heading up. Sounds like you're making progress."

"Thank you sir, but we're not where I'd like to be yet."

Polk laughed. "Once an investigator, always one, eh? Never satisfied with the pace."

"No sir."

Nat looked at him curiously and Dutch shrugged, indicating he didn't have an idea yet what the man wanted.

"Dutch, as I said we're out straight over here at the Mansion. These next two weeks are going to be brutal. I need to call in more agents and I'd sure like to have you back on the POTUS detail. What do you say?"

"Thank you, sir. But I thought you'd want me to stay on the investigation."

"Nonsense. We've got plenty of agents that can handle things over there. Besides, you were the one that gave them their biggest lead in identifying Aguilar. Hell, we need you and your eyes back here protecting the President. What do you say?"

The excitement in his voice was infectious. The thought of getting back on the PPD was tempting. As much as he wanted answers to the many questions about the investigation, to be back on the road with the President was an exciting offer.

"Sir, I'd be honored. Thank you very much."

"That's great Dutch, just great! Get your ass over to the Mansion in an hour. Report to me when you get here."

Polk hung up before Dutch could say anything.

Nat looked at Dutch. "Is he putting you back on the POTUS detail?"

"Yup." Dutch couldn't wipe the smile off of his face.

"Full time or are you going to split between the investigation and the detail like I'm doing?"

"He didn't say, but it sounds like I'm going to be back on the detail full time."

Nat held out his hand. "Congratulations Dutch. They just can't keep a good man down."

Dutch paused before saying, "Nat, can you please keep me in the loop with the investigation?"

"Not a problem."

Chapter 37
Twelve days before the election

The days flew by. The President was scheduled to shuttle between the White House and Capitol Hill, trying to bring the leaders of both parties back to the bargaining table over proposed changes to the collective bargaining process for Federal employees. In between the shuttling, she was holed up in the Oval Office trying to get ahead of as much work as possible. She would be out on the campaign trail the rest of the way so it was crunch time.

Dutch had been assigned Mansion Duty. He fell back into the routine of periodic sweeps inside and out, checking with the guards at the gates, and assisting with security for visitors with appointments to see the President. Also, as one of the agents assigned to the travel team, he attended numerous briefings on every aspect of security for Mission one seven two.

It was Thursday morning. He hadn't told anyone about the meeting that night with Roger Graham. Although he was back on the POTUS detail, his mind was still turning over the ongoing investigation in his head. The more he did so the more things pointed to Graham. He thought this meeting would be an opportunity to make some real progress without any of the red tape handcuffing him.

"Agent Brown, please report to the firing range," said a voice in his ear.

Dutch depressed a button under his coat and raised his sleeve to his mouth. "Roger."

He was at the East end of the White House. The Secret Service firing range was in the middle between both ends, four floors beneath ground level. It took him ten minutes to get through security.

"Dutch! I'm glad I caught you today. Thanks for coming down."

Dutch shook hands with White House ordnance officer, Peter McLean. McLean was a lean man in his late fifties with thick gray hair. His skin was gaunt, most likely from spending a lifetime four stories underground in an expansive section holding enough firepower to take down the entire White House.

McLean was a munitions specialist. He was the last word when it came to anything weapons related. Around the White House, he was affectionately called Q, after James Bond's famous fictional Quartermaster of the Research and Development Division of the British Secret Service.

"How have you been, Q?"

"Great. Listen, I'm awfully sorry to learn about your fiancée. I heard she was one hell of a woman."

Dutch managed a nod and thanked him.

McLean changed to a much more upbeat tone. "Now that you're back, I've got a surprise for you." He walked around a corner and came back holding a bullet proof vest. "Here you go," he said, handing it to Dutch.

The weight caught Dutch off guard, and he almost dropped it. It was much heavier than standard issue.

"Q, I've already got a vest."

"New orders. With all the excitement these last few months, Homeland Security decided to open its wallets to equip us a little better. That Bouncing Betty was the last straw. So here you go."

Dutch looked at the vest. "What's so special about this one?"

"Put it on," McLean urged. "I think you'll find it surprising."

McLean retreated while Dutch swapped his old vest for the new one. He was buttoning up his shirt when McLean came back. "What are you doing?" he said.

Dutch looked bewildered. "Putting my shirt back on. Why?"

"Take it off," McLean said matter-of-factly.

Dutch did a double take, then removed his shirt, leaving only a white cotton t-shirt under the new vest.

"Agent Brown, please follow me."

Dutch wondered why the sudden formality, but followed McLean to a far corner of the range. There was a gymnasium mat hanging on a concrete wall and another directly underneath it. The mats were surrounded on three sides by a hip-high concrete cinder block wall.

"This would be a good place for an execution," Dutch said, rather tongue-in-cheek to try to hide his growing unease.

"Agent Brown, are you wearing the new bullet proof vest I gave you?"

The formality of his voice gave Dutch pause for concern. "Yes, I am."

227

"Do you have any sharp objects in your pockets?"

Dutch instinctively looked down at his pockets, then back up. "No."

"Good. Then please stand directly in the middle of that mat," he said, motioning to the square red mat in the center of the small boxed off area of the room.

Dutch did as instructed. McLean stood on a green X that was stenciled on the concrete floor about twenty yards from where Dutch stood.

McLean reached under his coat and pulled out a gun. Before Dutch could react, McLean pulled the trigger.

Dutch felt the bullet hit his abdomen with such force he was lifted off his feet. He crashed into the mat hanging on the back wall. The impact knocked the wind out of his lungs. He lay still on the red mat for a moment, allowing his brain to catch up with what had just happened. He reached his hand under his vest, feeling for blood, but there wasn't any.

Mclean began laughing so loud it reverberated off the walls of the empty shooting range. Dutch looked up and saw him still standing on the green X. Dutch pulled himself up to his knees shakily and looked in disbelief.

"What the fuck are you doing, you sadistic mother fucker?" Dutch yelled. He was pissed at McLean, who laughed harder as he closed the distance and held out a hand to help Dutch up. Dutch wouldn't take his hand. His face was red and he shook all over, and the absolute last thing he wanted at that moment was help from the man who just shot him. Shakily, he got to his feet.

"How do you like your new best friend?" McLean asked, pointing to the vest.

Dutch looked at it. There wasn't even a depression where the bullet hit him.

McLean reached into his pocket and Dutch flinched.

"Relax," McLean bellowed and threw him a half full bottle of Advil. "Here, take three of those and you'll be fine in ten minutes."

Dutch shook the bottle until four pills fell into his quivering hand. He threw them into his mouth and swallowed without anything to chase it. His heartbeat began to slow and he felt his anger dissipate. It was hard to stay mad at Q.

"What you're wearing is the newest technology in bullet proof vests. It's a hybrid polyester and nylon combination, which absorbs energy. That sucker you have on can withstand a .357 Magnum at point-blank range."

"Cut the shit. Nothing can do that."

"Wanna bet?" McLean asked, and turned over the weapon he shot him with to reveal it was a .357 Magnum.

Dutch whistled, his heart still pounding so hard it felt like it was going to break out of his chest.

"And to top it off, the vest was designed by none other than Miguel Callabero."

"Who the hell is Miguel Callabero?"

McLean laughed. "If the President were here, she could tell you. Callabero designs luxury high-end bulletproof clothes. Some of the most famous people in the world have worn his vests without the public ever knowing."

"Why don't we all wear them?"

"Hah!" boomed McLean. "If we sold the one you're wearing, we could take a chunk out of the national debt. Only special people get to wear them. Congratulations. You made the list."

"Hey Dutch, how did your execution go?" yelled Meadows.

Dutch was leaving the West Wing on his way to the parking lot. It was seven p.m. and the last briefing before the next day's trip had wrapped up an hour late.

"Ha ha. Very funny."

Meadows bent over laughing. "I couldn't resist it, man. That prank never gets old!"

"You've done it before?"

"Hell yeah! Anyone who gets issued one goes through the same routine. That is, except for the Presidents, with one exception. George W. liked it so much we ended up shooting him five times. Marcus Reed almost went through the roof, but The Man had the last word."

Dutch was astonished. He thought he knew everything about the world of protective gear.

"Who else wears these?"

"Visiting heads of state, mostly. Sometimes we loan them out to agents, like yourself, who have been wounded in the line of duty. It helps with peace of mind."

There was an awkward pause while Dutch thought about the shrapnel he caught in the back.

"Thank you," Dutch said.

"Enough said. Are you all set for the trip?"

"Please. I don't think I've ever been so prepared in my life."

"Good. Make sure you get enough sleep tonight. PAG tells me that Harvey put us on the clock. Andrews is in full lockdown."

"No problem, and thanks for the vest. It's my new best friend."

Dutch passed the Washington Monument for the fourth time. His dashboard clock read 9:45, and there was no sign of Graham. He rounded another corner, wishing there were more traffic. A lone car making circles every ten minutes around a national monument didn't exactly blend in.

As he drove, he laughed at the absurdity of it all. He was about to meet a candidate for the nation's highest office and he had his Glock, an ankle Remington, two extra clips holding twenty-five rounds each, an Arrowhead throwing knife under his vest, and his newest piece of clothing from the Miguel Callabero line.

Dutch pulled over in one of the many unoccupied parking spaces. A cold October chill replaced the unseasonable warmth the day had brought. As a result, there was a wispy fog hovering at ground level. The moon was almost full, but a cloud cover cast a muted brightness over the memorial.

He had a clear view of the main entrance. The digital clock on his dashboard hit ten o'clock. As if on cue, a stretch black limousine pulled around the corner and stopped directly in front of the entrance.

A rear door opened. A dark figure stepped out and walked a few yards away from the car and stood alone, standing at an angle that suggested he was admiring the monument. The person was dressed in a long black coat with a hat popular with Hollywood actors portraying CIA agents from the 1960s. From where he sat, Dutch couldn't tell if it was Graham.

After another minute, Dutch opened his door and stepped out. He mentally inventoried his armaments as he walked toward the man. Something bothered him. If this man he was heading toward was Graham, then where was his protection detail? It unsettled Dutch that the Presidential Candidate would be alone.

As he approached, the shadowed figure turned. Dutch recognized Graham peering at him from under the brim of his hat. He had never met the man in person.

Graham reached up and removed his hat, smiled, and extended his hand.

Dutch's eyes darted around the area looking for—he wasn't sure what. He wordlessly took Graham's hand and the two shook.

Graham smiled and said in a friendly voice, "Agent Terrance Brown, it's a pleasure to finally meet you."

"Thank you, Congressman. It's nice to meet you, as well."

"Please, call me Roger."

Dutch considered a moment, then said, "Thank you, Roger."

"And may I call you Dutch?"

Dutch shrugged.

Roger motioned for them to walk past an angular black chain that encircled the monument. They approached the Washington Monument Lodge, a small building that served as a gift shop located two hundred yards in front of the monument itself.

Dutch fought the dryness in his throat and asked, "If you don't mind my asking, Roger, where is your security detail?"

"Security detail? Do you think I need one tonight?"

Dutch was at a loss, and Roger seemed to sense it.

"Please Dutch, you can speak candidly here. It's just the two of us."

Dutch looked toward the limo and motioned questioningly with his head.

"Oh, sorry. I do have a friend in the car waiting for us to finish."

"I take it your friend's paychecks aren't written by the same agency mine are?"

Roger laughed. "No."

He motioned for Dutch to sit with him on the long sloped marble bench facing the monument. It was lit like a beacon, casting the only light around them. The trees around them blew in the cold wind that had picked up during their short walk. Both men reached for their collars to protect themselves against the biting air.

Dutch had a random thought that for a stone bench, it was very comfortable.

"Sir, I mean Roger, it's my job to protect people. Does Agent Rolleston know you're here tonight?"

Roger laughed again. "No, I don't think I'll need extra security, unless you're planning to kill me. Then it's probably too late. Agent Rolleston has been reassigned to the POTUS detail. He'll now be protecting...'Widow' is it? That's the President's code name, right?"

"Agent Rolleston has been reassigned? That's news to me."

"The transfer took place tonight. It wouldn't have been in your briefing yet. You along with the rest of the detail will notice a few new faces tomorrow at Andrews."

Dutch tried not to look surprised while simultaneously seizing this man up. He always prided himself on being able to read people instantly, but so far Roger Graham was the exception.

"Besides, sometimes the best place to hide is in plain sight. Don't you agree, Dutch?"

Dutch thought about it, then laughed. "Yes Sir, I guess you're right."

The two sat silently for a moment, then Roger sighed. "I absolutely love this time of the year. The cold air smells so clean. It's as if nature is washing away the sweat of the summer. I hope to have at least four more years of this weather."

Dutch let the statement hang in the air.

"Dutch, I'm afraid I'm being guilty of what I accuse the President of all the time, wasting time and saying nothing."

"I am curious why you wanted to meet with me. And why did you pass the message through Willie Tanner?"

Roger laughed again. "I just love Willie. Don't you?"

Dutch turned so he was facing Roger. "How do you know Willie?"

"Oh, Willie and I go way back. You don't think you're the only one who knows his value, do you? Don't forget, I used to be a spy."

Dutch shifted uneasily.

"Dutch, let me just come out with it. I know you suspect me."

Dutch was struck with the straightforwardness of the comment.

"And what do you think I suspect you of?"

"Well, now, that's the question."

"Excuse me?"

"I said that's the question, isn't it?" Roger looked around. "I'm assuming you have some of your coworkers here somewhere, don't you?"

Dutch followed his gaze. "Actually, no. I didn't tell anyone."

Roger raised his eyebrows. "Really? I underestimated you Dutch."

"Underestimated, sir?"

"Yes. You see, I know you've heard things about me. Things that I'm sure don't make sense."

"Go on."

"Dutch, let me say what I came here to say. Your investigation into the assignation attempts on the President is being manipulated to implicate me."

Dutch tried to remain expressionless while studying Roger's face. If he played poker, he could be a millionaire he thought.

Roger paused as a car drove past them down Madison Avenue. Dutch took the opportunity to scan the area again. The thickening mist swirled around them, and he could feel the bench's cold seeping through his clothes.

"I would like to convince you that what you've learned about me— well, how can I put this? Not everything is as it seems."

Dutch laughed. "Sir, please don't take this the wrong way, but I'm a tough sell."

"That's the funny part, Dutch. I said I'd like to convince you, but I didn't say I had to. You see, this meeting isn't for me; it's for you."

"Sir, I'm sorry, but now you've lost me."

"Let me try this another way."

Roger paused for a moment and rubbed his chin. It appeared to Dutch like he was having a hard time figuring out how to say what he wanted to say. But he wasn't prepared for what came next.

Roger looked to either side of him, then squarely in Dutch's eyes. "Dutch, I believe your fiancé was murdered."

Dutch froze, his mouth agape. Never in his entire career had he ever been caught so off guard. His head spun as his mind tried to process what was just said.

Roger didn't wait for Dutch, but continued, "Do you believe the medical examiner's explanation of a placental abruption that killed her? C'mon, Dutch. Didn't you wonder how closely that medical examiner looked at her or did you just accept the diagnosis?"

Roger never broke eye contact. His face was expressionless. "I think it was a tragedy what happened. But there's more going on than you've noticed. Don't get me wrong, I understand your pain, your grief. It's personal so it's much easier to miss something. I think, no, I guarantee whoever did this was banking on just that.

Finally Dutch felt a part of him begin to take back control of his emotions. "Sir, you've got to be kidding me. Are you suggesting—"

"Dutch, I'm ex CIA. As such, it's in my nature to, let's just say, notice things. Just as you, by nature, are an investigator. But you can't be objective in this case."

"And you are?"

Roger nodded. "Let's just say that what I've seen watching from afar is a jumble of things that don't add up. I can't say I've figured it out, but old habits die hard. I can't leave a mystery alone."

Dutch started shaking his head, more in a manner of trying to take what Roger was telling him in. "Sir, I've got to tell you that this sounds far-fetched."

Roger replied quickly. "As I said before Dutch, I'm hoping to convince you of something."

"And that something is?"

"That you will stop viewing me as the enemy. My point in bringing your fiancé into this isn't to cause you more pain. Believe me, I am sincerely sorry for what happened to her. But in telling you my suspicions, I hope to gain some…good faith perhaps?"

He paused dramatically. Dutch couldn't tell whether he was sincere or just a well-rehearsed politician doing what he did best, deflecting suspicion any way he knew how.

"However, I'm afraid with so much that has already happened and so little time before the election…well, I'm just not sure. About the only thing I can do is give you a little advice."

"Advice?"

Roger stood and removed a sealed manila envelope from his coat and dropped it on the bench. Dutch stared at it without moving to retrieve it.

"Advice, and some direction. Where it leads, well, that's up to you. But I know what you suspect about me and the direction you're being led. So, I thought you should be the one to benefit from my observations."

"What's in the envelope?"

Roger began to walk back toward his limo. He shrugged his shoulders and said, "Maybe nothing, maybe something. You're the investigator; you have to do the work. I'm just trying to get votes. I hope I can count yours as one of them?"

Dutch watched Roger saunter down the incline. The Capitol Building at the end of the National Mall framed the scene like something out of a movie. Someone inside the limo opened the door as Roger approached. He turned to look at Dutch before getting in.

"Dutch, wouldn't you agree that sometimes the best place to hide is in plain sight?"

Entering his empty apartment, Dutch flipped the light switch by the door and threw his coat on the couch. He headed for the kitchen, and he threw the envelope onto the table as he walked by.

Taking a beer from the refrigerator, he sat at the table and stared at the envelope. After a long gulp, he reached for it. The envelope had a string stretched around two tabs, keeping it shut. He twirled the string around and opened the flap. He reached in and pulled out a stack of paper. The top page was blank. He wondered what the hell Graham had given him.

The clock read 11:30. He had to be up in five hours.

He stared at it a little longer then, taking another long swig of beer, peeled the blank page off to reveal a report with a picture attached to it. He frowned as he examined Trevor Sirois's face attached to pages of facts and figures about the Secretary of Homeland Security. "File Copy" was stamped in red on top of each page.

Dutch skimmed through them. It contained all the normal things one would expect to find in a bio. Sirois's schooling, job history, committees and boards of directors he participated in, philanthropically exploits, family background. The list went on.

The back page contained a quick editorial breakdown of his entry into public service. Based on the way it read, Dutch guessed it was put together by one of Congressman Graham's campaign staff. He read:

> Prior to his entrance into public office, the Director was the CEO of The Meehan Group based out of New York, and with offices in Washington, D.C., Los Angeles, and twenty other prominent cities worldwide, he was responsible for portfolios reaching tens of billions of dollars.
>
> He won the highly sought-after seat of Governor of the great state of New Jersey because of his keen mind for anything fiscally related and a strong endorsement from the then Senator from Arizona, Lorraine Burton, who was the Republican party's rising star.
>
> When Lorraine Burton became President, she bucked the norm once again and appointed him Director of Homeland Security. When asked why she would pick someone with a strong financial background instead of a legal one as most

past Directors had come from, she didn't shrink from the question. She correctly pointed out that the DHS was the third largest cabinet position with an annual budget of over fifty-five billion dollars. What better way to oversee the proper use of taxpayer dollars at that level than to bring in someone unparalleled in financial and organizational management? She said she had known and worked with and against Trevor Sirois when she was with Waverly Investments and respected his vast knowledge of the financial world and couldn't think of a better selection for this important post.

Dutch skimmed it again, thinking he may be missing something. Everything on the bio was common knowledge. Dutch tried to see if there were pages stuck together that could contain a revelation about Sirois, but there wasn't.

That was it. No secrets, no smoking guns, no dirt or pictures of torrid affairs away from the public's scrutiny. Just plain dry facts and figures.

Dutch decided to leave his beer and the papers sitting on his kitchen table. "That was a friggin' waste of time," he mumbled as he meandered into the bathroom.

Chapter 38
Eleven days until the election

His alarm clock seemed louder than usual when it woke him at 4:30. He was still getting used to waking up before the sun rose, and for the briefest of moments he missed the days of sleeping in.

As he packed, he glanced to his right where Alexis would customarily pack beside him. Then he looked to the right side of the closet, void of her clothes other than a few dresses still hanging that he didn't have the will to donate yet, if ever. His throat knotted and he looked away.

He finished packing and went downstairs. Passing by the kitchen, he noticed the previous night's paperwork still strewn on the table. He put everything back in the envelope and stuffed it into a pocket of his suitcase. Maybe there was something he'd missed.

After passing through the rigorous security screening at Edwards, Dutch stood on the tarmac and caught a quick glance at the runways, where twin VC-25s sat one behind the other, looking like two race horses yearning to leave their stalls. Then he noticed a large gathering of agents near the hanger.

Nat walked up behind Dutch.

"How many agents are on this trip?" Dutch asked and began silently counting heads.

"Sixty" Nat replied.

"Sixty? Is Polk expecting World War III to break out on this trip? Where did they all come from?" Dutch thought he knew based on information Roger gave him last night, but didn't want to let on.

"From what I hear, we have ten agents on loan from five branches around the Midwest, then another ten from Graham's detail."

"Ten from Graham? That's leaving him kind of thin, isn't it?"

"Hey, he's got the CIA guys with him as well, don't forget. By the way, you're wanted in the PAG barracks. Something got screwed up somewhere, and Max Ford is pissed."

"Why do I need to be there?"

"Because whoever the liaison for this trip was, he's not here yet. He and a few others are taking care of last minute briefings back at the Mansion. They're about ten minutes behind us but Ford wants someone from the Service in that room ASAP. You drew the short straw. He seems to like you."

"Gee, thanks," Dutch said and headed inside to the PAG meeting room.

Dutch was the last one to arrive. Ford was holding off the meeting until he got there.

"We have a problem with Mission one seven two." The formality with which Ford said this was unsettling. Dutch wondered why he didn't just say, "Something got screwed up and we have to fix it." But that wasn't the PAG's way, especially with Max Ford at the helm.

Dutch scanned the room and saw unblinking eyes locked on Ford. No smiles were in evidence, and many frowns and crease marks on people's faces seemed to be more pronounced.

"There was a gap in security at Carswell Field in Fort Worth. As a result, the fuel that had been delivered there for our return trip was left unguarded for twenty minutes. Because of that we cannot use it."

People shifted uncomfortably in their seats. By their reaction, Dutch could tell this was a big deal. He knew that among the many assets needed for any Presidential Air Group mission, they were required to bring their own fuel for Air Force One. The fuel was tested constantly to ensure no one tampered with it in any way. The only way to safeguard it while at a forward destination was to keep it under twenty-four hour guard. Even a gap of twenty minutes was unacceptable.

Ford continued, "The good news is we have two days to get new fuel trucks to the site. That's the last stop on Widow's trip and she won't be there until then. I would like a volunteer to fly down with the new fuel and babysit it until it gets pumped into our bird. I told the sergeant on site that I was insisting on additional oversight."

Every hand in the room shot up except for Dutch's. He was surprised by the enthusiasm of the Air Force personnel willing to volunteer for such a boring mission. But he had come to learn it was one very dedicated group.

As he looked around, he felt awkward he hadn't raised his hand. But he wasn't on the PAG group. It wasn't his place to volunteer for this mission. However, Max Ford was looking straight at him.

"Thank you," he said. "You can all put your arms down. Let me define the parameters of who I would like on this mission. I need someone with extensive experience guarding assets of the United States of America."

Again all hands in the room went up but Dutch's.

"Thank you. But I feel the need to further define the parameters of the volunteer I'm looking for."

He was once more staring at Dutch, who shifted as he felt all eyes fall on him.

"I need a volunteer that has experience guarding our nation's assets and who works for the Secret Service."

Chuckles all around. Dutch was cornered, realizing this wasn't a request. Sheepishly he raised his hand.

Ford smiled brightly. "Good, that's better. Agent Brown, you would fit the bill nicely. Thank you for volunteering. Ladies and gentlemen, we are on the clock for Mission 172 at T minus twenty minutes. I appreciate your participation with this impromptu briefing, but let's make up for lost time."

Chairs and bodies moved all at once except for Max Ford and Dutch.

Once everyone filed out of the briefing room, Dutch said, "Excuse me, Captain, but why did you have to convene a meeting with the entire PAG group if you were going to select me for this mission?"

"Because there are no secrets or information withheld from my group. Someone screwed up, and I needed to make sure everyone knew that. I have no tolerance for screw-ups, as I'm sure you can appreciate."

Dutch nodded. "I respect that. But sir, I'm not the liaison for this mission. Agent Shaklis is."

Ford pointed to the paper in front of Dutch. "You'll notice that the order doesn't contain your name, just 'Secret Service Liaison.' Shaklis is late, so you drew the short straw."

He stood and walked behind Dutch on his way out of the room. "Sometimes Agent Brown, life just isn't fair."

Dutch grimaced as he thought of being taken off the protective detail until the last stop of the trip just to babysit two truckloads of fuel.

From just outside the PAG offices, Dutch watched as the first VC25 exploded down the runway in advance of the President's plane. The heavier weight and extra thrust compared to a regular plane made it sound more like a squadron of jets rather than one airplane taking off. He let out a long sigh and cursed his luck for having his first road trip since he had been back taken away from him. A voice from behind startled him out of his thoughts.

"Agent Brown?"

Dutch nodded and shook hands with the tall officer.

"Nice to meet you sir. I'm Major Thompson. It looks like we'll be traveling together."

"Major," Dutch said. "By the way, I've never gone on the cargo planes that carry assets to the advance points. What will we be flying?"

The Major smiled knowingly, obviously getting a kick out of the agent who had no idea what he would endure for the next two days.

"Come this way, sir," he said and pointed across to another hanger whose doors were just opening. A tractor was backing out with a long metal bar attached to the nose of a giant green propeller plane.

"There it is. There's nothing like riding in a C-17 transport. Have you ever had the pleasure?"

Dutch had never seen up close one of the giant cargo planes, which were large enough to transport the HMX1 helicopters used by POTUS, along with the Beast and multiple backup vehicles.

Dutch watched it taxi to a halt and the huge cargo door in back slowly drop like a mouth opening wide. Three ten-wheeled tanker trucks drove out from one of the secure fueling stations and lined up in front of the ramp. Slowly and methodically, they took turns driving up the ramp and into the belly of the plane.

Dutch thought of his spacious leather chair assigned to him on Air Force One, the wonderful food, climate control, and staff that made each mission better than first class on any commercial airline. Then he looked back to the hulking green plane as a thought occurred to him. He had no idea where the seats were located.

"Riding in the lap of luxury, sir. It's your lucky day," said the major, who slapped Dutch on the back and turned to jog to the plane.

Chapter 39
Nine days before the election

The hanger was dingy. It was the only word Dutch could think of to describe the dank, hot, rusted Quonset hut housing the three tankers holding Air Force One's jet fuel for the return trip to D.C.

He sat on an uncomfortable wooden chair with his feet up on a weathered square table and examined his surroundings. The hut was cavernous, with the apex of the arch towering over a story high. A row of what could loosely be called offices ran along the east side, but the rest of the area was kept open for storage. He peered upwards and noticed the tangle of cobwebs hanging from the worn wooden rafters. Skylights had been cut into the roof, but they were too high for anyone to clean. Sunlight streamed through layers of dust, adding to the already humid air. Dutch yearned for the cold October wind of Washington D.C.

Currently, the three trucks were the only things parked on the expansive, oil-stained concrete floor. The sight of them dwarfed by their surroundings only enhanced the desolation the mission afforded Dutch.

He watched guards pace back and forth, machine guns hanging by their sides. The boredom on their faces seemed to exemplify the mood.

Dutch and the cargo had been there for two days. Once they touched down, guards from the Air Force assigned to this military base in Fort Worth surrounded the C-17 as the huge door slowly made its way down and the three tanker trucks backed straight into the Quonset hut where they currently sat.

Dutch switched between looking at the rotation schedule on the table to watching the four guards, who worked in two-hour rotations, circle the three trucks looking for who knew what. Everyone on the detail knew no matter how bored they were, theirs was an important job.

"Coffee?" asked the major from behind Dutch.

The two switched off sitting at the table, making sure there were no lapses in security.

"Sure. Black, please," Dutch answered. He watched as the hulking form of the major disappeared into one of the doors that led to a small kitchen area about as modern as the rest of the rickety hut. He looked at his watch, which read two p.m. The President was scheduled to arrive at four-ten, at which time he was to rejoin the protection detail.

He had been out of touch with the detail since they departed on separate flights at Andrews, but was able to follow their progress on CNN, which had been kept on the television in the corner. The television looked to be as old as the Quonset hut, but the picture wasn't bad.

With two weeks to go before the election, tension was high. Security had been air-tight.

Dutch watched some of the stops the President made in New Orleans and Dallas. He noticed the agents at each stop in the formations that were agreed upon during the countless hours of planning for this trip. He credited that to Bill Polk's attention to detail, plus his being on this trip didn't hurt. Normally he would stay out of the field working logistics at the home office, but this last push on the campaign of this far-from-typical election couldn't keep him behind a desk.

Bored, he leaned down to his travel case sitting next to his chair and pulled out the file Graham gave him. He'd read it through at least ten times since he'd been babysitting the fuel, but it still hadn't yielded any secrets. He once again scanned the dossier for the Secretary of Homeland Security.

Why the hell would Graham give him this? Why the cryptic and veiled references instead of just saying what he thought? Undercover agents, Dutch thought.

"Here you go," Major Thompson said appearing out of nowhere. He placed the cup down and walked toward the guards.

Dutch went back to the pages laid out in front of him. He flipped them over again to see if anything had been written on the back. He held them up to the light, hoping there was something small or hidden he somehow missed, but there was nothing. He tapped the pages together to straighten them out.

Sirois's background in the financial industry was difficult to read because it made Dutch think of Alexis and all her potential. Dutch swallowed hard to force a lump back down. He shook his head and went back to reading.

To his credit, Sirois had enough foresight to stay in good graces with the power brokers and opinion makers back in his home state of New Jersey. Was Graham pointing to the endorsement by Lorraine Burton when he was running for Governor? It had been a surprise because of her strong ties with Michael Harvey, but she was always known as a woman who wasn't influenced or swayed easily. But then Trevor Sirois owed the President much. She was instrumental launching his post-Wall Street life.

He was jolted out of his thoughts when his phone vibrated next to him.

"You're going to love me," came the familiar voice of Richard Flecca.

Chapter 40

"Whizzer! Where the hell have you been?" The surprise and relief in his voice was evident.

"I'm sorry buddy, but I had to lay low for a while. I've been busy working on a project for Roger Graham. Strictly top secret. I couldn't even tell Ken Needle I was transferring to the CIA."

"The CIA? What are you talking about?"

"Oh Dutch, trust me, we've got a lot of catching up to do. But we can't right now, I've just uncovered a major problem for the President. Where are you right now?"

Dutch snapped forward in his seat. "Sitting in a Quonset hut waiting for the President to arrive."

"When is she expected?"

Dutch glanced at his watch just as his earpiece crackled with activity. He heard Meadows's voice. "Widow is five minutes out. Status report, Agent Brown."

"We're secure. Ready for Widow" Dutch said into his mic, then back to Whizzer.

"Five minutes. What's wrong?"

Whizzer began speaking much quicker. "Shit, that's not much time. Listen, you've got to move fast on this. Here's a quick recap. I've been working on a lead Graham wanted me to very quietly run down. Somehow he gets wind of some questionable financial transactions Trevor Sirois is involved in. Don't ask me how, he just knows of it. So I did a little poking around."

"As only you can" Dutch said, still relieved to be talking to his friend.

"You know it buddy. Anyway, he was dead on. This guy Sirois has been stashing millions of dollars over the last few years. Where he's been getting it I have no idea. But I was able to pick up on a very clever way he was hiding it. You see, he'd log onto these private bank accounts from his personal laptop and move the money around every few months to covert accounts he had set up around the world. The laptop never recorded any of these transactions."

"How did you get access to the man's personal laptop?"

"I'm sitting in his den right now. We got here about half an hour ago and I got straight to work."

"What? You're in the Secretary's house now?"

"We've got a warrant, and it's a good thing too."

Dutch looked quickly at his watch. "Whizzer, I'm up against the clock here. What did you need to tell me?"

Whizzer spoke quickly and over the course of three minutes filled him in on the evidence that was being uncovered as they spoke. It pointed to Secretary Sirois being a serious threat to the President of the United States.

A crackling in Dutch's ear broke the silence.

"Widow is two minutes out. Agent Brown, report."

Dutch raised his sleeve to speak into the mic, but paused not knowing what to say. The silence hung in the air. He turned back to the phone.

"Whizzer, are you sure?"

"Right now I've got federal agents all around me taking this house apart. The case just turned damned fast from money laundering to attempted assassination of the President of the United States. Dutch, as soon as I got here I did a quick inventory of his laptop and found a file with the map of Day Street where the Bouncing Betty was planted!"

As Whizzer continued, Dutch looked down at the papers Graham gave him, showing Sirois's work history. The section about his glaring departure from Wall Street orchestrated by Michael Harvey suddenly jumped out. It ruined his financial career. It was all about revenge!

A concerned voice came through his earpiece again, "Agent Brown, report."

"Whizzer, what type of security did you have to bypass at the house? Is there any chance Sirois knows you're there?"

"Well, I had to take out the alarm system when we got in, but that wasn't a problem. We've been here..al...st..n..hou..."

The connection was beginning to break up.

"Whizzer. You're breaking up."

"Dutch? Can...me? Up...wait...som...shit!"

The line went dead. Dutch felt like his heart stopped as suddenly as the call was disconnected.

In the distance he could see Air Force One descending toward him. All at once, the area was flooded with Air Force personnel who went into a routine they had practiced countless times. Dutch stood rooted in the middle of it all.

If he alerted the agents onboard it might spook Sirois into making a move. Having an incident arise within the confines of Air Force One while in flight was too risky. If he hadn't found out the government was onto him yet, then it would be a normal landing and Dutch could make sure Widow was secure before confronting Sirois. Waiting was a gamble, but a decision needed to be made.

He lifted his sleeve to his face. "Agent Brown reporting all clear."

Now what he needed to focus on was the quickest and most effective way to secure the President without alarming anyone on board.

He moved to his position on the tarmac where Air Force One would taxi. He watched the graceful blue and white plane emblazoned with the Presidential Seal effortlessly touchdown and glide toward them.

Dutch lifted his sleeve and gave an unusual request. "Agent Brown requesting status update."

A pause, then a concerned sounding Meadows said, "Agent Brown, please confirm your status."

"Secure on the ground, sir. Can you confirm the same?"

The silence lasted an eternity. He hoped his veiled warning worked.

Now it was Polk's voice. "Status unchanged, Agent Brown. Please take up position under the port wing."

Dutch hadn't realized he'd been holding his breath when he exhaled. His gamble paid off. Polk's order confirmed to Dutch that he picked up on the cryptic warning and, he was sure, at this moment putting the detail on high alert. Being ordered to move under the port wing afforded him a better position to scan the crowd in case of a threat. Dutch knew this wasn't necessary as the threat was inside the plane, but Polk couldn't have known that. But Dutch's warning would ensure extra precautions would be taken to secure Widow as she disembarked.

After what seemed like an hour but was only a few moments, the hulking presence of Air Force One stopped directly above the painted X on the tarmac. Dutch moved to the port wing. That's where Polk or Meadows would go before anyone on board disembarked.

The rolling red-carpeted staircase had barely stopped when Polk bounded out. Dutch watched as he quickly scanned the perimeter making a quick assessment to see what could be wrong.

Once under the wing he said, "Report Agent Brown."

"Sir, I have an unconfirmed report there is a credible threat to the President's life onboard Air Force One."

Polk reacted without asking any questions. He knew the priority was to remove POTUS from possible harm, regardless of the credibility of the threat.

He raised his sleeve and spoke. "Agent Meadows, that's a go for debarkation. Security measure one. Get her into the Beast."

Dutch and Polk watched as President Burton jogged down the stairs surrounded by her Secret Service detachment. She quickly disappeared into the Beast without acknowledging the press or onlookers, and was spirited away.

The usual entourage of black SUVs were replaced by four Army Humvees complete with turret gunners flanking the Presidential limousine to the front and rear. A not-so-subtle bevy of agents in black Chevy Suburban's followed closely on the heels of the heavily armed escort. All these vehicles had emerged from what otherwise looked like an empty hangar bay five hundred yards from the point the plane had stopped. The contingency plan had taken less than 30 seconds.

Polk motioned to a lone black SUV idling at the rear of the plane, and the two men climbed into the back.

Polk said, "Driver, please step out and report to Air Force One."

As soon as the driver left, Kevin Brady swooped in and sat behind the wheel.

Before Dutch could say anything Polk said, "Agent Brady, follow the assigned route."

They pulled away, heading in the same direction as the President.

"All right Agent Brown, what the hell is going on?"

"Sir, I've just been informed that a joint task force between the FBI and CIA is currently turning Secretary Sirois's home upside down."

Polk's forehead creased, but he stayed silent.

"A map of the route taken by Widow in Alabama with the exact location on Day Street of the Bouncing Betty clearly marked was found on his home computer. The date stamp on the document read two weeks before the attempt."

Polk sat silently and absorbed this information. After a long moment, he thrust out his arm deliberately and spoke gruffly into the microphone.

"Agent Fowler, remove the passengers to a secure area until further notice, except for Secretary Sirois. Detain him on board under guard while your team conducts a security sweep of the entire VC-25."

Dutch exhaled loudly. "Thank you, sir."

Polk leaned over and shook Dutch's hand. "No son, thank you. I don't know what the fuck is going on, but if any of this is true you just saved Widow's bacon."

"Sir, should we fill in Agent Meadows? I'm sure his team with Widow is on high alert right now."

Polk nodded and chuckled. "I'm sure of that."

Dutch waited, but Polk didn't move.

"Sir, about the alert?"

Polk kept looking straight ahead.

Dutch turned to look at the section of I-30 they were traveling, then at Agent Brady behind the wheel. They were slowing and moved into the breakdown lane.

"Sir, where are we going?"

"We're taking a different route, Dutch. I want to make sure we stay on Widow's flank."

Brady took a sharp right onto a winding, bumpy dirt road surrounded by tall strands of bull grass that reached as high as the SUV.

Dutch hesitated for a moment before asking, "In case of what, sir?"

Polk cupped his earpiece. Dutch heard muffled sounds coming from Polk's ear, but nothing came through his own.

Dutch asked, "Kevin, are you picking up anything in your headset?"

Brady nodded. Dutch tapped his earpiece, then took it out of his ear and shook it. Still nothing.

Polk spoke into his sleeve. "That's affirmative; all clear."

Dutch reached inside his pocket and twisted the knob to channel two to see if he was on the wrong setting. Still nothing.

The SUV rocked as Brady traversed crater-like holes in the dirt road, forcing Dutch to brace himself against the door. On either side of the narrow road, the high-reaching bull grass gave the effect of an artificial green wall that seemed to move with the wind.

"Kevin—hey, Kevin..." Dutch said uneasily.

Brady tilted his head back slightly and said, "Relax Dutch, this is one of the alternative routes we were going to use in case anything went wrong. Didn't you get the changes we sent last night?"

Dutch was about to say he didn't when Polk said, "Okay Agent Brady, this should do,"

The hulking SUV pulled to a stop in the middle of the desolate road.

Dutch looked to either side. He'd studied the main route for Widow as well as the three alternates, but there was never any mention of this dilapidated road.

Polk motioned for Dutch to climb out. "Agent Brown, please join me. We need to talk."

Dutch stepped out. Instinctively he checked his Glock, making sure the safety was off.

The two met at the front of the vehicle. Polk then motioned for Brady to join them.

Dutch looked off in the distance to a ninety-degree turn about fifty yards in front of them. The bull grass acted as a shield for both sight and sound in front and behind them. The noises from the highway were muted in this desolate spot.

Polk reached into his jacket and Dutch stiffened. Polk seemed to notice this, because he slowed his motions as he pulled a pack of cigarettes out.

Polk chuckled and said, "Relax Agent Brown. You're too jumpy."

He flicked the top of a Zippo lighter and held it to the cigarette. He turned and held the pack out to Dutch, who shook his head. Polk shrugged and put everything back in his jacket pocket.

He took a long drag on the cigarette, then formed a circle with his mouth and blew out smoke rings.

"Quite frankly I'm surprised it took them this long," Polk said.

"Sir?" Dutch asked.

"Dutch, let me tell you something about politicians. They couldn't cover their tracks if they were walking on the ocean."

Polk laughed at his own joke, although Dutch couldn't see what was so funny. Polk took another drag.

The hair on the back of Dutch's neck stood up. He calculated the distance between himself and Polk, then behind him to the wall of grass and what might lie behind. He glanced at Brady, who had a puzzled look on his face as his eyes switched between Dutch and Polk.

Dutch stifled a cough from the smoke that wafted over to him.

"I'm not sure what you mean, sir."

"Then let me show you."

Polk smiled and removed his Sig P226, pointing it at Dutch's head. "You know the drill, Agent Brown. Throw your weapon at my feet." He flashed a twisted smile. "And if you flinch, well—I may live behind a desk now, but I can still shoot straight."

Dutch looked to Brady for help. Kevin's mouth hung open as he started for his gun. Polk casually looked at the agent and shook his head.

Anger pulsed through Dutch's veins as he slowly reached into his jacket. He pursed his lips and stared at Polk, who had a twisted sort of smile on his face while pointing the gun at Dutch's head. His arm didn't waver.

"There you go, Dutch, you thought about it. But now it's time to throw it on the ground."

Dutch threw his gun at Polk's feet.

Polk glanced at Brady, who seemed frozen, then slowly picked up the gun at his feet. He tucked his own gun back in the holster and chambered a round in Dutch's gun.

"You see Dutch, politicians can't cover their tracks, but I certainly can."

He quickly pivoted to Brady and, with the accuracy of a sharp shooter, shot him between the eyes.

For a moment, Brady stayed on his feet, eyes widened in shock. But then a small circle of red appeared on his forehead and he crumpled like a rag doll.

Immediately Polk turned back to Dutch who was looking around, hoping someone heard the gunshot.

Polk was laughing when he turned back to Dutch. "I give you credit there, Dutch. Most people would have tried to run by now."

Dutch desperately searched for a way to buy some time. He knew his chances weren't good, but even a few extra seconds might present an opportunity.

"You can chalk it up to morbid curiosity," he said. "You've certainly got me dead to rights, so to speak. I didn't see this coming. If you were me, wouldn't you want an answer before you checked out…sir?"

Polk let out a booming laugh. "You're right. I would. You see, this isn't like the movies. You're going to be dead in a moment, and you know there's nothing you can do. I don't even care about the revolver you keep in your right sock, or the Arrowhead knife you have hanging behind that new bullet proof vest. You won't have time to reach either of them. But let's cut the shit, because I really don't have a lot of time. Information is a two-way street, so why don't you let me know what you've pieced together so far?"

Being careful not to move his eyes to give away his intent, Dutch used his peripheral vision to assess the ground around him, then focused on Polk who still had the gun trained between his eyes. He was sure if he did try for one of those weapons, he'd be shot before he moved an inch. Training told him to keep Polk talking.

"Well, sir, you've just killed Agent Brady with my weapon. No doubt you will blame it on me, for which I'm eternally grateful."

Polk laughed again. "I never knew you were this funny, Dutch. But you're right so far. Please continue."

Dutch tried to give his best disarming smile. "Thank you, sir. Anyway, after you call in that I killed Brady and tried to kill you, you'll head back to Widow. Because my communications gear is no good, I don't have any idea what orders you issued on Air Force One. But I don't think it's a stretch to believe you didn't say anything about Trevor Sirois being a threat to the President. As a result, my warning was never heard and Sirois is still in the clear."

"Congratulations Dutch. You're close, but I'm afraid you're out of time."

Dutch said quickly, "Sir, about that 'two way street?'"

"Quickly."

"Sir, why does Trevor Sirois want the President dead? Revenge? Money? What is it?"

Polk shook his head and made a tsk, tsk sound. "Dutch, it would take too long to explain the errors in your hypothesis. You'll just have to take that question to the grave."

Very slowly, Dutch lowered his eyes hoping it went unnoticed as Polk spoke. The moment had arrived, and they both knew it.

Polk reached into his jacket for his own weapon. In doing so, his unwavering aim holding the Glock moved just enough. With lightning speed, Dutch drove his hand into his vest and buckled his knees so he would crumble straight down instead of at an angle. Polk snapped off a shot at the place where Dutch should have been.

Dutch drew out his Arrowhead knife. With a flick of his wrist, he threw it and struck Polk in the throat. Polk grabbed at where the blade had penetrated, but it was futile. The knife had severed everything in its way. Polk landed on his side facing Dutch, his expression a mixture of horror and shock.

Dutch got to his feet and picked up his gun next to where Polk lay. He stood momentarily over the man whose eyes were still open but glazed over, his mouth hung slack. Dutch kicked the gun from the dead man's hand.

Dutch had to move quickly. He realized that the last time his earpiece had worked was when he was ordered under the wing of Air Force One. Now, without the radio, he had no way of knowing who else was involved in the plot to kill Widow.

Dutch checked the chamber on his Glock and slammed it back in place. Then, kneeling, he plucked the curled radio wire from Polk's ear and pulled the system up through his shirt. But he didn't want to broadcast a warning now, uncertain who in the security detail might be involved in the plot against the president.

He stuffed the system into a jacket pocket in case he needed it. His Navy Seal training kicked into high gear, and he searched Brady for other gear he might need. In his jacket, he found Brady's Sig 229 and a cell phone. Dutch checked to see if it worked. On duty agents were forbidden to have cell phones on their person. Kevin Brady never struck Dutch as a rule breaker, but at that moment he was grateful for it.

He looked at the phone. Who could he call who was with the President? It had to be someone he could trust, or at least thought he could trust. Who always had a cell phone attached, no matter the circumstances?

Dutch punched in one of twelve numbers he had long before committed to memory.

A clipped voice answered. "Harvey."

"Mr. Harvey, this is Agent Brown. Sir, has the President taken the stage yet?"

Dutch heard rustling and crackling on the other end, which he guessed meant that Harvey was moving. He wondered if Harvey had been within earshot of the President.

"Agent Brown? What the fuck is this, a joke? Where are you?"

"Sir, I don't have time to explain, but the President is in trouble. Bill Polk just killed Agent Brady and tried to kill me as well."

"What, who? Polk? Bill Polk just tried to kill you? Brown, have you lost your mind? Why aren't you here on the detail? Where are you?"

"Sir, I'm on a dirt road about a half mile east of the President's route, but that doesn't matter. The President's life is in danger!"

"Danger? From whom?"

Dutch paused before blurting out, "Sir, I believe Secretary Sirois is trying to kill the President."

"What?" Harvey's voice sounded strained, as though he were trying, but failing, to keep as quiet as possible.

"As we speak, agents are uncovering evidence in his house. It won't take long before the Secretary finds out. Once that happens, there's no way to predict what he may do. Sir, it is imperative to keep him away from the President at all costs."

Harvey retorted in an angry, loud whisper. "Sirois? Trevor Sirois is trying to kill the President? Agent Brown, have you lost your fucking mind? Do you realize what you're saying?"

Dutch didn't have the time for this.

"Hey, Mike, do you realize what the fuck will happen to you if your squeeze has her head blown the fuck off after I told you to pull her and you didn't? You're choice pal, but you'd better make it quickly!"

After what seemed like an eternity, Harvey's voice came back. "Okay, Okay. Shit! What the fuck should I do?"

Dutch could tell he wasn't getting through to Harvey quickly enough.

He had to take charge as best he could so he calmly said, "Mr. Harvey, here's what you need to do. Has the President begun her address?"

"Yes, ahh…yes, she just took to the podium."

"All right. Where is the Secretary now?"

"Ahh, right now? He's supposed to be—Shit! I don't know. Shit, I can't see him!"

Dutch swore under his breath. Time was up.

"Mr. Harvey, I don't know who else may be involved in this plot, but my gut tells me Byron Meadows is the safest to turn to. Tell Agent Meadows what I told you. He'll take it from there."

"Brown, do you know how ludicrous this sounds?"

Dutch turned back to the lifeless body of Bill Polk, pointed his cell phone, and snapped a picture. Within seconds the image was sent to Michael Harvey.

"Sir, this image tells you all you need to know. Just tell Meadows what I told you. He'll take care of the rest."

"What the…" Harvey's voice trailed off, but came right back and said, " I'll get him. Agent Brown, thank you."

"No problem, sir. I'll stay on the line if—"

The line went dead. He looked at the screen and saw he still had a signal. What just happened? He couldn't let that distract him, though. He was confident he got word to the right people.

He took a deep breath and thought through his next move. Harvey would contact Meadows in a few seconds, and that would get the convoy moving. He turned to the two bodies on the ground. There was no time to take them. He had to get to the main road and help get the President safely on board Air Force One. The agents staying behind could take care of Sirois.

Dutch looked at Polk's body, bent down, and removed the knife protruding from his throat. He wiped the blood on the dead man's torso before putting the knife back in its sheath, then ran back to the empty Suburban.

Lorraine Burton waited for the applause to die down. For the previous few weeks, she hadn't felt that supreme confidence she once had while standing in front of the podium with the Presidential Seal. Could it have been the dead heat in the polls or the thought of someone trying to kill her? She wasn't sure.

She flashed her best smile and held her arm high, waving as she slowly turned, making sure to encompass the entire audience. The numbers in the crowd had surpassed what they expected, which was a good thing.

Snippets of the security briefing for this trip flashed through her head. She could almost hear Bill Polk say, "This will be the stop where we will have the highest level of security. This is where the President will deliver her longest address of the trip," and, "That's thirty-three minutes during which our primary will be exposed. It will mark the longest time spent in an outdoor venue since Juan Diego Martinez's attempt on her life."

She did her best to shake the thoughts from her head as she looked out at the elevated hill in front of her which was full of thousands of cheering people rising above her podium. Being at this angle was not the norm.

"Thank you. Thank you," she said between waves, her voice emanating from the speakers surrounding the amphitheater.

She glanced at the teleprompter. Her speech hadn't materialized on the strategically placed glass reflectors on either side of the podium. Reading a speech while trying to make it look like you're not reading wasn't the problem, but not seeing the speech at all, well, that was a different matter entirely. She was good, but she hadn't yet memorized her stump speeches.

She fought to keep her concentration. This wasn't good. The last thing she wanted to do was wipe sweat off her face on a cloudy, mid-sixty degree afternoon.

The applause was beginning to die down. She looked at the prompters again. Still no speech. Shit, she thought, someone's fucking head is going to roll for this one!"

"Thank you. Thank you. It's great to be here at Texas Christian University and the wonderful city of Fort Worth!"

Another roar rose up from the crowd. But this time she wasn't in a hurry to quell it, instead letting it rumble around like a sports stadium in order to buy time. She didn't want to stand there any longer than she had to, but there was no choice. Where is that fucking speech?

"Thank you, one and all. How are you all doing today?"

Another roar from the crowd.

"I want to thank you for coming out and supporting me. It's been quite a ride these past four years. But we still have work to do, and lots of it."

Flash, the speech lit up both sides of the teleprompters. She tried not to make it look as if someone just saved her, but she stood a little taller and adjusted her fitted skirt.

"For a long time now, our country has been tied up in what seems to be endless debate about one subject or another. In a way, it's what makes a democracy great; the ability to peacefully debate and disagree while keeping an eye on compromise for the common good. But for many years now, it seems that politicians care more about arguing than resolving their differences. It's as though Washington D.C. keeps score to see who's on top: Republicans or Democrats."

She paused, allowing for more applause as she scanned the vast number of people in front of her, but something wasn't right. She could almost sense activity going on behind her. She tried to use her peripheral vision. There it was. She spotted movement. Was Michael Harvey leaving the stage? What the hell was going on?

She struggled to keep her game face on and continued, "But for the average citizen of this country, the only scorecard that counts is what your overall quality of life is. Do you have a roof over your head, are you able to pay your bills, save money for your children's education? Will your hard earned dollars be there when you retire, or has the government taken that away from you as well?"

Now she was sure of it. People behind her were moving. What the hell was going on? When she spoke, everyone was supposed to stay still.

"Since I have been in office, one of the tenets of my administration has been fiscal discipline. My record shows the promise I made to you four years ago to be true."

Pause for applause. It certainly was a friendly crowd, or was it? She could see Secret Service agents on the edges suddenly begin to move. This wasn't a good sign. Nor was it a good sign that she was paying more attention to everything around her rather than on her campaign address.

Her eyes fell back on the speech scrolling in front of her, but she had looked away for too long. She lost her spot and couldn't remember what she last said. Shit, she was going to stammer.

Instead, she cleared her throat awkwardly as she searched for where she left off. Despite herself, she couldn't help but let out a loud, "Ahh…"

During the long pause, a murmur emanated from the crowd.

Finally she found it, but fought hard to keep her voice from wavering as she continued.

Moments later she reached the spot where she was supposed to turn things over to Sirois.

"For these reasons, it is my pleasure and honor to request a key member of my staff to come on stage and be recognized for playing such a critical role in keeping our nation's costs under control while at the same time keeping our citizens safe from harm."

She smiled and turned to her left, holding her arm out in a welcoming fashion.

"Would the Secretary of Homeland Security, Trevor Sirois, please join me out here."

People applauded as they waited for Sirois to come out. Lorraine peered through the makeshift curtains surrounding the stage, but no one emerged. Her heart raced. Where was he? This was the critical part of her speech, setting up the points of emphasis for the next twenty-four minutes.

"Secretary Sirois, please come on out here," she said once again.

Still nothing. She hadn't felt this nervous in front of a crowd since she was in seventh grade playing the role of Girl Number Four in Oklahoma.

Where is this fucking idiot? He was supposed to have been five minutes behind me after I left Air Force One.

She tried her best to improvise, but she knew it wasn't going to fool anyone.

"Folks, I think our Secretary of Homeland Security is busy at the moment. He may be on the phone more than I am, if that's possible."

Another murmur resonated throughout the crowd. The movement around her was more pronounced, and she felt someone appear at her right side and clasp her shoulder.

Harvey cupped his hand around her left ear and whispered, "Madame President, we need to move you out of here. Now."

She caught herself just before her jaw dropped. She harnessed every finely tuned instinct to keep from showing shock or concern.

"If you would excuse me for just one moment, we seem to be having some technical difficulties," she said and turned toward Harvey.

Now the murmur was much louder, and the tension around her seemed to increase. People were no longer whispering, but now questioning openly and loudly what could be happening on stage. The Secret Service outwardly brandishing their weapons didn't help quell this fear.

Lorraine stepped down from the podium keeping a shaky hand on the corner to imply she was coming right back to finish her speech. She kept a smile while saying, "Michael, what is going on? Did something happen to Sirois?"

Meadows stepped in between the President and Harvey. "Madame President, we have reason to believe your life is in danger. We must get you out of here now."

This time Lorraine couldn't hold back the look on her face. Her mouth gaped open and her eyes were so wide they looked as though they would fall out of her head. "What?" she tried to say quietly, but she could hear her voice amplified out over the crowd.

Meadows wasn't waiting any longer. He signaled the detail to move. He stepped up and locked his arm into hers. Seemingly out of nowhere, more bodies appeared around the podium. She lost sight of the crowd as a ring of bodyguards encircled her. Hands and arms affixed themselves onto her as she was muscled off the podium.

She tried to grab for Harvey, but her feet lifted from the ground. As the agents quickly removed her she yelled out, "Who is it?"

Harvey watched her being spirited away. Without trying to shield the microphone or lower his voice he yelled loudly, "Special Agent Dutch Brown."

Chapter 41

Settling in behind the wheel of the Suburban, Dutch gunned the engine and jammed the transmission into drive, spinning the wheel around as he did so. The truck kicked up dirt and gravel as it headed back out toward the highway. He tried his best to maneuver around the deep holes in the road, but some were unavoidable.

He started a mental stop watch. He estimated Harvey would have taken about a minute to give Meadows the warning. Surreptitiously securing Sirois would take another. Then one more to get Widow into the Beast, which made three. Assuming Meadows had the convoy rolling after those three minutes, Dutch estimated it would take them no more than eight minutes to reach the point in the road where he was currently stationed.

In the distance, he could hear police sirens wailing. That was good. They had been called in to help escort Widow back to the plane. Meadows had gotten his message. Things were working as they should.

Dutch turned the last corner but had to slam on the brakes before hitting one of the police cruisers heading right for him.

"What the fu—" he cried out as he watched three more cruisers skid to a stop, blocking his exit from the dirt road.

Dutch began yelling as soon as he threw open the door. "She's coming from that road, not this one, you idiots!"

Every police officer jumped from their cars and crouched down behind their doors, guns drawn.

Dutch stepped in front of the SUV and looked at every gun trained on him.

"What the fuck are you doing? The President is in danger! You've got to secure the road!" he yelled.

The guns stayed trained on him. After a long moment, one of the officers in the rear grabbed his dashboard receiver. A stern voice bellowed from the loudspeaker on top of the cruiser.

"Don't move. Remain exactly where you are."

"Hey asshole, I'm not the one you're looking for." Dutch pointed diagonally behind the officers. "The President is coming from that direction."

"Agent Brown, put down your weapons."

Dutch was baffled. He wasn't holding any weapons. He took a step away from his vehicle, which was beginning to feel more and more like the backdrop to a firing squad.

"I said don't move!" yelled a wavering voice.

Dutch saw the face of the cop speaking to him. He didn't look to be over twenty-five years old.

"Officer, may I ask what you're doing?" Dutch tried to say in as measured voice as he could maintain.

"Agent Brown, I asked you not to move. Now turn around and place your hands on the hood of the truck."

"May I ask what for?"

"For the murder of two Secret Service agents and attempting to assassinate the President of the United States."

Dutch felt his heart skip a beat. What was happening? His attention was momentarily diverted to the screaming caravan that whisked the President past them. Dutch watched until they disappeared.

"Sir, you've got five seconds to comply."

Dutch didn't know what the hell was going on. He counted six cops; which was not exactly the odds he preferred. Something was rotten, but he didn't have time to think of that. He didn't trust these cops. They looked so nervous they might just be stupid enough to shoot him.

"Agent Brown this is your last warning."

"Okay! Okay!" he yelled and began to turn around.

Like a flash, he feigned to the right then darted left through the wall of bull grass. He could hear gunshots. These guys weren't fooling around. He crouched and ran deeper into the grass. The area was marsh like, and Dutch stumbled as he sunk into a combination of mud and water that climbed over his ankles.

Bullets showered all around him. Pieces of tall grass exploded on either side. A bullet hit him in the back, throwing him forward into the marsh. He checked himself for injury, silently thanking his vest for doing its job. He flattened in the mud as a fresh round of bullets splashed everywhere around him. These cops were fucking crazy. Shoot first and ask questions—never. He knew he only had seconds before they would be on top of him.

He moved his arms through the mud and searched for something he could throw. His fingers curled around a stick and rock.

Carefully he drew himself up on his knees, but not high enough to emerge from the tall grass. He hurled the stick ahead as far as he could, then took the rock and did the same. The effect made the top of the grass look as though someone was running in a straight line away from his position. He hoped the cops would follow his feign.

Moments later he heard them sloshing through the mud, following the rudimentary decoy. He knew it would give him only a precious few moments.

He raised himself slightly and, as quickly as he could without drawing attention, slinked back to his SUV. He poked his head around the bumper and saw his ruse had worked. There was only one officer standing by the middle car, and his attention was fixed in the wrong direction.

Dutch figured he had about ten more seconds before they realized their mistake. Crouching low, he moved around the lead police car and down the row of cars on the opposite side of the officer, whose attention was still transfixed elsewhere.

Dutch reached the driver's door of the last car in line. It was open and, to his good fortune, the engine was still running. He jumped in, threw it in reverse, and pushed the pedal to the floor.

He could hear the officer yell as the cruiser backed into the highway. Dutch stayed low and rammed the car into drive. The wheels squealed, and he started to move forward. Bullets hit the car everywhere and shards of glass rained down around him as he headed down the highway.

In a few seconds he cleared the area and could sit up. To his dismay, the windshield had been hit twice, making it difficult to see the road. But he only had about a mile before he'd reach the airfield. He estimated the other two cruisers would be on him in a few moments, so there wasn't much margin for error.

Dutch knew what he did in the next few moments would determine whether he would live or die, and the thought made him furious. He was being framed for something he didn't do, and the President was still in danger. What could be worse than dying in disgrace?

He pushed the thought away and reached into his pocket for Polk's communication system. Nothing to lose now, he thought as he raised the microphone to his mouth and depressed the send button.

"Agent Byron Meadows, this is Agent Dutch Brown."

The response was immediate. "Agent Brown, what the hell are you doing?"

"No time to explain, but I will be at the airfield in less than a minute. I am driving a Texas State Cruiser. I'm telling you this in the hope you will realize I am not a threat."

"Agent Brown, if you attempt to enter the airfield you will be shot. Do you understand?"

"Byron, look. I don't know what's going on here, but things aren't as they seem. The President is in danger. Bill Polk tried to kill me because I found out the truth. I don't know who else is involved, so you've got to get Widow into lockdown."

A brief pause.

"Agent Brown, I'm warning you. Don't come near Air Force One."

Through the cobweb of cracks in the windshield, Dutch could see the gates leading into Carswell Airfield come into view. They were closing. A security shack was on one side of the thick, barbed wire fence. Guards fanned out with their machine guns aimed at Dutch's cruiser. Beyond the fence, agents and Air Force personnel took up defensive positions on the tarmac. He was only going to have one chance at this.

He said more forcefully, "Agent Meadows, I've got to get into the airfield. I will stop in the middle of the tarmac and not advance any further toward Air Force One, but I have to get through those gates!"

No response.

The gate was fast approaching. He knew his time was up, so he aimed the car straight ahead and pushed the gas pedal hard to the floor. He felt the cruiser lurch forward as he lay sideways across the seat. The engine roared and the sheer power of the police modified Interceptor V-8 engine pushed his body deeper into the vinyl seat.

The gunfire was explosive, and the car was riddled with bullets. Glass and metal rained down around him. He could hear the engine whine as it was hit multiple times but kept going. He felt the car swerve as it hit the gate and he hoped he was still pointed straight ahead.

He counted, "Seven, six, five, four, three, two, one," then slammed on the brakes. The cruiser careened to one side and nearly flipped over before stopping. He reached for the microphone. "Meadows, I'm on the tarmac but will not move any closer. It's imperative I speak with you—now!"

Dutch heard security running toward him. He lay prone across the seat and waited for the inevitable.

"Agent Brown, get out of the car with your arms in the air. There will be no other warning."

Dutch knew that, unlike the greenhorn policeman back in the marsh, whoever just issued this warning knew what he was doing.

Slowly, Dutch pulled himself up with his arms raised above his head. The cruiser was riddled with bullets and had no windshield left.

He kicked at the door, and it fell off its hinges and crashed to the ground. Dutch inched his way out of the car leaving a line of blood from the cuts he sustained from all the broken glass. A quick inventory of his body showed blood seeping out from under his ripped pants and shirt. All told, he considered himself lucky that the cuts and bruises were all he sustained. Before being ordered to do so, he laid himself spread eagle on the concrete runway.

He turned his head and saw Air Force One in the distance. He estimated he was about one hundred yards away. He hoped it was far enough to convince Meadows he wasn't trying to get on the plane.

Immediately hands were on him. His weapons, bulletproof vest, communications, and just about everything else but the clothes on his back were expertly stripped from his body.

"On your knees," barked an Air Force sergeant, who held a machine gun inches from the bridge of his nose.

Dutch complied. He scanned the ring of security surrounding him, hoping to see a friendly face, but to no avail. There were no Secret Service agents there.

Shit, he thought. Just one person I know could make a difference here.

His hands were wrenched behind him and handcuffs wrapped both wrists tightly—a little too tightly. Dutch grimaced but tried not to show any pain.

Then there was silence. It was as if no one knew what to do next. Dutch was on his knees, handcuffed, with more firepower aimed at him than existed in most police stations.

The sirens of the other police cars entering through what was left of the gate broke the silence. He didn't dare look. His eyes stayed fixed on the red carpeted staircase attached to Air Force One. The door to the plane was closed, and agents were positioned around it.

The moments that ticked by felt like hours. His knees were sore from the unforgiving hardness of the tarmac, but he didn't move or try to shift his weight. He had a sinking feeling his fate was being determined at that very moment. He looked at the Air Force security around him. Most were gripping their weapons tightly, some shifted from one foot to the other. Most avoided eye contact with him.

Finally, one of the men standing in front tilted his head and spoke into a receiver attached to his lapel. "Affirmative, sir."

He kept his gun trained on Dutch and said, "Sir, we've been instructed to allow you to use your communication device to speak with Agent Meadows."

He nodded at a soldier Dutch couldn't see. He felt the cuffs come off. Dutch brought his arms around and rubbed his wrists.

The officer continued. "Sir, I am going to hand you the device. I want you to slowly take it. Do not make any sudden or unexpected moves."

"Thank you."

The sergeant handed it to him. Slowly, he put the earpiece in and depressed the microphone button. "Agent Brown reporting in."

"All right Dutch, you've got one minute."

Dutch was relieved it was just Meadows on the channel, but he needed to get out as much information as he could in a short time, so he spoke quickly.

"Sir, I have reliable intel that implicates Secretary Sirois with at least one attempted assignation on the President's life. It's imperative you keep Widow from the Secretary."

"That's a pretty serious accusation—"

Dutch interrupted. "Sir, you don't have time. I implore you to put Widow in lockdown now."

"She already is. Now, can you tell me where you received this intel from?"

"Right now there are federal agents recovering evidence in the Secretary's house. If you call Richard Flecca, he can tell you exactly what's going on. He gave me this information just before Air Force One touched down."

"Under whose jurisdiction is Flecca working?"

"A joint task force of FBI and CIA."

There was a pause before he heard, "Stand by."

Dutch's heart raced and his back ached, but the President was safe—which for the moment was all that mattered.

Dutch looked again at the hulking presence of Air Force One. The engines idled, ready to take off on a moment's notice. Dutch peered into the cockpit and could swear he saw Max Ford's silhouetted figure there, probably glaring at him.

The door of Air Force One opened, snapping him back to the present. Meadows jogged down the stairs and over to him. He was holding something in his hand.

"Gentlemen, please stand down," he said tersely.

The guards lowered their weapons and took a couple paces back, allowing Meadows into the circle.

He held out a hand and helped Dutch up.

"Before I show you this, can you please tell me what the fuck is going on?"

Dutch tried but couldn't see what was in Meadows hand, so he stood up straighter and looked him straight in the eyes.

"Sir, I received a phone call from Richard Flecca. He used to be the techie in Omaha, but about a week ago Roger Graham offered him a spot in the CIA. The first job he was given was top secret and time sensitive. So much so he couldn't report in to even alert his superior in the Service of his transfer. He was told to find out why tremendous amounts of money had been flowing surreptitiously from accounts covertly owned by Secretary Sirois."

Meadows crossed his arms.

"Sir, I swear to you I don't know how Graham found out about this. But once Flecca began sniffing around in cyber-space, it didn't take long to find enough evidence to get a search warrant."

"For Secretary Sirois's home?"

"Yes sir, which brings us to this moment. While Whizzer, I mean Flecca, was searching Sirois's home computer, he stumbled upon a file containing a detailed map of the route the President took in Alabama. The location of the bomb was clearly marked on the document—"

Meadows interrupted. "But that doesn't prove—"

Dutch cut him off. "According to the time stamp on the file, it had been created two weeks before the assignation attempt."

Meadows expression didn't change.

"Immediately, I radioed during your approach to warn of a possible threat onboard. I didn't want to announce specifics because I wasn't sure where the Secretary was in relation to the President. That's when Polk ordered me to take up position under the wing."

"When Agent Polk deplaned, he came over, but instead of asking for my report, he indicated for us to move to a car so he could hear me. Agent Brady got behind the wheel, and before I knew it we were following Widow. I told Polk the information I had about Sirois, but I wasn't paying attention to where we were driving. Before I knew it, we were off the route and onto a dirt road. About half a mile in, we stopped and got out. That was when Polk shot and killed Agent Brady. He turned to me and said something about covering his tracks, then he turned his gun on me. I avoided being shot, but killed Agent Polk in the process."

Meadows finally showed some expression, furrowing his eyebrows as he said, "Agent Brown, I've been in contact with Bob Fleming, Special Agent in Charge of the Washington Office of the FBI. He confirmed your story and was also asking why Bill Polk didn't raise the alert level once his office contacted him about the warrant. Now that question's been answered." He turned to the officers surrounding them. "Who has Agent Brown's weapon?"

A lanky serviceman presented the Glock. Meadows handed it back to Dutch and barked out, "Agent Brown is no longer a suspect. Please go back to your designated positions."

"Sir, what about Secretary Sirois? Shouldn't he be removed from Air Force One?"

Meadows paused, looking thoughtfully at him. "No one seems to know where the Secretary is at present. He was supposed to have joined Widow on stage during her speech but wasn't there. A search hasn't turned up anything. It seems he has disappeared. We're working with the local police and have our own team fanning out, but we don't know how long he's been missing. Your hunch may be correct that he found out about the search warrant and took off after we landed. If so he has a good head start, but we'll find him."

Meadows handed him what he had been holding and said, "This was sent to Air Force One. Mr. Flecca said it would be of great interest to you."

Dutch took what looked like the back of a five-by-eight-inch photograph.

"This was hanging on the wall in Sirois' home office. They scanned it over to us."

Dutch took it tentatively and turned it over. The picture was of two men taken during a fishing trip, one holding a large trout. He didn't recognize one of the men, but Dutch stared at the other and his heart skipped a beat. The man with a silly smile holding a large trout was Trevor Sirois, and he wore a white fedora. Dutch had only seen one other hat that looked as distinctive as this, and that was in China.

"Does this mean something to you?"

"Yes it does. But how this is—I mean—what the hell does this have to do with...?" His voice trailed off.

"Dutch?" Meadows asked, snapping his fingers.

"Huh? I'm sorry, what did you say?"

"Stay with me here. Does this photo have anything to do with the President?"

Dutch shook his head. "No, it doesn't. But things just got more personal between me and Trevor Sirois."

Meadows' eyes snapped from Air Force One, then back to Dutch. "Well, you can worry about that later. I need you to stay focused and help me. There's something I'm confused about."

"What's that?"

"Why you were blamed for killing Polk?"

The question hit Dutch like a brick. He had been so singularly focused on protecting the President, he hadn't ever thought of why he was implicated.

"I'm—I'm not sure."

"Dutch, this is critical. Retrace your steps from the time Polk tried to kill you."

"Well," he began, trying to retrace everything that had happened in the previous half hour. "Knowing we had been compromised, I didn't want to send a broadcast over the Service airwaves. But I knew the President was in danger because the Secretary was supposed to be with her. The only person I knew who would have an active cell phone was Mr. Harvey. He's the only person I spoke with."

Meadows face turned white as a sheet. "Widow is with Harvey right now."

The two men stared at one another for a split second, then in unison turned and sprinted toward Air Force One.

Meadows raised his sleeve and shouted, "Isolate Widow, repeat isolate Widow immediately!"

The panic in Meadows voice chilled Dutch to the bone. But it was nothing compared to what he heard next.

"Sir, we have a situation."

Chapter 42

Meadows and Dutch took the red carpeted stairs three at a time and bounded through the open hatch of the plane. Immediately, Dutch heard loud voices permeate through the hallways, but he couldn't understand what they were saying.

He followed Meadows as they pushed and strong-armed past invited guests and staff running and screaming in the opposite direction. Air Force One was luxurious, but even this plane had its limits as to the width of hallways. As a result, more than one person found themselves bruised from a forearm to the face or upper body as the pair rushed against the flow to get to the President.

They launched themselves up the short staircase leading to the nose of the plane. There stood five Secret Service agents, weapons drawn, just outside the President's private quarters.

They moved when Dutch and Meadows announced themselves. Meadows positioned himself squarely in the threshold of the President's sleeping quarters. Dutch couldn't see past him, but by his stance he guessed whatever was happening inside wasn't good.

Meadows said in a measured voice, "Mr. Harvey, please drop your weapon."

Dutch's blood froze. None of this was making any sense.

It became more complicated when the Chief of Staff replied, "Agent Meadows, am I correct in assuming that Agent Terrance Brown is behind you?"

After a long moment, Meadows said, "Yes, sir."

"Then if you would be kind enough to step out of the way and let him into the room, I would greatly appreciate it."

"Mr. Harvey, you are in no position to—"

Harvey shouted over him, "And you are in no position to dictate terms of what is happening right now. I want to see Brown now, or I'll blow the President's head off."

Meadows looked back at Dutch, then slowly withdrew. Dutch took his place in the doorway. No training the Secret Service could ever have given would prepare him for what he saw inside.

Lorraine Burton, the President of the United States of America, was being held against her will in a corner by her Chief of Staff, who had his arm wrapped tightly around her throat. His left hand held what looked like a Browning 9 mm semi-automatic pressed against her temple.

His weapon trained on Harvey, Dutch said, "Mr. Harvey, release the President."

The Chief of Staff responded calmly. "Agent Brown, I'm surprised. I didn't think you had been on the job long enough to be able to control your emotions so well. Please, step inside the room."

Dutch slowly passed over the threshold, keeping his weapon trained at what little could be seen of Michael Harvey, who was using the President as a human shield.

"Sir, I'm not sure what you mean by that, but you have been warned."

Harvey laughed, and his body pitched back, causing his grip on the President's neck to tighten. She looked at Dutch with an odd expression. He couldn't tell if it was loathing directed toward her Chief of Staff or impatience with her security detail for not ending this already.

"Agent Brown, please, let's dispense the formalities shall we? We both know what's happening here."

Dutch sized up Harvey in a way he never had before. He tried to calculate what this man, who was suddenly the enemy, was capable of.

"Mr. Harvey, you're a smart man. You've done the math, and there are only two possible outcomes here, both which will end badly for you."

The private quarters drew deadly quiet. Although agents were just outside, at that moment he was the only one who could save the President. He tried not to let the gravity of the situation affect him as he frantically searched for a solution.

"Well that doesn't give me much hope then, does it?"

"True, but I'm here to present you a third option you may not have considered."

Harvey's face flushed, and he pressed the gun harder against the President's temple, causing her to wince in pain.

"Not considered? Ha! That's rich!" he boomed. "The only thing I didn't consider was you, Agent Terrance Brown." He enunciated each word of the name as if he were spitting them out in disgust.

Dutch was confused, but couldn't allow himself to be caught up in the dialogue. He mentally calculated there was approximately twenty feet between himself and Harvey. Although a big man, Harvey was doing a good job hiding his bulk behind the narrow frame of the President. There was no clear shot. Dutch had to keep the man talking, which at the moment didn't seem to be a problem.

"Sir?" Dutch said, finally. "I'm not following you."

The President thrashed within the confines of Harvey's hold. Harvey moved his hand and tightened his grip, momentarily cutting off her air supply. She gasped, so it was evident she could still breathe—but barely. Dutch tightened the grip on his Glock.

Harvey let out another sarcastic laugh. "Dutch Brown, the great detective. Ha! You're nothing more than a glorified flatfoot. That's what makes this so infuriating for me."

The insult didn't bother Dutch, but it was enough to cause him to pay attention to what the Chief of Staff was actually saying.

"You think you're a detective, but you never saw what was right in front of you!"

"Well sir, I'll admit I don't know the reasons you'd want the President assassinated."

Harvey turned and nuzzled his nose into Lorraine's ear. "The Service is so easily deceived," he said, then kissed her ear before pulling his face away.

Her eyes were struggling to catch a glimpse of Harvey full on, but it was impossible given the angle at which he held her. Dutch could see pure, unfettered fury in those eyes and imagined that the President would be able to rip her former lover apart if given the chance.

Harvey continued. "Of course you would be puzzled. It's because you're a trained military man. You don't have the mental capacity someone like me possesses. I'm always three steps ahead of the common man. That's how I rose to the apex of the financial world. There was no one better, and the world knew it."

Dutch allowed Harvey to continue, not changing his expression or moving his Glock. But as Harvey spoke, Dutch surreptitiously moved his feet apart allowing for a more balanced center of gravity.

"Was that it, sir? Jealousy? You were jealous that a woman who had been your subordinate became the most powerful person in the world?"

Harvey's eyes narrowed in disgust.

"If that's what you think, then you're a bigger fool than I thought you were, Brown. A man of my stature is above such vain ways of thinking."

Dutch stiffened when he saw Harvey slightly relax his grip on the President. He needed to keep Harvey talking until he could find an opening.

"Well, sir, then why would you want her dead? You'd be out of the White House as soon as she was laid to rest. What motivation did you and Secretary Sirois have?"

Harvey raised his voice, his frustration obvious. "You're a fool, Brown. You really are. For someone who's heralded as a great detective, you're still blind to who the real target was. The assassination attempts weren't meant for the President, the target all along was you!"

Chapter 43

Dutch's mental calculations of angles and firing solutions halted immediately. His mouth hung open and his Glock lowered halfway as the shock of what was just said set in.

"You see what I mean? You never had any idea." Harvey chuckled quietly, almost to himself. "In a way, it was a shame your partner had to buy it first. It was so easy to kill Harry Ludec."

Dutch felt heat flush throughout his body as his blood pounded through his veins. His eyes narrowed as his hatred of this man grew.

"You bastard! Why did you kill Harry? Why did you try to kill me?"

"Why do men do anything?"

Dutch recoiled, recalling the picture of Trevor Sirois wearing the white fedora. "Money! It was you and Sirois who were smuggling money out of the country!"

Harvey nodded. "That's very good, Brown. Now you're using your brains. You were getting too close to us from your office in Omaha. Didn't your fast track onto the PPD ever bother you? Did it ever not make sense, or were you too hung up on the pomp and circumstance of it all? By taking you and your partner out of investigations, we could get back to the business of feathering our retirement."

It took every ounce of strength for Dutch to maintain a steely resolve.

"All right, I'll buy that. But why did you kill Harry?"

Harvey smirked. "After he got injured on the job, he went home. He was so bored while rehabbing, all he did was pop in and out of your old office. My sources told me he began to re-immerse himself in the stale investigation that had gone nowhere since you two left. Inevitably, he got too comfortable being back home, so he put in for the transfer. Surely you can understand we couldn't let him go home and get back on our trail."

Dutch set his jaw. "So you offered him the chance of a lifetime, one road trip guarding the President. You bastard!"

Harvey laughed. "I love how he flew through the air like he did. Martinez couldn't have missed him if he tried." Harvey's expression instantly flipped back to fury. "But you, you're different. We couldn't kill you. You're the luckiest son of a bitch alive. It was the perfect plan, but suddenly she decided to grab even more headlines by inviting you into the limo. You should have been lying in pieces that day."

The President again struggled, resulting in a tighter grip around her neck.

Dutch knew he was running out of time. With great resolve, he was able to rein back his anger and again assess the situation while he kept Harvey talking.

"But how did you convince Martinez to take the shot? He must have known it was a suicide mission."

"Martinez? He was a dead man walking before he woke up that morning. He crossed his bosses one too many times, and he knew it. Let's just say the drug money he was in charge of didn't always balance. I don't know how much experience you have with drug lords, but that practice is—" he paused, "—frowned upon." Actually, I give Martinez credit; he died for a noble cause. He knew he couldn't save himself, but he ensured his family was taken care of before his ticket was punched."

Dutch could almost hear a piece of the puzzle click into place. "Green cards."

"Very good. You see, there are some advantages to working with the Secretary of Homeland Security. It's easy to cut through governmental red tape if you're using the right pair of scissors. That moron Sirois had his usefulness; I'll give him that."

"I thought you hated him."

"I do; even more so now. It's because of him that I'm stuck here."

"Michael, it doesn't have to end this way. You've got a choice."

"Ha!" he bellowed. "Don't insult my intelligence. By the time those agents leave Sirois's house you'll have enough evidence against us for five life sentences. I'm sure that fool left a trail a mile long."

Dutch tried not to allow his eyes to stray, but as surreal as the scene unfolding in front of him was, pieces from a case two years before were quickly coming together. But as tempting as it was to find out the answers to an old investigation, Dutch knew he had to negotiate a resolution to the stalemate he faced at the present, and quickly.

"Michael, listen. You know cooperation goes a long way. Lower your weapon, and we can work with you. Things may not be as dire as you think."

"Oh that's priceless, Brown. I've got a gun to the President's head, but the situation isn't dire." His demeanor turned darker. "And you want me to trust you? Trust the system? That's bullshit, and you know it. I've worked my entire life to manipulate the system. I know it doesn't work." He shook his head. "I am not a man who lets others dictate my future. I write my own destiny."

"Is that what you're doing now? Writing destiny?"

Harvey's face turned stone cold. "Yes, that's exactly what I'm doing. I'm sure I don't have much time left. But I want to make sure this President dies on your watch so I can ruin your life as you've ruined mine. Your name will go down in infamy as the agent who stood idle while the President got her head blown off."

With great effort the President thrashed and managed to slightly loosen the choke hold he had on her.

"You fucking pig!" she yelled.

Harvey laughed and kissed her cheek. "If only CNN were here to carry that sound bite. But look on the bright side, sweetheart. We had some good times. Now both our names will be immortalized. The shooter always gets the front page."

Dutch finally had his legs separated enough and he locked them in place.

"However there is one more thing I'd like to tell you before I leave this world, so I give you this. Your fucking girlfriend? We killed her!"

The room seemed to spin as Dutch's eyes shot wide and his blood boiled with rage.

"Oh yes, my friend. It still hurts, doesn't it? Now it will hurt even more, and it will never leave you." Harvey sighed. "If it's any consolation Brown, I told him not to do it. But poor Trevor, he panicked. He thought by taking Alexis out, you'd mentally pack it in and wash out. I told him it wouldn't work, but he impetuously decided to take the chance when he found out she was staying in his hotel. It's too bad that Alexis was so fond of ginger ale. It masks the flavor of almost anything you put into it. One too many glasses at dinner was to blame."

This final piece was all Dutch could handle. Time had run out, but only for the man hiding behind the President.

Harvey pushed the gun harder into her temple.

Dutch slowly raised his Glock.

Harvey grinned. "Do you think you can—"

Dutch squeezed the trigger and sent the 9 mm round through Michael Harvey's left eye socket and out the back of his head. The man's body slumped straight down, only bending when his girth collapsed onto his legs, sending the President sprawling away from him. He lay lifeless on the carpeted floor.

The President had shrieked when the bullet passed within inches of her own head. Clambering to her feet, she stood over the body of her former Chief of Staff. Her hands raised to cover her mouth and she began to cry, slowly shaking her head while tears trickled down her face.

"You bastard!" she yelled at the lifeless body.

No one made an effort to stop her. Dutch knew it to be a cathartic and needed moment for the President.

She stopped as suddenly as she began. Then her hands raised once more to her face and she closed her eyes, wiping the tears away. When she dropped her hands, she once again had her trademark look of control. Her face was emotionless and cold.

Then she calmly walked to the bed where lay her high-heeled Jimmy Choo shoes and put them on. Very deliberately, she walked to the crumpled body and stomped on it, making sure the tip of her heel hit all the important parts.

The agents watched silently.

Dutch looked at Michael Harvey's lifeless face, still frozen in disbelief, and wished he could shoot him all over again.

EPILOGUE
Two years later

Detective Timothy Mackenzie placed the steaming cup of coffee in front of Dutch and sat behind his desk. Lifting his own, he took a sip of the steaming liquid and winced.

"I don't know why you Secret Service guys get all the perks. I can't even get a good cup of coffee here."

Dutch raised the styrofoam cup in a mock toast and said, "It's not that bad, Tim."

"Bullshit. Next time you want to talk, it'll be in your office, with your coffee, your comfortable leather couch, and your secretary with the blue eyes and big tits."

They shared a laugh.

"So what's up?" Mackenzie said.

"We got a lead about some pretty damn good twenties making their way around the Northeast corridor. I was hoping I could talk you into kicking over some rocks with me this afternoon."

"How good a lead?"

Dutch arched his back and pulled out a twenty dollar bill from his front pocket.

He handed it to Tim and said, "We picked up a couple of these from Bank of America on Market Street in Camden yesterday. Branch manager had a watch list and picked this one out of a deposit made earlier in the day."

Tim whistled as he spun the bill front to back, and to the front again. "Any video?"

Dutch laughed. "Yeah. It was part of a deposit a little old lady was putting into her passbook savings account. We have her name and address, but I'm not holding out much hope she's the mastermind."

"Now, now, Agent Brown, one must follow up every lead. You never know if Granny has an Epsilon in her basement cranking these babies out ten sheets an hour."

Dutch sipped the coffee and choked it down. "You weren't kidding. This is horrible."

"All right, I'm sure I can take a couple hours this afternoon to help our Federal Government. When do you want to go?"

Dutch was about to answer when his phone vibrated. He held up a finger and answered. "Agent Brown."

A woman's voice said, "Please hold for the President."

"Who is it?" Tim asked.

Dutch placed one hand over his phone and glanced up. "The President."

"Ha! Oh, sure. Wait a minute, I've got a message here from Oprah Winfrey. I should probably call her back."

Dutch was about to give a smart rebuke when a loud voice interrupted him. "Dutch! How the hell are you?"

"Mr. President. I'm doing fine, sir. This is a pleasant surprise. To what do I owe this honor?"

"Cut the shit, son. It's just you and me on the line."

"I'll try, sir. What can I do for you?"

"I've got to take a quick trip tomorrow to meet some trade delegation down south, and I'd like you to come with me."

"Come with you, sir?"

"Sure, I can always use an extra bodyguard."

Dutch paused. "Sir, I'm sure Director Meadows has everything covered."

"He certainly does. But even Meadows thought it would be good if you tagged along with us. Come on, Dutch, don't you miss the thrill of guarding the President of the United States?"

"Although it is an honor, sir, I much prefer being back in investigations."

"And you will return there in three days."

Dutch was suspicious. "Sir, how far south are you talking about?"

The President laughed. "Son, just pack your suntan lotion. It's more appealing than looking at a dreary downtown Atlantic City from Tim Mackenzie's window."

"May I assume there's a car outside waiting for me?"

The President laughed and hung up.

Dutch looked at Tim, whose jaw hung open.

"Really? Just like that?" Tim said.

"Yup. Good old Roger and I are like this." He held up two intertwined fingers.

"Cut the shit, Dutch. You've been back in Jersey for two years and he still calls?"

Dutch shrugged. "What can I say?"

"In my next life, I'd like to come back as Dutch Brown."

Dutch's face sank for a moment, and he quietly said, "No Tim, you wouldn't."

The next day found Dutch in a tropical paradise.

"Dutch, please have a glass of champagne," the President said, removing a glass from the private bar nestled next to him.

They rode along a beautiful coastal road on the island of Tahiti. The sun shone, and the temperature was a good fifty degrees warmer than Jersey.

"Sir, I can't drink that. I'm on duty."

"You're allowed a few liberties when you're around me. Besides, today is a great day. You'll agree when I tell you where we're going."

"Mr. President, no one on the detail would give me any information about this trip."

The President handed Dutch the long stemmed glass. "Listen, it's just the two of us in here."

"About that, sir. Don't you usually travel with a car full of people?"

The President laughed. "Normally you'd be correct, but not today."

Dutch took a sip of champagne. It was dry and delicious. "Sir, will you join me?"

"Naw, I wish I could, but I've got this trade meeting in an hour. Although it might go better if I had a couple beforehand. But back to business."

Dutch stiffened.

"As you know, I was a field operative in the CIA for many years. But what you may not know is I continued working for them after entering the world of politics. I did some highly classified work for a few more years. Once I became fed up with the way the government ran, I decided to run for President. That's when I retired from my other job. But I kept in touch with the many connections I cultivated through the years. They were too valuable not to."

Dutch took another sip and listened in rapt attention.

"Bottom line, I hate a mystery I can't solve. I've read all the reports of what unfolded that day in Fort Worth. But I've spent more time writing government reports than you have, so I know they never tell what really happened. I wanted you to fill in the blanks for me."

"Fill in the blanks, sir?"

"Yes. You wrote the damn report. Your name is listed first and in bold letters above the other twenty agents who investigated this for over a year. You're the only one who truly knows the whole story. So why don't you tell me what wasn't in that report."

"Good point."

"All right, Dutch, I knew about Sirois and his money problems. Shit, when he lost out to Harvey on the Drumm Pharmaceutical deal, it was the last straw. The writing was on the wall. Like any Wall Street hot shot, he didn't know what to do with himself after The Meehan Group bought out his contract. Between his divorce and living a flamboyant lifestyle, he pissed away most of his money in no time. So with a penchant for living an extravagant lifestyle and no job, and the only skill he possessed was a natural bullshitter, it made sense he'd turn to politics. But what I don't understand is why the endorsement from Lorraine Burton when he was running for governor? And then to bring him into her cabinet once she was elected President? It never made sense to me."

"Sir, this has to stay between the two of us. I could lose my job if I told you any of this."

Roger Graham held his arms apart. "I'm the President. I think you can trust me."

Dutch held back the witty retorts that came to mind and sat back, making himself comfortable.

"Well sir, I have to go back a bit before the endorsement. You were correct about Sirois, as I'm sure you already know. But as it turns out, Sirois wasn't the only one with money problems. Michael Harvey blew a shitload of money in some very—shall we say—unwise and borderline criminal investments. Like Sirois, he realized his shelf life on Wall Street was limited, so he glommed onto Burton. He knew the family stock she heralded from, and he also knew she was being groomed for bigger and better things. So he played ball by moving her up the ranks quickly and making her feel indebted."

President Graham held up a finger and said, "That's not exactly a new phenomenon."

"True, but nothing was ever as it seemed with Michael Harvey. Sure he got off on all the power and perks, but he knew those wouldn't last.

He needed to tangibly cash in on his relationship with her. He needed to score, and score big. What better way than to work closely with the most powerful person in the world? Despite popular belief, people are hesitant to suspect you when you're tied in with the President."

The President looked as though he were hanging on every word. Dutch was glad he could finally tell someone the entire story.

"Now, some of this is speculation on my part, but I'm confident based on the piles of documents I've pored over from the Federal Trade Commission and they all point in one direction. It appears Harvey had the inside track for the Drumm deal, and he knew it. But he also knew Sirois would be in the running. Harvey needed this last deal so he could go out in a blaze of glory. I believe Harvey reached out to Sirois and the two met covertly. It was during this meeting that Harvey convinced him to throw the bid."

"Throw the bid? Why the hell would he do that?"

"It doesn't take much to imagine what he got in return."

President Graham clapped his hands. "Enter a surprise endorsement from one Lorraine Burton during his run for Governor of New Jersey. Son of a bitch."

"But that's only half the story. The hardest part was getting Burton into the White House. None of this would have worked without that critical piece. That bastard wasn't lying when he said he was always three steps ahead of his competition. He ran one hell of a campaign for Candidate Burton."

"You can say that again. I've got three people from her staff working with me now."

"He knew all the right buttons to push and put the right people in the right places. Once she became President, he became Chief of Staff, and he had her ear in determining the makeup of her cabinet."

"In comes the unexpected pick of one Trevor Sirois as Secretary of Homeland Security."

Dutch nodded. "The ironic thing is Sirois really was a smart pick for the job. When it came to budgeting and allocation of money, many believe he wrote the roadmap for years to come in that department."

"Agreed," said the President.

"So now both Harvey and Sirois were in place. Better yet, no one in the world would have suspected them working together."

"I thought they hated each other."

"Actually they did, but you know as well as anyone you don't have to like the people you work with. Some would have called it a marriage of convenience."

The President reached for a glass and the bottle. "I think I'd better join you for the rest of this story."

He filled his glass and topped off Dutch's.

"Bottom line was money. How do you get a lot of it in a short period of time?"

"Steal it?"

Dutch held his glass in salutation.

The President narrowed his eyes. "Stolen money? I thought it was counterfeit."

"Nope, it was real honest to God American script."

"But how did they do it?"

"A masterful piece of money laundering. Michael Harvey kept his friends close and his enemies closer. I believe this whole scheme came up during that secret meeting with Sirois. I've got you to thank, sir, for this part of the puzzle."

The President smiled. "Sirois's background? But I was trying to get you to look at Sirois because of the rumors I was hearing about his off shore accounts."

"That was part of it, yes. But what I learned from his biographical information was that he wasn't born in New Jersey. He moved there when he was twelve. But before he moved he grew up in the small town of Dalton, Massachusetts."

The President looked confused.

"That's all right sir, most people would have no reason to know this. But the United States purchases all of the paper it prints its money on from the Crane Paper Company, a third generation business located in Dalton, Massachusetts. After a lot of digging I found out that Sirois grew up with and stayed close with the CEO, Oliver Crane. I have to admit, it really was ingenious."

"Come again?"

"Extra paper."

The President shook his head in amazement. "Do you mean to tell me no one noticed extra paper being delivered to the Treasury?"

"Sir, the checks and balances never took into account a coordinated effort by top members of the President's cabinet."

"But that still doesn't explain how they printed it. I have to believe the machines they use at Printing and Engraving have encrypted counters that would need a litany of access codes."

"That's where Harvey comes in. What Chief of Staff couldn't get anything they wanted in Washington? If you found the right person and offered enough money, access codes can be bought. And when the Chief of Staff is involved, it's just about a lock that you won't get caught."

The President slowly nodded and said, "Ingenious."

"But no crime is perfect. There was one thing they couldn't hide. And it was that one thing that got me looking in that direction, otherwise I may never have figured it out." Dutch paused for dramatic effect before saying, "Ink."

"Ink?"

"Ink. The one thing they couldn't hide was the extra ink used."

The President still looked confused.

"Something stuck in my head the day I visited A.J. Burke. He said he was trying to track down ink supplies that occasionally ran short. Governmental cost overruns are part of life, except at the mint where everything must balance. Part of the beauty of this plan was the patience they exercised. They calculated the time it would take for the ink shortages to show. My estimates were they made two runs per year."

"Just two a year? Was it worth it?"

"I'd say it was good for fifty million at a time."

"Fifty million! Son of a bitch!"

"My thoughts exactly. I was kicking myself I didn't pick up on it sooner, but I was handicapped by proximity. My first assignment was Omaha, which never made sense to me. I thought I was a lock to be assigned to my home state of New Jersey. It turned out Sirois pulled a few strings to get me sent to the middle of nowhere."

"Why would he care where a rookie agent was assigned?"

"Because he was shipping the stolen money overseas from the docks in Jersey. He couldn't risk my stumbling onto it, especially because I had a good network of contacts along those docks. It was bad luck for him that Harry and I were assigned this case that led us back to Jersey after all."

The men drained their glasses. The President moved to refill Dutch's but he held his hand over the top. "No thank you sir, one is my limit when I'm with you."

"Suit yourself." The President replaced the bottle in the bar before continuing. "Now how about this guy Martinez? What the hell would have happened if he missed and hit the President?"

"Well… it wouldn't have been ideal. They would have been forced to close up their operation sooner than planned. But this guy Martinez was smart. I watched video footage of the murder over and over, and something just didn't seem right. Finally it hit me what was wrong."

"I've seen the footage as well but didn't notice anything."

"If you're trying to kill the President, the last thing you want is to bring attention to yourself. Martinez yelled just before he pulled out the blow gun. You could tell because it caused the crowd around him to part. More importantly, it sent Harry in motion to shield the President."

The President looked off in the distance and said, "Risky."

"Yes it was, but too many questions would have been asked if Harry had been shot while simply standing his post."

The President whistled loudly and said, "How about when you almost bought it?"

"That was bad luck for them. I was supposed to be alongside the Beast when the bomb detonated, but President Burton unexpectedly called me inside." Dutch's face reddened. "Fucking Harvey thought nothing of taking other agents out as long as he got me." Dutch took a deep breath and continued. "As you know, sir, these windows are nearly impossible to penetrate."

To emphasize his point, Dutch rapped on the one next to him. "Even a Bouncing Betty detonated at close range only sent pieces of shrapnel inside. That bomb was meant to kill me. And I guarantee it was Polk's idea. He had a strong background with explosives while in the Army."

The President looked suspiciously at the window then asked, "Speaking of Polk, where does he fit into all of this?"

"That was another brilliant move. Marcus Reed, the longtime head of the Presidential Protection Detail, retired after President Burton was elected. As Chief of Staff, it was Harvey's job to pore over the candidates to replace Reed. But he did so with an eye toward finding the most likely person he could seduce for an ally. Bill Polk's name stood atop an extremely short list. Polk was injured while with the Rangers and had to accept a medical transfer. The problem was, it happened before he accrued enough time to receive his full pension with the Army. Working administratively with the Secret Service didn't help because he was only a few years from retirement and couldn't put in enough time to get full pension here, either. It made him ripe for the picking. Harvey threw enough money around to convince him to play ball."

The President nodded and said, "I remember when that appointment was made. Not many people agreed with it. Polk had the military experience but lacked the practical. The people who made the most noise ended up chalking it up to another Washington screw up."

Dutch pointed at the President. "Correct. You have a good memory, Mr. President."

Roger nodded his appreciation.

"Polk was very instrumental in throwing me off the trail by redirecting me toward the mystery surrounding your candidacy."

"Mystery, Agent Brown?"

Dutch chuckled. "Yes sir. You see, he knew Kevin Brady and I were friends. He nudged Brady to come to me with concerns about your—how can I say—interesting choice for covert meetings without your security detail?"

"I'm sure the picture of me with Otto Torres really fanned the flames."

Dutch raised his eyebrows and said, "And how. That was an added bonus even they didn't expect."

The President raised a hand. "Say no more, Dutch. I understand. However, my keeping ties with Torres really helped bring stability to Mexico."

"Mr. President, I was hoping one day to get a chance to ask you about that."

The President nestled himself between the seat and the door. "I can give you an abridged version."

Dutch sat back. Now it was his turn to listen.

"The drug lords had pushed the Mexican government to the verge of collapse. Legalizing marijuana in the U.S. caused them to lose their foothold on the market. Otto Torres played a major role in brokering the peace and bringing marijuana out of the shadows by working with the government instead of against it. Now the United States is able to divert the billions of dollars fruitlessly spent for the war on drugs and allocate it toward other critical needs. But if word had leaked about my meetings with Torres, chaos would have broken out all over Mexico, and the government would have collapsed overnight."

Dutch nodded, duly impressed.

The President paused, then in a somber voice said, "Dutch, I've only got one more question for you, and it's a delicate one. I don't mind if you chose not to answer it."

Dutch knew what it was going to be before he asked, but nodded anyway.

The President looked him in the eye and said, "I'm very sorry about Alexis. How did they do it?"

Dutch said in an almost whisper, "Warfarin."

Roger shrugged his shoulders, raising his eyebrows questioningly.

"It's an anticoagulant prescribed to prevent blood clots. Any pharmacy would have it in stock. However, it's contradictory to use it while pregnant because it easily passes through the placental barrier and causes bleeding in the fetus. The dose that Alexis had been poisoned with was more than enough to cause her to bleed out and die. Because of her scare with the placental abruption earlier in her pregnancy, the medical examiner assumed that was the cause of death. It all fit together."

The President stayed respectfully quiet for a time before saying, "They underestimated you, Dutch. You came back to work."

"Thanks to Meadows. I owe him much. Polk was doing everything he could to keep me home without my even realizing it."

"But they had to know you wouldn't stay in your house forever."

"It didn't matter. President Burton's term was coming to a close. Even if she won a second, they were getting out of town. Their time was up, and they had more than enough money salted away in banks all over the world."

"Couldn't they have kept going another four years?"

Dutch shook his head. "Remember the ink discrepancies? Their plan had a shelf life."

The President looked at Dutch. "Harvey must have worked on this for years."

"He literally did. That's why he lost his mind when it fell apart."

"Any thoughts on why he ended it the way he did?"

"Only conjecture on my part, but a man like Michael Harvey either had to live like a king or go out in a blaze of glory."

The two shared looks before Dutch said, "That's about it, Sir. But the investigation wasn't one hundred percent successful. I do regret one thing and that's not getting my hands on Trevor Sirois. He got away clean. I killed Michael Harvey because it was my job. But if I ever get Sirois in my sights, it's personal."

Roger smiled and patted him on the shoulder saying, "I don't doubt it."

The limo rolled gracefully to a stop and a door opened. The President stepped out and signaled for Dutch to follow.

They stretched in the warm glow of sunshine in front of a private beach resort.

"Dutch, I want to thank you for sharing that information. It would have gnawed at me forever."

"Sir, it was my pleasure."

"Agent Brown, I'm not one to take and not give back. Therefore, you are hereby granted a twenty-four hour pass from your duties protecting me. I want you to enjoy this beautiful resort and all it has to offer."

"Sir?" Dutch was baffled.

The front passenger door of the Beast opened, and to Dutch's surprise, Meadows stepped out. He walked to the rear of the limo and opened the trunk. He pulled out an overnight bag and handed it to Dutch.

"I didn't know you were here. Why didn't—" Dutch said before being interrupted by the President.

"Agent Brown," the President said, "In that bag you'll find everything you need for a day's worth of enjoyment here on this island paradise."

Dutch unzipped it and found typical beach attire and general lounging around clothes that anyone would pack for vacation. As he zipped the bag up, he caught Meadows smiling at him.

"What?" Dutch asked.

"Nothing," he said, but continued smiling and nodded toward the bag. "I put some extra stuff in there I thought you could use."

The President patted him on the shoulder and said, "I'm going to be late for my meeting. Enjoy your stay at the Papeari Resort."

A moment later Dutch was alone on the sidewalk, bag in hand. He looked through gates hidden behind shrubbery and caught a glimpse of a swimming pool surrounded by thatched-roofed cabanas. He had never heard of the town of Papeari, Tahiti, and based on the route they took to get here, it was a hidden gem.

He walked inside and a dark skinned beauty with oval-shaped brown eyes greeted him. A mesh skirt hung loosely around her waist, and her bikini top wasn't doing a very good job covering what it was supposed to.

She smiled and said, "Mr. Brown, we've been expecting you."

Dutch was really confused. He tried not to look clueless as she took him by the hand and led him to the men's lounge.

"You may change in here," she said sweetly. "When you're done, I'll escort you to your cabana. Please, take your time."

Dutch walked into a plushy decorated spa. Palm leaves adorned bamboo walls, soothing music played, and the scents of body oils highlighted what a sign on the far wall told him was called the Tranquility Room.

He passed comfortable-looking recliners separated by silk curtains that hung from ceiling to floor. Recessed lighting cast a soft glow as he moved to the next room.

Here was the changing area. He found an open locker and began to undress as he took in his surroundings, trying to estimate what a day's stay here cost. He opened the bag to find a Hawaiian patterned shirt and white shorts. Although almost empty, the bag still seemed heavy. He peered around to be sure he was alone, and then worked his fingers under the cardboard bottom and uncovered a hidden compartment.

He gingerly lifted the cardboard, revealing a Kurki knife with a ten-inch blade and nylon sheath. Next to it was a Sig Sauer P226, complete with silencer and two clips loaded with .357 copper flat-top bullets.

He turned the false bottom over, revealing an envelope taped to the back with his name on it written in the President's handwriting. He opened it and found a note and two pictures. The note read, "Enjoy your time off. I suggest cabana number five."

Dutch looked at the pictures. His heart raced and his face flushed.

He collapsed into the chair adjacent to his locker and just stared for a long time into nothingness. Slowly, his lips formed a smile.

He stood, put the pictures in his pocket, and replaced the false bottom. The gun and knife fit nicely inside his outfit. He stored the bag in his locker and walked back to the lobby where he was greeted once more by the beautiful attendant. She smiled and directed him outdoors.

Trevor Sirois slurped loudly at the ice on the bottom of his glass, then set it down and lay back. He adjusted his white fedora and enjoyed the ocean breeze gently blowing through the palm trees. He took a deep breath and slowly let it out. His freshly massaged body settled into a perfect spot on his plush lounge. A perfect time for a nap, he apparently thought.

He placed his hat on a table and closed his eyes. He didn't seem to hear the footsteps until they were right behind him.

Sirois held the empty glass over his head and without looking, said, "I'll take another."

"Absolutely," came a man's voice from behind.

If anything about the voice sounded familiar, Sirois must have shrugged it off because he shifted into an even more comfortable position. His body seemed to relax and within a few minutes he seemed to be sleepy. His hands dropped from the arms of the lounge chair. He didn't open his eyes until a small disturbance on his lap woke him He opened his eyes and saw two pictures sitting there.

"What the—" he said and held them up.

Staring back at him were the smiling faces of Harry Ludec and Alexis Jordan.

He sat bolt upright and frantically looked around for the man who moments ago had been standing behind him taking his order. No one was there. Sweat exploded from every pore on his body. He jumped out of his chair and looked around in a panic.

Sitting on a barstool across the pool, Dutch smiled, watching the man dart his head in every direction. He took a sip from his drink and looked at the bartender.

"Yes, I agree. This is going to be a good day."

About the Author

Adam is a 48 year-old small business owner from Stow, Massachusetts. Since graduating from Framingham State College in 1987 with a Communications Degree, he has worked in his family business as a marketing specialist and property manager.

For many years Adam was a bartender, and collaborated on the "Harvard Student Agencies Bartending Guide" released by St. Martin's Press.

"I think the spark that got me interested in writing occurred during my many years behind the bar observing people. The drama that would unfold night after night provided me with many a resource to draw from."

Adam's first published work was "Love on the Line" whose idea had been taken from being amazed at watching and hearing what personal information people would share with others they just met.

He has been married to his wife Kim for twenty two years and has two college age children. In his spare time he enjoys soccer refereeing and has worked games not only in the New England area but has traveled as far away as Norway to referee. Adam says that he enjoyed his time as an international referee because those were the only venues where he couldn't understand what fans were yelling at him about!

CPSIA information can be obtained at www.ICGtesting.com
Printed in the USA
LVOW08s0855240114

370766LV00004B/331/P